THE UNKNOWN

CONVERGENCE WAR
BOOK 2

M.R. FORBES

Published by Quirky Algorithms
Seattle, Washington

This novel is a work of fiction and a product of the author's imagination.
Any resemblance to actual persons or events is purely coincidental.

Cover illustration by Tom Edwards
Edited by Merrylee Lanehart

CHAPTER 1

Soren stared at the viewscreen, Montoya's ultimatum hanging in the air like a guillotine blade. *Surrender or be destroyed.* The words echoed in his mind, a bitter irony considering all he had done and risked to protect the Federation. He didn't blame Montoya for the situation. He had created it himself, initially to find Dana. But it had become something so much more. Something so unbelievable he could hardly resolve it. The admiral was following orders. Doing his job. Just like Commodore Clarey and everyone else in Strike Force Seven.

Beside him, Jack shifted uneasily. "Soren," he said softly, "what's the plan here? We can't fight the Navy."

Soren nodded. Jack was right, of course. For all the Wraith's advanced technology and the skill and bravery of his crew, they were hopelessly outmatched. Strike Force Seven had them surrounded, their weapons locked and ready. One wrong move, and they would be nothing more than a cloud of expanding debris. Besides, those were their people out there.

He met Jack's gaze. He didn't need to say what he read

in Jack's eyes. It was the same thing he knew Jack read in his. "Your son could be on one of those boats, Jack."

A flicker of pain crossed Jack's weathered face. "Knowing what's coming, I wish that weren't true."

"Knowing what's coming, there's nowhere for anyone to hide. Better to be on the front lines. To have a chance to do something about it."

"But what would they even be fighting for? To become merged with their counterparts from another dimension? It still sounds so crazy, I can't put my head around it."

"Let's not get ahead of ourselves. We aren't exactly in a position to do anything about anything right now."

"You know what that means, right? Court-martial. Prison. For all of us."

"I know," Soren replied, the weight of his decision settling on his shoulders like a physical burden. "But we knew the risks when we set out. We knew there would be consequences."

He glanced around the bridge, taking in the faces of his crew. They had followed him into this and trusted him to lead them through the fire. And now, because of his choices, they would all pay the price.

"I'm sorry," he said softly, the words woefully inadequate. He raised his voice. "I'm sorry for getting you all into this mess."

Ethan shook his head, a sad smile on his lips. "Don't be, Soren. We volunteered for this. We knew what could happen. But none of us would have even had the last thirty years of our lives if not for you."

Murmurs of agreement rippled through the bridge, each crew member nodding their support, their loyalty. It was humbling and heartbreaking.

Soren took a deep breath, squaring his shoulders. "Ethan, power down all systems except life support and comms. Samira, open a channel to the Die Hard."

"Aye, Captain," they answered, moving to comply.

"Channel open," Samira reported a moment later.

"Commodore Clarey," Soren said, his voice steady despite the turmoil inside him. "This is Captain Strickland. We surrender."

There was a pause, a heartbeat of silence. Then Clarey's clipped and professional voice filled the bridge. "Understood, Captain Strickland. Open your hangar bay. A boarding party will be en route in five minutes."

"Acknowledged," Soren replied. "Wraith out."

Samira cut the connection. Soren slumped in his seat. Around him, the bridge lights dimmed as Ethan carried out his unspoken orders, the ship's powerful systems winding down into standby mode.

The door hissed open, and Alex burst onto the bridge, his face a mask of confusion and growing anger. He took in the scene, the somber expressions, the darkened consoles.

"What's going on?" he demanded, his gaze locking on Soren. "Why are we powering down?"

Soren met his son's eyes, seeing the fire burning there, the stubborn defiance that was much like his own. "We're surrendering, Alex."

"What?" Alex exploded, his hands balling into fists at his sides as his eyes shot to the viewscreen. "Is that Strike Force Seven?"

"It is. Admiral Montoya has ordered us to stand down."

"How did they even see us? I thought this ship was invisible?"

"I'm led to believe that Rashad may have included some way for the Navy to detect ships using this technology. A failsafe, as it were."

"Probably an active system," Ethan added. "Something that needs to be intentionally used, which is why Recon Three never saw us."

"They might not have even been looking if the enemy hadn't destroyed the skunkworks," Jack agreed.

"So this is it?" Alex growled. "You're just going to roll over? After everything we've been through, everything we've learned, you're just going to give up?"

Soren rose from his chair, crossing to stand before his son. He placed his hands on Alex's shoulders, feeling the tension thrumming through his frame. "No. I'm the Wraith. I never give up. But we can't fight the Navy. They're not our enemy."

"They're trying to stop us!" Alex argued, pulling away from his father's grip. "They're getting in the way of us finding Dana and stopping this whole convergence disaster before it's too late!"

"I know," Soren said, his frustration bleeding into his voice. "Because they don't know any better. And I know you don't really want me to attack them. I know you're upset. I'm upset, too. But that's not who you are. That's not who we are as Stricklands."

Alex deflated, the fight draining out of him. He looked suddenly young, lost and frightened beneath the anger and bravado. "So, what then? We just let them take us in? Lock us away while the whole universe goes to hell?"

"For now, yes." Soren held up a hand, forestalling another reply. "But only for now. We'll find a way to make them understand, to convince them of the threat we're facing. But we can't do that if we're dead or branded as traitors."

"What's going to happen to me?" Alex asked softly. "To my team?"

Soren sighed, the question twisting like a knife in his gut. "You didn't volunteer for this, Alex. You and your squad came aboard because you had wounded and because there are no operational facilities on the planet to treat them. As far as the Navy is concerned, you were just in the wrong place at the wrong time."

"But that's not true," Alex protested. "I want to stay and help. We all do."

"I know," Soren said, a sad smile touching his lips. "But there's no value, emotional or tactical, in you going to the brig with us. The galaxy is going to need the Scorpions out there, fighting the enemy. Enough so that the enemy came to Jungle specifically to kill you." He offered a sly grin. "And failed."

Alex nodded back. "It won't be the last time for them."

"That's my boy," Soren replied.

"Captain," Mark said. "The shuttle is on its way."

Soren looked to the viewscreen, where a small silver craft had emerged from Die Hard's side, coming their way. Not an Armadillo at least. They didn't expect him to put up a fight.

Soren squared his shoulders. "Let's go welcome our guests," he said to Alex before turning away. "Samira, open shipwide comms."

"Channel open, Captain."

"Attention all hands. This is Captain Strickland. Unfortunately, we've been forced to surrender to the Navy. They're sending a shuttle across now to transfer us to the Die Hard, under Commodore Clarey's command. I know this is unexpected and not anything we had in mind, but it was a risk we knew we were taking. For my part, I'm sorry for dragging you into this mess, but I'm incredibly proud of each and every one of you for the way you've comported yourselves throughout this mission. I'm honored and grateful to have served with you all." Soren paused, fighting back emotion. "Report to the hangar bay for transfer. I repeat, report to the hangar bay for transfer. Soren out."

The comms disconnected. Soren stared at the

viewscreen for another moment, breathing in deeply and setting his resolve. Then he glanced at Alex and Jack. "Let's go."

The Marines were waiting for them in the hangar bay, a full platoon in combat armor, their weapons held against their chests. At their head stood a young lieutenant, his face serious beneath his helmet.

"Captain Strickland?" the Lieutenant asked, stepping forward and coming to attention.

"At ease, Lieutenant," Soren answered. "I'm Strickland."

"Lieutenant Moffit, sir. I have orders to take you and your crew into custody and escort you to the Die Hard."

Soren nodded, unsurprised. "I understand, Lieutenant. We'll come quietly."

Moffit seemed to relax slightly, some of the tension easing from his posture. He gestured to the man beside him, a dark-skinned officer with lieutenant commander's bars on his collar. "This is Lieutenant Commander Bashir. He and his team will be taking command of the Wraith for the trip back to Earth."

Bashir stepped forward, his expression neutral but his eyes alight with curiosity as he took in the Wraith's sparse hangar bay. "An honor, Captain Strickland," he said. "I must say, I've never seen a ship quite like this before."

"And you never will again," Soren replied. "She's the first and last of her kind, I'm afraid. Do you need help locating the bridge?"

Bashir smiled. "I don't know, do I?"

"I got lost more than once my first few times through the passageways," Soren answered. "This is Ethan, our chief engineer. He can show you the way."

"Thank you, Captain," Bashir said as Ethan gestured for him and his crew to follow. Soren could see the withheld sadness and anger on his friend's face as he led them away.

Moffit cleared his throat, drawing Soren's attention back to him. "The rest of you are under arrest. I imagine you'll come quietly?"

"Of course, Lieutenant," Soren said.

Moffit motioned to the shuttle. "In that case, if you'll find seats on board."

The crew hesitated at first. Keira was the first to break, though Soren knew she moved out of respect for him, not wanting to leave the Wraith. Their eyes met as she passed, tears welling in hers.

"Lieutenant," Alex said, getting Moffit's attention. "I'm Sergeant Alexander Strickland, First Company, Force Recon Marines. Scorpion Squad. I was stationed on PX-2847 when the enemy attacked." He paused, glancing at Soren, who nodded encouragement. "My unit and I had nothing to do with whatever my father and his crew are being arrested for."

"I understand, Sergeant," Moffit replied. "And I'm glad you survived your ordeal on the planet."

"Because Captain Strickland arrived to help us," Alex said. "Px-2847 would still be under enemy control other-wise. And it's possible everyone on the planet would be dead."

"I'm sure these last few weeks have been difficult for you and your team, Sergeant," Moffit said. "I commend you personally for your bravery, and I also personally have no doubt that Captain Strickland is a brave man, and loyal to the Federation. But for now, you and your squad need to join Captain Strickland's crew on the shuttle."

"Yes, sir. I'd like to comply with that order, but two of my Scorpions, Corporal Chen and PFC Holt are still in the healing pods. They can't be moved yet."

"I see," Moffit said. "I didn't realize you had injured. One minute." The Lieutenant activated his comms.

"Die Hard, this is Moffit. We have wounded Marines

from PX-2847 aboard requiring ongoing medical attention. Please advise."

There was a pause, and then Clarey's voice came over the link. "Understood, Lieutenant. The Marines can remain aboard the Wraith for now, along with any necessary medical personnel. We'll sort it out once we reach Earth."

"Acknowledged," Moffit replied. He turned to Alex, his expression softening slightly. "You and your team may stay with your wounded for the duration of the trip. But I'll need you to surrender your weapons and remain under guard."

Alex hesitated, clearly torn. But a glance from Soren, a small nod of encouragement, seemed to decide him. "Understood, sir. Thank you."

"Lieutenant," Soren said. "There's also the matter of the Pinto's crew." He motioned to the small group, who had remained outside the shuttle, waiting to plead their case.

"Pinto?" Moffit asked.

"A Hermes class vessel assigned to Recon Three," Soren replied. "They were attacked by the enemy. We rescued them from their stricken ship after we defeated their attackers."

Moffit shook his head in disbelief. "More unwilling crew members, then?"

"Not entirely unwilling, Lieutenant," Aiko said. "We're privy to what Captain Strickland and his crew are facing out here. In my opinion, removing him from command and locking him up would be a grave mistake."

"Noted," Moffit replied. "I'm sure you won't face any consequences for your actions, considering your situation. But it's not up to me to decide. I'll be sure to relay your concerns on to Commodore Clarey."

"Thank you," Aiko said. The entire group of Pinto survivors moved toward the shuttle.

"Is all of your crew accounted for, Captain?" Moffit asked.

"Our doctor, Asha, is remaining behind with the injured Marines," Soren said. "And Ethan is assisting Commander Bashir." He paused as Ethan returned to the hangar bay.

"They're all set up there, Captain," he reported.

"The rest of the crew is already in the shuttle," Soren replied.

"I'll go join them, then."

"Anyone else?" Moffit asked.

Soren had noticed Wilf and Tashi were both missing. He only had a split second to decide whether to inform the lieutenant of that fact or not. As unlicensed spacers, they would be in deep trouble no matter when they were picked up. So would Asha, though he had to imagine they would show some leniency for saving multiple lives.

"No, Lieutenant," he answered. If Wraith was docked somewhere, possibly even landed at NAS Pensacola, maybe Wilf and Tashi could sneak off and disappear. It would be a long shot, but at least it was a shot.

"Very well, follow me."

Commodore Clarey was waiting for them when the shuttle arrived, her presentation fully professional. Soren noticed a glimmer of respect in her eyes as she looked over the assembled crew of the Wraith.

"Captain Strickland," she greeted, her voice cool but not unkind. "Admiral Harper. I wish we were meeting under better circumstances."

"As do I, Commodore," Soren replied. "I know I'm not in a position to make requests, but I need to speak with Admiral Montoya. The things we've seen, the information we've uncovered...it's vital that he hears it, and soon. Every minute we delay puts the FUP, puts our entire universe, at greater risk."

"No, I'm afraid you aren't in a position to make any

requests," Clarey replied, though it was clear by her expression that she was considering it. "Though I believe you've earned the right with your years of loyal service to the FUP. Both you and the Admiral." She considered for a long moment, then nodded slowly. "Very well, Captain. You and Admiral Harper, come with me. Lieutenant Moffit, please escort the others to the brig for now. We'll sort out more permanent arrangements later."

As his crew was led away, Soren felt a pang of guilt for what he had brought upon them. But there was no time for regrets, no room for second-guessing. He had to focus on the mission, on convincing Montoya and the rest of the FUP leadership of the danger they faced.

He and Jack fell into step behind Clarey. She led them through the ship's corridors, past groups of curious sailors who watched them pass with wide eyes and hushed whispers. Finally, they arrived at her office, a small but well-appointed space just off the bridge.

As the door slid shut behind them, Clarey turned to face them. "Alright, Captain. You have my attention. What is so important that it can't wait until we reach Earth?"

"I'd prefer to pass what I've learned directly to Admiral Montoya," Soren answered. "Rather than repeat it twice."

"I've allowed you this far out of respect for both of you," Clarey said. "But I'm not going to trouble the admiral if your intent is to make excuses for your actions."

"Excuses?" Jack replied. "Legally, there is no excuse for what we did. But that doesn't change what we've accomplished or learned. And it won't change the ramifications of failure to act decisively. Please, Commodore. Put us through to Admiral Montoya. He needs to hear what we have to say."

"Believe me, Commodore," Soren added. "You don't want to be responsible for the potential consequences if you purposely delay a response."

Clarey made a face before tapping on her intercom. "Comms, open a transSat connection request to Admiral Montoya."

"Request sent, Como," came the reply a moment later.

Clarey turned back to Soren. "Alright, Captain. You've got your chance. Make it count."

Soren nodded, steeling himself for the conversation to come. He had to make Montoya understand, had to convince him of the urgency of their situation.

He just hoped it wasn't already too late.

CHAPTER 2

Soren and Jack stood in Commodore Clarey's office, a palpable tension hanging in the air as they waited for a connection to be established with Admiral Montoya. The minutes ticked by with agonizing slowness, each second feeling like an eternity.

At last, Clarey's desk surface flickered to life, and Anton Montoya's familiar face appeared above it. The admiral's expression was a mix of concern, frustration, and a hint of relief at knowing Soren and Jack were alive and well.

"Admiral Harper, Captain Strickland," Montoya greeted, his voice tight. "I had a feeling you would convince Commodore Clarey to contact me as soon as you were on board. I'm trying to be patient, but there really is no excuse for what you've done, and no way for you to escape the consequences. I know we're friends, but we both know there's only so much I can do."

Soren leaned forward, his gaze intense. "Admiral, forget about what we've done, and forget about consequences. This isn't about me, my crew, or the Wraith. This is so much bigger than all of that, and you need to know what's happening so you can react before it's too late. Dana's disappearance, the loss of Recon Three, the attack on PX-2847, the attacks in other parts of the galaxy, they're all connected. And they aren't being carried out by the Outworlders or a reformed Coalition. This isn't even some kind of rebellion within the FUP itself. I wish it was. I've seen the face of the enemy, Anton. And it was me."

Soren nodded to Clarey to send his response. They waited in tense silence for Montoya to answer.

"Soren, you should know better than to be so cryptic over tranSat. What the hell are you talking about?"

Soren almost laughed. He had neglected his tranSat protocol. He went into great detail about the alternate Dana's message and how he had encountered his duplicate from another dimension in orbit around Jungle. He also told Montoya how Alex had found his doppelgänger on the planet's surface and killed him.

"The Convergence," Jack finished. "Two universes, two realities, drawn together until they merge into one. It's already begun, Anton. The enemy's decided the best solution is to wipe us out to ensure they remain unique. We're already playing catch-up, and the longer we delay, the further behind we fall." He nodded to Clarey to send the message.

"This can't be real," Clarey said once it was sent, while they waited for the reply. "How can two universes collapse into one another? Scientifically, how is it possible?"

"Normally, we want science to prove a thing is possible," Soren answered. "But when that thing is already occurring, I don't think the science matters. Only the reality of the situation."

"I accept that, Captain. But, how do we know this convergence will join us to our counterparts in this other dimension? How do we know it won't destroy us?"

"We don't," Jack said. Clarey's face paled.

"So if this convergence happens…"

"Both our dimensions may be destroyed," Soren confirmed. "That's why we need to stop it before it's too late."

They waited again for Montoya's reply. When it came, he was as doubtful as Soren expected.

"That's...that's impossible. Parallel universes? Even if I believe you, which I'm struggling to do, there's no way I can convince the Joint Chiefs of this unless you have verifiable proof."

"I thought so too, at first," Soren admitted. "But we do have proof. Dana's message, and the coordinates of the dimensional rift. Anton, let me return to Wraith so I can send you the coordinates. Then, you can send a flotilla to check it out. Hell, send Strike Force Seven. We can go take a look, and return to Earth if we come up empty."

They sent the message. Soren tapped his foot while he impatiently waited for the response. The suggestion was outside standard operating procedure but not beyond the realm of possibility. Montoya had the power to make it happen, and it would settle the question of proof once and for all. If there was some portal to another dimension, no one could deny it.

Finally, Montoya's response made it back to them.

"I need to bring this to the Joint Chiefs, Soren. There are too many factors at play, and I can't make a decision of this magnitude on my own. If what you're saying is true, if we really are facing a threat of this scale, it's going to take a coordinated effort from the entire Federation to even begin to address it. There's also the matter of exactly what to do with you. Like it or not, you and your crew are criminals, and you need to return to Earth for prosecution. Even the Wraith doesn't get out of jail free."

Soren could tell both by the time it took for Montoya to reply and the sudden strain in his voice that he had paused the recording while he decided on his next step.

"Here's what we'll do. Commodore Clarey, maintain position around PX-2847 while I escalate this to my superiors. Also, keep Soren and Jack comfortable but confined to quarters. I know your hearts are in the right place, gentlemen, but you have to understand the position you've put us in. There are protocols, a chain-of-command that needs to be respected and adhered to. I'll do what I can to make the Joint Chiefs understand the urgency of your intel and stress who provided the information, but I can't make any promises."

Soren clenched his jaw, biting back the arguments that rose to his lips. He knew Montoya was right, knew that he couldn't just bypass the entire command structure of the Federation, no matter how dire the situation. But it galled him—the bureaucracy, the red tape. Lives were at stake, the very fabric of their reality. They didn't have time for debate and deliberation.

"I understand, Anton," he said at last, his voice tight with barely restrained frustration. "Just...please, stress to them the importance of acting swiftly. Every minute we delay is a minute our enemy has to prepare."

"I'll do my best, Soren. That's all I can promise. Montoya out."

The screen went dark. Clarey turned to Soren and Jack. "You heard the Admiral," she said coolly. "Quarters will be prepared for you. You'll be escorted there, and guards will be posted outside each of your doors. I expect full compliance."

"And you'll have it, Commodore," Soren replied. "Whether the top brass understands it or not just yet, we're all in this together."

Clarey tapped on her comms. "Lieutenant Moffit, I need four Marines at my office immediately to escort Captain Strickland and Admiral Harper to their quarters. They're to be confined there, under guard, indefinitely."

"Copy that, Commodore," Moffit replied, passing the order on over his personal comm. "They're on the way."

Soren and Jack exchanged a glance, a silent understanding passing between them. There was nothing more they could do, for now at least. Fate and circumstance had placed them in the hands of the very system they had sought to circumvent in the first place. Neither one of them had much hope that things would end well.

The Marines arrived within a minute, and Clarey opened her office door to allow them in. With a curt nod, Soren and Jack followed the Marines out of the office. A final glance over his shoulder showed Clarey watching them go, her expression inscrutable.

Minutes later, Soren found himself alone in a small but comfortable room, a stark contrast to the brig he had been expecting. But the locked door and the armed guards outside made it clear that this was no mere guest quarters.

He paced the room, his mind racing, replaying Dana's message repeatedly in his head. The coordinates she had provided, the urgency in her voice...he knew with absolute certainty that if they could get there, they would find the rift, whatever it looked like.

And they might find something much worse along with it, like a massive enemy fleet gathering for invasion. And how many in that fleet might be people he knew from this universe? Might Clarey's doppelgänger be commanding one of the attacking Valkyries? Could Montoya be heading up the assault? It was all too strange to consider.

Instead of onboard Wraith and on their way to find out, he was here. Locked away, useless, while the gears of bureaucracy ground with agonizing slowness. Soren tried to rest, but sleep eluded him. His mind was too busy trying to come to grips with their new reality, planning for the unlikely scenario that he could return to Wraith and try to do something to prevent Dana's fears from coming to pass.

A knock on the door startled him from his dark thoughts. "Come."

One of his guards opened the door. "Sir," he said, "Commodore Clarey wants to see you in her office."

A surge of adrenaline flooded Soren's veins. This was it, the moment of truth. He could only hope the heads of the FUP military had made the right decision.

He joined Jack and the other guards outside his door. Fearing the worst but hoping for the best, the two men shared tense glances at one another as the guards escorted them through the corridors.

Clarey looked up as they entered, her expression giving nothing away. "Captain Strickland, Admiral Harper. Please, have a seat."

'I'll remain standing if you don't mind," Soren said, too keyed up to even consider sitting. "What's the word, Commodore? What did they decide?"

Clarey sighed, a sound of mingled resignation and frustration. "Believe it or not, Captain, after what you said, I was pulling for you. However, our orders are to return to Earth, as ordered. The FUP will handle the situation from there."

It was the worst response they could get. But like he had told Alex, he would never give up. If Clarey was pulling for them, she might listen to reason.

"Commodore, you have to understand, we don't have time for this! Every second we delay—"

"Enough, Captain," Clarey snapped, her voice cracking like a whip. "This isn't up for debate. The decision has been made, and I have my orders. The FUP will handle this situation, through proper channels. From their perspective, there's no room in the Navy, retired or otherwise, for rogues or vigilantes, especially if war truly is coming."

Soren exhaled his frustration, voice returning to calm. "Will they at least allow us to recover the coordinates so they can send ships to verify the intel and see for themselves?"

"They didn't mention any such thing, but the Wraith has a Navy crew on board. Beyond that, I'm not privy to the details of the FUP's strategic decisions. And frankly, neither are you. Your clearance, your need to know, ended the moment you entered retirement. I'm sorry. I have boundless respect for both of you gentlemen. But you are to return to your quarters and remain there for the duration of our trip to Earth. Am I clear?"

Soren stood there, his fists clenched at his sides, his entire body vibrating with impotent fury. He wanted to argue, to fight, to make them see the folly of their inaction. But he knew it was futile. In their eyes, he was nothing more than a rogue element, a wild card to be contained and controlled.

"Yes, Commodore," he snapped at last, the words bitter on his tongue. "Perfectly clear." He turned towards the guards before pausing and pivoting back toward Clarey. "One more question. How did you locate the Wraith while she was cloaked?"

Clarey smiled. "I suppose you'll find out soon enough, anyway. The ship transmits a beacon at the top end of the spectrum, higher than our comms equipment are programmed to go because the range is so short."

Soren raised an eyebrow. Not so much a failsafe as he had thought but a means to avoid accidental collisions with a vessel they wouldn't otherwise be able to see.

"Thank you, Commodore."

With that, he allowed himself to be led from the room, Jack by his side. Soren's mind raced as the door closed behind them and the guards escorted them back to their gilded cages. This couldn't be the end, couldn't be how it all played out. They'd come too far, sacrificed too much.

But what could he do? What options did he have,

confined and watched as he was, entirely cut off from his ship and his crew? How could he fight an enemy that no one else wanted to believe in?

He didn't know. But as he entered his quarters and heard the door lock behind him, one thing was certain.

He would find a way. He had to.

The fate of their entire universe hung in the balance.

CHAPTER 3

Alex, Malik, and Zoe stood over two healing pods in the small compartment connected to the Wraith's sickbay, staring down through the small transparencies into the serene faces of Sarah and Jackson. The two Marines floated, sedated, in electrically charged gel while an array of lasers emitted a light show of flickering, flashing lights. Although the three Scorpions couldn't see the lights through the protection of the transparencies, they knew they were there, accelerating the healing of their squad mates.

"They look peaceful. Pain free," Alex said. None of them had ever been in a healing pod before. With their Karuta armor, they'd never suffered anything worse than a sprained ankle.

Asha moved from her terminal in the corner to stand beside him and look in on her charges. "They're going to be just fine. The gel and lasers are doing their job, stimulating their natural healing processes. Besides the broken bones and internal bleeding, they had a number of lacerations, bruises, and muscle strain from the fighting, just like you." She turned to him, her eyes searching his face. "Speaking of which, how's your head feeling?"

Alex touched the bruise on his forehead where he'd suffered a minor concussion from one of his lookalike's punches. "Still sore," he said, wincing slightly, "but the headache isn't too bad now. I've had worse."

Asha nodded, seeming satisfied. "Good. They'll need another day or two in the pods, but once they're out, they'll be better than new. This ship didn't come with many amenities, but these pods are top-notch. Next generation, I'm guessing."

"I'm so glad they're going to be okay," Zoe said, relief evident in her voice.

"I heard Captain Strickland's announcement," Asha said. "I thought I would have to go with the others. I'm glad I didn't, but…" She trailed off, looking at Alex hesitantly.

"What's wrong?" he asked, picking up on her anxiety.

Asha bit her lower lip. "The thing is, I'm not supposed to be here. I'm a rev."

"What?" Malik snapped. "And you're working on fixing up our squad mates? No, I don't think—"

"Cool it, Mal," Alex said. "My father trusts her, which means I trust her."

"Thank you," Asha replied. "When the Navy finds out, they're going to skin me alive for agreeing to this mission."

"You are a doctor though, right?"

"Medical officer," she replied. "I was a Lieutenant before…" She trailed off.

"Before what?" Malik asked.

Asha shook her head. "I'd rather not talk about it if that's okay with you. It's not a fun story."

"It's alright, Asha," Alex said. "You don't have to tell us if you don't want to. Do you mind if I ask where my father found you?"

"At a medical clinic in the Dregs. I was working there,

trying to help people who couldn't afford real care. It wasn't much, but it was something."

"That's a pretty damn honorable place to practice your training, if you ask me," Zoe said.

"Agreed," Alex added. "Asha, I'll do my best to get you off this ship without any trouble. I don't have a lot of pull, but I have some. Maybe I can convince them to give you a pass, considering the circumstances."

She looked at him, a small, grateful smile tugging at her lips. "Thank you, Alex. I appreciate that. You know, you're a lot like your father in that way. Always looking out for your people, no matter what."

Before Alex could respond, the side door to the pod bay door slid open. Wilf and Tashi hurried through it, their eyes wide and nervous as they pulled up short at the sight of the Marines, Wilf's fingers twitching in agitation.

"Oh, uh...hey there," he said, his voice strained. "We were just looking for Asha. Didn't mean to interrupt. We'll come back later."

They turned to leave, but Alex called out, stopping them. "Wait a minute. Why are you two still on board? I thought everyone went over to the Die Hard with the rest of the crew."

Tashi and Wilf exchanged a glance, a silent conversation passing between them. Finally, Tashi spoke, his voice low and urgent. "We couldn't go with the others. If the Navy finds out we're revs, with all the trouble we're already in...we'll get life in prison for sure."

"You're revs, too?" Alex said. "How many civilians with revoked licenses did my father bring with him?"

"Just the three of us," Tashi said.

Wilf nodded vigorously. "We're planning to hide on the ship for as long as we can. Maybe try to sneak out once we dock somewhere. It's our only chance."

Alex frowned, shaking his head. "That's not going to

work, guys. This ship is crawling with Navy personnel now. They'll find you sooner or later."

"We don't have a better choice," Tashi said, desperation creeping into his voice. "Unless...hey, maybe you want to help us retake the ship from the Navy?"

Alex barked a laugh, the sound harsh and humorless. "Retake the ship? With what, the six of us? Even if we could overpower the crew, it won't help unless my father is back on board with the rest of your crew. Unless you know how to fly the ship?"

"I can handle the helm," Wilf said, his fingers nodding their agreement.

"What about sensors, tactical, comms?" Zoe asked.

"There's only two of us," Tashi replied.

"My point, exactly."

Wilf's fingers slumped dejectedly, rising as a thoughtful expression emerged on his face. "Still...it might not be a bad idea to start working on a plan. Just in case, you know? We could figure out how to do it without hurting anyone, maybe create a distraction or something and get them locked down in one of the compartments."

Alex hesitated, torn. It was a crazy idea, reckless and dangerous. But a part of him, the part that chafed at the idea of his father being locked away, couldn't help but consider it.

"Alright," he said at last. "Work on it. Quietly. Come up with something and let me know. But be careful. We're on thin ice as it is."

Tashi and Wilf nodded, their expressions a mix of relief and determination. But before they could say anything more, the sound of boots on the deck plating echoed from the corridor approaching the main entrance to sickbay. Heavy, purposeful footsteps, drawing closer with each passing second.

"Someone's coming," Zoe hissed. "You two better make yourselves scarce."

They didn't need to be told twice. With a final, grateful look at Alex, they slipped back out of the side door to the pod bay, vanishing down an empty corridor just as the main door to sickbay slid open.

Lieutenant Commander Bashir entered, his dark eyes sweeping the room until he spotted the Marines and Asha through the windows in the wall separating sickbay from the adjacent compartment holding the healing pods. He headed for them, and came to a stop before Alex as soon as he moved through the doorway, his posture ramrod straight.

"Sergeant Strickland," he said, his voice deep and resonant, his expression a mix of respect and regret. "I wanted to check in on you and your team and make sure you have everything you need right now."

Alex met his gaze, a flicker of appreciation warring with the anger and frustration that simmered beneath the surface. "We're fine, Commander. Thank you for your concern."

Bashir nodded, a faint smile touching his lips. "Good, good." He glanced at the pods. "I assume these are your injured squad mates. How are they faring?"

"They're doing well, Commander," Asha answered. "But they need two more days in the pods."

"Understood. It won't be a problem. It's two weeks back to Earth."

"What happens to us then?" Zoe asked.

"I assume you'll be part of a reformed First Company. I can only imagine what you went through on Jungle. That you survived when none of the other Marines did is nothing short of—"

"A lot of training, a little skill, and a dose of good luck, sir," Alex interrupted. "And as you can see, we weren't all as lucky as the three of us."

Bashir swallowed hard as he nodded. "Of course. I understand if you don't like me being here, Sergeant. Considering the circumstances, I'm an unwanted replacement. I get it. I want you to know, I'm a big fan of your father's. The things he's done, the battles he's won. He's a legend in the Navy. I just wish things hadn't come to this."

Alex did his best not to direct too much anger at Bashir. "You and me both, Commander. But based on what I've seen, what we've been through...this is just the beginning of bad things to come. Things are going to get worse. A lot worse, especially with my father not on board this ship. If we're going to stand a chance against what's coming, we need him back in the command chair. And fast."

Bashir's face paled, his eyes widening slightly. "What do you mean? What exactly are we facing out there?"

Alex shook his head, a bitter laugh escaping his lips. "You wouldn't believe me if I told you. Hell, I barely believe it myself."

Bashir stared at him, a look of growing unease on his face. He opened his mouth as if to ask another question, then seemed to think better of it. With a final, uncertain nod, he turned and left sickbay the same way he came in, his footsteps echoing down the corridor until they faded into silence.

CHAPTER 4

Soren lay on the small bed in his quarters, staring up at the featureless white ceiling. Sleep eluded him, his mind occupied by a thousand thoughts and worries. They were headed back to Earth, back to a court-martial and a prison cell, while the very fabric of their reality unraveled around them.

He couldn't let it happen. He wouldn't. Except he didn't have much of a choice, locked away like this, cut off from his ship and his crew. He had to find a way to convince the FUP leadership of the danger they faced and make them see the urgency of the situation.

But how? They had dismissed his warnings and refused to see his evidence, at least so far. They had chosen to bury their heads in the sand, to cling to protocol and procedure even as the wolves circled ever closer.

A sudden, sharp buzz at the door jolted him from his thoughts. He hopped to his feet and went to answer the call, hoping maybe Clarey had reconsidered her position. Perhaps they weren't on their way to Earth after all. The door slid open, revealing the face of his guard, a young Marine with a nervous expression.

"Captain Strickland," the Marine said, his voice tight. "You have a visitor."

Soren raised an eyebrow as Jack stepped into the room with a sly smile on his weathered face. The door slid shut behind him, leaving them alone. An overwhelming sense of apprehension settled over Soren as he eyed his old friend.

"How?" he asked simply.

"Apparently, my status as a retired flag officer still carries some weight," Jack replied. "I convinced my guard to let me talk to Clarey, and Clarey to let me talk to you. It helps that her mother served under me back when she was still in diapers. She's being lenient given the circumstances, but she's not going to allow for anything untoward under the watchful eye of her superiors."

Soren nodded, a flicker of hope kindling in his chest. "What's the status on board the Wraith?"

Jack shook his head, frustration etched into every line of his face. "Clarey's keeping a tight lid on most things. You know how the media keeps tabs on FUP comings and goings. She told me that the official story is that we're just another patrol group, heading back to Earth for routine maintenance and resupply."

"The Wraith is part of a routine patrol?" Soren asked dubiously.

Jack smirked. "My guess is they'll bring her in cloaked."

Soren sighed. "They're really going to sweep this all under the rug, aren't they? Pretend like none of it ever happened?"

"It looks that way," Jack agreed. "At least until they can figure out a way to spin it, make it fit into their neat little narrative. I can picture Anton trying to convince them to see reason based on our message. But I think our 'unsanctioned' actions are working against us, despite your reputation and mine. They've spent so long at peace, thinking our dominance is unquestionable, that they don't want to

believe war is coming, so they're choosing to ignore everything we've said."

"We can't let them do this, Jack. Not when so much is at
stake."

Jack held up his hands, a placating gesture. "I know,
Soren. Believe me, I know. But we need to be smart about
this. We're not going to do any good if we're locked away in
a cell, or worse."

Soren took a deep breath, forcing himself to calm down.
Jack was right. They needed to play this carefully and find a
way to work within the system, even as they sought to
circumvent it.

"What about the crew?" he asked. "Do you think they'll
go to prison, too?"

"They have to take into account the fact that we rescued
those spacers from Pinto, saved your son's unit, and helped
liberate Jungle. Not to mention, we found the data recorder
they were searching for and unlocked it for them. They'll
review the contents eventually. The only question is
whether they'll believe it."

"By then, it'll probably be too late," Soren added.

"There is that," Jack agreed. "If we play our cards right,
I think we can get most of our crew released once we reach
Earth. Questioned, maybe given a slap on the wrist,
possibly revoked.

"If we can keep them out of prison with their pensions
intact, I'll be happy," Soren replied.

"You and me both, old friend. As for us...we won't be
getting let off so easily."

"I don't care about myself," Soren said, waving away the
concern. "I'll face whatever consequences come my way.
But the others...they don't deserve to have their lives ruined
because of my choices. You, either."

"I knew the risks. So did they. They believed in you, in

what we were doing. That's a testament to the kind of leader you are, the kind of loyalty you inspire."

Soren shook his head, a bitter laugh escaping his lips. "And look where it got them. Look where it got all of us."

"We're not done yet," Jack said, a fierce light in his eyes. "We'll find a way to make this right, to finish what we started. We have to."

A heavy silence fell between them. Finally, Soren spoke, his voice low. "Did you notice that Wilf and Tashi never boarded the shuttle?"

"I noticed. Why?"

"They're on board Wraith, Alex is on board. I know my son, and if I know Wilf and Tashi, the three of them are probably trying to figure out how to regain the Wraith and spring us from captivity the second we get to Earth."

"That's a bad idea."

"I know, and hopefully it won't come to fruition. Alex is a good Marine, but if there's one thing he's more loyal to than the FUP, it's his family. And you heard the other Soren. He said Dana's gone, not dead. I've been thinking a lot about what that means."

"Do you think she went looking for the rift?"

"Not exactly. The other Soren isn't exactly like me. From what his Dana said, I see him as much more ruthless. He wanted to kill me and Alex because he saw us as threats. But Dana's a scientist at heart. Always was. Even their version was talking about her team and stopping the Convergence. My Dana never crossed him, so he had no reason to kill her. Especially since she was the only Dana left, if that makes any sense."

"In a twisted way, it does," Jack replied. "So you don't think she went searching for the rift. You think the other Soren told her where to find it."

Soren nodded. "Precisely. The other Soren might have

even given her information on how to contact his Dana's team."

"Then why did she just disappear, instead of contacting her superiors?"

Soren raised an eyebrow. "Come on, Jack. She's still my kid."

Jack laughed. "She knew the FUP wouldn't believe her or would turn a blind eye. Or both. She took matters into her own hands."

"And obviously, she wasn't wrong to do so."

"I've got to hand it to you, Soren. Your family dynamic is…interesting to say the least."

Soren grinned. "You should see us at Christmas."

"I'd say we should inform Clarey about your theory on Dana, but we both know it won't get us anywhere."

"No. Not yet. My best hope is that I can get a live audience with someone on the Joint Chiefs' staff or maybe a senator on the Planetary Defense Committee, and convince them to wake up before it's too late."

"I think we'll have better luck with Alex stealing the Wraith and breaking us out of prison."

"Not exactly a positive attitude, Jack."

"I'm just calling it the way I see it. But I've been known to be wrong from time to time. I mean, thirty years in the service, ten of them as a flag officer, doesn't count for much, right?"

"It means we have a higher hill to climb, but we need to climb it."

Before Jack could answer, the door to the room slid open, and the Marine guard stepped in. "Admiral Harper, your time's up, sir."

Jack squeezed Soren's shoulder. "I'll see if I can get us some time every day. Solitary confinement is bad for the psyche, and we aren't violent criminals. Until then, keep doing what you're doing."

Soren smiled. "Failing miserably at falling asleep? I can do that. You, too, Jack."

Jack followed the guard out of the room. Soren laid back down on his bunk, his thoughts setting out on a new track. He had to convince the FUP that the threat from the alternate dimension was real before Alex did something with the best intentions that would make everything so much worse.

CHAPTER 5

As the journey to Earth stretched on, the monotony of confinement began to wear on Soren and Jack. The stark walls of their quarters seemed to close in a little more each day, the endless hours blending together into a haze of restless energy and mounting frustration.

But on the fourth day, a glimmer of hope broke through the tedium. Commodore Clarey, perhaps taking pity on her prisoners or simply recognizing the futility of keeping them isolated, loosened the restrictions on their movements. They were still confined to the ship, of course—there was nowhere to go while they were jumping through the vast emptiness of space—but there was really no reason they couldn't be allowed to access the public areas of the ship, like the gyms and chow halls.

Soren wasted no time in taking advantage of this small mercy. Wanting nothing more than to clear his mind by pushing his body to the max, he changed into a set of plain Navy issue workout shorts and a t-shirt. Although he could still access officer territory on their separate deck, away from the enlisted personnel, he'd quickly found upon retirement that he much preferred the more relaxed atmosphere among the rank and file. Leaving his quarters, he made his way to the enlisted gym.

It was a large and well-equipped space, with rows of treadmills, weight machines, free weights, and other equipment. A group of spacers were already there, going through their paces, their faces glistening with sweat. They looked up as Soren entered, a few recognizing him immediately.

"Captain Strickland," one of them said, a young man with a classic Marine haircut—high and tight—and a lean, muscular build. "It's an honor, sir."

Soren waved away the formality, a small smile tugging at his lips. "At ease, Marine. I'm just here as another man looking to get in a workout."

The Marine nodded, a flicker of admiration in his eyes. "Of course, sir. The equipment is all yours."

Soren moved to one of the treadmills, starting out at an easy jog to warm up, but as the minutes ticked by and his muscles loosened, he found himself picking up the pace.

He lost himself in the rhythmic cadence of his feet pounding the belt, his mind drifting back to his academy days, to the grueling physical training that had honed his body into a weapon. Even now, decades later, he could feel that old strength, that old endurance, flowing through him. Too focused after a while on the burn in his legs and the sweat pouring down his face, he barely noticed the looks of awe-filled respect from the other spacers.

An hour passed, then two. Finally, Soren slowed to a stop, his chest heaving, his body thrumming with a pleasant ache. He stepped off the treadmill, nodding to the spacers as he toweled off. "Not bad for an old man," he quipped, drawing a round of chuckles from the gathered crew.

"Old man?" one of them scoffed. "Sir, with respect, you just put most of us to shame."

Soren grinned, a rare moment of levity in the midst of so

much uncertainty. "Stick around long enough, and maybe you'll be in my shoes one day. Well, without being under arrest that is."

As he left the gym, the spacers' laughter and good-natured ribbing followed him out, a reminder that even in the darkest of times, camaraderie and shared purpose could light the way.

The enlisted chow hall was next on his agenda. It was a bustling space, crammed with long metallic tables and a veritable sea of charcoal uniforms.

He moved through the line, helping himself to his choices of the limited fare the Navy could offer on board ship when resupply wasn't often possible. He chose the reconstituted pot roast with mashed potatoes and gravy, the hydroponic broccoli, vegetable soup, and a slice of fresh baked chocolate cake with vanilla frosting. As he turned to find a seat, he found himself confronted by a passel of eager faces.

"Captain Strickland! Would you like to join us?"

"Sir, it's an honor to have you aboard. Can I get you a coffee?"

"I read about what you did at Praxis IX. Is it true you took out a CIP destroyer with a single railgun shot?"

Soren held up a hand, overwhelmed by the sudden onslaught of questions and invitations. He had known he was respected within the Navy ranks. But this? This was something he'd never really experienced since retiring.

"I'm surprised so many of you have even heard of me," he admitted.

"Are you kidding, sir?" one of them, a young woman with short brown hair, replied. "There's a statue of you and a whole display case about your time in service at the Naval Academy in Seoul."

"There is? Huh," Soren replied, surprised. "I didn't know that." They had offered him a teaching job at the academy the day after his retirement, which he'd turned down because he wanted to get home to see Jane and go fishing on the lake. If he had known then what he knew now...he would have accepted the position.

"Sure is, sir," another spacer replied. "If you have time, we'd love to hear any nuggets of wisdom you'd like to impart to us."

"Since I've got nothing but time, and you're all giving me a swelled head here," he joked, "how can I say no?"

Soren soon found himself seated at a table surrounded by eager faces and steaming mugs. He sipped a coffee, savoring the bitter warmth, and let the conversation wash over him.

They wanted to hear his stories, to glean anything they could from the man who had become a living legend, at least in this circle. Soren obliged, regaling them with tales of battles won and lost, of sacrifices made and bonds forged in the crucible of war, while at the same time shifting all the real glory to his crew where it belonged. A captain was only the head of a ship, useless without the body.

As he spoke, he could sense an undercurrent of something else, a hunger for more than just stories. These men and women, they were the best of the best, the pride of the Federation. And yet, they had spent their careers in a time of peace, their skills and courage untested.

They yearned for a challenge, for a chance to prove themselves. And as much as it pained him to admit it, Soren knew that chance was coming. Sooner, perhaps, than any of them realized.

As the days stretched on, Soren found himself spending more and more time among the crew, in the gym and the chow hall, on the observation deck and in the rec rooms. He listened to their stories, their hopes and fears, and he shared his own in turn.

And slowly, subtly, he began to plant the seeds of readiness and resolve. He spoke of the importance of staying sharp, of being prepared for anything. He hinted at the dangers that lurked in the vast reaches of space, at the threats that might soon come calling.

He never spoke openly of the Convergence or alternate dimensions, of the nightmarish reality that haunted his every waking moment. But he made sure they understood the gravity of their situation and the weight of the responsibility that rested on their shoulders.

It was on the seventh day that Commodore Clarey summoned him to her office. Soren went willingly, his head held high, his step sure and steady. Being around a starship crew again had reinvigorated him and given him a purpose during his time on board.

Clarey's face was an inscrutable mask as she gestured for him to take a seat. "Captain Strickland," she said, her voice cool and measured. "We need to talk."

Soren raised an eyebrow, settling into the proffered chair. "Of course, Commodore. What's on your mind?"

Clarey leaned forward, her elbows resting on the desk. "I've been watching you, Captain. Observing your interactions with my crew. And I have to ask—what game are you playing?"

Soren met her gaze unflinchingly. "I'm not playing any games, Commodore. I'm simply trying to make the best of a difficult situation."

"By fraternizing with the crew? By filling their heads with tales of adventure and glory?" Clarey's voice had an edge to it now, a hint of accusation. "If I didn't know better, I might think you were trying to incite a mutiny."

Soren laughed at that, a short, sharp bark of amusement. "A mutiny? Commodore, with all due respect, that's the last thing on my mind. My only concern is for the safety and readiness of this crew. Of all our people."

Clarey studied him for a long moment, her eyes searching his face for any hint of deception. "And what exactly do you think they need to be ready for?"

Soren sighed, leaning forward to mirror her posture. This was probably his last chance. "Commodore, I know the idea of an impending war with another universe sounds impossible. But I'm telling you, it's real. And it's coming, whether we're ready for it or not."

"And you think building up my crew's resolve is going to help us weather that storm?" Clarey asked.

"I think," Soren said carefully, "that when the time comes, every single one of us is going to need to be ready. Physically, mentally, emotionally. We're going to need to be strong, Commodore. Stronger than we've ever been before. Because if we're not..."

He trailed off, letting the implication hang heavy in the air between them. Clarey stared at him, her expression unreadable. And then, to Soren's surprise, she nodded.

"I understand," she said quietly. "I suppose there's no harm in preparing the crew, no matter what happens in the future."

Soren felt a flicker of hope, a spark of possibility. "It can only help them, regardless of the outcome," he agreed. "Let me help, Commodore. Let me do what I can to prepare your crew and make sure they're ready for whatever comes."

Clarey was silent for a long moment, weighing Soren's words, his offer. And then, with a heavy sigh, she nodded once more. "Okay, Captain. I believe you. And you've made an excellent case. You have my permission to continue. More than that, I'm granting you access to the bridge. I'd like you to work with the crew there as well."

"Thank you, Commodore," Soren replied, a small smile tugging at his lips.

As he left Clarey's office, a flickering ember of hope sprouted in the darkness of his fears. It wasn't much, but it was something. A start.

The next day, as he made his way to the enlisted gym for his usual workout, he noticed a flurry of activity throughout the ship. Spacers hurried through the corridors with a new sense of urgency, their faces set with determination.

And then, over the ship's intercom, Commodore Clarey's voice rang out. "Attention all hands, this is the Commodore. As of this moment, Die Hard is entering a state of heightened readiness. All departments, begin preparations for potential hostile engagement. This is a drill. Repeat, this is a drill."

Soren felt a thrill run through him, a surge of adrenaline and anticipation. He didn't know if Clarey truly believed his warnings and was fully convinced of the danger they faced. But she was taking action, preparing her ship and her crew for the worst. To Soren, that was more important than belief. When the time came, it could be the only thing that saved the lives of these brave men and women.

Diverting from the gym, he made his way to the bridge, which accepted his thumbprint to allow him access. He moved to where Clarey sat at the command station. She spared him a look, her eyes running down his less than bridge appropriate attire and then up again. His eyes settled on her smirk and he shrugged. "I was on my way to the gym when you made your announcement." She grinned at him before returning her attention to her crew, barking orders as they continued running through the drill. Soren moved around the bridge, watching and gently correcting any inefficiencies or mistakes he noticed in their operations.

When the drill ended, Soren turned back to Commodore

Clarey. She wore a proud grin, her confidence visibly improved from any of their prior meetings.

Whatever happened next, at least one ship in the fleet would be ready.

CHAPTER 6

Alex and his team had taken to practicing on the lower decks of the Wraith, making the most of the limited equipment and space. The rhythmic pounding of boots on metal grating and the sharp exhalations of controlled breathing filled the air as they pushed themselves through agility drills and sparring sessions.

Sweat glistened on their skin, soaking through their utilities as they moved, ducked, and struck with a precision born of countless hours of training. Alex watched with a critical eye, calling out corrections and encouragement as needed.

"Come on, Zoe!" he barked as the petite Marine faced off against the much larger Malik. "Use your speed, don't let him pin you down!"

Zoe danced around Malik, her fists up and her eyes narrowed in concentration. She feinted left and then darted right, landing a rapid series of jabs to Malik's ribs before spinning away.

"That's it!" Alex grinned. "Keep him guessing!"

Malik laughed, shaking his head as he rubbed his side.

"Damn, Zoe. For such a tiny thing, you hit like a freight train."

Zoe smirked, bouncing lightly on the balls of her feet. "And you move like a slug, Mal. All that muscle slowing you down?"

"Oh, it's like that, is it?" Malik raised an eyebrow. "Alright, little mongoose. Let's see how you handle this slug rolling over you."

He charged forward, arms wide, trying to engulf Zoe in a bear hug. But she was too quick, ducking under his grasp and executing a perfect leg sweep that sent Malik tumbling to the mat with a surprised grunt.

"Boom!" Jackson crowed from the sidelines. "That's how it's done! Zoe: 2, Malik: Zip."

Malik flipped Jackson the bird as he clambered back to his feet. "I let her do that. Just to make it interesting."

"Sure you did, big guy," Sarah laughed. "Just like you *let* me put you in that chokehold yesterday."

Alex clapped his hands, drawing their attention back to him. "Alright, Scorpions. Let's reset. Jackson, you're up against Sarah. Let's see if you've learned anything from watching Zoe school Malik."

Jackson and Sarah moved to the center of the mat, settling into ready stances, but before they could engage, a scraping sound echoed from the far wall. Instantly, the Marines were on alert, and they turned in combat stances to face the potential threat. A small maintenance hatch swung open, and a messy head of hair poked out.

"Whoa, whoa, don't shoot!" Wilf yelped. "It's just us!" Grinning sheepishly as his tattooed fingers waved frantically, he climbed out of the hatch, Tashi right behind him.

Alex straightened, both relieved and annoyed. "What the hell are you two doing sneaking around down here?"

Tashi brushed himself off, his expression turning serious. "We think we might have a plan to get your father and the others back."

That got everyone's attention. "What kind of plan?" Alex asked.

"Yeah, this better be good," Malik added.

"Well," Wilf hedged, "it's probably a bad one. Like, more-likely-to-get-us-all-killed-than-actually-work bad."

"But it's something," Tashi added quickly. "We figure, first step, we sabotage the Wraith. Manually lock out the controls so the ship can't leave without us."

"At least until they figure out how to fix whatever we do, which could take a while. Then, once we land on Earth, or if we get a chance to sneak on a shuttle in the case we don't land on Earth, we make our way to wherever the captain and the others are being held."

"We'll disguise ourselves as their attorneys," Tashi picked up the thread. "You can vouch for us, get us access. Then, while we're 'meeting' with them, you Scorpions knock out the guards and we all make our daring escape. We steal a shuttle and fly back to Wraith, turn off the lockouts, and whoosh! We're on our way!"

There was a beat of silence. Then Malik burst out laughing, his deep guffaws echoing off the metal bulkheads. "Oh, man," he gasped, wiping tears from his eyes. "That's...that's just precious."

Wilf's fingers twitched indignantly. "What's so funny?"

"You two? Passing as attorneys? *Please*." Malik shook his head. "You're way too baby-faced. And those finger tattoos aren't exactly screaming legal professional."

The tattooed faces looked quite put out at that.

"And that's not even touching the part where we go from prison break to waltzing onto a shuttle," Jackson pointed out. "Feels like you're missing a few crucial steps there."

"And a few screws," Sarah muttered.

Wilf deflated, his shoulders slumping. "Okay, okay, so it needs some work. But it's a start, right?"

"Yeah, we told you it was a bad plan, but it's the best we could come up with," Tashi added. "Let's see you do one better."

Alex held up a hand, his expression thoughtful. "The finer details might need tweaking. But the core idea…" His lip curled as if he didn't quite like what he was about to say. "…it has potential."

Zoe turned to him, surprised. "You can't be serious, Gunny. This whole thing about trying to break your father out of prison is wacky as hell."

"Wackier than letting him and the others get locked away when the fate of the universe is at stake?" Alex met her gaze, his jaw set. "If what they told us is true, if this convergence is really happening, then we have to do something. Even if it means court-martial, even if it means losing the uniform…at least we'll still be us. Not some merged version of ourselves."

A heavy silence followed his words as the weight of their reality settled over them all.

"You don't have anything to worry about, boss-man," Jackson said. "You already killed your body double. You're home free."

"You might be, too," Alex replied. "We don't know if my double was fighting with his Scorpions or not, and we never had a chance to get a look at the bad guys we killed on Jungle."

"Huh. You know, I never thought about that."

"Either way, I'm not too enthralled with the idea of billions of people losing themselves or their loved ones." He turned back to Wilf and Tashi. "Focus on the sabotage part of your plan. Find ways to disable the Wraith and keep it grounded without putting any crew at risk. Force Recon will handle the actual extraction."

Tashi and Wilf nodded, a glimmer of hope chasing away their earlier disappointment. "We won't let you down," Tashi promised.

He turned to his Marines, resolve hardening his features. "We have a new mission, Scorpions. Planning and executing an asset recovery under the most challenging conditions imaginable. We come up with an approach, and then we start drilling for every contingency, every scenario. But whatever we come up with, the most important thing is that none of our fellow Marines or our brothers and sisters in any of the other services are hurt. This has to be quick and clean."

"You're asking us to do the impossible, Gunny," Sarah said, not ready to buy into his enthusiasm.

"Maybe, but a week ago I would have said inter-dimensional rifts and evil twins are impossible, too. "

"Damn good point," Jackson said.

"We have eight days until we reach Earth. Let's see what we can come up with. Hopefully, we'll never need to even attempt a rescue."

"Fingers double-crossed," Malik said, showing his hands with his fingers in their right positions. "Hey Wilf, do your fingers feel naughty when they cross like that?"

"What?" Wilf looked down at his hands, crossing his fingers. He quickly uncrossed them. "No."

"We should go," Tashi said. "Wraith has lots of these little access passages. Makes it easy for us to move around without being seen."

"Until next time," Wilf said before they disappeared back into the maintenance hatch.

Alex turned to his squad. "Alright, Scorpions. We have our work cut out for us. Huddle up. Let's get to it."

As they began brainstorming strategies and possibilities,

a new sense of purpose settled over the group. Yes, it was a desperate plan, fraught with risks.

But, as they had so many times before, Scorpion Squad would find a way to make the impossible possible.

They had to.

CHAPTER 7

The journey back to Earth felt interminable, each day stretching into eternity as the ships of Strike Force Seven and the Wraith hurtled through the vast emptiness of space. Soren and Jack spent their waking hours helping Commodore Clarey train her crew, preparing them for a war they were certain would come but that the powers that be had so far refused to accept as real.

As the predominantly blue-green jewel of humanity's homeworld finally swelled in the viewports, a mix of trepidation and resolve settled in Soren's gut. Whatever awaited them on the surface, he would face it head-on and fight with every fiber of his being to make the FUP leadership understand the true nature of the threat they faced.

The Marine guards came for them as the flotilla entered orbit, politely but firmly insisting on escorting them to the hangar bay. Commodore Clarey and Second Lieutenant Wells, the junior officer in Moffit's outfit, waited beside a prepped shuttle, their faces somber and carefully neutral.

Soren could sense the conflict within them, the unease from having come to believe the truth but being bound by

duty and protocol. Clarey, in particular, seemed to be struggling, her jaw tight and her eyes shadowed.

"Captain Strickland," she said as they approached, her
voice carefully formal. "Admiral Harper, your shuttle is
prepared for departure. Your crew is already on board."

"And my ship?" Soren asked, his voice level. His
thoughts weren't only on the Wraith, but also Tashi and
Wilf. "What's going to happen to her?"

Clarey hesitated, glancing around the hangar bay to
ensure they weren't overheard. When she spoke, her voice
was low and urgent. "Bashir and his crew are bringing her
down at NAS Pensacola," she murmured. "From what I
gather, your little adventure proved her worth."

"Funny, the Navy was ready to mothball her a month
ago," Jack replied.

"I don't think they intend to build any more. But why
waste a perfectly good ship? Especially one with confirmed
kills against a Komodo and a Rhino. It should help make
short work of the *Outworlder pirates*." She rolled her eyes at
the last bit, telling Soren she didn't believe what the FUP
was trying to sell. Not anymore.

Soren nodded, unsurprised. "And my crew?" he asked.
"Alex and the Scorpions?"

"Already en route," Clarey assured him. "You'll be
reunited on the surface." She hesitated, looking as if she
wanted to say more, but a pointed glance from Wells had
her straightening, her face smoothing back into a neutral
mask. She had already said too much, but Soren sensed that
she felt she owed him that much for helping prepare her
crew.

Soren and Jack boarded the shuttle to greetings from the
rest of the crew, including the survivors from Pinto. Soren
was pleased to see they all looked rested and well-fed, and
they'd all shaved, showered and dressed in Navy charcoal
for their next destination. He sat in the empty seat next to

Keira while Jack sat a few rows back with Harry. Clarey and Wells both boarded as well, along with two units of Marines.

"Keira," Soren said. "How are you feeling?"

"After two weeks in Die Hard's brig?" she replied. "I feel great now that I'm not staring at the same three drab gray walls. You?"

"Commodore Clarey afforded me the luxury of a guarded officer's quarters," he replied. "And I've had free movement around the ship for the last eight days."

"It's good to be the king, huh?"

"You may say that now, but the king is the one who most often loses his head when things go sour."

"I can't really argue that. Do you want to take bets on where we'll land? Ethan thinks FUP HQ in Geneva. I'm going with the Washington Navy Yard. And of course, Harry's convinced they're going to make us disappear in some unlisted black site. Which, given those options, I'm kind of hoping is the case. It'll at least be a whole lot more interesting."

Soren smiled, happy to see Keira had retained a sense of humor through the ordeal. "I want to apolo—"

"No," she said, cutting him off. "No more of that. We all made our decisions. Nobody put a gun to our heads. We're in this together."

Soren nodded. "I appreciate you, Keira."

"Back at you, Captain. Twice over."

The shuttle lifted off with a muffled roar of thrusters, the hangar bay of the Die Hard falling away below them. Soren stared out of the viewport as they descended through the atmosphere, watching the landscape resolve from the swirling white of clouds to the rich greens and browns of the continents.

Their destination soon became clear.

"Looks like you win," Soren said, eyeing the Pentagon

as they broke through the last of the high clouds. Maintaining its iconic shape, it had been transformed over time into a towering beacon of military might, not just for the United States but for all of Earth and beyond. The reinforced composite alloys made it gleam in the sunlight, practically daring any enemy to challenge the strength and sovereignty of the Federation of United Planets.

The Washington Navy Yard sat within view of the building, a few miles to the north along the Anacostia River. Joining the original 18th-century brick buildings were more modern structures, all glass and steel, the FUP flag waving high at the top of the main administrative building. While there were no boats docked at the Yard anymore—water-based navies had gone out of use with the advent of counter-mass generation—the docks had been repurposed into landing pads for small to medium-sized air and spacecraft.

The shuttle touched down on one of those landing pads, the slight bump of contact barely registering. As the hatch hissed open and they were led out into the bright sunlight, Soren caught sight of another shuttle settling onto the adjacent pad. A familiar figure soon emerged from within.

Alex. His son looked much better than the last time he had seen him. His eyes were clear and his bearing proud as he fell into step behind Lieutenant Moffit and his Marines, the rest of the Scorpions close behind.

The two groups merged into one as they neared the building. Soren and Alex exchanged greetings through eye contact and short nods. Together, the expanded assembly was escorted into the administration building. Of course, their presence drew attention from everyone present, who offered everything from shy glances to full-on stares, no doubt wondering why all of them were there.

They boarded the elevators and ascended to the fourth floor, where they were shown into a large conference room.

The viewscreens lining the walls, a holographic projector in the center, currently projected the FUP logo.

At the head of the table, Admiral Montoya and another man who Soren immediately recognized, were already seated, their expressions serious and foreboding. Jack, ever the consummate salesman, started to greet them with an easy smile and a friendly hello, but a stern look from Montoya had him subsiding, his face falling into lines of sober respect.

"Be seated," Montoya said, his voice tight with barely restrained frustration. He waited until they had all found a place at the table before continuing.

"I'm not sure if introductions are needed here, but the gentleman to my right is Senator Jason Huff, the head of the Senate Planetary Defense committee."

The senator nodded. A slightly overweight man with short brown hair and a cherubic face, Soren knew he was known for his biting personality.

"You are all here because you were, in some way, involved with the unauthorized operation of the experimental vessel which I understand you took to calling the Wraith, in honor of her captain," Montoya said, his eyes sweeping the assembled group. "The operation was launched from a top-secret FUP facility you should never have known about, let alone found transportation to, and which has since been destroyed under suspicious circumstances."

Soren could feel the tension in the room ratchet up a notch, and could see the flicker of unease on the faces of his crew. They had all known the risks, had all understood the potential consequences of their actions. But to hear it laid out so starkly, in the cold, formal tones of an official reprimand...it was sobering, to say the least.

Montoya glanced down at the datapad before him, his

finger scrolling through some unseen document. "Now, I understand that not everyone here bears equal responsibility for these events," he said, his voice softening slightly. "We will be examining the evidence and conducting interviews to determine the degree of culpability for those gathered here. Some of you may be dismissed to await further orders. Others may be allowed to return to your normal duties or sent home. And some," his eyes locked with Soren's, hard and unyielding, "may face more serious consequences."

Soren leaned forward, a protest rising to his lips, but Senator Huff forestalled him with a raised hand. "Captain Strickland," the senator said, his voice smooth as oil, "there will be ample time for you to present your case. But for now, Admiral Montoya and I will be conducting these proceedings."

Huff turned to Alex, his eyes glinting with calculating interest. "Gunnery Sergeant Strickland," he said. "I understand you and your team were present on PX-2847 during the recent attack. Is that correct?"

Alex stood, his posture rigid with military discipline. "Yes, Senator," he said, his voice steady. "The Scorpions were stationed on PX-2847 when the colony was attacked by unknown hostiles."

"And by unknown hostiles, you mean Outworlders?" Huff asked.

"No, Senator. I don't believe the attackers were Outworlders."

"And what brings you to that conclusion, Sergeant?"

"Mostly, because of what I experienced at the end of the occupation, sir."

"We'll get to that in a minute," Huff said. "Right now, I want to understand something. From what I understand, there were eight thousand Marines stationed on PX-2847. Is that about right?"

"As far as I know, sir. I never paid much attention to full roster counts."

"Nor would you be expected to," Huff said. "You can probably guess where I'm going with this. What I'm curious about, Sergeant, is that out of those eight thousand Marines, there were only five survivors. You and your unit. Is that correct?"

Alex's jaw tightened, a flicker of pain crossing his features as he remembered the fallen. "That's correct, Senator."

Huff nodded, his expression unreadable. "A tragic loss, to be sure. And you attribute your own survival to, what exactly? Skill? Providence?"

"A little bit of everything, sir. A lot of things had to go right for us to be standing here before you."

"They sure did, didn't they."

"Are you trying to imply something, Senator?" Alex asked.

"Sergeant, I'm sure you can put yourself in my shoes, and in doing so see how this looks. And maybe you would find yourself thinking the same thing I am. From where I'm sitting, it looks damned convenient that your squad, and your squad alone, made it out alive."

CHAPTER 8

Soren surged to his feet, his blood boiling. "Now wait just a minute, Senator," he growled. "My son and his team are heroes. They fought with courage and honor, against impossible odds. To suggest that they had anything to do with—"

"Captain Strickland." Huff's voice cracked like a whip, sharp and commanding. "You will sit down and remain silent until addressed. This inquiry is not about you, not yet. Sergeant?"

Soren sank back into his chair, his fists clenched and his heart pounding. Beside him, he could feel Jack's restraining hand on his arm and could sense the warning in his old friend's eyes. Steady, the look seemed to say. Don't play into their hands.

"It does look convenient, sir," Alex agreed. "But I assure you, there was nothing convenient about it."

Huff grunted, tapped on his datapad, and then looked at Alex. "Please, continue your account. And spare no detail."

Alex took a deep breath, visibly collecting himself before speaking again. He quickly provided an overview of everything that happened on Jungle, from the initial surprise attack to the liberation of Hut and the Scorpion's assault on Fort Brix. Huff listened with rapt attention, though Soren sensed it was so he could identify holes in the story, not because he truly cared as much as it seemed.

"It was during the assault on the fort that I encountered...him. The other me."

Huff leaned forward. "Did you just say, the 'other' you? Please elaborate."

"An enemy Marine, sir. He's the reason I know it wasn't the Outworlders who attacked PX-2847. He's the reason I know my father is onto something big, and you should listen to him when—"

"Stick to answering the question, Sergeant," Huff interrupted.

"It was as if I was looking into a mirror," Alex said softly. "Same face, same voice. Same skills and training. But twisted, somehow. He was stronger, faster, and utterly ruthless. We fought, and it was like nothing I've ever experienced. Like battling my own shadow."

Soren's heart clenched at the pain and confusion in his son's voice. He understood the shock of confronting one's doppelgänger, the sickening wrongness of it. And to imagine Alex facing that horror man-to-man, instead of wrapped inside the cocoon of a starship, without any context or understanding.

Senator Huff shook his head, his lips curled in a condescending smirk. "A fascinating tale, Sergeant," he said. "I've reviewed your medical report. It seems you took a blow to the head during that fight. I understand you believe you saw some evil twin out there. But I find it more reasonable to think your memory of that particular individual may be faulty."

"It's not faulty," Malik spoke out. "Gunny saw it right. I was there. I saw his doppelganger, too.'

"In the fog of war," Huff said. "In the heat of battle. It could be this enemy Marine had a similar face, that's all. And don't speak out of turn again, Corporal."

"Sorry, Senator," Malik replied. "But it wasn't a similar face. It was Gunny's face. I'd bet my life on it."

"Me, too, sir," Zoe said.

"I see. Well, I'll humor you for a minute, Sergeant. If it wasn't the Outworlders, then who was it?"

"I can't answer that question without providing much more context, sir. And my father is better suited to giving that context than me."

"Conveniently enough," Huff grumbled. "You're free to sit, Sergeant." He swiveled his chair towards Soren as Alex returned to his seat. "Captain Strickland. The Wraith. A former POW, a decorated war hero. A man of action. A loving father and husband. And yet, here you are, in front of me not as an asset to the FUP, but as a disgrace. And the only question I can think to ask is, why?"

Soren stood. "You already answered it, Senator. Because I'm a loving father, and my daughter went missing. Because I'm a man of action, and couldn't sit idly by while the FUP made a half-assed attempt at a search before sweeping the whole thing under the rug as some sort of accident or insurgent event supposedly orchestrated by outworlders."

"Captain!" Huff snapped, clearly angered by the statement. "How dare you speak of your fellow spacers that way. Half-assed?"

"I didn't call them half-assed, sir. I'm referring to our leadership and its desire to avoid the existence of confrontation at every possible opportunity. You asked me why. That's my motive, sir. But what I've learned since then has turned what I saw as a search and rescue mission into something much bigger and far more important. A fight for not only our galaxy, but for the very definition of ourselves as individuals."

Huff didn't look happy. "And what do you mean by that?" He gestured to Soren to keep talking.

Soren recounted their search for the data recorder and what they found stored on the device. He also related his interaction with the other Soren and their duel in space.

"Senator, Admiral, please," he said softly. "I know how this must sound. I know the idea of alternate realities, of a threat from beyond our own universe, seems like the ravings of a madman. But I swear to you, on everything I hold dear, that it's the absolute truth."

He gestured to the others, his voice low and urgent. "We have evidence, hard data that supports everything my son has said. The missing data recorder from the derelict ship, the readings of dimensional instability. It's all there, if you'll just let us show it to you."

Montoya hesitated, a flicker of doubt crossing his face. Soren pressed on, sensing an opening.

"And the attacks, the destabilization efforts, it all fits a very obvious strategic pattern. The other side is testing our defenses ahead of a massive invasion. We need to act now, to mobilize our forces and fortify our defenses, before it's too late."

For a moment, it seemed as if Montoya might relent, or at least entertain the possibility. But then Senator Huff was there, his voice dripping with condescension.

"A thrilling narrative, Captain," he said. "And you can produce this evidence?"

"I told you, sir. It's on a data recorder, on board the Wraith."

Huff turned to Montoya. "What do you know about this, Admiral?"

"Lieutenant Bashir has the recorder, Senator," Montoya replied. "It's en route from Pensacola as we speak."

"I know once you've reviewed it, you'll understand," Soren said.

"We'll see about that," Huff countered. He swiveled his chair again. "Can the survivors from the Recon Three assigned starship Pinto please make themselves known?"

The crew members all rose to their feet.

"Can any of you corroborate Captain Strickland's story?"

"I can, Senator," Sophie said. "It's all exactly as he says, sir. Captain Strickland saved our lives and took a big risk to himself, his ship, and his crew in doing so. I hope you'll take that into consideration."

Soren glanced at Montoya. He seemed willing to consider the good they had done with their stolen starship, not only that they had stolen it. Huff, on the other hand…

"Serious crimes have been committed," the senator said. "But not by you. You're all free to go. You'll be escorted to the nearest Naval base until you can be reassigned."

"Thank you, Senator," Sophie said. She offered Soren a comforting glance before she and the rest of Pinto's crew were guided from the room.

Senator Huff swiveled his attention back to Alex but spoke to Montoya. "Admiral, I remain suspicious of Sergeant Strickland's story. However, most of the events he described have witnesses and occurred before the Wraith ever arrived in orbit. I can't find any fault in the actions these Marines took in the face of overwhelming odds. In fact, if it turns out that everything is as Gunny has said, I would recommend the highest commendation for their bravery and courage under fire. However, I believe our investigation needs to be completed to make a final determination."

"I recommend transferring them to Camp Pendleton," Montoya said. "They can train there while we await the results of the inquiry."

"As you say, then," Huff said. "Sergeant, you and your unit are dismissed."

Alex didn't say anything to Soren before he walked out. He didn't need to. As he and his squad stood up, he laid his hand on his father's shoulder, his fingers tightening in a comforting squeeze.

Soren patted the back of his hand and smiled at him before he and the others left the room. Soren watched them leave, wondering when he would see Alex again or if he ever would. Considering what they were facing, he could take nothing for granted.

Soren turned back around to find Senator Huff looking directly at him and Jack once more. "Captain Strickland, Admiral Harper...you may think what you did was a victimless crime. And as a man with children of my own, I commend your love for your daughter, truly. But your reckless actions have put the peace and security of the FUP at risk. You may have saved some lives out there, but your actions may cost so many more. For that, you are to be remanded to custody pending formal charges of treason and theft of Federation property. Your crew will remain for further questioning. Guards, take them away."

CHAPTER 9

Soren and Jack were silently led from the conference room, their footsteps echoing hollowly in the long corridor. The Marine guards flanked them on either side, their faces impassive, their grips firm on their weapons. Soren could feel the bitter taste of anger rising in his throat, his fists clenched as he mentally replayed the senator's dismissive words.

How could the man be so blind? So willfully ignorant of the danger that loomed over them all?

Beside him, Jack walked with his head held high, his bearing as proud and dignified as ever. But Soren could see the tension in his old friend's shoulders, the tightness around his eyes. This was also a blow to Jack, a painful reminder of how quickly the tide could turn and how easily a lifetime of service could be forgotten in the face of political expediency.

They were loaded into a waiting prisoner transport, the heavy doors slamming shut behind them with a resounding clang. The vehicle rumbled to life, carrying them away from the Navy yard, away from any hope of making their case heard.

Soren slumped against the wall, his head falling with a dull thud. "This can't be happening," he muttered, his voice rough with barely contained fury.

Jack sighed, settling onto the bench beside him. "I know, Soren. Believe me, I know. But we have to stay calm, stay focused. Losing our heads now won't help anyone, least of all ourselves."

Soren turned to him, his eyes blazing. "How can you be so damned calm about this, Jack? They're going to bury us, bury the truth. And while we rot in some cell, the enemy will be preparing to strike. We can't let that happen!"

"We won't," Jack said firmly, his hand resting on Soren's forearm. "But we have to be smart about this. We have to trust in the system, in the people we know. Montoya is on our side. He'll do what he can to make this right."

"I didn't get the impression he was on our side."

"Because you're letting your frustration get the better of you. That's not the Wraith I knew from the Navy. Montoya can't ignore the facts the way Huff can. Once he has the data recorder, once he sees Dana's message—"

"What if he thinks it's fake? That we created it to support our claims?"

"That would be a tall order. You know AI creations are all watermarked."

"They can still make the claim, even if it isn't true."

Jack sighed. "If the FUP wants to bury us, they can bury us. There's nothing anyone can do about that. But we both know Anton. He'll come through."

"And if he can't?" Soren asked, his voice barely above a whisper. "If Huff and his ilk have their way?"

"Like you said. We never give up."

"Oh, I'm not giving up, Jack. I'm just trying to plan my next move."

"Now that's the Wraith I know."

The journey to Naval Support Activity Bethesda only

took a few minutes. They were processed quickly and efficiently, stripped of their uniforms and personal effects, and given bright orange jumpsuits with PRISONER stenciled on the back. As he donned the plain, ill-fitting garment in place of his tailored uniform, Soren felt a profound sense of loss, as if a piece of his identity had been stripped away.

The adjacent cells they were led to were small and spare, little more than a bed, toilet, sink, and a mirror. The bars slammed shut behind them with cold finality, the locks engaging with a heavy clunk.

For a long moment, Soren simply stood there, staring at the bars, his mind racing with a thousand thoughts and emotions. Then, with a snarl of rage, he slammed his fist against the wall, the impact sending a jolt of pain up his arm.

"Damn them," he hissed, his voice shaking. "Damn them all."

Suddenly feeling the weight of exhaustion pressing down on him, he sank onto his bunk. The loss of the adrenaline that had sustained him throughout the long journey and the tense confrontation had left him feeling drained and hollow. He hadn't seen anyone in any of the other cells as they were led midway down the corridor between the two rows of cells, the overwhelming silence only adding to his sense of isolation and shame. All despite his belief that he had done the right thing for his family and for the FUP.

"Montoya will come see us," Jack said from the adjacent cell. "Before the day is over, I think."

"I hope you're right, Jack," he murmured. "For all our sakes, I hope you're right."

Soren laid down, and feeling the need for solitude, turned to face the wall.

The hours crawled by with agonizing slowness, each minute feeling like an eternity in the confines of their cells. As usual, Soren couldn't sleep, his mind too occupied with scenarios and possibilities, and the fear of what might be happening beyond these walls. Mostly, he was afraid for his crew, though the fact that they had yet to be delivered to Bethesda to join them was a positive sign.

Soren rolled back over and looked at Jack. He sat quietly on his bunk, his eyes closed and his breathing steady. He seemed almost at peace, as if he had found some inner reserve of calm to draw upon.

"Are you meditating, Jack?"

The older man grinned but still didn't open his eyes or move. "Maybe. You should try it sometime. It's very beneficial. It clears the mind of all frustration and worry."

Soren snorted. "Right. Running does that for me. Do you think they'll allow us rec time?"

"Probably. But not today. If I were you…"

Jack stopped speaking and opened his eyes when footsteps echoed down the corridor. Soren hopped to his feet and moved to the bars, his hands gripping the cold metal, straining to glimpse who approached.

And then, Admiral Montoya appeared, walking toward their cells. He looked tired, the lines of his face deeper than Soren remembered, but there was a steely determination in his eyes.

"Anton," Soren breathed, relief and gratitude suffusing his voice.

Montoya held up a hand, forestalling any further words as he stopped before Soren. "Not here," he said quietly, turning to the guard who walked up behind him. Keys jangled as he unlocked Soren's cell and then Jack's.

"Come with me. Both of you."

Soren and Jack fell into step behind Montoya as he led them down the corridor into a small, nondescript room. The door had barely closed behind them before Soren was speaking, the words tumbling out in an urgent rush. "Anton, you have to listen to me. What we told you at the meeting, it's all true. Every word. The threat is real, and it's coming. We have to prepare. We have to—"

"Soren," Montoya cut him off, his voice gentle but firm. "I know. I believe you."

Soren stared at him. "You do?"

Montoya nodded, a wry smile tugging at his lips. "Of course I do. I've known you too long and trust you too much to doubt you now. What you've done, the lengths you've gone to, to find Dana and uncover the truth...it's exactly what I would expect from a man like you." He sighed, shaking his head. "The FUP isn't what it used to be. Everyone wants peace, but peace has its downsides, too. It brings complacency and breeds weakness. As men of war, we both know that. People like Huff don't. They care more about their own agendas or their polling numbers than the truth or what's right. War is bad for re-election, you know."

"How inconvenient," Soren agreed with a sigh. "Is there anything you can do to make them see reason?"

"I'm doing everything I can, Soren. Believe me. I've seen the data recorder, watched the video. It's...it's chilling. The implications are staggering. I still haven't fully wrapped my head around it."

"That was my initial reaction, too," Soren replied.

He leaned forward, his expression intense. "I'm pushing to get approval on a mission to the coordinates Dana provided. If what she says is true, if there's a rift out there, a way to another dimension, we need to know. We need to be prepared."

"And what about us?" Jack asked, speaking for the first time. "What about the charges against us?"

Montoya's face hardened. "If war is coming, if this threat is as real as you say...then we're going to need every able-bodied fighter we have. Every ship, every weapon. That includes you two. And especially the Wraith." He met Soren's eyes, a fierce light burning in his gaze. "I'll do everything in my power to get you out of here, Soren. If it comes to it, I'll call in every favor, pull every string. Because when the time comes, we're going to need you out there, on the front lines. Not rotting in some cell back here."

"And what about my crew?" Soren asked.

"Lucky for you, most of them were honorably discharged and had multiple commendations on their records." Montoya smiled. "I can't believe you got Ethan to come out of retirement to join you on your quest."

"He was bored," Soren replied.

"They broke the law, but Huff is willing to settle for revocation and probation over jail time. A slap on the wrist, as long as the masterminds don't get away without punishment. As for your medical officer…she's already revoked." Montoya shook his head. "I know you took her on because you were desperate, but it was a bad idea."

"You can't get her off the hook for saving the lives of the spacers from Pinto, not to mention two special forces Marines? There's a lot of value in those lives."

"Again, I'm trying. She was already in the Dregs, so best case is she'll end up right back where she started."

"Better than prison."

"Not by much."

Soren nodded. "Anton, thank you for everything you're trying to do. I owe you one."

"You owe me more than that," Montoya replied. "Anyway, don't thank me yet. We've got a long road ahead of us, and like you pointed out, my hands are tied. But I'm using them as best I can." He stood, straightening his uniform. "For now, though, I need you to sit tight. I know it's hard, but we have to let the process play out. Give me time to work on approvals and call in favors. I'll let you know when I have news." Montoya clasped his shoulder, a gesture of solidarity and support. "You're a good man,

Soren. A damned good man. We'll see this through, one way or another."

With that, he was gone, the door closing softly behind him. Soren slumped back in his chair, feeling as if a weight had been lifted from his shoulders. For the first time since their arrest, he felt a glimmer of hope, a sense that maybe, just maybe, they could still turn the tide.

Beside him, Jack let out a low whistle. "Well, that went about as well as we could have hoped."

Soren nodded, a small smile tugging at his lips. "It did. Anton, he's always been a straight shooter. If he says he'll fight for us, he will."

"Damn right he will," Jack agreed. "Now we just have to wait, see how it all plays out."

"I've never been good at waiting," Soren admitted, a note of wry humor in his voice.

"Well, now's a good time to learn," Jack chuckled. "Because something tells me we're going to be doing a lot of it in the days to come."

CHAPTER 10

Alex had no idea why they'd been brought to this stark, impersonal room with hard chairs that sprouted from bare white walls or even what they were waiting for. All they'd been told was to wait. Typical for the military.

"This is boring as hell," Jackson griped. The monitor in the corner was running through the day's news, but it was on mute, and there was no way to turn on the sound. Under the circumstances, all they could do was sit there and twiddle their thumbs until someone came to get them.

"It sucks," Zoe said, finally losing her patience. Slapping her palms against her thighs, she got up to pace the length of the tiny room and back again. "They told us we were off the hook and leaving for Pendleton." She was talking as much with her hands as with her mouth. "What are they waiting for? We've been here two hours and there's not even a drink machine in here."

"You dying of thirst or something?" Jackson asked.

"Maybe she's got a hot date waiting for her at Pendleton." Malik suggested.

"I wish," Zoe replied. "I just want to get out of here

before Gunny here can convince us to jailbreak his dad or something just as stupid."

"Hey!" Alex put a finger to his lips. There was no telling what kind of listening devices they had hidden in the room. "I have no intention of trying to get my dad out of the mess he's gotten himself into. He's my father, not the other way around."

"She has a point, though, Gunny," Malik said. "I can see the wheels turning in your head. Not that you're really thinking about doing something as crazy as trying to break your old man and the Admiral out of stir. We've helped them all we can. It's time to go fight the interdimensional hordes that are headed our way. That's where we belong."

Alex sighed. "I guess you're right. I just hate the way Huff is treating my dad, and this waiting around wasting time is getting on my nerves."

Each second that passed was a torturous tic in Alex's head, bringing his headache to a pounding crescendo. When, at last, the door opened. he jumped to his feet, surprised when a pair of Marine guards led the rest of Soren's crew into the room, their faces weary. It was immediately obvious that Senator Huff had put them through the wringer.

"Wait here," one of the Marines said, closing the door behind them.

"Great. More waiting," Zoe groused, dropping back down in her chair. Folding her arms across her chest, she let out a weary sigh.

"What do you want to bet they're standing guard out there," Kiera said, her voice strained. "Like we're about to jump ship or something."

"What happened in there?" Alex asked her, observing everyone else's grim expressions. "Are you all okay?"

Keira shook her head and took the last open seat next to

Alex. "They're revoking our licenses, and putting us on probation."

"No prison time, at least." Ethan slid down the wall to sit on the floor.

"And we get to keep our pensions," Bastian added from where he'd leaned against the wall.

"Thank the stars for that," Harry muttered, looking grim.

Alex noticed Asha standing apart from the others, her eyes distant. "Asha, what about you?" he asked.

"They haven't decided about me yet," she said softly. "The rest of you have these exemplary military records. Mine is a disaster. I'm not allowed to leave. I'm afraid...I'm afraid they'll send me to jail."

"I'm going to put in a good word for you with Admiral Montoya first chance I get," Alex said. "You saved people's lives. You don't deserve to be treated like this."

"Thank you, Alex. I—"

Before the conversation could continue, the door opened again, and a staff officer entered, Lieutenant E. Weber according to her name tag. She pushed in a cart laden with duffel bags.

"Your personal effects from the Wraith," she explained briskly. "I'm sure you can sort out which bag is whose better than I can."

"Does that mean the data recorder is here as well?" Mark asked.

"I wasn't made aware of any other items delivered on the shuttle."

Alex eyed the packs. With all that had happened, his and the rest of his team's personal effects had been abandoned on Jungle. They literally had nothing that was their own, not even a toothbrush.

Lieutenant Weber handed out small envelopes next, her expression softening slightly. "A stipend, to help you through the next twenty-four hours. We've also arranged rooms at a hotel near the airport for you."

She turned to Alex, holding out a handful of plastic cards. "Shuttle tickets for you and your squad, Sergeant. Your flight leaves in the morning. The rest of you," she addressed Soren's crew, "will need to purchase your own tickets to your destinations. A bus is waiting outside to take you to the hotel, whenever you're ready to leave."

"That includes me?" Asha asked, holding up the envelope she'd been handed.

"Why wouldn't it?"

"Well, I was under the impress..." She had second thoughts. "Nevermind." She shoved the envelope into her back pocket, and with that, the staff officer left them to find the duffels holding their individual belongings.

The Marine guards returned a few minutes later to take them outside, where a large bus waited to take them to the hotel. They piled into the vehicle, riding in near silence as they made their way to the hotel positioned on the outskirts of Washington, D.C.

The hotel itself was nice enough, a blend of sleek, modern lines and retro-futuristic flourishes. Under different circumstances, Alex might have appreciated the aesthetic and maybe even booked a personal stay. But right now, all he could feel was a growing sense of unease and urgency.

As soon as they departed the bus, Alex moved to the head of the line and turned to address the others. "I'd like to have a few words with you when we get inside."

"What is it, Alex?" Ethan asked.

"Inside," he repeated, leading them into the lobby. He found a quiet corner, his gaze intense as he looked at each of them. "We need to talk about what happened back there," he said, his voice low. "Now that we're away from prying eyes and ears."

"What's on your mind?" Keira asked. "It seems everything has already been decided."

"By Senator Huff," Alex scoffed. "Not by us. Are you really ready to just pack it up and go home? After everything that's happened? Considering what you know?"

Keira shook her head, her expression pained. "What can we do? We're lucky we're not behind bars, which is where we were told we'd end up if we divulged any of what we saw and did out there."

"My father is behind bars," Alex countered. "So is Admiral Harper. And let's not forget my sister's ship is still missing. Maybe if this was just about Dana and her crew, I could find a way to accept that. It wouldn't be easy, but I would try. But this isn't only about Dana. And if the FUP won't act, somebody has to. I think you all know that."

"What are you suggesting?" Ethan asked.

Alex took a deep breath. "We've been working on a plan to rescue my father and get him back to the Wraith since we left Jungle." He lowered his voice even further. "Wilf and Tashi sabotaged the ship to make sure it can't leave before we have a chance to get to it. They also found ways to manipulate the controls without access to the bridge, so even if they try to lock us out, we can still get the ship into space."

"Those two never fail to impress," Lina said, shaking her head in disbelief.

"What I can't believe is that they're working together on something," Ethan added.

"I think in their eagerness to help Soren, they forgot they hate each other's guts," Asha said.

"Once we have my father and the Admiral, we get them to the Wraith and we get the hell out of here. We go to the coordinates on the data recorder, and we find a way to stop the Convergence before it's too late."

"You make it sound so simple," Sang said.

"I know it won't be simple, which is why I can't do it without your help, but..." He turned to his team. "I know we planned all this out, but there's a big difference between planning it and actually doing it. I'll understand if you want to forget about all of this and continue on to Camp Pendleton without me."

The Scorpions stared back at Alex. Zoe spoke up first. "I knew this was going to happen. Give Gunny five minutes alone with us..." She gave her arm an agitated wave. "...and he ropes us into following him on another fool's errand."

"I didn't say anything to try to convince you of anything," Alex countered.

"It happens like this every time," Jackson agreed. "Gunny makes this big impassioned speech, and we just follow along like he's the pied piper."

"I didn't make a speech," Alex argued.

"It's like he hypnotizes us or something," Sarah said.

"Damn straight. It's subliminal messaging," Malik explained. "Subconscious words beneath his spoken words, convincing us to do whatever he wants."

"What?" Alex said, confused.

The other Scorpions began laughing. Malik clapped him on the shoulder. "As if we'd go to Pendleton or anywhere else without you, Gunny! We didn't spend all those hours planning this just to leave you holding the damn bag. We're with you, man. All the way."

Alex grinned, finally getting the joke. He wrapped his arm around Malik's neck and hugged him. "Thanks, man," he said, fighting back his emotions. "I'm happy to have you with me. But I'll need all of you." His attention skimmed over every other face. "What do you say? Will you help us?"

After a moment, Bastian sighed heavily. "I don't know

who's got the best gift of persuasion, you or your old man." He grinned at Alex. "Count me in, kid."

"Me, too," Lina said.

"I think that goes for all of us," Ethan said, eliciting nods and mumbled affirmations from all the others. Except Harry.

"Harry?" Alex raised his eyebrows.

"We just barely got out of this first mess," he said, his expression troubled. "And now we're diving headfirst back into another? I want to help Soren as much as any of you, but...is this really wise?"

"Let me just ask you this," Alex countered. "Knowing what we know, how can we just walk away?"

A murmur of agreement passed through the group. Harry sighed but nodded his understanding.

"Asha, what about you?" Alex asked. "If we try to get back to the Wraith, are you in?"

She didn't hesitate. "Absolutely. I'd do pretty much anything to help your dad after what he did for me."

"Alright," Alex said, scrubbing his palms together. "Thank you all for sticking with me." He zeroed in on Kiera. "Do you know where they might have taken my father and Jack?"

She hesitated, thinking. "NSA Bethesda is most likely," she said at last. "It has the closest brig from here, and it's a major Navy installation."

"Which means we can't just walk in, grab them, and walk out," Ethan added.

"I never planned to. But we need a location before we can get into the details. I don't suppose I can get a map of the place online?"

"The surrounding area, sure," Ethan answered. "But the base itself? Not a chance. I can get you one, though. Give me a few hours with a terminal. I'll find what we need."

"I think I can help you, too," Sang said. "I have a friend

stationed at Bethesda. I can talk to her and tell her I want to come see her. If she signs me as a visitor, maybe I can sneak you inside."

"You don't think Montoya will notice you're on the visitor list where my father is locked up?" Alex asked.

"Of course he will, but hopefully not until it's too late."

"I like the way you think, Sang," Sarah said.

"Next steps," Alex said, "we'll split up for now and get what supplies we need. Scorpions, we need to pick up black clothing, gloves, new DAs so we can stay in contact, and something to use for local comms. And freezers, so we can take out anyone who gets in our way without hurting them."

"Where are we going to get freezers?" Sarah asked. "They're illegal." Every eye turned to her. "What?" They all began laughing. Considering what they were planning, obtaining illegal non-lethal paralysis guns hardly registered.

"It should take about five minutes for me to find a guy on a dark corner who's selling them," Malik said.

"The rest of you will need to book tickets," Alex continued. "The Wraith is in Pensacola. I suggest shuttle flights taking a circuitous route to Florida, with multiple stops so the FUP can't trace you until it's too late. Sang, work on getting us that way inside. Ethan, the map. We'll meet back here at 2100 hours."

CHAPTER 11

The hours flew by as Alex and his team made their preparations. They moved through the city, using the stipends the lieutenant had given them in a manner the Navy least expected. They gathered everything they needed, every action deliberate, every interaction subtle and beyond the public eye. They couldn't afford any slip-ups or to leave a trace of what they were really doing. This was the kind of mission they had trained for.

As the appointed time drew near, everyone regrouped in the hotel lobby, their faces tense beneath the otherwise sedate, comforting nighttime lights. Sang was the last to arrive, a triumphant gleam in her eye.

"It's set," she said without preamble. "My friend thinks I'm coming to pick her up so we can have a ladies' night out with some other friends of ours. She put me on the approved list and everything. I've got us a shuttle rented, but..." She hesitated.

"But what?" Alex prompted.

"We'll need something faster and with longer range if we want to reach Pensacola before they realize what's happened and scramble interceptors."

Alex digested the problem. Stealing a military craft was no small feat, but what choice did they have? "Once we're in, we'll have to split up into two teams. One to the brig, the other to pick up a shuttle."

"We won't be able to grab a shuttle unnoticed," Sarah pointed out. "It's going to up the ante."

"I don't see any way around it," Alex replied.

"Then Malik and I will take care of it," Sarah said.

"Copy that," he agreed.

Ethan produced his digital assistant, holding it up with a grin. "The map," he said simply. "I had to slice my way into a couple databases, but I got what we needed. Do you have a DA for me to pass it to?"

Alex retrieved his burner device. "Brand new, unmarked, harder to trace. We got it off a guy in an alley, along with the freezers." He tapped on the burner to activate it. Ethan passed the map to the device. Alex passed it to the other Scorpions. "The rest of you have tickets?"

Keira nodded. "We'll be on our way to the airport while you're on your way to Bethesda. None of the flights we planned are less than three hops."

"Good work. I hope you all enjoy safe flights." The comment drew chuckles from the group.

"Good hunting out there, Scorpions," Harry said. "Do us a favor and give us a ring if you get caught. We can skip our connecting flights and deny everything."

That drew another round of soft laughter, except for Alex. "You may be on to something there, Harry. Everyone, send me your DA identifiers. If things go south, I'll send a group message out before I smash this thing to pieces."

The others passed him their identifiers, which he loaded into his DA and prepped the message. All he needed to do was open the application and hit the send button.

They said their goodbyes, the weight of the moment hanging heavy over them all. Then, as Soren's crew headed for their airport transfer, Alex and the Scorpions fell into step behind Sang, following her to the rooftop landing pad, where dozens of personal shuttles were parked.

She brought them to a small, nondescript craft with its counter-mass rods positioned along the hull rather than on separate nacelles. Easily affordable for someone on a basic salary and plentiful in the skies worldwide, the aircraft wouldn't draw a second glance. They piled in, nervous energy crackling between them as Sang took the controls and lifted off.

The flight to Bethesda was short, the shuttle eating up the dozen or so miles in a couple of minutes while Alex went over the map with the Scorpions. Sarah and Malik focused on the route to the shuttle bay while Jackson found the path to the brig, and Alex looked at the building blueprints to get the exact layout and location. They didn't have a lot of time, but it was enough.

Sang guided the shuttle towards the landing pad at Bethesda, her hands steady on the controls despite the nervous energy thrumming through her veins. As they neared the base, a gruff voice came over the comms.

"Approaching shuttle, identify yourself and state your purpose."

Sang took a deep breath, her reply calm and even. "This is Sang Hee Brooks, visitor ID SW-4421. I'm here to visit Petty Officer June Larson."

There was a pause, the silence stretching a heartbeat too long for Alex's comfort. Then, "ID confirmed. You're cleared to land on pad seven, Ms. Brooks."

"Acknowledged," Sang replied. She glanced back at Alex and the other Scorpions, her expression urgent. "You all need to hide. Now."

"Hide?" Malik's eyebrows shot up. "Where, exactly? This thing's not exactly spacious."

"There's a storage compartment in the rear," Sang

explained, already descending towards the designated landing pad. "It'll be a tight fit, but it's the only option."

Malik dubiously eyed the small hatch leading to the compartment. "All of us are going to fit in there?"

"Yes, all of you," Sang snapped. "And unless you want to get caught before we even start, you better get your butts in there…now."

Alex cut off any further protest with a sharp gesture. "You heard her, Scorpions. Into the compartment, double time."

There was a flurry of movement as the team scrambled to comply, squeezing into the cramped space with muffled grunts and curses. It was a tight fit, their bodies pressed together, the air quickly growing hot and stale. Alex was the last one in, pulling the hatch closed behind him just as the shuttle touched down at the security shack with a gentle bump.

Wedged between Jackson and the hatch, hardly able to breathe, Alex strained to hear what was happening outside. He could make out Sang's calm and controlled voice as she greeted the base security. Then, the tramp of booted feet as a guard came aboard, ignoring Sang's suggestion that there was no need to check the interior as June would arrive at any moment.

A guard insisted briefly but firmly that he had to have a look inside her shuttle, his voice growing louder as he entered. Alex's heart pounded, his hand reaching for his freezer, sweat beading on his brow. He imagined the hatch being wrenched open and their hiding place discovered. But then he heard the guard inform Sang she was approved to taxi ahead and that June was on her way before departing the shuttle. The shuttle moved forward and came to a stop.

Sang quickly opened the hatch from the outside, Alex and the others spilling onto the shuttle's deck. "Let's go,

Marines," she said. "Get off my ship. That way." She pointed to the closed hatch opposite the open one the guard had used and then exited the shuttle through the open hatch to keep a lookout.

Alex rolled to his feet, stretching cramped muscles and gulping down lungfuls of fresh air as they stumbled to the closed hatch.

"Coast is clear for now," Sang said. "But June will be here any second. You need to hurry."

Alex nodded, already shoving a comms device in his ear and pulling a black balaclava out of his pocket and tugging it over his head. The others did the same, transforming themselves into anonymous infiltrators in seconds. He opened the hatch, and they slipped out of the shuttle, darting across the tarmac toward a nearby alley. Just as June appeared in the distance, moving towards Sang's shuttle, they disappeared between two storage structures.

As they melted into the shadows, Alex heard Sang greeting her friend, spinning a tale of sudden illness. A quick glance over his shoulder showed June guiding Sang towards the admin building, no doubt in search of a restroom. They had bought themselves a small window, but they would need to move fast.

"You all know what to do," he said.

"Oorah," the Scorpions quietly replied.

Sarah checked her freezer before moving farther down the alley with Malik, the two of them disappearing around the corner of the building. Alex followed them but led his small team in the opposite direction, his mental map of the base guiding them toward the brig. Slinking through the darkness, they stopped in the shadows multiple times to allow personnel to pass before sneaking behind them to their next hiding spot.

"Approaching the brig now," Alex murmured into his comm as they neared their target.

"Copy that," Sarah replied. "We've reached the hangar." There was a pause, then, "Going in, stand by."

Alex guided his team around the building to a side door before motioning Zoe and Jackson to watch their six as he pulled out his Marine-issued DA and approached the reinforced entrance. A bead of sweat trickled down his spine as he lowered the device towards the access panel.

And all hell broke loose before he could use it.

CHAPTER 12

An alarm blared across the base, the sudden wail freezing everyone where they stood. Red lights strobed along the outer walls of the building.

"Malik, Sarah, what the hell happened?" Alex barked into his comm, activating his DA to crack the door's security.

"A damn technician came out of nowhere," Sarah replied, her voice shaky with shock and adrenaline. "Malik froze him but he triggered the alarm before he went down. We're blown!"

"Damn it," Alex growled. "We've come too far to turn back now. Get us a shuttle, we'll be there in five mikes."

"I don't know if we can wait that long."

"You have to." Alex gritted his teeth and turned to his companions. "We're out of time. Breach on my mark and sweep fast. They'll be on us right away."

Zoe and Jackson nodded, readying themselves for confrontation. The security panel on the door flashed green, and they burst through into the corridors beyond, freezers at the ready.

The coast was clear, but only for the first few seconds. A

pair of guards came around the corner right in front of them. Jackson and Alex went low while Zoe swerved and charged, diving into the guards to press her freezer against the chest of one and then the leg of the other. They both toppled to the floor, frozen in place.

The three Scorpions sprinted ahead, Alex navigating the corridors to the brig. It was a running battle, a desperate sprint through a gauntlet of shouting guards firing stunner blasts at them while they avoided the shots and moved in close to press their freezers into the bodies of their Navy brothers and sisters. In no time, the air reeked of ozone and sweat as they fought deeper into the facility, dropping threats with precision as they appeared.

Two guards leaped out from an adjoining passageway, energy pistols raised. Jackson dropped into a slide, his freezer snapping to catch them in the knees, sending them both toppling backward. Alex took out guard number three as he tried to move in from behind them. He threw the freezer at the man as though it were a knife, the active side hitting him in the shoulder, putting him on the floor.

Picking up his weapon, Alex led an increasingly desperate charge. A squad of guards poured from a doorway ahead, trying to form a firing line. Alex threw himself into a forward roll, coming up in their midst like a coiled snake, his freezer like fangs biting into them.

Caught off guard, they fell static to the floor. But more were coming, the alarm still blaring, and even the Scorpions couldn't fight an entire base.

At last, the brig door came into view, a single guard standing wide-eyed before it. He swung to face the attackers, energy pistol steady, but Zoe was faster. She shoved her freezer against his groin, his body folding as he slumped to the floor.

"Ouch, sorry," she said in response to her aim.

Alex stepped over him, slamming his DA against the

lock. The mechanism disengaged with a heavy clunk, and he burst through, Jackson and Zoe right behind him.

"Dad! Jack!" he cried.

Soren and Jack were already on their feet, roused by the alarms and commotion. Their faces registered shock, disbelief and a flicker of pride as Alex engaged his DA to unlock Jack's cell door and then Soren's.

"What the hell are you doing here?" Soren demanded as he pushed his cell door open and stepped out to clasp Alex's shoulder, checking him for injury with a father's eye.

"What do you think? We're busting you out," Alex replied.

"Not exactly stealthy," Jack said, coming up behind Soren.

"It didn't all go according to plan." He returned his attention to his father. "We need to move."

"That we do."

They hurried together, a tight unit surrounding Soren and Jack as they retraced Alex's route. The opposition seemed to have slackened, looking to have been called off by some other crisis, but they all knew it was only a momentary reprieve.

Back outside the admin block, they oriented towards the shuttle hangar. "Sarah, Malik," Alex called over comms. "We're out. Where are you?"

Neither of them answered. That didn't stop Alex from leading the others at a run—boots pounding on tarmac, hearts racing—towards the hangar. They rounded the corner of a prefab structure and came to a sudden stop. Just in front of the hangar were Sang and the two Scorpions, balaclavas removed, disarmed and on their knees with their hands folded behind their heads. Four Military Police surrounded them. The one woman was on her comm.

"Shit," Jackson cursed. "It's over."

"No," Alex snapped. "We can still…"

Soren put a hand on his shoulder. "It's over, son. It was a good effort, but we can't win this."

Alex cursed under his breath, pulling out his burner DA and quickly sending the message to the others. Then he dropped the device and stomped on it to destroy the evidence.

Hearing the commotion, two of the MPs swung around and raised their rifles, their weapon lights illuminating the group. When they spotted Soren and Jack in their prison orange, red dots appeared in the center of their foreheads. Both men raised their hands.

"Drop your weapons," the woman ordered Alex and the others as she stepped forward and raised both her handgun and a handheld flashlight, further illuminating them.

Alex tossed his freezer down and pulled off his balaclava, dropping it, too. "Do as she said," he ordered, scowling at the female MP.

The Scorpions obeyed Alex, discarding their freezers as she and the two men with Soren and Jack in their rifle sights moved toward them. When she stopped within ten feet of them, Alex identified the rank of Master Chief on her uniform.

"Over there, with the others," she growled, directing them with a jerk of her chin to where Sarah, Sang, and Malik waited.

"Sorry, Gunny," Sarah said, hanging her head in remorse.

"We messed up...bad, boss-man," Malik added.

"I can explain—" Alex started.

"Shut up," the Master Chief barked before pressing a finger to her ear comm, listening to someone giving her orders. "Are you sure, sir?" A moment later, she added a crisp, "Yes, sir."

Everyone turned toward the whirring of an electric ground vehicle as it approached them, its headlights cutting through the darkness engulfing the tarmac. The white command car approached quickly, stopping just short of them.

The driver quickly emerged, walking around the front of the car to open the back door. She stood at attention as Admiral Montoya got out, followed by a staff officer carrying two duffle bags. Montoya's expression reflected more concern than anger, surprising Soren. He stepped forward, hands raised. "Anton...I can—"

"Quiet, Soren," Montoya snapped, but his voice had more exasperation than true anger. "I wish I could say I was surprised by this, but with everything that's been going on these last few weeks, this is just par for the course." He sadly shook his head.

That was when Soren noticed the alarms were still going off, even though they'd been captured. "Anton, what's going on?"

Montoya locked eyes with Soren, his expression pained. His voice was heavy with a new kind of urgency when he spoke again. "I was coming to get you and Jack before your son and these well-meaning hoodlums decided to dress up and try to break you and Jack out of jail. My intention was to release you into protective custody."

"Why?" Jack asked. "What happened?"

"We just got word from Proxima. They've been hit hard. An enemy fleet showed up just outside of orbit. Komodos and Rhinos, like the kind that you said attacked Recon Three. They took out our orbital defenses in minutes."

A shocked silence fell, the implications sinking in with sickening clarity. Soren found his voice first, rough with dread. "The planet?"

Montoya shook his head. "We lost contact. But from what came in before that, we have to assume Proxima is lost." He straightened, his voice hardening. "It looks like that war you warned us about just kicked off ahead of schedule."

"Let's see Senator Huff blame the CIP for this one," Jackson spat.

"How?" Soren asked, his voice rough. "How could they take an entire planet so quickly?" Stunned, he shook his head. "Our defenses…?"

"…were unprepared," Montoya finished. "And outmatched. Just like you said they would be."

"If we hadn't wasted the last two weeks, we would have reached the rift by now," Alex said. "We might have had a chance to warn them. To warn everyone. Not that you would have listened."

"Be careful, Sergeant," Montoya said. "You're still talking to a superior officer."

Alex met his gaze unflinchingly. "My apologies, Admiral."

Soren looked around, noticing activity from the hangar bays and barracks. Ambivalence had so quickly been replaced by fear of being caught off-guard like Jungle and Proxima. Like Dana.

"Soren," Montoya continued. "I was coming to get you because I need you. Our entire universe needs you."

"What about Huff?" Jack asked. "Does he need us?"

"I haven't spoken to Huff yet. I don't care if he approves of what I'm about to do or not. This is war. It's better to act first and apologize later."

"It seems to me that's exactly what you threw us in prison for doing, Anton," Soren growled. "You chose not to believe me when I tried to warn you. You decided to—"

Montoya put up his hand. "That was Huff's decision, not mine. You can blame me now and hate me later, but the shit is hitting the fan." He turned his attention back to Alex. "You're right, Sergeant, we already wasted too much time. Let's not waste another second."

He turned to the staff officer who handed him the duffles when he reached for them. "Here," He handed one to Soren, the other to Jack. "Can't have the two of you commanding an FUP ship in prison orange. You'll find your uniforms in there and the personal belongings you left onboard the Wraith when you were arrested. Both of you are being recalled to active duty, effective immediately. Soren, you've been reinstated at your rank of Captain. Sorry, Jack, you're busted down to Commander. Can't have a captain giving orders to an admiral, now can we?"

"And I suppose we've already signed the proper paper-work," Jack quipped.

"Of course. I don't leave things to chance." He glanced at Sang, then back to Soren "Where's the rest of your crew?"

"Scattered," he answered. "But they were all headed to Florida, to join us in Pensacola."

Montoya laughed bitterly. "Of course they were."

"I called them off when we failed our mission," Alex added. "I don't have their DA identifiers to call them back."

"I do," Soren said, looking at Montoya. "If you return my DA to me."

The admiral turned to one of the SPs. "Go back to the brig and fetch the personal effects that were taken from these men when they were incarcerated. Double-time!"

"Yes, sir," the SP replied, racing off to retrieve the items.

"The universe doesn't care about our rules or decorum," Montoya said. "We both know the Wraith is our best asset in this fight and we need both the man and the ship out there as soon as possible. You'll take your team, you'll take the Wraith, and you'll follow this lead to its end, be that to damnation or glory. Is that understood, Captain Strickland?"

"Yes, Admiral," Soren replied.

Montoya straightened, addressing the assembled SPs.

"As of this moment, I'm classifying this mission as top secret under FUPN protocol. No records, no reports. As far as the world knows, none of this ever happened. Understood?"

A chorus of "Yes, sir!" rang out, crisp and unified.

The breathless SP came running back, carrying two baggies with Jack and Soren's things. Montoya handed them over, his expression deadly serious.

"Go with my blessing, and more importantly, a warning —you screw this up, there might not be anyone left to court martial you afterwards."

Soren chuckled at that, a humorless bark. "Understood, Admiral. We won't let you down." as they hurried into the nearby hangar.

"See that you don't," Montoya replied. "Take your pick of whatever ship you want to fly to Pensacola. I'll make sure you have a clear route, and that the Wraith is loaded up for your arrival."

"Thank you, sir," Soren said. "We'll be in touch."

With that, they were moving, the Scorpions falling into step around Soren and Jack, Alex at Soren's elbow. "You know, Alex," he said, "breaking us out was the stupidest thing you've ever done, but thank you for coming,"

He grinned. "You're welcome, Dad. Anytime."

"Actually, I think it all went quite well," Jackson said.

"Not for Proxima," Jack replied somberly. Nobody had anything to add to that as they hurried into the hangar. Behind them, Montoya was already barking orders over his comm, setting the wheels of the coverup in motion.

"Let's hurry and get airborne," Soren said. "I have some calls to make."

CHAPTER 13

Soren and the others hurried into the hangar, their eyes scanning the various craft parked within. Sang's gaze immediately locked onto a sleek, angular shape nestled in the corner.

"There," she said, pointing it out. "That's our ride."

"Is that a Stinger?" Sarah asked.

"Sure is," Sang answered. "I've always wanted to fly one. The fastest, most maneuverable, and most well-armed VIP shuttle in the Navy."

"I don't think we'll need to do much maneuvering or shooting," Soren said. "It's a straight shot down to Florida."

"Maybe not here, but once we get into space and through the dimensional rift," Sang explained. "It couldn't hurt."

"Thinking ahead. I like it."

They hurried over to the shuttle, Sang taking the lead. She ran a hand along the smooth, composite hull, which had a bulge along each of the wings where weapons pods were hidden. A grin spread across her face as the hatch slid open, and they piled inside.

The interior was more utilitarian. It was a military craft, after all. A dozen lightly padded seats were arranged in six rows, each with three-point harnesses. Curved displays along the fuselage offered camera-fed views of the outside.

Everyone but Sang was strapped into the rear seats. Jack took a seat alongside Jackson, and they immediately struck up a conversation as Soren hurried forward to the flight deck. He slid into the co-pilot seat beside Sang and buckled himself in. She was still flipping switches and tapping on the control interface, bringing systems online with practiced ease.

"I thought this thing would at least have a tray table and cup holders," Soren heard Jackson quip from the rear.

Sang chuckled as she activated the counter-mass generators, lifting the transport off the deck and retracting its landing skids. She eased the craft forward through the hangar door, giving the MPs and other base personnel time to clear a path. Soren found Admiral Montoya standing to their right by his car and offered him a thumbs-up. The Admiral waved back.

"Bethesda Control, this is Stinger Alpha Six Bravo requesting clearance to launch," Sang said, contacting base operations.

"Stinger Alpha Six Bravo, you are cleared to launch," came the reply. "Good luck, and godspeed."

"Thank you, control." Sang closed the connection and drew in a deep breath. "Alright, everybody," she threw over her shoulder, her voice loud enough for everyone to hear over the hum of the engines coming to life, "pull your belts tight. These birds have a kick." She glanced at Soren, a huge smile on her face that he knew wouldn't last. The exhilaration of a dream would only last so long before the reality of their situation returned.

With a roar of thrusters, the Stinger lifted off, pivoting

on its axis before streaking into the sky, pressing Soren back in his seat. Sang banked hard, angling them southward, the Florida coast a distant glimmer on the horizon.

"I think I'm gonna puke," Jackson joked, groaning as the shuttle ate up the distance, quickly leaving the smear of D.C. behind.

Soren pulled out his DA from the baggie the MP had handed him. He had to get his crew headed back in the right direction. He started with Keira.

Her face materialized above the screen, lined with worry. "Soren! Thank the stars. We saw Alex's message. What happened?"

"Change of plans," Soren said. "We've been...unofficially sanctioned."

"What caused that sudden about-face?" Her expression hardened. She was smart enough to realize it was nothing good. "What happened?"

"Our fears are being realized ahead of schedule," he answered. "Proxima's been hit. We've lost contact with them."

"Oh, no..." Keira gasped.

"Admiral Montoya decided he was done playing games, come what may. I need you on the next direct flight to Pensacola. The Wraith is waiting for us there."

Keira nodded, her initial shock morphing into firm resolve. "Understood. I'll be there as quickly as I can."

He nodded. "I'll see you there."

The call ended, and he moved down the list: Ethan, then Harry, and Lina, each expressing the same mix of concern and determination. They were happy to see him free but saddened by the circumstances.

As the Florida coast grew larger in the viewscreen, Soren made one final call. He'd saved the best for last.

Jane's face appeared, her eyes tired. Soren could tell right away that she hadn't been getting much sleep.

"Soren," she breathed, her voice thick with emotion as she burst into happy tears. "Oh, thank the stars. It's so good to hear from you. To see you. Are you...is everything...this isn't tranSat. You're on Earth?"

"Yes, I'm on Earth," he replied, his tears blurring his vision. He was so damn happy to see her and hear her voice. "It's a long story. I'm doing just fine. But…"

"Dana?" The hope and fear in that single word broke his heart.

"Not yet," he said softly. "But we believe she's alive. And we're going to find her. I promise you that."

"I...I don't understand. You know she's still out there, but you're here on Earth?"

"Not by choice," Soren replied. "Anton caught up to us. He brought us back here. I spent most of the day in the brig."

"But you're free now." Like Keira, she caught on quickly. "Something's happened. Something bad."

"I'm afraid so. The FUP is under threat. There's been an attack. I've been reinstated in the FUPN, and we're going after the attackers."

"What about Dana?"

"She's part of all this. Going after this new enemy will lead me to her." Soren unbuckled his harness and rose to his feet. "I'll explain the whole thing in a minute. I have someone here I know you'll want to see and speak to."

He moved to the rear of the Stinger, keeping the DA facing him so he wouldn't reveal the surprise too soon. He squatted in the aisle beside Alex and repositioned the DA, bringing him into the frame. Jane's gasp was audible, fresh tears springing to her eyes.

"Alex," she whispered. "Oh, my boy..."

"Hi, Mom," Alex managed, his own eyes glistening. "I...I've missed you."

"I…I can't believe you're there with your father. How? What is going on?"

"It's a long story," Alex replied. "And most of it isn't very good. We're in trouble. Not just Dad and me, but the whole galaxy."

"That's kind of what your father told me," Jane said. "Whatever it is, I'm so comforted to see you and Soren together. To know that you're both safe in the present and are taking care of each other."

They continued talking for a few minutes, words tumbling out in a rush of love and longing. Soren watched, his heart full to bursting. This, right here, was what he was fighting for. His family, his loved ones. The chance for moments like these, even in the midst of chaos and uncertainty.

As promised, Soren filled Jane in on the broad strokes of their situation—the attacks, the Convergence, the desperate race against time. She listened, her expression a mix of awe, pride, and worry.

"I believe in you, Soren," she said at last. "In both of you. If anyone can find Dana and stop this madness, it's the Strickland men." Her smile was watery but fierce. "Just…come back to me. All of you. Come home…safe."

"We will," Soren promised. "I love you, Janie. More than anything."

"I love you, too, Mom," Alex said.

"I love you. Both of you. Always."

The call ended, leaving a heavy silence in its wake. Soren stared at the blank screen for a long moment, gathering himself. Then, with a deep breath, he straightened and squeezed Alex's shoulder, before reaching for his bag.

"It wouldn't do to show up in Pensacola in these jump-suits, would it Jack?" Soren asked, digging out his uniform and changing in the aisle. It wasn't the ideal dressing room, but he made do. So did Jack, taking his place as he regained his seat.

"If I had a dollar, I'd give it to you," Malik joked behind them.

"Coming up on Pensacola," Sang announced a few minutes later.

Soren nodded, his gaze drawn to the windshield. There, illuminated by dozens of lights in the darkness and growing larger with each passing second, was the Wraith. His ship, his mission. The key to saving everything he held dear.

To his surprise, the ship wasn't cloaked. It occupied nearly half of the base's massive tarmac, its sleek lines and battle damage plainly visible for all to see. A small crowd swarmed around it—mechanics, technicians, and other non-coms—making hasty repairs and loading supplies.

As they touched down, Soren spotted a familiar figure striding across the tarmac towards them. Captain Broz, the base commander. Soren had met him once, years ago, at a mutual friend's change of command ceremony at Devonport. He recalled Broz as a straight-backed, no-nonsense officer with a reputation for getting things done.

Broz reached the shuttle just as they disembarked, his face a mix of confusion and tightly controlled urgency. "Captain Strickland," he said, voice clipped. "I received an urgent call from Admiral Montoya. He said I'm to give you and your ship our full support. Anything you need, anything at all." His eyes narrowed, a mischievous grin spreading across his face. "He also said to remember that neither you nor that ship were ever here. I'm not sure how I'm supposed to do that since I'm certain civilian crews have spotted that black beauty by now, but I don't ask those kinds of questions. Otherwise, I would be asking what a retired Captain is doing with a starship whose design doesn't match anything in our database and is loaded with advanced tech. No sir, I just follow orders."

Soren shrugged. "Have you heard about Proxima?"

"It just came down the wire." Broz shook his head. "Bastard Outworlders."

"It isn't the Outworlds," Soren replied. "I wish it were that simple. That's all the answer to your non-question you're going to get."

Broz nodded. "Understood. Well, in that case, what do you need from me?"

"Foremost, I need ordnance and provisions," Soren replied. "Full loads of both, as much as you have. Second, any spare parts or equipment you may have on hand for field repairs. Third, and least important, but still needed, furniture, bedding, exercise machines, weights, and other creature comforts. We're on a long journey into the black, and I don't know when we'll be able to resupply."

"Well, the first two are already in progress," Broz said. "But our initial orders were to sit tight and wait for techs from R and D so we're behind where we could have been, I'm sorry to say. As for your third request, I'll see what I can do. It just depends on how quickly you want to get spaceborne."

"As quickly as possible," Soren replied. "Balanced by enough amenities to keep my crew happy during a long trip."

"Understood."

They reached the Wraith, her hull absorbing the harsh lights illuminating the tarmac. Technicians and forklifts went in and out of the loading ramp like an army of ants, loading supplies. It was controlled chaos, a frenzy of activity driven by the knowledge that every second counted.

Soren noticed when Commander Bashir joined the techs coming down the ramp. The Commander hurried over to him and Broz, coming to attention. "Captains," he said. "Commander Bashir reporting, sirs."

"At ease, Commander," Broz said. "What do you need?"

"I just got off the line with Admiral Montoya," Bashir said. "Captain Strickland, I have orders to report to you for duty, sir. My crew is yours."

"I see," Soren replied, wondering if Montoya had reassigned the commander and his crew to him to help spell his team or if he planned to use the man to keep him in check. More likely the former, he decided. "While I can certainly use the extra hands, I'm hesitant to take you on board. Where we're headed is extremely dangerous."

"From what I hear, everywhere will soon be extremely dangerous, Captain," Bashir replied.

Soren snorted. "I can't argue with that, Commander. Welcome aboard."

"Thank you, sir. Also, the Admiral wanted me to inform you that additional resources are on their way to you. Additional attack drones, a squadron of starfighters, and pilots to fly them. Along with enough Marines to fill out a platoon."

Soren was surprised. That was a lot of additional resources for what he had taken as a clandestine mission. The way he was going, Anton would find himself in the brig.

Then again, the Joint Chiefs had bigger problems to keep them busy. They all did.

"Commander, I want you to work with my logistics officer, Harry, when he arrives, to make sure every piece of equipment and every new crew member is properly cared for."

"Harry?" Bashir asked, confused. "Just Harry?"

"Every member of my crew is either retired or revoked," Soren explained. "Where we're headed, none of that means a damn thing. So we go by first names. What's your first name, Commander?"

"Victor, sir. But you can call me Vic."

"Welcome aboard, Vic," Soren said.

"Thank you, sir."

"You have your orders." He turned to Broz. "And you have my requests. Let's make it happen."

CHAPTER 14

Soren paused just after crossing the threshold onto Wraith's bridge, Jack at his side. The compartment was empty, the stations dark and silent, the viewscreen inactive. Peaceful in a way he hadn't experienced since he'd boarded the ship nearly two months earlier.

A peace he knew wouldn't last for long.

"You missed her, didn't you?" Jack said, watching Soren smooth his hand along a console as he passed it, his eyes sweeping across the other consoles, drinking in the familiar sight rather than taking in the quiet.

"I don't know if I missed the ship so much as what she represents," Soren replied.

"What is that?"

"Hope," Soren answered. "For Dana and my family. And for our galaxy. The Wraith has exactly what we need to make it into the dimensional rift to the enemy's universe and try to stop this madness."

"We'll have even more than that, soon enough. A squadron of starfighters? A platoon of Marines? Anton isn't holding anything back."

"He's just as upset about the delay as we are. He

didn't have us delivered back to Earth because he wanted to. He was following orders. He should still be following orders."

"Well, I for one am glad he decided to act first and apologize later. And I can tell, you missed the ship for the ship, too."

"Guilty as charged, Jack," Soren admitted, approaching the command station. "Though I'd give her up in an instant if it meant this was just a bad dream."

"Me, too," Jack agreed.

The irony of the situation wasn't lost on him. Just a couple of hours ago, he had been a prisoner, his ship confiscated, and his crew scattered, his very freedom hanging in the balance. And now, by a twist of fate and the machinations of war, here he was again, poised to lead them all into the dark unknown.

Soren settled into the command seat and activated the controls, the displays flickering to life under his touch. He quickly navigated to system status reports to get a feel for Wraith's current condition. She was scuffed but unbowed, her hull scarred but her spirit unbroken. Just like her captain's.

He navigated deeper into the system, searching for the data they had copied from Dana's data recorder. A surge of relief washed through him when he confirmed that Dana's data was still intact, the precious coordinates and recordings safe within the ship's memory banks. They wouldn't get very far without it.

The soft hiss of the parting bridge doors drew his attention. Wilf and Tashi burst through, their faces alight with unabashed joy at the sight of him.

"Captain!" Wilf exclaimed, his tattooed fingers wiggling with excitement. "Alex told us you were back and…well…you're back!"

"We knew you would be," Tashi added, grinning from

ear to ear. "We knew they couldn't keep the Wraith down for long.

"Wilf, Tashi." Soren stood, clasping each of them by the shoulder. "It's good to see you both. Are you well?"

"We're great, Captain," Wilf said. "Even better now that you're here."

"I heard about how you two planned to sabotage the ship to keep her grounded for me while Alex broke me out of the brig."

Wilf's smile turned sheepish. "Yeah, well, it seemed like a good idea at the time. Guess we kind of botched it, huh?"

"Nonsense," Soren said firmly. "You showed courage and loyalty, both of you. And I couldn't be more grateful or proud to have you on my crew. It was my wife's idea to hire additional crew from the Dregs, and I don't regret it for a minute."

"Uhh...I don't mean to sound ungrateful, Captain," Tashi said. "But you said hire, and...well, we've never been paid."

Soren stared at them, a river of guilt crossing his face. "With everything that's happened, I never actually sent you any payments, did I?" He reached for his DA. "We should fix that right away."

Tashi laughed. "Don't worry about it, Captain. You saved us from the Dregs. Gave us a purpose, a place to belong. That's worth more than any paycheck."

Wilf nodded vigorously, his fingers echoing the sentiment. "He's right. Besides, what are we going to do with money while we're out in space? You can pay us whenever we get back."

"I definitely will," Soren replied.

The bridge doors parted once more. Tashi and Wilf quickly moved around Soren's station as if to hide behind it, though there was no longer a need. Commander Bashir entered, along with Lieutenant Moffit.

"Captain Strickland," Vic said, coming to attention. "Lieutenant Moffit has some additional orders from Admiral Montoya for you, sir."

Moffit nodded to Soren. "Captain. Admiral Montoya has assigned my platoon to the Wraith."

Soren's eyebrows rose. He hadn't expected Montoya to send him reinforcements from the same unit that had taken him into custody.

"In that case, welcome aboard, Lieutenant…?" Soren trailed off.

"Moffit, sir."

"Liam Moffit, Captain," Vic filled in.

"Thank you, Vic. Welcome aboard, Liam. I'm happy to have you and your platoon as backup should we have need of your kind of expertise on this mission. I don't suppose you brought a dropship with you?"

"Yes, sir," Liam replied. "An Armadillo. She's last generation though, not next generation like the Wraith."

"That might actually come in very handy where we're going," Jack said.

"Admiral Montoya believed the same, sir," Liam replied.

"Liam, I want to keep one thing clear from the outset," Soren said. "While I'm happy to have you and your Marines, I require Scorpion Squad to fall under my direct command, following my orders. And only my orders."

Liam's jaw tightened, a sharp glint of protest in his eyes. "With respect, sir, Scorpion is a Marine unit. Their chain of command belongs—"

"With me, Liam," Soren cut him off, his voice unwavering. "No offense to you, but right now I'm not ready to fully accept that the Admiral has no ulterior motives in your assignment to this ship. As such, I need to retain control of a unit I trust completely. Besides, I need their expertise and direct knowledge of the enemy at my immediate command."

"Or is it so you can keep your boy out of the line of fire?" Liam asked.

The question hit Soren like a sucker punch to the chin. His jaw clenched with barely restrained anger, his voice low and cold when he replied. "You're out of line, Lieutenant. I would never demean myself, my son, or you and your Marines by intentionally withholding him and his team from a fight. Do you understand me?"

Liam nodded. "Yes, sir."

"Good. I'll let this one go. Make another comment like that, and we'll have a problem. Am I making myself clear, Lieutenant?"

For a moment, Moffit looked like he might argue further. But then, with visible effort, he swallowed his objections and nodded curtly. "Understood, Captain. Your ship. Your crew. Your command. We'll pull our weight, sir. Just point us where you need us."

"Glad to hear it, Liam. Dismissed."

As Vic and Liam retreated from the bridge, the stalwart figure of Ethan walked in, nearly colliding with the equally brawny Marine. The Chief Engineer's face broke into a wide smile as he locked eyes with Soren and Jack.

"Damn, if you two aren't a sight for sore eyes," Ethan exclaimed, crossing the deck in a few long strides to shake Soren's hand with both of his and then reaching out to Jack for a quick handshake. "When I heard you two were returned to active duty…" His eyes danced back and forth between them. "and that you needed your crew back, I couldn't get here fast enough." And then he frowned at the rank boards on Jack's shoulders, his eyes lifting. "They demoted you, sir?'

Grinning, Jack shrugged. "You know how it is. Montoya needed to make things official and couldn't have a lowly captain…" He smirked at Soren, eliciting a grin from him. "…giving an admiral orders, or some such shit."

Soren grinned. "Well, you beat the rest of the crew here. So in a sense, you definitely got here fast enough."

"Yeah." And then Ethan's expression sobered. "Hell of a thing, what happened at Proxima."

"It is," Soren agreed, the words heavy with regret. "But we can't change what's already done. All we can do now is try to keep it from happening to any more planets."

Ethan nodded. "Copy that." His gaze shifted to Wilf and Tashi. "I heard you two have been mischievous gremlins. I assume you can fix whatever you sabotaged?"

"Oh, aye, Chief," Wilf replied. "It's more like an on-off switch than unplugging a fridge. So, everything should be working just fine right now."

"Have you tested your switch to make sure?" Soren asked.

They both made a face. "Not the easiest thing to do," Tashi answered, "when we've had to sneak around everywhere to avoid capture."

Ethan turned to Soren. "I think I should have these two show me what they've done."

"Agreed," Soren replied. "Go ahead."

Ethan nodded and motioned for Tashi and Wilf to follow him from the bridge.

The rest of the crew began arriving quickly thereafter, each arrival lifting Soren's spirits higher—Keira, who wrapped him in a fierce hug, Bobby and Mark who looked more energized and focused than ever, and Bastian who clapped him on the shoulder with a knowing grin.

Harry, ever the diligent quartermaster, only stayed long enough to welcome Soren back before hustling off again. "Already met with Commander Bashir outside," he assured Soren. "We'll make sure this ship is stocked and everything stowed proper like before we break atmo. You can count on it."

Samira, the last of his crew to arrive, finally walked onto the bridge at 15:20 hours that afternoon, sliding into her station at comms with a brisk nod to Soren. "Sorry I'm late, sir. Flight delays."

"No problem, Samira," he said.

No sooner had the doors slid closed behind her than they opened again, his attention drawn to the Marine officer who walked onto the bridge and approached him. A compact man with sharp eyes and an unmistakable air of cocky confidence, Soren didn't recognize him.

"Captain Strickland sir." The man snapped to attention in front of him. "Lieutenant Colonel Minh Pham, CO of VMFA-16, the Hooligans, squadron of twelve Pilums, armed for bear and ready to fly, sir."

"At ease, Minh." Soren firmly shook the man's hand. "Welcome aboard. Glad to have you and your pilots with us."

"Thank you sir. I'm excited to serve under you, Captain."

"Are your fighters loaded onto the ship?"

"Not yet, sir, but they're being racked as we speak."

Soren nodded. The Pilums were compact craft, generally stored in modular racks when not prepped for launch. This made it easy to transfer them from ship to ship and use them with little extra available hangar space. Since the Hooligans had flown their birds to Pensacola, they needed to be loaded up before they were brought in. "Please oversee their stowing, Colonel."

"Yes, sir!" Minh snapped before executing a sharp about-face and marching out to promptly carry out Soren's order.

"Intense, isn't he?" Jack contemplated.

Soren chuckled. "He'll loosen up once he's seen non-simulated combat."

"Well, the gang's all here. Samira was the last crew member in, and the Marines and starfighters Montoya promised are all here."

"Almost time to go then," Soren said. "Samira, can you get Captain Broz on the horn for me?"

"Aye, Captain." she replied.

"Captain Strickland," Broz came across the comm a minute later. "I'm glad to hear the comms are in working order. I assume you're contacting me about the status of your resupply."

"That's right," Soren replied.

"Ordnance and provisions are all squared away. As for the creature comforts...let's just say we had to raid some dusty back rooms to meet your needs, so if any of your crew has allergies..." He paused to laugh. "In all seriousness, you should be eighty percent of the way to a fully-equipped starship. Not bad for a few hours' work."

Soren shook his head, a smile, playing on his lips. "No, not bad at all. We'll take what you've given us with gratitude. Once your current delivery is unloaded, clear all base personnel from the ship." His voice hardened with resolve. "We've waited long enough. It's time to launch."

"Copy that, Captain," Broz said. "I'll send word. Should only be another ten minutes or so."

A wave of excitement rippled through the bridge as Soren closed the comm. All eyes locked on him, waiting for the word, ready to leap into an uncertain future.

Before that word came, a different communication arrived.

"Captain," Samira said. "We're receiving an inbound comm from Admiral Montoya."

"Open the channel," Soren replied.

"Soren," Montoya said. "How are the preparations going?"

"All of the crew is on board, and I've received your parting gifts. Thank you for your generosity, Admiral."

"Don't thank me yet. I contacted you to deliver your revised orders."

Soren raised an eyebrow in confusion. "Revised orders? Admiral, the rift—"

"Isn't going anywhere, from what you've said. I need you to make a stop at Proxima. We need to know the outcome of what happened there, and your ship is the only one that can go in without being seen."

"Yes, sir," Soren replied. "But that isn't entirely true. We can't cloak until the jump cycle is complete. We'll be visible and vulnerable for nearly fifteen seconds. Long enough for enemy sensors to pick us up."

"That's still better than any of the other ships in our fleet. Set a course for Proxima. Find out the status of the planet and the people on it, and report back to me. Then you can continue on to the rift."

"Yes, sir," Soren said.

"Good luck out there, Soren. I know you'll make us proud. Montoya out."

The comms disconnected, leaving Soren stunned and frustrated. Depending on what they encountered near Proxima, the possibility existed that they might not make it to the rift, which should be the priority.

"Well, we have orders," Jack said.

"That we do," Soren agreed.

"Are we going to follow them?"

"There's a reason Anton put all of these additional personnel on the ship, and it's not only to help us succeed."

"Good point."

"Captain, incoming communication from Captain Broz," Samira said.

"Put it on."

"Captain Strickland, our deliveries are complete. My team is all off your ship. You're good to depart at your convenience."

"Thank you, Captain," Soren replied. "For everything."

"Thank you in advance for kicking the shit out of those assholes who attacked Proxima," Broz sent back. "Good hunting, Captain. Broz out."

Soren looked around the bridge at his crew. They were practically vibrating with their eagerness. "Samira, open a ship wide comm."

"Comms open, Captain," she replied.

"Attention all hands. This is Captain Strickland. Prepare for departure." He nodded to Samira, who disconnected.

"I thought you were going to make a speech," Jack said.

"Maybe later," Soren replied, eager to be on their way after nearly ten hours of resupply and repairs. "Ethan, initiate prelaunch checks and confirm all systems ready for departure."

"Aye, Captain," Ethan replied, his hands already running over the control surfaces. "Prelaunch initiated. All systems are green. Ready for docking clamp release."

Soren nodded. "Sang, confirm the tarmac is clear and and release the clamps."

"Copy that, Captain," Sang answered. "Tarmac is clear. Clamps disengaged. We're free to launch."

"Sang, take us up," Soren ordered. "Nice and easy."

"Aye, Captain," she replied. "Activating counter-mass generators."

A heavy thudding sound echoed through the hull as the counter-mass coils came alive, pressing back against gravity. It took a minute for the system to spool up, leaving the ship shuddering lightly in its docking cradle before it finally began to lift from the tarmac and drift upward like a helium-filled balloon.

"Reactors online," Ethan announced. "Thrusters online. All systems nominal."

"Sang, make haste," Soren said.

"With pleasure, Captain," she replied, putting her hand on the throttle.

The Wraith shuddered as her thrusters roared to life, the sudden kick pressing Soren back slightly as the ship climbed out. On the viewscreen, the tarmac and structures of Pensacola rapidly fell away, dwindling into toylike specks against the backdrop of the coming night. They rose with gathering speed, the sky darkening from blue to indigo to inky black as they punched through the atmosphere and into the void beyond.

"Sang, all stop."

"Aye, Captain," she replied. Sang flipped the ship around, its main thrusters firing to slow and then stop its forward momentum, leaving it orbiting Earth.

"Bobby, set a course for Proxima."

"Coordinates locked in," Bobby announced.

"Initiate jump," Soren ordered.

"Initiating," Sang responded. The viewscreen went dark as spacetime shifted around the static vessel, moving them without being in motion. "Jump active. Estimated time to arrival, four days, seven hours, sixteen minutes."

"And we're on our way," Jack said softly.

"Time to get some answers," Soren muttered, half to himself. Proxima and whatever lay beyond were looming directly in their path, whether they were ready or not.

CHAPTER 15

A few hours later, Soren stood from the command station, groaning as he stretched his back. "Jack, you have the conn."

Jack nodded. Having just returned from a four-hour nap, he slid into the vacated seat with practiced ease. "I have the conn. Go stretch your legs, Soren. Maybe get some sleep if you can. I'll hold down the fort."

Soren clapped his old friend on the shoulder in silent thanks before exiting the bridge, the doors hissing shut behind him. The corridors of the Wraith stretched out before him, no longer the bare, unfinished maze they had been when they first set out. Now, there was a sense of life, of purpose, the ship humming with the activity of its expanded crew. He wanted to meet them, check in with them, and let them put a face and personality to their captain, so when the time for fighting came, which it would, they would know exactly who they were fighting for.

His first stop was upper deck berthing. As he entered, he was struck by the transformation. Where once there had been little more than bare bulkheads and exposed wiring, and then mattresses on the deck and nowhere to stow gear except the duffels they were brought in, now there were orderly rows of individual racks, each outfitted with a mattress, bedding, a footlocker, and a regular locker. It was still sparse and utilitarian, but it was a far cry from the spartan conditions they had endured before. He was sure it wouldn't be long before Ethan, Keira, and the others added photographs, doodles, and other personal effects.

He went to the far end of berthing to check on the head, noting with satisfaction the stacks of folded towels and the standard-issue toiletries. The little things, the creature comforts, they mattered on a long journey.

Soren was leaving the head when he nearly collided with the spacer entering. He pulled up short, an apology on his lips, only to blink in surprise at the familiar face.

"Yeoman Noguchi?" he asked.

Hiraku snapped to attention. "Captain Strickland, sir. My apologies for nearly knocking you over. I should look where I'm going."

"At ease, Yeoman," Soren said automatically. "What are you doing here? I thought you and the others from Pinto were headed to Virginia for reassignment."

Hiraku smiled, a glint of pride in his eye. "Admiral Montoya asked for volunteers, sir. To join you on this mission. I volunteered. So did Sophie and Aiko."

Soren felt a swell of gratitude and respect for these brave men and women who had already endured so much and yet were still willing to put themselves on the line. "I'm honored to have you aboard, Hiraku. Truly."

"The honor is ours, Captain," Hiraku replied. "After what you did for us, how could we not stand with you now?"

Soren nodded. "Are there any other crew members on board I should know about?"

"Yes, Captain. We arrived with nearly thirty other

enlisted. I don't know all of their names and roles yet, but I'm sure you'll meet them soon enough."

Soren shook his head, marveling at Montoya's speed and efficiency. The man had managed to assemble and dispatch a full complement of crew in a matter of hours.

"Thank you, Hiraku," Soren said. "As you were."

Soren left the berthing area with a newfound spring in his step, his faith in his mission and his crew stronger than ever. He went down to the hangar bay, eager to see what other surprises awaited him.

The cavernous space was a hive of activity, a deck crew he didn't know had boarded, scurrying about like industrious ants. And there, tucked against the rear bulkhead, Soren found more of the admiral's sudden, unexpected benevolence.

The Pilums, sleek and deadly, were nestled in their racks like a rattlesnake waiting to strike. Three across and four high, the compact fighter craft represented a potent addition to the Wraith's arsenal. And perched atop the Pilum racks, three times that number of Pilum-linked semi-automated assault drones, their angular forms promising swift and merciless destruction.

In the midst of it all stood Lieutenant Colonel Pham, his critical gaze sweeping over the assembled craft. The Hooligans' commander exuded an air of coiled energy, like a rattlesnake poised to strike.

Soren approached, a grin tugging at his lips. "Minh," he called out. "I see you've settled in nicely."

Minh turned, and Soren was glad he'd relaxed enough to match his grin with one of his own. "Captain Strickland! Just checking on the birds, sir. Making sure they're all comfortable in their cages." Minh waved over a man studying a data pad by the Pilums. "Allow me to introduce my second, Major Jamie Walcox. We were just going over the ordnance reports. It's good to know how much ammo you have before you use it, wouldn't you agree, sir?"

"Definitely," Soren replied.

Walcox, a tall, lanky man with a shock of brown hair, stood at attention. "Captain, it's an honor."

"At ease. The honor is mine, Jamie. The Hooligans' reputation precedes you. I'm glad to have you watching our backs out here."

He let his gaze drift over the other nearby pilots, noting their eager, determined faces. "In fact, I'm glad to have all of you here with us. We've got a tough fight ahead, and I can think of no one I'd rather have at my side than the men and women of VMFA-16."

A chorus of "Oorahs!" and "Yes, sirs!" rang out, the pilots standing a little straighter, their eyes shining with pride.

Minh grinned. "We won't let you down, Captain. The Hooligans always come through."

"Of that, I have no doubt," Soren replied.

As he spoke, his eye caught a flurry of activity at the far end of the bay. A group of deckhands in color-coded jump-suits were bustling about, hefting crates and boxes, checking manifests on glowing data pads.

Soren excused himself and made his way over, having already recognized them by their red shirts—aerospace ordnancemen—who kept the fighters and drones armed and ready.

He paused, watching them work, marveling at their effi-ciency, their precision. Each move was practiced, honed by countless hours of drills and real-world experience. It was like watching a well-oiled machine, every cog and gear turning in perfect harmony.

One of the ordnancemen looked up as Soren approached. His eyes widened, and he snapped to atten-tion. "Captain on deck!" he barked, his voice cutting through the din of the hangar, prompting his fellows to snap to attention, too.

"As you were, gentlemen. I just wanted to come by and see how you were settling in."

The lead ordnanceman, a chief petty officer by his insignia, stepped forward. "We're doing just fine, sir. Just making sure these birds have everything they need to give the enemy hell."

Soren nodded, pleased. "And we all thank you for that. What you do is vital. Never forget that. Without you, those fighters are just fancy paperweights."

The chief grinned, pride evident on his face. "Yes, sir. If you ain't ordnance, you ain't shit!" he crowed.

Soren chuckled at the old saying that came out of the bygone era of the waterborne Navy. "Isn't that the truth, Chief," he agreed.

"Yes, sir, we'll keep 'em loaded and fightin', come what may."

"I know you will, Chief," Soren said, clapping the man on the shoulder. "Carry on."

With a final nod to the ordnancemen, Soren turned and made his way out of the hangar. His next stop was the lower deck berthing, where his grunt Marines, old and new, were quartered.

He found them gathered in the common area, a buzz of conversation filling the air. Alex and the Scorpions were there, holding court, regaling their new comrades with tales of their exploits on Jungle. The other Marines listened with rapt attention, eyes wide, occasionally interjecting with questions or exclamations of awe.

But as soon as Soren entered, a hush fell over the room. The Marines leapt to their feet, snapping to attention with a crisp snap of booted heels on deck plating.

"Captain on deck!" someone shouted, voice ringing with respect.

His gaze found Lieutenant Moffit standing ramrod straight, his expression carefully neutral. But there was a flicker of surprise in his eyes, a hint of confusion at Soren's presence.

"At ease," Soren said, his voice carrying in the sudden stillness. "As you were."

There was a moment of hesitation, but then the Marines complied, settling back onto their bunks and chairs. Their posture was still straight, and they were still attentive.

"Lieutenant Moffit," Soren said, nodding to the officer. "I just wanted to come down and personally welcome your Marines aboard."

Moffit blinked, clearly taken aback. "I...thank you, Captain. That's very kind of you."

Soren smiled, sensing the man's unease, his uncertainty. He couldn't blame him, really. It wasn't every day that a ship's captain made a personal visit to the Marines' domain.

"Kindness has nothing to do with it," Soren said. "You're part of my crew now, part of this mission. And I make it a point to know my crew, to let them know that I'm here for them, no matter what."

He let his gaze sweep the room, making eye contact with each Marine. "That goes for all of you. I know this mission, it's not what you signed up for. It's not what any of us signed up for. But here we are, on the edge of the unknown, facing a threat unlike any we've ever seen."

Soren paused, letting his words sink in. "I won't lie to you. It's going to be tough. It's going to be dangerous. I'm sure the Scorpions have filled you in on what they encountered and survived on Jungle. I know that each and every one of you has the strength, the courage, the sheer stubborn grit to see this through, just as they did."

A murmur of agreement rippled through the room, heads nodding, spines straightening.

"We're in this together," Soren continued. "One crew, one fight. And I promise you, I will do everything in my power to bring us all home safely. But I need you to promise me something in return."

He let the silence stretch, heavy with anticipation as he looked at each face peering back at him. "I need you to have each other's backs out there. I need you to fight for each other, to bleed for each other if necessary. Because that's what it's going to take. That's how we'll win this."

"Oorah!" the Marines chorused, the word ringing like a battle cry.

"Lieutenant Moffit, do you or your Marines need anything before we reach Proxima?"

Moffit shook his head. "No, Captain. We're squared away down here. Ready for whatever comes."

Alex spoke up from his bunk. "The gym's fully stocked now too, Captain. Weights, machines, the works. And you'll never guess what else we've got," he said, grinning like the Cheshire Cat.

Soren raised an eyebrow, the look on Alex's face reminding him of his ninth birthday when he got the mini trail bike he'd been asking for, but of course, he wasn't about to bring that up here and now. "What's that?" he asked him instead.

Alex's grin turned predatory. "Karuta power armor. A full set for each Marine. We're talking top of the line, state of the art. With that kind of firepower at our backs, those bastards won't know what hit them."

"Glad to hear it," Soren said.

With a final nod to Moffit and his Marines, Soren took his leave. His people were ready, as ready as they could be. Now it was just a matter of time.

Soren navigated the passageways from the lower berths to the elevator, riding it back up and heading to sickbay. He found Asha there, as he knew he would, along with two others he didn't recognize, all bent over a terminal, studying something intently. They looked up as he entered, Asha's face breaking into a warm smile.

"Captain," she said by way of greeting. "I didn't expect to see you here."

Soren returned the smile. "Just making the rounds, checking on my crew. Making sure we're ready for whatever comes next."

Asha gestured to her companions. "Of course. Allow me to introduce my new team. This is Ensign Eric Alonzo, our surgical technician, and Ensign Ava Dern. They came on with the new personnel from Pensacola."

"Welcome aboard," Soren said. "I know things are a bit unorthodox around here, but I'm glad to have you two with us."

"Happy to be here, Captain," Ava said, her voice soft but filled with conviction.

Soren nodded, turning back to Asha. Clearly, no one had told the two ensigns that she was a dishonorably discharged revo. He didn't plan to be the one to spill the beans. "So tell me, how are we looking in terms of medical supplies?"

"All stocked up, Captain," Asha replied. "Medicines, bandages, pod gel. A lot of it. If the need arises, we'll be ready."

Soren felt a knot of tension ease in his gut. With Asha and her team on the job, with their sickbay fully equipped, he knew his people would be in good hands, no matter what trials lay ahead.

"Glad to hear it," he said. With a final nod, he left them to their preparations, stepping back out into the corridor. As he did, a familiar voice hailed him.

"Captain! A moment, please!"

Soren turned to see Harry hurrying towards him, data

pad in hand, his face creased with a mix of excitement and concern.

"Harry," Soren said as the other man drew near. "What is it?"

The quartermaster waved his data pad, a grin tugging at his lips despite the worry in his eyes. "Just going over the manifests, Captain. I have to say, I'm impressed. Admiral Montoya really came through for us."

The two men walked side-by-side, their footsteps echoing in the quiet corridor. "He did indeed. We're better equipped now than we ever were before. It feels like a real Navy ship."

Harry nodded. "Just like old times, eh? Makes you feel like we might just have a shot at this after all."

There was a note of hope in his voice, fragile but undeniable. Soren clapped him on the back, a gesture of reassurance and solidarity. "With this ship, this crew, and all the extra ordnance and supplies Montoya loaded us up with, I think we might just pull this off."

Harry met his gaze, a flicker of his old fire burning in his eyes. "Damn right we will, Captain. We'll show those bastards what happens when you mess with the FUP."

"That we will," Soren agreed. "If there's one thing I know I can count on, it's you keeping this ship running smoothly."

"Aye, Captain. You can count on me."

With that, Harry hurried off, already lost in his data pad once more. Soren watched him go, a smile tugging at his lips. Some things never changed. And in a universe turned upside down, that small constant was a comfort.

Soren decided against a nap. Too wound up to sleep, he returned to the bridge to find the lights of the consoles playing across all the faces. The return to space made him realize just how much the ship had changed in the last two weeks. From a near empty shell with a crew of only a dozen strong to a proper warship crewed by nearly a hundred.

"Captain," Jack said by way of greeting. "How's our crew?"

"Settling in," Soren replied. "And more than ready for whatever's coming. Montoya did us a hell of a favor."

"If you ask me, he owed us one," Jack countered. "Though I'm sure he had his reasons beyond the goodness of his heart. No nap, huh?"

He shook his head. "I have the conn, Jack," Soren said as his best friend moved out of the command chair, letting him settle back into it. He immediately opened a comm to Bashir. "Vic, your rotation begins in eight hours. Make sure your team is ready to take over."

"Aye, Captain," Vic's voice came back, crisp and professional.

Soren leaned back and closed his eyes, trying to center himself, to find a moment of peace. He knew this was the calm before the storm. The deep breath before the plunge. And when that tempest hit, when they finally faced the darkness head on, there would be no room for doubt, no margin for error.

They would have to be ready and strong. For each other, for the mission, and for the very fate of their universe.

CHAPTER 16

Over a week later, Soren sat at the command station, his eyes fixed on the viewscreen, waiting for Proxima to come into view as the jump drive began spooling down and spacetime flattened out. The tension on the bridge was palpable, every crew member poised at their station, ready for his orders.

"One minute to ingress," Bobby announced, watching the jump countdown at his terminal.

"Keira," Soren said, his voice calm but firm. "Prepare to cloak as soon as possible."

"Aye, Captain," Keira replied. "I'll execute as soon as the jump drive disengages from the main power core."

Soren pivoted toward his operations officer. "Mark, the moment we arrive, I want a full sensor sweep. I need to know the situation immediately."

Mark nodded. "You'll have it over the barrel, sir."

"Sang," Soren continued, addressing the helmsman. "Evasive maneuvers the second the thrusters are available. We can't afford to linger."

"Understood, Captain," Sang replied, her hands poised over the controls.

"Ten seconds to ingress," Bobby said.

"Here we go," Jack commented from beside Soren.

With a shudder and a flash of light, they were there. Proxima B, a once-thriving colony world, immediately filled the viewscreen, positioned half an AU away.

But it wasn't the Proxima Soren remembered.

Sang immediately engaged the thrusters, propelling them forward as Mark projected the sensor grid, clogged with hundreds of large contacts. Not all ships. At least, not anymore.

The sight that greeted them was one of utter devastation.

The once-pristine orbit of Proxima B was now a grave-yard of shattered spacecraft and drifting debris. The proud vessels of the FUP Navy, broken and lifeless, tumbled slowly against the starry backdrop. It was a sight that struck Soren to his very core, a visceral reminder of the stakes they were playing for.

"My stars…" Bastian said, trying and failing to put into words what everyone on the bridge was thinking. The destruction was absolute, hard to look at, and even harder to believe.

"Zoom in on the surface," Soren ordered, his voice tight.

The image shifted, the cameras focusing on the domed habitats that housed Proxima's populace. What he saw there made his blood run cold. Enemy troops were entering the structures, a ground invasion to cement their orbital victory. But it was worse than that. The domes, once trans-parent and gleaming, were now hazy with a swirling, sickly yellow mist—chemical agents.

"My god," Jack breathed from beside him. "They're not just invading. They're exterminating."

Soren's grip tightened on the armrests of his chair, anger and revulsion warring within him. "The convergence," he realized, his voice deadly cold. "If they damage the domes, the buildings, when it happens…"

"The destruction will become part of the flattened universe," Jack whispered. "They have to kill as many of our people as they can without harming the infrastructure."

"And it looks like they came prepared for just that," Soren agreed.

Mark's voice broke through the suffocating tension, strained and brittle. "Captain, I'm picking up dozens of ships in low orbit. Troop transports, by the looks of them. Massive ones, designed for heavy planetary assault."

Soren tore his gaze from the domes and looked to the skies above Proxima. There, hanging like bloated ticks, were the transports. Ugly, brutish things, each one capable of ferrying thousands of enemy soldiers and releasing a number of dropships. They were the first unique vessels Soren had seen from the enemy. Their FUP had no parallel. Clearly, they had been designed for the exact task they were now carrying out. It was just another disgusting revelation that left his body cold, his blood boiling.

A protective cordon of warships surrounded the transports, the angular silhouettes of too many Komodo-class destroyers standing out amid the swarm.

"How many?" he asked, his voice sounding distant to his own ears.

"Fifty...no, fifty-two capital ships," Mark replied. "Plus the transports. It's a full-scale invasion, sir. A damned armada."

The number hit Soren like a physical blow. Fifty-two ships. It was a staggering force that dwarfed anything the Federation had ever fielded in a single battle. The enemy had come prepared for a war of extermination, and they had the numbers to see it through.

"But how?" Bastian asked, his voice trembling. "How

could they assemble a fleet that size without us knowing? Where did they all come from?"

Soren shook his head slowly, a grim understanding dawning. "They've known," he said, the words heavy in his mouth. "They've obviously known about the Convergence far longer than we have. While we were in the dark, they were preparing, building their strength."

The revelation settled over the bridge like a shroud, a palpable weight of dread and despair. It was one thing to understand the situation, another to warn that it was coming, and another entirely to see it in person.

They were up against an enemy that had planned for this moment for years, perhaps decades. An enemy that had the will and the means to complete their task and wipe out all human life in their universe.

At that moment, Soren realized how badly he'd underestimated the enemy and how much trouble they were truly in.

"Captain, the cloak is active and stable," Keira said, but there was no triumph in her voice, only a hollow note of fear.

Not a moment too soon. On the screen, a small group of Valkyrie-class vessels broke away from the main enemy fleet, angling towards the Wraith's position.

They had been spotted.

"Sang, change course," Soren ordered. "Take us out of their line of fire. We can't let them trace our trajectory."

Sang complied instantly. The Wraith veered hard to starboard, the stars wheeling on the screen as they cut a new path through the void.

But the enemy ships kept coming, closing the distance with alarming speed. They opened fire, railgun rounds stitching the void, hunting for their invisible prey.

Sang continued updating their trajectory, keeping the Wraith one step ahead of the attack. The enemy's fire flashed past them, searing the void, sometimes coming close to the hull but never quite finding its mark.

Finally, they slipped the noose, vectoring in a direction the enemy didn't anticipate. The Valkyries' searching fire passed further and further away until it was obvious they were clear.

"Nice flying, Sang," Soren said. They had seen what they came to see and gathered the intelligence they needed. It was time to report back to Admiral Montoya and get out of there.

"Samira," he called out. "Try to establish a connection to Proxima's tranSat relay. We need to get a message out."

There was a pause, then Samira's voice, tight with frustration. "Negative, Captain. The relay is offline. Likely destroyed in the initial attack."

Soren wasn't surprised. The horrors on Proxima's surface and the junkyard of debris in orbit weren't the only reason they'd lost contact with the planet.

"Captain," Bobby spoke up from the nav station. "I recommend we jump to Tau Ceti. We can contact Admiral Montoya from there and report what we've seen."

"I'm not sure that's a good idea," Jack countered. "If Proxima was hit this hard, Tau Ceti could be next on their list. Hell, it might already be under attack. We might want to choose a system a little further out, in the direction of the rift."

Soren hesitated, weighing the options. Jack had a point. Tau Ceti was a major colony, a linchpin of the Federation's presence in this sector. If it fell, the enemy's path to Earth would be much clearer, making it a prime target.

But at the same time, if Tau Ceti was under attack, the Wraith might be able to make a difference—to help evacuate civilians or at least buy them some time. Admiral Montoya needed to know what they were up against, the sheer scale of the enemy's forces.

"We stick with Tau Ceti," Soren decided, his voice firm. "If they're under attack, we do what we can to help. And either way, we get this intel to the Admiral. He needs to know what he's facing. Sang, get us a bit further out. Bobby, set the course."

"Aye, Captain," he and Sang replied.

Soren watched the sensor grid, keeping a close eye on the Valkyries as they finally gave up the hunt, adjusting their vectors to return to the larger fleet. A wave of exhaustion washed over him, his entire soul weighed down by everything he had just seen.

"Coordinates set," Bobby announced.

"Sang, all stop," Soren ordered. The ship immediately began to flip over, the mains pushing against their momentum to bring them to a faster standstill. "Keira, deactivate the cloak. Bobby, initiate the jump."

"Cloak deactivated, Captain," Keira said. The Valkyries immediately began adjusting their course again, swinging around to face the static, defenseless warship.

"Incoming missiles," Mark announced.

The projectiles were invisible from their current distance, but the sensor grid tracked them unerringly, small blips moving at increasing speed toward them.

They were too late.

The Wraith jumped, the blinding flare of transition engulfing them, carrying them away from the nightmare of Proxima and toward an uncertain future.

CHAPTER 17

The tension on the Wraith's bridge was palpable as they emerged from their jump into the Tau Ceti system. No one knew what to expect after the horror they had witnessed at Proxima. Soren leaned forward in his command chair, eyes fixed on the viewscreen as the darkness between folded spacetime vanished, revealing the familiar sight of Tau Ceti, the system's habitable world.

For a moment, all was quiet. Then, relief rippled through the bridge crew as they took in the scene before them. Tau Ceti hung in space, its surface unmarred by the devastation they had seen on Proxima. The orbital defenses were intact, and a network of gleaming satellites and defense platforms formed a protective shell around the planet.

But what truly caught Soren's attention was the fleet. Dozens of FUP warships hung in high orbit, their sleek forms a welcome sight after the graveyard of Proxima.

"Thank the stars," Jack murmured beside him. "Looks like we got here in time."

Soren nodded, allowing himself a moment of cautious optimism. "Let's hope it stays that way."

"Captain, we're being hailed," Samira said.

"Go ahead," Soren replied.

A stern, authoritative voice filled the bridge. "Unidentified vessel, this is Rear Admiral Lane of the Fourth Fleet. You have entered a restricted area. Identify yourself immediately or you will be fired upon."

"Captain, we're being hit with multiple target locks," Mark announced.

Soren exchanged a glance with Jack before leaning forward to respond. "Admiral Lane, this is Captain Soren Strickland of the FUP starship Wraith. Transmitting ship identifier now."

There was a pause, and then Lane's voice returned, a note of confusion evident. "Captain Strickland? I...your ship identifier checks out, but I'm not familiar with any vessel called Wraith, or the configuration on our sensors. And last I heard, you were retired. I need more information before I'm ready to stand down my guns."

"Admiral Lane," Jack said. "This is Jack Harper. I'm sending you cryptographic keys which should verify my identity, and confirm we're on the same side." He moved beside Soren at the command station, using it to enter his keys while Soren looked on.

"Target locks are breaking," Mark said. "The fleet is standing down."

"Jack, you're supposed to be retired, too," Lane said.

"Desperate times," Jack answered. "By the way, I'm a Commander now."

"What? Can one of you please tell me what's going on?"

Soren took a deep breath, knowing how outlandish his explanation would sound. "Admiral, we've been recalled to active duty by Admiral Montoya for a special mission, the first part of which was to check in on Proxima. We've just come from there, and I have urgent intelligence to report back to the Admiral."

The silence that followed was heavy, pregnant with tension. When Lane spoke again, his voice was tight with barely contained alarm. "Proxima? We lost contact with them days ago. What did you find?"

Soren's jaw clenched as the memories of what they'd witnessed flooded back. "It's gone, Admiral. The enemy hit them hard and fast. The orbital defenses were obliterated, and they were using some kind of chemical agent on the surface to wipe out the population." A sharp intake of breath was audible over the comm. "I've seen a lot of war. I've never seen anything more horrible in my life."

When Lane spoke again, his voice was strained. "How... how many enemy ships?"

"Fifty-two capital ships, sir," Soren replied, the number still staggering. "Plus a significant number of troop transports. It's a full-scale invasion force."

"Stars above," Lane whispered. Then, more firmly, "Captain Strickland, I need to debrief you. Please switch over to a private channel." He gave Soren the frequency he was to use.

Soren didn't really want to waste more time speaking to Lane, but he couldn't argue with a superior officer, either. Technically, he didn't need to answer to the man, but there was no sense creating problems from the outset. A short conversation could spare him much longer delays.

"Yes, sir. Standby."

As the communication ended, Soren turned to his crew. "Keira, keep us ready to cloak at a moment's notice. Mark, eyes on the sensors for enemy contact. Don't even blink. Sang, be ready for evasive maneuvers."

The crew acknowledged his orders, a flurry of activity sweeping across the bridge as they prepared for their unexpected stop. Soren felt the weight of responsibility settling heavily on his shoulders. The information they carried could be crucial in mounting a defense against the coming storm.

He activated his comms patch. Thanks to the many extras Rashad had provided, they'd distributed one to everyone on board. "Vic, I need you on the bridge immediately."

"Lieutenant Commander Bashir reporting, Captain," the man said, reaching the bridge so quickly it seemed as though he'd been standing outside the door, just waiting to be called in. He stood at attention beside the command station.

"Vic, you have the conn," Soren said, getting to his feet. "Jack, you're with me. Keep the ship at ready stations, Vic. If anything so much as twitches on long-range sensors, I want to know about it."

"Aye, Captain," Vic replied, sliding into the command chair as Soren and Jack made their way off the bridge.

Entering the conference room, Soren used the newly installed terminal and projection system to resume the connection to Admiral Lane. He tapped on the terminal, activating the video feed as well. The admiral immediately appeared projected above the table. Not on the bridge, he looked to be in the Combat Information Center. The CIC was a hub of controlled chaos. Officers huddled around holographic displays, voices raised in urgent discussion as they pored over tactical readouts and sensor data. Admiral Lane stood at the center of it all, ready to relay orders to the entire fleet if needed. His weathered face was creased with worry as he studied a large strategic map of the sector. The estimated entry points for the enemy fleet, depending on which system they arrived from, were marked on the map.

"Admiral, I'm sorry to keep you waiting," Soren said. "Jack and I are on a private channel."

"Captain Strickland, Adm...Commander Harper," Lane said, looking away from the map toward them. "I'm sure you understand the irregularity of this situation. Under normal circumstances, I'd have a lot more questions about your presence here and the nature of your mission. But these are far from normal circumstances."

Soren nodded, understanding the man's position all too well. "We appreciate that, Admiral. And we're prepared to share everything we know."

Lane finally looked up, his piercing gaze sweeping over them both. "Then let's get to it. Tell me everything you can that might help us fight these bastards. Leave nothing out."

For the next half hour, Soren and Jack recounted their discoveries in painstaking detail. They explained what they had learned about the Convergence before going on to describe the outcome on Proxima. The shattered wreckage of the defense fleet, the chemical attacks on the surface, the massive invasion force that had descended upon the helpless world. With each new revelation, the atmosphere in the war room behind the Admiral grew heavier, the faces of his assembled officers more pale and somber.

When they finished, Lane leaned heavily on the edge of the holotable, his knuckles white. "This...this is worse than we feared. We knew something had happened, but this..." He shook his head, visibly gathering himself. "You say these ships, they're identical to ours?"

"In many ways, yes," Soren confirmed. "But there are differences. The troop transports, for instance—we have nothing like them in our fleet. They're massive. And their tactics...these people are organized and ruthless, Admiral. They've been planning this for a long time."

Lane nodded slowly, clearly considering the possibilities. "It fits with what Admiral Puk believed. That's why the Fourth Fleet is here. We're expecting Tau Ceti to be their next target."

Jack leaned forward, his voice urgent. "With all due respect, Admiral, you're going to need more ships. A lot more. Fourth Fleet has thirty-four. Even with Planetary Defense, you're still outnumbered.

Lane's face hardened. "I'm well aware of that, Commander Harper. But we didn't have a count of the enemy's assets until you arrived. Even if we did, there aren't any other ships in the area right now. We're spread thin as it is, trying to cover all the potential targets. I hate to admit it, but we're completely unprepared for this."

It was nothing Soren didn't already know. Still, to have Lane admit it sent a chill down his spine. "Admiral," he said, his voice low and urgent. "If you'll excuse us, I need to contact Admiral Montoya immediately. He needs to know what we've discovered. The fleets need to be reorganized to better meet this threat."

"It certainly seems that way," Lane agreed. "Brief me on the outcome when you're finished."

"Yes, sir," Soren said, contacting the comms station. "Samira, put the current channel on hold and open a tranSat comm to Admiral Montoya. Route it directly to the conference room."

"Aye, Captain," she replied.

A couple of minutes later, the projector activated in the secluded conference room, revealing Montoya's face lined with exhaustion and worry. "Soren," he said without preamble. "I'm sure the news isn't good, but tell me it isn't as bad as I fear."

Soren shook his head grimly. "It's worse, Admiral. Proxima is gone. Completely overrun. And the force that took it is larger and better prepared than we anticipated."

He quickly outlined what they had discovered, repeating most of what he had told Lane and watching as Montoya's expression grew darker with each passing moment. When he finished, the admiral was silent for a long moment, his eyes closed as he processed the news.

"This changes everything," Montoya said at last, his

voice heavy. "I've been in talks with the Joint Chiefs. They're less than thrilled about my going behind their backs and handing Wraith back over to you. But in light of the situation, and because of who you are, they agreed to extend their support. Conditionally, of course."

Soren raised an eyebrow. "Conditionally?"

Montoya's lips twisted in a humorless smile. "Let's just say that if you create any kind of incident between the planets of the FUP or the Outworlds, they'll deny all knowledge of you and your mission. But for now, you have their backing. To that end, I'm assigning Strike Forces Seven and Eight to your command."

Soren blinked, taken aback. "Strike Forces Seven *and* Eight? Admiral, I appreciate the support, but I don't need or want a fleet where I'm going. It'll only make it harder to move around undetected. Surely they'd be put to better use here, defending against the enemy ships?"

Montoya shook his head, his expression dark. "You don't understand, Soren. What happened at Proxima changes the equation. We were ambushed, caught flat-footed. An entire world's population wiped out in a matter of hours. And poisoned? That only makes things worse. You told me yourself that the enemy sent their Soren Strickland to kill you because they fear you. That's something we can use. Something we need to use. We don't need a covert mission anymore. We need a counterstrike."

Soren felt his heart sink. He understood the logic, but he didn't agree with it. They were reacting emotionally, letting the enemy dictate the terms of engagement. But he knew better than to argue the point. Not now, when time was so precious.

"Understood, Admiral," he said. "When and where should I expect to rendezvous with the strike forces?"

"They'll meet you at the rift coordinates," Montoya replied. "Soren, I know this isn't what you had in mind. But we're at war now. A war unlike any we've ever faced. We have to show that we have a bite of our own."

Soren nodded, the weight of responsibility settling even more heavily on his shoulders. "I understand. We won't let you down."

As the communication ended, Soren turned to Jack, seeing his own concerns mirrored in his old friend's eyes. "Well," he said quietly. "It seems our mission parameters have changed."

Jack nodded, his expression troubled. "A full-scale assault on an unknown dimension. It's madness, Soren. We don't know what we're walking into."

"No, we don't," Soren agreed. "At least Montoya gave me command of the flotilla. I'll have orders prepared for them, just not the orders the Joint staff expect."

"Once a renegade, always a renegade," Jack agreed.

"I wouldn't go that far. But I'm not going to sacrifice brave men and women for no good purpose."

After a short silence, Soren reconnected to Lane's channel. "Admiral," he said, getting the man's attention.

"Well, gentlemen?" Lane asked. "What's the word from high command?"

Soren took a deep breath. "We have new orders, Admiral. We're to proceed to the coordinates of the dimensional rift immediately. Strike Forces Seven and Eight will be joining us there."

Lane's eyebrows shot up. "Seven *and* Eight? That's...that's a significant commitment of forces. Are they pulling them from our defensive lines?"

"I'm afraid so," Soren confirmed. "The thinking is that we need to take the fight to the enemy, hit them where they're not expecting it."

Lane's face darkened. "Leaving us even more vulnerable here. Didn't you explain the situation?"

"I'm afraid we've been at peace so long, we've forgotten how to fight a war," Soren answered.

Before Lane could say anything more, a young officer burst into the CIC, his face pale. "Admiral Lane! Sir, we have multiple contacts on long-range sensors. They just appeared out of nowhere. It's...it's them, sir. The enemy fleet."

The room erupted into controlled chaos, officers rushing to stations, voices raised in urgent commands. Lane spun towards the main tactical display, his face set in grim lines as the sensor data resolved into a chilling picture.

Dozens of ships, their configurations matching what Soren and Jack had seen at Proxima, were materializing at the edge of the Tau Ceti system.

It was happening again, just as they had feared.

CHAPTER 18

The moment the young officer's words registered, Soren and Jack were in motion. They disconnected from the terminal and rushed from the conference room, the urgency of the situation propelling them. As they raced through the corridors of the Wraith, Soren felt the telltale vibration beneath his feet that signaled the ship's acceleration. Sang was already taking initial evasive maneuvers, and Keira had no doubt activated the cloak.

They burst onto the bridge. On the main viewscreen, the horrifying scene unfolded. The enemy fleet had materialized a relatively short distance away.

Lieutenant Commander Bashir rose from the command chair as Soren approached, but there was no time for formalities. Soren slid into place, his eyes locked on the screen as he barked out orders.

"Status report!" he demanded.

"Enemy fleet has completed their jump, sir," Mark answered, his fingers flying over his console. "Forty-eight capital ships, matching the configurations we saw at Proxima."

Forty-eight? They had either left a few ships behind, or

this was a different enemy fleet. Soren's bets were on the latter. The enemy forces on Proxima couldn't have finished their work there already.

With the enemy ships forced to a full stop to jump, the defenses had a limited window to hit them as hard as possible.

They didn't waste it.

"All hands, battle stations!" Soren ordered on ship-wide comms. "I repeat, all hands to battle stations! This is not a drill!"

The blaring gong of red alert sounded on all decks as Soren watched a brilliant flash light up the viewscreen. The FUP defense fleet had seized the initiative, launching a massive barrage of railgun rounds and swarms of missiles against the still-immobile enemy.

For a moment, hope flared in Soren's chest. A powerful enough initial blow could turn the battle in the first few seconds. But as the barrage struck home, that hope withered and died. The enemy ships' shields flared to life, absorbing the punishing assault with sickening ease. As the last echoes of the attack faded, the enemy began to move.

"Keira, charge the vortex cannon."

"Aye, Captain," Keira replied. "Cannon charging. Time to full power, two minutes."

"Soren, we might be better served heading for the rift," Jack suggested.

"You aren't wrong, but I can't just surrender the field without doing my part. We're going to assist in the defense, but I agree, we can't afford to burn through our limited resources. No fighters. No drones. No limited ammunition."

Soren turned away from Jack and settled back into his seat, looking at the projected sensor grid and analyzing the unfolding battle with a tactical eye. The enemy fleet had begun to advance, their formation tight and disciplined.

The FUP defenders responded, spreading out to engage them on multiple fronts.

Shields flared and hulls buckled as the two fleets exchanged missiles and high-velocity railgun projectiles. A FUP destroyer caught a full broadside of railgun fire, its shields failing. Hundreds of punctures appeared in its port side before secondary explosions tore it apart from within. In retaliation, a wing of FUP drones slipped through the enemy's defenses, their explosive payloads tearing gaping holes in a Valkyrie's hull. Fighters from both sides screamed into the fray, their weapons strobing in the darkness as they danced between the lumbering capital ships. Soren watched with pride and despair as the FUP ships fought valiantly against the superior numbers of the invaders.

"Captain," Keira called out, her voice tight with concentration. "I've identified a potential firing solution. Two enemy destroyers, moving in close formation."

Soren leaned forward, studying the tactical display. "Good eye. Status of the vortex cannon?"

"Fully charged and ready, sir," Keira responded.

"Then let's introduce ourselves," Soren said grimly. "Sang, bring us into position. Keira, on my mark."

The Wraith glided through the chaos of battle, her cloaking device rendering her invisible to friend and foe alike. Sang's piloting was masterful, weaving between dueling ships and fields of debris with skill gained from years of experience.

"In position," she reported.

Soren took a deep breath. This was it. The moment they revealed themselves, they'd become a priority target for the entire enemy fleet. But they couldn't stand by and watch their comrades slaughtered.

"Decloak and fire!" Soren ordered.

The Wraith shimmered into visibility, and for a split

second, the nearby ships seemed to pause in confusion. Then the vortex cannon spoke.

A twisting, writhing beam of energy erupted from the Wraith's bow, cutting across space like the finger of an angry god. It struck the first enemy destroyer dead center, the vortex of destructive force tearing through the first ship's shields and hull alike. The beam continued onward, barely diminished, to strike the second ship with equal fury.

Both vessels simply ceased to exist, consumed by the awesome power of the vortex cannon. Where two proud warships had floated moments before, only expanding clouds of debris remained.

"Shields up!" Soren commanded. "Sang, get us clear! Keira, say the word when we're ready to cloak!"

It took time to make the transfer from cannon to cloak, and in that time the enemy began changing vectors, a few of the ships wheeling around to attempt a firing solution. Sang expertly worked the helm, creating maneuvers that weren't in any academy textbook. Even so, railgun rounds peppered their shields as they sped away from the thick of battle.

"Cloak is ready, sir," Keira reported.

Soren watched the grid. The Navy ships had forced the enemy to turn away from Wraith, giving them an opening to drop their shields.

"Shields down, cloak up," he said.

"Aye, Captain," she replied.

The Wraith vanished once more, slipping away as the enemy fleet reacted to the devastating attack. Soren watched as the invaders' formation began to change, spreading out to minimize the effectiveness of another cannon strike.

"They're adapting," Jack observed, his voice grim. "But at least we've given them something to think about."

Soren nodded. "And bought our people some breathing room. But this is far from over."

The battle raged on, a titanic struggle that stretched across the space just beyond Tau Ceti e. The FUP defenders fought with desperate courage, their ships maneuvering through the storm of enemy salvos. Swarms of fighters and drones clashed in furious dogfights, their agility allowing them to slip past capital ship defenses to wreak havoc on vulnerable systems. A squadron of Pilums screamed past an enemy cruiser, their cannons blazing as they dug through its shields and into its reactor core, leaving a blinding flash of light in their wake.

But for every invader they managed to cripple, the Navy lost at least one of their own, and in many cases more. The enemy crews were more prepared and better trained, and fought with a familiarity to war that their side simply didn't possess. Seeing it, Soren could only imagine what the alternate dimension threatening to collapse onto their own was like. Its Dana had claimed it to be different, it was more aggressive, but that seemed an understatement now.

The Wraith continued to strike from the fringe, decloaking just long enough to unleash the fury of its vortex cannon before vanishing once more. Each attack bought the defenders precious time, forcing the enemy to reconsider their tactics. But Soren had fought in enough battles to know, with a sinking feeling in his gut, that it wouldn't be enough.

"Sir!" Mark called out, his voice strained. "Admiral Lane's ship is under heavy attack!"

Soren's eyes snapped to the tactical display. Lane's ship, a Komodo-class destroyer, was surrounded by enemy vessels, its shields flickering weakly under the relentless assault.

"Sang, get us there now!" Soren ordered. "Keira, prepare to fire as soon as we're in range!"

The Wraith surged forward, racing towards the beleaguered flagship. The order to use missiles and railguns reached the edge of Soren's lips, ready to put in the extra effort to save the Admiral and his crew. But even as he opened his mouth to give the order, it was already too late.

A final barrage from the enemy ships overwhelmed Lane's weakened defenses. The proud vessel's hull split apart, secondary explosions rippling along its length. In a matter of heartbeats, the ship that had organized the system's defense was reduced to an expanding cloud of debris and bodies.

A stunned silence fell over the Wraith's bridge. Soren closed his eyes for a moment, offering a silent thought for Lane and his crew. But there was no time for mourning, not now.

"Status report," he demanded, his voice tight with barely contained anger.

"It's not good, Captain," Mark replied, his tone somber. "We've lost nearly a third of our fleet. The enemy's numerical advantage is starting to tell. I...I don't think we can hold them much longer."

Soren's jaw clenched as he studied the tactical display. Mark was right. The defense was crumbling, the remaining FUP ships fighting valiantly but increasingly overwhelmed. It was Proxima all over again, and the realization hit him like a physical blow.

They couldn't win this fight. Not here. Not now.

"Samira," he said, his voice heavy with the weight of command. "Open a tranSat channel to Admiral Montoya. Priority One."

"Channel open, sir," Samira reported a moment later.

"Admiral," Soren began, not waiting for pleasantries. "Tau Ceti is under attack. The enemy fleet arrived in force, just as we feared. Admiral Lane is dead, and the defense is collapsing. We can't hold them."

There was a moment of silence, and Soren could almost see Montoya wrestling with the implications of his words. When the admiral spoke again, his voice was heavy with resignation."Understood, Captain. What's your status?"

"We're still operational, but we can't turn the tide of this battle. We're pulling out, sir. We can't do any more good here, and we can't risk losing the Wraith. Our only chance now is to reach the rift and find a way to stop this at the source."

"Agreed," Montoya replied. "Godspeed, Soren. And... good hunting, my friend. And Soren, I—"

The channel suddenly went silent.

"We've lost tranSat," Samira said.

A heavy silence settled over the bridge. Soren looked around, meeting the eyes of each crewmember in turn. He saw fear there, yes, but also determination. They were with him, come what may.

"Sang," he said at last, "get us clear for a jump. Bobby, set a course for the rift coordinates."

"Aye, Captain," they responded in unison.

As the Wraith turned away from the dying battle, Soren felt a deep ache in his chest. Every desire screamed at him to stay, to fight to the bitter end alongside their comrades. But he knew that this retreat, painful as it was, might be the only thing that could save them all in the long run.

"This isn't over," he said quietly, as much to himself as to his crew.

"Captain, jump calculations are complete," Bobby said. "Estimated time to arrival, eighteen days, twelve hours."

"Sang?"

"Almost clear," she replied.

They all waited in tense silence, watching the flashes from the shrinking battlefield lessen in volume and intensity as the final group of Navy ships, sensing their loss, blinked out of the system, surrendering the planet and it's sixty million inhabitants to the enemy. Cold fury pulsed through Soren's veins, the defeat one of the quickest and most decisive he'd ever seen.

The aftermath would be even worse.

He swallowed the bitter bile rising up his throat, hands clenching the armrests of his seat. Sang flipped Wraith over, reversing the burn and quickly slowing the ship.

"Full stop, Captain," Sang announced.

With a final, silent, painful farewell to the brave defenders of Tau Ceti, Soren gave the order, and the Wraith jumped away.

CHAPTER 19

The rhythmic thud of combat boots echoed through the modified cargo bay as Alex led the Scorpions through their training regimen. The space, hastily converted into a sparring arena, was filled with the grunts and controlled breathing of Marines pushing their bodies to the limit.

Alex watched critically as Zoe and Malik circled each other on the practice mat, their movements fluid and precise. The rest of the platoon, including Lieutenant Moffitt, stood in a loose circle around them, observing the bout.

Zoe feinted left, then darted right, her fist snapping out in a lightning-fast jab. Malik, anticipating the move, pivoted and deflected the blow, using Zoe's momentum against her to throw her off balance. She recovered quickly, dropping low and scissoring Malik's legs out from under him.

The big man hit the mat with a resounding thud, the air rushing from his lungs. Before he could recover, Zoe was on him, her forearm pressed against his throat in a submission hold.

"Yield," Malik gasped, tapping the mat twice.

Alex nodded approvingly as Zoe helped Malik to his feet. "Good work, both of you. Zoe, excellent use of your opponent's momentum. Malik, next time, watch your footing when she goes low."

As the two Scorpions stepped off the mat, Alex noticed the look of begrudging respect on Lieutenant Moffitt's face. The officer had initially been skeptical of the Scorpions' unorthodox training methods, but even he couldn't deny their effectiveness.

"Alright," Alex announced, addressing the entire group. "Let's switch it up. Jackson, Sarah, you're up. Remember, this isn't just about winning. It's about learning, adapting, and improving. Every bout should teach you something new about yourself and your opponent."

As Jackson and Sarah took their positions on the mat, Alex felt a presence at his side. He turned to find Lieutenant Moffitt standing there, arms crossed, with a contemplative look.

"Interesting techniques," Liam said, his tone neutral. "Not exactly standard Marine Corps hand-to-hand."

Alex nodded, keeping his eyes on the sparring match. "No, sir. First Company incorporates elements from various martial arts and combat styles outside of the manual. It gives us more options and makes us more unpredictable in a fight."

Liam grunted, neither approving nor disapproving. "And you think this approach is better than tried-and-true Marine Corps training?"

Alex chose his words carefully, aware of the delicate balance between respect for authority and the need to push for improvement. "With all due respect, sir, I think there's always room for growth and adaptation. The enemy we're facing...they're not like us, but they're also just like us. They have the manual, too, so to speak. Against equivalent adversaries, we need to find every edge we can get."

On the mat, Sarah executed a perfect armbar, forcing Jackson to tap out. The assembled Marines murmured appreciatively, clearly impressed by her display of skill.

Liam's brow sank as he watched the Marines' reactions. "You may have a point, Sergeant. But introducing new techniques this late in the game could do more harm than good. We don't have time to retrain the entire platoon."

Alex turned to face the lieutenant fully, his voice low and urgent. "Sir, we have eighteen days before we reach the rift. That's more than enough time to at least introduce some basic concepts that could save lives. The Scorpions could run training sessions, share what we've learned."

Liam's jaw tightened, a flicker of something—perhaps pride, perhaps stubborn hubris—passing across his face. "I'll take it under advisement, Gunny. For now, carry on with your training per the book."

The Lieutenant turned and strode away, leaving Alex frustrated and concerned. He knew the skills the Scorpions had developed could make a real difference, but Liam's reluctance was a significant obstacle.

As the training session wound down, Alex gathered the Scorpions around him. "Good work today, team. Hit the showers and get some chow. We'll reconvene at 1400 hours for tactical simulations."

The Marines filed out, their bodies glistening with sweat, a mixture of exhaustion and satisfaction on their faces. Alex lingered behind, his mind churning with thoughts of convincing Liam of the value of additional training. The idea of going over Liam's head to his father didn't sit well with him, but neither did the idea of potentially watching good men and women die when he might have been able to teach them something that could save their lives.

It was that thought that made the decision for him. That, and the fact that he and his Scorpions were directly under his father's command. It didn't completely remove Liam from his chain of command, but it gave him the avenue he needed to go over his head without suffering the most significant of consequences. If Liam wouldn't listen, maybe his dad would, and not just because he was his dad.

If Alex found Soren in the captain's ready room, poring over tactical reports and sensor data from the battle at Tau Ceti, no doubt reliving the fight in his mind and looking for things he could have done better, or maybe trying to find holes in the enemy's tactics that he could exploit. Like him, his father was a consummate student, always trying to improve despite his years of experience.

That's why Alex was so sure his father would understand his position.

The weight of command was evident in the lines of his father's face, the slight slump of his shoulders. But when Soren saw Alex, a warm smile spread across his features.

"Alex," he said, gesturing to a chair. "Come in. How was training?"

Alex took a seat. "That's actually what I came to talk to you about, Captain."

Soren raised an eyebrow. "So you're speaking to me as Sergeant Strickland then?"

Alex nodded. "This is a professional visit, sir."

Soren turned off his datapad and placed it on the desk.

"In that case, what can I do for you, Sergeant?"

"I wanted to discuss a conflict I've run into. The truth is, the Scorpions are in top form, but the rest of the platoon...they're good Marines, don't get me wrong, but I've seen the enemy up close. They're not prepared for what we might face on the other side of that rift."

Soren's expression grew serious as he listened to his son's concerns. "What do you mean, exactly?"

"They're trained for conventional warfare," Alex explained. "But what we saw on Jungle, what we're up against now...it's anything but conventional. The enemy is more focused. More violent. What's more, they're also FUP Marines. They're training from a similar manual, if not the same manual. That means they'll anticipate whatever we throw at them because they would do the same thing."

Soren nodded. "When my doppelgänger challenged me, I had Wilf take the conn because I knew the other Soren would guess what moves I might make more accurately. As a result, Wilf came up with a strategy I wouldn't have, and we won the fight."

"Yes, sir. It's like that. They're good Marines, and I want them to survive. The Scorpions have developed techniques, strategies that could give them an edge. But Lieutenant Moffitt is resistant to the idea of us training the rest of the platoon."

Soren leaned back in his chair, his brow furrowed in thought. "I can understand Liam's hesitation. Changing established training protocols, especially on such short notice, can be risky."

"That's what Lieutenant Moffitt said," Alex replied. "But I'm telling you, he's selling his platoon short. I'm sure that, given the chance, they'll rise to the occasion."

"I'm not saying I disagree with you. In fact, I think you might be onto something important. But you need to approach this carefully. Liam is a good officer, and we need him fully on board if we're going to implement any changes. Otherwise, you undermine his authority and he loses the trust of his subordinates. I'm sure you understand."

Alex nodded, acknowledging the wisdom in his father's words. "So what do I do? How should I approach him? I don't care if he takes all the credit. I just want to help those Marines become better weapons."

"I know you do," Soren replied. "And I appreciate that, Gunny. Let me talk to Liam. I'll hear him out, try to understand his reservations. Then we'll see about finding a way to integrate some of your advanced training into the platoon's regimen."

"Thank you, Captain," Alex said, a wave of relief washing over him. "I just can't shake the feeling that we're not as prepared as we need to be. And after what happened at Proxima and Tau Ceti..."

Soren turned back to his son, his eyes filled with pride and concern. "I know, Sergeant. Believe me, I feel it, too. We're facing an enemy that's been preparing for this fight for far longer than we have. But that doesn't mean we're beaten. Not by a long shot."

Alex stood, squaring his shoulders. "You're right. We'll find a way to even the odds."

As Alex left, Soren called, "Can I talk to my son for a second?"

Alex paused at the door, looking back with a smile. "Sure, Dad."

"I'm proud of you," Soren said softly. "The way you're looking out for your fellow Marines, pushing for improvement. It's what a good leader does."

A lump formed in Alex's throat, and he nodded, unable to find words. With a final glance at his father, he left the ready room, his determination renewed.

Soren watched the door slide shut behind Alex, a complex mix of emotions swirling within him. Pride in his boy's leadership and initiative warred with concern over the challenges ahead.

Shaking off the moment of introspection, Soren activated his comm patch. "Liam, report to the ready room."

A few minutes later, Liam entered, his posture rigid, his face a mask of professional neutrality. "You wanted to see me, Captain?"

Soren gestured to the chair Alex had vacated. "Have a seat."

Liam sat down. "Sir, if I may. I think I know what this is about."

"Then we can skip right to the meat of it."

"Permission to speak frankly, Captain?"

"Go ahead."

"I have to admit, I'm not pleased about the idea of your son coming up here to tell his daddy that he didn't get his way."

"A completely understandable position," Soren agreed. "But Sergeant Strickland made it clear he was coming to me as squad leader for Marine Special Forces."

"Even with that being the case, I don't appreciate an enlisted man going over my head like that."

"Please keep in mind he and his Scorpions are directly under my command. I know that seems a bit unconventional considering he's my son, but he came in here as Sergeant Strickland, a damn good SpecOps Marine, not the kid I taught how to ride a bicycle. Did he speak to you about his ideas?"

"Yes, sir, he did."

"And what did you tell him?"

"I told him I think it's too late in the game to add new training to my guys' routines. And I'll say the same thing to you."

"Normally, I might agree with you, Liam. But you have to admit, nothing about this whole fight is normal."

"I'll give you that, sir. It's not that I'm against improvement. But we have established protocols, training methods that have been proven effective. Introducing new elements this close to a potential engagement...it could disrupt unit cohesion, create confusion in the field."

Soren nodded, acknowledging the point. "I understand your concerns, Liam. But let me ask you this. Do you believe our current training protocols adequately prepare our Marines for the kind of enemy we're facing?"

Liam opened his mouth to respond, then closed it, giving the question more consideration. Finally, he admitted, "No, sir. I don't think any of us were prepared for what we've seen."

"Exactly," Soren said, leaning forward. "We're facing an enemy that knows our tactics, our strategies, possibly better than we do. They've been preparing for this conflict for months, maybe years. We need every advantage we can get."

"With all due respect, sir, I'm not comfortable with Sergeant Strickland taking over the platoon's training."

"Why not?" Liam didn't answer right away, face flushing. "Does it have anything to do with me keeping the Scorpions under my direct command, does it?"

"Well..I..." Liam shifted in his seat, clearly uncomfortable.

"Liam, no one is suggesting that Alex take over. But the Scorpions have valuable experience and skills that could benefit the entire platoon. Wouldn't you agree that as their commanding officer, it's your responsibility to ensure they have every tool at their disposal?"

"Yes, sir. But—"

Soren held up a hand, cutting him off. "What if we approached this differently? Instead of Alex leading the additional training sessions, what if you were to oversee them? You could work with the Scorpions, integrate their techniques into the existing training regimen. It would be your initiative, your program."

Liam blinked, surprised by the suggestion. "I...I suppose that could work, sir."

"Think about it, Liam," Soren pressed. "You'd be pioneering a new approach to Marine combat training, one specifically tailored to the unique threats we're facing. It could be a significant achievement in your career."

Soren could almost see the wheels turning in Liam's

head as he considered the possibility. The Lieutenant's expression shifted from reluctance to cautious interest.

"And Sergeant Strickland?" Liam asked. "How would he feel about this arrangement?"

Soren smiled, feeling the tension in the room begin to dissipate. "Alex isn't interested in taking credit, Lieutenant. He just wants our Marines to be as prepared as possible for whatever we might face. He wants them to come out of this alive. I'm sure he'd be more than willing to work with you on developing the program. All you have to do is listen to his suggestions and go from there."

Liam nodded slowly, his posture relaxing slightly. "I see. Well, in that case...I suppose it would be negligent of me not to explore every avenue for improving our combat readiness."

"I'm glad you see it that way," Soren said, standing and extending his hand. "I look forward to seeing what you and the Scorpions can put together."

Liam stood as well, shaking Soren's hand with renewed confidence. "Thank you, sir. I'll start working on a training plan with Sergeant Strickland immediately."

As Liam turned to leave, Soren called out, "Liam?"

Liam paused at the door, looking back.

"Remember," Soren said, his voice gentle but firm, "there's no shame in learning from those under your command. The best leaders are those who recognize and nurture talent, regardless of rank."

A flicker of embarrassment crossed Liam's face, but he nodded, accepting the gentle rebuke. "Understood, sir. I'll keep that in mind."

As the door slid shut behind Liam, Soren let out a long breath. He'd managed to navigate a potentially divisive situation, but he knew the real challenge lay ahead. Eighteen days to prepare for an enemy they barely understood in a universe that wasn't their own.

Soren returned to his desk, again pulling up the reports on the Proxima and Tau Ceti attacks. A cold determination settled over him as he pored over the data, looking for any pattern, any weakness they could exploit.

Whatever lay on the other side of the rift, they would be ready. They had to be. The fate of their entire universe depended on it.

CHAPTER 20

The next morning, after putting together a new training plan, Liam and Alex stood at the front of the makeshift training area, the rest of the Scorpions standing off to the side. A sea of expectant faces, the rest of the Marine platoon stood at ease before them.

"Alright, Marines," Liam began, his voice strong and clear. "Over the next few weeks, Gunny and I will be introducing some new combat techniques and strategies. These aren't meant to replace your existing training but to supplement it.

He paused, making eye contact with several Marines and gauging their reactions. Most seemed curious, if a bit skeptical. That was good. Skepticism was something they could work with. Outright resistance would have been harder to overcome.

"I know some of you might be wondering why we're doing this now, so close to a potential engagement," he continued. "The truth is, the enemy we're facing is, essentially, us. They know our tactics, our strategies. We need to be unpredictable, adaptable."

A hand went up in the crowd. "Sir," a young corporal

called out, "how do you know these new techniques will be effective against the enemy?"

"Because the Scorpions used them effectively against the enemy on Jungle. And survived when no one else did. That, in itself, should answer your question. I've asked them to step up and teach you as much of what they know as they can in the time we have left in FTL. Gunny will be taking over from here," he said, stepping off to the side to watch.

Alex took a deep breath, pushing down the nervousness that threatened to rise in his gut. This was his chance to make a real difference, to potentially save lives when they finally faced the enemy. He couldn't afford to mess it up.

"My team and I survived for over a month on PX-2847 while it was occupied by these invaders. We fought them, and we succeeded in large part because of the added training we were given as members of Force Recon. There's no reason to think you can't benefit from them, too. Force Recon developed these techniques through trial and error in hundreds of high-tech training simulations. The kind regular leathernecks don't have access to. They carried the day more than once. And now…" Alex glanced at Liam, who gave him a small nod. "…thanks to the Lieutenant's foresight, we can share that knowledge with all of you. It was his idea to provide this additional training. He'll be overseeing the program, ensuring that what we teach integrates smoothly with your existing skill set."

A murmur of surprise rippled through the assembled Marines. They hadn't expected Liam to be the driving force behind such an unorthodox approach.

Liam stepped forward, his voice carrying across the room. "That's right, Marines. I want you all to consider this an opportunity to expand your combat repertoire. I expect each of you to give your full attention and effort to this training."

Alex felt a wave of relief wash over him. With Liam's explicit backing, any lingering resistance among the Marines would likely dissipate.

"Alright," Alex said, clapping his hands together. "Let's get started. We're going to begin with some basic evasion techniques. These are designed to make you a harder target in close-quarters combat. All of these techniques are equally applicable in power armor, which we'll train with once you get the basics down. Zoe, if you could demonstrate?"

Alex and the Scorpions led the platoon through a series of drills and exercises for the next several hours. They focused on various aspects of offense and defense, pushing the Marines to their physical and mental limits.

By the time Alex called for a break, the entire platoon was drenched in sweat, breathing heavily. But there was an energy in the air, an excitement that hadn't been there before. The Marines were starting to see the potential in these new techniques.

As the platoon dispersed for a quick meal and rest, Liam approached Alex. The lieutenant's expression was thoughtful, almost impressed.

"Good work, Sergeant," Liam said, his voice low. "I have to admit, I was skeptical at first. But I can see the value in what you're teaching."

Alex nodded, wiping sweat from his brow. "Thank you, sir. I appreciate you giving us this opportunity."

Liam nodded, his eyes scanning the room as the Marines filed out. "I've been thinking about what your father said," he admitted. "About learning from those under my command. It's not always easy to set aside one's pride. But watching you work with the platoon today, I can see why the Scorpions are so effective."

Alex felt a surge of respect for the Lieutenant. It couldn't have been easy for him to admit that. "Thank you, sir. We're all on the same team here. The more we can learn from each other, the better our chances when we face the enemy."

"Agreed," Liam said. "Excellent work, Sergeant."

"Thank you, sir."

Over the next few days, the training intensified. Alex and the Scorpions pushed the platoon to their limits and beyond. They introduced advanced hand-to-hand combat techniques, unorthodox weapon handling, and other skills to improve their coordination and mobility in any environment.

One afternoon, about a week into the new training regimen, Alex watched as Sarah led a group through a particularly challenging close-quarters combat drill. The Marines moved through a makeshift obstacle course, engaging holographic targets with a combination of standard Marine Corps techniques and the new methods they'd been learning.

"Looking good," a familiar voice said from behind him.

Alex turned to find his father standing there, arms crossed, a look of approval on his face.

"Thank you, Captain," Alex replied. "They're picking it up faster than I expected. Liam's been a big help, too. Once you got him on board, everything fell into place. He's even done some of the training himself."

Soren nodded, his eyes tracking the Marines as they navigated the course. "I'm glad to hear it. We're going to need every edge we can get."

"I've been thinking about that," Alex said suddenly. "What if we expanded the training to ship-to-ship combat as well? If the enemy knows our standard naval tactics, maybe we should be preparing alternative strategies there, too."

Soren's eyebrows rose, a thoughtful expression crossing his face. "You know, that's not actually a bad idea. We could run some simulations, war games with the bridge crew. Maybe even bring in Captain Pham and his Hooligans."

Alex nodded eagerly, his mind already racing with possibilities. "Exactly. We could set up scenarios based on what we saw at Tau Ceti and try to develop better counter-measures. Obviously, the benefit to the Wraith alone is limited, but I heard the Seventh and Eighth Strike Forces are meeting us at the rift coordinates."

"I'm going to do everything I can to keep those ships out of the rift, but I agree that we may need them at some point. And whatever we develop can still be passed back to Montoya for further refinement. I'm sure the Navy analysts are working on the problem, too."

"Navy analysts exist on the enemy's side as well," Alex pointed out. "There are only one Soren and one Alex Strickland."

"I'll talk to Jack and Ethan about the viability of setting up those kinds of simulations," Soren said, clapping Alex on the shoulder. "Good thinking, son. This is exactly the kind of innovative approach we need."

As Soren turned to leave, Alex called out, "Dad?"

Soren paused, looking back.

"Thanks," Alex said softly. "For trusting me with this, for giving me the chance to make a difference."

A warm smile spread across Soren's face. "You've more than earned it, Alex. I'm so damn proud of you."

With that, Soren left, leaving Alex with a mix of emotions swirling in his chest. Pride at his father's words, determination to live up to the trust placed in him, and a gnawing fear of what lay ahead and whether or not what little training they were giving the Marines would be enough.

Pushing the fear aside, Alex turned back to the training area. There was still work to be done, skills to hone, strate-gies to perfect. Whatever awaited them on the other side of that rift, they would face it head-on, as prepared as they could be.

"Alright, Marines," he called out, his voice carrying across the room. "Reset the course. We're going to run it again, but this time, I want you to focus on situational awareness. The enemy we're facing isn't just strong, they're focused and determined to the point of reckless abandon. We need to be ready for anything."

Alex felt a renewed sense of purpose as the platoon scrambled to reset the obstacles. They had eight days left before they reached the rift. Eight days to turn this group of already elite Marines into something even more formidable.

It wasn't much time. But it would have to be enough.

CHAPTER 21

The next morning, Soren stood at the end of the table in the Wraith's briefing room, surrounded by a mix of Marine, Navy and civilian personnel. Alex and Liam were there, along with Minh and his top pilots, plus Jack, Vic, Ethan, Keira, Lina, Tashi and Wilf.

"Some of you may have already heard that Liam and Alex have put together an advanced training regimen for the Marines on board," Soren said, his expression serious as he addressed the assembled group. "It's been brought to my attention that similar innovation may benefit our entire tactical apparatus. To that end, we will also expand our training to our naval personnel. The enemy knows our standard playbook, so we must write a new one."

He noted an array of unspoken reactions among his crew. Shock. Surprise. Anxiety. Tension. Nervousness. Even a little eagerness. Wilf's fingers tapped out an excited staccato beat on the table before him. Vic looked at him like he'd lost his mind. Jack looked thoughtful, his fingers plucking at his lower lip. Alex, of course, was already on board since this was his idea, and Milf and Minh were the only other ones who looked even a little bit enthusiastic.

He would obviously have to put on his salesman's hat to sell this idea to several of the others.

"We're going to run a series of simulations," he explained, tapping a control on the table. A holographic display sprang to life in the center of it, showing a tactical representation of the battles in the Wolf system, on Jungle, and at Tau Ceti. "Based on what we've seen of the enemy's tactics so far, our goal is to develop new strategies and unconventional approaches that might give us an edge."

Minh leaned forward, his eyes fixed on the holographic display. "What kind of unconventional approaches are we talking about, Captain?"

Soren nodded, appreciating the question. "Good question. We're looking at everything from changes to our drone AI programming to novel uses of our existing weaponry. We even need to consider squadron formations and targeting, especially when we account for the vortex cannon. Nothing is off the table."

He paused, his gaze sweeping the room. "I know this is unorthodox. I know some of you are skeptical. But the stakes couldn't be higher. We're fighting for the very existence of our universe. We need every advantage we can get."

The room fell silent as the weight of Soren's words sank in. He met Alex's gaze, bolstered by the pride he saw in his son's eyes and in the interest he saw in Minh's.

"Thank you for including me in this, Captain," Minh said. "I'm sure we can come up with some approaches the enemy won't expect." Suddenly, Minh's enthusiasm seemed to spark the same in the doubters.

"We'll be dividing into teams," Soren continued. "Some will play the role of our forces, others the enemy. We'll rotate these roles to get different perspectives. I want everyone thinking outside the box, pushing the boundaries of what we think is possible. Any more questions or concerns before we get started?"

"Alright then," Soren said when all he got in response were thoughtful looks and a shake of the head from Lina and Minh's XO. "Let's get to work. The engineering team has built a basic simulation that will allow us to review existing enemy tactics and build on our own. It may take a bit of trial and error to get everything running smoothly, but I have every confidence we can push the envelope. If nothing else, this will be a good team building exercise, and a good way to productively pass the time before we reach the rift. We'll start with a basic scenario and build from there."

The briefing room quickly transformed into a bustling command center as the teams dove into the simulations. Holographic displays flickered to life around the room, each showing a different aspect of the simulated battlefields. Soren watched with satisfaction as his crew, both Navy and Marine, divided into teams and settled into their roles with enthusiasm.

They ran through the simulations, enjoying the camaraderie as much as the process, trying different tactics, some of which ended in spectacular failure and others they filed away for possible use. All the while, Soren moved between the groups, offering suggestions and encouragement. He paused by Keira's station, where she was working with Ethan and Tashi to explore new applications for the vortex cannon.

"What if we modulated the beam?" Tashi suggested, his fingers moving in excited patterns. "Instead of one continuous burst, we could pulse it, create a kind of...I don't know, vortex shotgun effect?"

Keira's eyes lit up. "That could work. It might reduce the overall power, but it would give us a wider area of effect. Ethan, is that something we could actually implement?"

Ethan stroked his beard thoughtfully. "It would require some significant tweaks to the emitter array, but...yeah, I think we could make it happen. Let me run some simulations."

As the day wore on, the teams cycled through various scenarios, each more challenging than the last. They paused frequently, huddling together to discuss new ideas or consult with the engineering team about the feasibility of some of their more interesting proposals.

By the end of the session, Soren could feel the energy in the room, the buzz of excitement and possibility. Ideas that had seemed outlandish at first were being refined. Novel uses of existing technology were being explored and tested in the simulations.

As they wrapped up for the day, Soren addressed the group once more. "Excellent work, everyone. I've seen some truly innovative thinking today. We'll reconvene tomorrow to build on what we've started. Remember, no idea is too crazy to at least consider. Keep pushing those boundaries. And speak to all your people. There are some sharp minds among them and any one of them could trigger a winning strategy or tactic. If one of them comes up with a feasible idea or two, invite them to the session tomorrow."

The crew filed out, their voices animated as they continued to discuss the day's simulations. Soren caught snippets of conversation—debates about drone tactics, discussions of unconventional uses for shield generators, even a heated argument about the potential applications of weaponized counter-mass fields.

Jack lingered behind, a smile playing at the corners of his mouth. "Well, old friend," he said, clapping Soren on the shoulder. "I'd say that was a resounding success."

Soren nodded, feeling a surge of pride in his crew. "Thanks to Alex. It was his idea. Did you see the way they were working together? Navy, Marines, the civillians...everyone contributing, building on each other's ideas."

"I did," Jack agreed. "And more importantly, I saw something else. Something we've been sorely lacking since this whole mess began."

"Oh?" Soren raised an eyebrow. "And what's that?"

"Hope," Jack said simply. "For the first time since Proxima, since Tau Ceti, I saw real hope in their eyes. They're starting to believe we might actually have a chance."

Soren nodded. He felt it too—a palpable shift in the ship's atmosphere. The fear and uncertainty that had plagued them since witnessing the devastation at Proxima was being replaced by determination, by a collective will to fight back.

"We've still got a long way to go," Soren cautioned. "And there's no guarantee any of this will work against the real enemy."

"True," Jack conceded. "But we're better prepared now than we were yesterday. And we'll be better prepared tomorrow than we are today. That's all we can ask for."

As they left the briefing room, Soren couldn't help but feel a glimmer of optimism. They were still heading into the unknown, still facing an enemy of terrifying power and ruthlessness. But now, at least, they were doing so with renewed purpose.

The next seven days would be crucial. They would refine their tactics, push their simulations to the limit, and prepare themselves as best they could.

Soren allowed himself a small smile as he headed to the bridge. They might be outgunned and facing impossible odds, but they weren't beaten yet.

Not by a long shot.

CHAPTER 22

Soren stood on the bridge of the Wraith, his hands clasped behind his back as he paced back and forth in front of the command station. They were moments away from completing the long journey to the rift. Moments away from balancing precariously on the edge of a knife, with no way to know which way their fortunes might turn.

They had set the jump coordinates to arrive beyond sensor range from the right flank, assuming the enemy wouldn't leave it unguarded. Even so, they had no idea what to expect or if the enemy might have anticipated their maneuver.

"One minute to arrival," Bobby announced from the nav station, his voice tense.

Soren nodded. This was it. The culmination of everything they had been through, everything they had prepared for. Beyond that invisible threshold lay not just an enemy fleet but the gateway to another universe—and perhaps the key to saving their own.

"Keira," he said, his voice calm despite the adrenaline coursing through his veins, "prepare to activate the cloak the moment it comes online after the jump."

"Aye, Captain," Keira replied, her fingers hovering over her console. "Cloak primed and ready."

Soren turned to Mark at the ops station. "I want a full sensor sweep the instant we arrive. Over the barrel, Mark. We can't afford to miss anything."

Mark nodded, his face a mask of concentration. "You'll have it, sir. Every scrap of data we can pull."

"Samira, broadcast ship wide," Soren ordered. "All hands to ready status."

"Aye, Captain," Samira responded. A moment later, her voice echoed through the ship's intercom system. "All hands, this is the bridge. We are one minute from arrival at the target coordinates. All hands to ready status. Repeat, all hands to ready status."

Soren felt a surge of pride as he imagined his crew responding to the call, each moving to their assigned post with practiced efficiency. They had trained for this, prepared as best they could. Now, it was time to put that preparation to the test.

"Ten seconds," Bobby announced.

Soren took a deep breath, centering himself as he dropped into the command chair. "Here we go. Stay sharp."

The final seconds ticked away, followed by a flash of light and the sudden appearance of space in the primary viewscreen.

"Jump complete," Bobby reported. "We've arrived at the designated coordinates."

"Sensor sweep initiating," Mark said.

Soren leaned forward, his eyes fixed on the main viewscreen as it resolved to show their new surroundings. At first glance, it seemed unremarkable—just another patch of empty space. However, a very different picture emerged as the sensor data streamed in.

"Sir," Mark called out, his voice tight with tension. "I'm

picking up multiple contacts. It's Strike Forces Seven and Eight."

Soren's eyebrows rose in surprise. "Where?"

"They're... they're much further out than expected, sir. It looks like they jumped in even farther back than we did."

A grim smile tugged at Soren's lips. "Smart move. They were being cautious, just in case."

"Captain, we're being hailed," Samira said.

"Put it on," Soren replied.

"Captain Strickland," Commodore Clarey said. "Admiral Montoya told us to be expecting you. I'm glad you've finally arrived. And, welcome back into the good graces of the FUPN, by the way."

"Thank you, Commodore," Soren replied. "How long have you been waiting for us?"

"Thirty-four hours, sir," Clarey answered. "If you'll switch to Channel Ninety-three, I have Captain Ling of Strike Force Eight on the comms with a status report."

"Samira," Soren said.

"Aye, Captain," she replied, changing the channel.

"Captain, our cloak is active," Keira announced before a new voice, deep and resonant, came over the channel.

"Captain Strickland, this is Captain Tao Ling of Strike Force Eight. I regret we have to meet under these circumstances. I've long been an admirer of yours."

"Captain Ling," Soren said. "Thank you for joining us. What have you got for me?"

""We arrived thirty-nine hours ago. Upon arrival, I deployed a tranSat relay at the far end of range from the coordinates we were provided. Since we're beyond sensor range, I've had my crews at ready stations full time, just in case anything unfriendly pops up. But if there are enemy ships nearby, they haven't noticed us, and we haven't noticed them."

"Good," Soren said. "We'll take care of recon."

"Of course. We lost you on sensors a few seconds ago. That's some ship, Captain."

"It is," Soren agreed. "Sit tight. We're going to sweep forward to get a look at what we're dealing with."

""Understood, Captain."

Soren cut the connection. "Sang, bring us in, nice and easy. I want to hug the edge of our sensor range, close enough to cover five AU around the rift position."

"Aye, Captain," Sang replied, putting the cloaked warship in motion.

"Mark, call it out as soon as you see it," Soren said.

The Wraith advanced slowly, a quick burn before drifting. Soren settled back, controlling his calm as the minutes ticked past.

"First contact," Mark called out forty minutes later.

"Configuration?" Soren asked.

"Not yet. Standby."

"Well, whatever it is, it means they didn't leave the rift undefended," Jack said.

"Not unexpected," Soren replied.

"No, but still annoying."

Soren allowed himself a small grin. "Agreed."

"More contacts, Captain," Mark said. "First ship is positively identified as a Komodo-class, matching the previously seen enemy configurations."

"There they are," Jack said.

"More contacts hitting the grid," Mark announced.

Soren watched the projection as more marks appeared at the edge of their range. A full defensive fleet, positioned around the rift coordinates.

"Put it on screen, full zoom." They were too far out to see much, but it wasn't as much the ships he was interested in seeing as the rift they were there to protect.

The viewscreen shifted, and Soren could see what he believed to be the lead Komodo, which was a speck of dust against the background of a star. He studied the screen intently, searching for any sign of the dimensional tear they had come so far to find. But there was no visible anomaly, no swirling vortex or shimmering portal. Just empty space and enemy ships.

"It looks clear, Captain," Mark said.

"It must be there somewhere," Soren said. "They wouldn't be defending nothing."

"It might just be invisible to the eye," Ethan said.

"Mark, run the feed through all available filters."

"Aye, Captain."

The image shifted as filters were applied. UV, infrared, polarization, and more.

"Still nothing," Jack said. "Do you think this is a trap? That we were led on a wild Bryce chase? They could have abducted your Dana and made up the whole alternate universe story. Forced her to record that message and lead you here."

"For what purpose?" Soren asked. "Besides, we fought my doppelgänger over Jungle."

"We never saw him. That could have been a trick, too."

"Alex and his squad saw his other. He said he was an evil twin. We'll just have to trust that it's there. For now, we focus on the threat we can see. Mark, do we have a full sweep?"

"Yes, sir."

"Sang, reverse course, bring us back out of range."

"Aye, Captain."

They retreated faster than they advanced, returning to the two Strike Force flotillas within half an hour.

"Samira, establish a tranSat link. We need to update Admiral Montoya on the situation."

"Aye, Captain. Standby." She paused, tapping on her console. "Connection confirmed."

Soren nodded. At this distance, it would take a little

over twenty minutes for a message to reach Earth. "Alright. Keira, I want you to transmit all our data and logs on the training we've been doing. We have no way of knowing if it will help, but it's better than nothing."

"I'm on it, Captain."

Soren used his command console to record a message. "Admiral Montoya. We've arrived at the rift coordinates, and made an initial reconnoiter of the area. The rift is invisible to the naked eye, as well as available filters on the primary camera. However, there is a defensive fleet encircling the area at regular intervals, creating a net around it. By our count, sixteen ships, including four Komodo-class destroyers. A formidable fleet. I'm also transmitting some work my crew and I have done on modifying our tactics to be less predictable based on current training methods, which the enemy also likely possesses. I don't know if any of these proposals will be effective in combat, but they're based on both my and Alex's experiences fighting this enemy. Perhaps you can put it to good use."

He ended the message and nodded to Samira to send it.

"Message sent, Captain," she replied.

"So, what's our plan?" Jack asked.

"Good question," Soren replied. "I'd love to sneak right past that fleet and enter the rift, except we have no idea if we can just fly into the middle and we get transported, or if we have to do something to activate it, or—"

"Maybe we find out there's no rift there in the first place," Jack provided.

"Yes. And there's a benefit to taking out that defensive line if we can. If we seize control of the space around the rift, we gain a massive strategic advantage. It becomes a chokepoint, a way for us to better control the flow of forces between our universes."

"True," Jack conceded. "But it could also become a meat

grinder. We could be committing our forces to a battle we can't win."

"You're not wrong," Soren said, his voice heavy with the weight of command. "It will be a meat grinder. But better here than on our worlds. If we can hold this point, we keep the fight away from our civilians, our homes. Our families."

Jack nodded slowly, understanding dawning in his eyes. "You're right, of course. I just hope the cost isn't too high."

"Ethan," Soren called out. "What's the status on that modulation update you and Tashi were working on for the vortex cannon?"

"We've got it ready to go, Captain. But we haven't had a chance to test it in real-world conditions yet."

"How long does it take to switch it over from the standard configuration?"

"About ten minutes to make the changeover," Ethan replied. "Wait. Are you planning to use it in shotgun mode?"

"I'm thinking about it."

"Are you sure? Like I said, we haven't tested it yet."

Soren felt the weight of the decision pressing down on him. It was a risk, certainly. But then again, everything about this mission was a risk. "I have faith in you, Ethan. In both of you. Make the switch. Put it in shotgun mode."

"Aye, Captain," Ethan said, standing and heading off the bridge. "We'll make it happen."

As Ethan and his team worked on modifying the vortex cannon, Soren turned his attention back to the tactical situation. They had surprise on their side, and now potentially a weapon the enemy wouldn't be expecting. But they would need more than that to overcome the defensive fleet.

"Samira, open a channel to Strike Forces Seven and Eight," he ordered. "I think I have a plan."

As soon as the connection was established, Soren described what they had seen, passing the sensor data to them before laying out his strategy. "We're going to use the Wraith's cloak to sneak into the midst of the enemy fleet," he explained. "Once we're in position, we'll hit them with the vortex cannon. We've modified it to work more like a shotgun, with a wider area of effect. It should damage multiple ships at once."

"And where do we come in?" Clarey asked.

"You'll be our backup," Soren replied. "And our diversion. The goal is to attract the defenders toward you so they bunch up a little more while you remain out of weapons range. With the ships more tightly grouped, we'll decloak and fire, putting the hurt on them. We need to keep pounding them from there, and you'll have to move up to your weapons range just after our attack. Timing is critical."

There was a moment of silence as the other officers considered the plan. Finally, Ling spoke up. "It's risky, but it could work. We'll be ready on your signal, Captain."

"My crew is up to the challenge thanks to you, Captain," Clarey added. "Good hunting, Wraith."

"Jack, who's our aerospace boss?"

"You don't know?"

"I'm sure I welcomed them and shook their hand, but I can't remember everyone."

"You're getting old, my friend."

"Look in the mirror sometime."

"Commander Phoebe Gates. Her mini-boss is Lieutenant Commander Ettore Puccini."

"Thank you." Soren made a mental note to go visit them later, to make sure he could put faces to the names. He activated another channel. "Phoebe, I want the Pilums and their drones launched immediately. Tell Minh to hang back with Strike Forces Seven and Eight, follow their squadrons into the fight."

"Aye, Captain," she replied in a slightly husky voice.

Soren checked their time. "Ethan, status of the cannon?"

"Just finishing up," Ethan's voice came over the comm. "We're in shotgun mode, Captain."

"Pilum squadrons launched, Captain," Phoebe reported a few minutes later.

"Captain, we're free birds dropping back to ready position," Minh announced.

"Strike Forces Seven and Eight are moving into position," Samira added.

Soren took a deep breath, feeling the familiar surge of pre-battle adrenaline coursing through his veins. This was it. The moment of truth.

"Sang," he said, his voice steady despite the tension thrumming through him, "take us in. Nice and easy."

"Aye, Captain," Sang replied, her hands moving with practiced precision over the helm controls.

The Wraith began to glide forward, invisible and silent, towards the unsuspecting enemy fleet. On the viewscreen, the hostile ships grew larger, their sleek, predatory forms a stark reminder of their destructive prowess.

They had trained for this, prepared as best they could. Now it was time to put that preparation to the test.

As they drew closer to the enemy formation, Soren felt the familiar tightening in his chest, the razor-sharp focus that always came with imminent combat. He glanced around the bridge, seeing the same intensity mirrored in the faces of his crew.

"Distance to target?" he asked, his voice low.

"Three AU and closing," Sang reported.

Soren nodded, his hand hovering over the comm panel. "Keira, status of the vortex cannon?"

"Charged and ready, Captain," Keira replied, her voice taut with anticipation. "Awaiting your command."

"All ships, begin your attack run," Soren ordered.

"Attack run commencing," Clarey replied.

The time passed with agonizing slowness as the Wraith

closed the distance. On the sensor grid, the sixteen Strike Force Seven and Eight ships began their advance, creeping up behind the invisible Wraith. He would know the instant the enemy spotted the incoming ships.

"Sang, pick up the pace," Soren said. "We need to arc around to the side to hit as many as we can."

"Aye, Captain," she calmly replied, taking the correction in stride.

"Looks like they see our not-quite-decoy," Jack said. Indeed, the enemy ships within sensor range had started moving, slowly gaining velocity as they moved to intercept the incoming strike forces.

"All ships hold steady," Soren said. "Here they come."

CHAPTER 23

The Wraith continued its advance, gaining velocity and changing vectors to move outside the firing line of the two approaching fleets.

"Sang, bring us about, let's drift across their broadsides. Keira, prepare to fire."

"Ready," Keira replied as vectoring thrusters pushed the Wraith's bow, turning it back toward the enemy ships.

"Ten seconds to firing range," Mark announced, plotting the distance between the strike forces and the enemy tangos, who loomed large in the viewscreen, the closest ship less than a thousand kilometers away. By his estimate, they could hit six ships with their first attack.

"On my mark," Soren said, taking one final, deep breath. This was it. No turning back now.

"Decloak and fire!" he barked.

In an instant, the Wraith shimmered into visibility, catching the enemy completely off guard. Before they could react, the modified vortex cannon roared to life.

Instead of the usual concentrated beam, a wide cone of swirling, destructive energy erupted from the Wraith's bow.

It swept across the enemy formation, engulfing multiple ships in its fury.

The effect was immediate and devastating. Enemy shields flared and failed under the onslaught. Hull plating buckled and tore. Two Valkyries in the firing range simply disintegrated, while larger ships were damaged. One Komodo suffered secondary explosions, which took the ship offline and sent debris careening across space.

"Three targets destroyed," Mark reported. "Four additional targets damaged."

But even as the echoes of the vortex cannon's fury faded, the enemy was already responding. Alarms blared across the Wraith's bridge as hostile targeting systems locked onto them.

"Multiple incoming!" Mark shouted. "They're launching fighters!"

"Evasive maneuvers!" Soren ordered. "Sang, get us clear of their firing solutions! Keira, shields to maximum!"

The Wraith lurched as Sang threw her into a series of maneuvers, reducing the impact of the first return salvo. But they were outnumbered, and the element of surprise was gone.

Only this time, they weren't fighting alone.

Space lit up with new energy signatures as Strike Forces Seven and Eight came into range, their weapons blazing as they unloaded on the disorganized enemy fleet.

"Minh," Soren called out. "You're clear to engage! Give 'em hell!"

"With pleasure, Captain," Minh's voice came back.

The battle erupted in earnest, with a chaotic maelstrom of projectiles, missiles, and dueling fighters. The Wraith skirted through it all, Sang's expert piloting keeping her one step ahead.

Soren watched the tactical display, his mind working furiously to process the evolving situation. They had bloodied the enemy's nose, yes, but the fight was far from over. And somewhere out there, invisible but undoubtedly present, was the rift, the very reason they had come all this way.

The Wraith shuddered as a volley of enemy fire slammed into her shields, the energy dissipating in a brilliant flare of light. Soren gripped the arms of his command chair, his eyes darting between the tactical display and the chaotic scene unfolding on the main viewscreen.

"Shields at sixty-eight percent," Keira reported, her voice tight with concentration. "That last hit took a chunk out of us."

"Understood," Soren replied. "Sang, keep us moving. Don't give them a static target."

"Aye, Captain," Sang answered, focused with deadly calm as she guided the Wraith through a series of intricate evasive maneuvers.

The space around them turned into a maelstrom of destruction. Strike Forces Seven and Eight had engaged the enemy fleet in earnest, their ships vectoring through the battlefield, doing their best to avoid the incoming fire while returning their own. Railgun rounds and missiles crisscrossed the void, while swarms of fighters and drones clashed in furious dogfights amidst them. Shields flashed and flared constantly, mostly hit by weapons fire, but also absorbing the growing fields of debris created by the fighting.

"Status of the vortex cannon?" Soren asked.

"Recharging," Ethan's voice came back over the comm. "The modified shot drained it more than we anticipated. It'll be another three minutes before we can fire again."

Soren nodded, filing away that information. The cannon's new "shotgun" mode had proven devastatingly effective, but the increased power drain was a significant drawback. They would need to use it judiciously.

"Sir," Mark called out from the ops station, "I'm picking up some strange readings. There's a localized distortion in spacetime about ten thousand kilometers off our port bow."

Soren's head snapped up, his heart racing. "The rift?"

"I think so, sir," Mark replied. "It's hard to get a clear reading with all the interference from the battle, but the energy signature matches what we were looking for."

"Can you get a visual?"

Mark's fingers danced over his console. "Trying to filter out the background radiation and electromagnetic interference...there!"

The main viewscreen shifted, zooming in on a seemingly empty patch of space. But as they watched, the stars beyond seemed to waver and distort, like light bending around a heat mirage. It was subtle, almost imperceptible, but unmistakably there.

"That's it," Jack breathed beside him. "The gateway to another universe."

Soren felt a chill run down his spine. After everything they had been through, all the battles and sacrifices, there it was. The source of the threat to their entire reality, and perhaps their only hope of stopping it.

But before he could fully process the implications, the ship rocked violently, nearly throwing him from his seat.

"Shields down to fifty-two percent!" Keira cried.

"Keep power diverted to our vulnerable sections," Soren said. "We can't repair the hull if it's damaged, and we can't afford to lose the cloak."

The battle raged around the Wraith, a chaotic dance of destruction and survival. Soren watched the unfolding carnage on the main viewscreen. The vortex cannon's devastating first strike had given them a significant advantage, but the enemy was far from beaten.

"Ethan, the cannon?" Soren again called out, his voice tense but controlled.

Ethan's reply came back over the comm, tinged with frustration. "Still recharging, Captain. It'll be another two minutes at least."

Much too long. They needed that cannon to go back online quickly. Every second it remained inactive was a second the enemy could use to regroup and press their numerical advantage.

"Divert all non-essential power to the cannon," Soren ordered. "Life support, artificial gravity, lighting, anything we can spare. I want that weapon ready to fire as soon as possible."

"Aye, Captain," Ethan replied. "Cutting power now."

Almost immediately, the bridge lights dimmed, and Soren felt the familiar sensation of weightlessness as the ship's artificial gravity disengaged. Around the bridge, unsecured objects began to drift lazily through the air. The crew, well-trained for such situations, barely missed a beat as they adjusted to the new conditions.

After addressing the immediate concerns, Soren focused on the broader battle. His eyes were drawn to the swarms of fighters darting between the capital ships, streaks of light marking their paths as they engaged in their deadly dance.

The Hooligans were in their element, their Pilums weaving through the chaos with a grace that belied the violence of their actions. Each fighter was accompanied by three semi-automated drones, their movements a near-perfect mirror of their parent craft. It was a sight to behold, a testament to the skill of Minh and his pilots.

Soren watched with fascination as Minh and his second, Bryce, broke from the main group to engage an enemy fighter squadron. Instead of charging in at full speed as traditional tactics would dictate, they decelerated, allowing their drones to take point.

The enemy fighters, caught off guard by this unexpected maneuver, scattered, breaking apart their formation. In that moment of confusion, Minh and Bryce struck. Their rail guns blazed to life, each shot finding its mark with devastating precision. Two enemy fighters erupted into expanding balls of plasma and debris.

But the Hooligans weren't done. As the remaining enemy fighters regrouped and moved to counterattack, Minh and Bryce split up, each taking their drones in a different direction. The enemy squadron, faced with two equally threatening targets, hesitated for a crucial second.

It was all the opening the Hooligans needed. Minh's drones suddenly broke formation, cutting sharp angles that would have been impossible for a human pilot to endure. They sliced through the enemy formation, their weapons blazing. Another fighter fell, its hull shredded by the unexpected assault.

Meanwhile, Bryce had looped around, coming at the enemy from behind. His rail gun spoke again, the hypervelocity rounds tearing through an enemy fighter's engines. The stricken craft spiraled out of control, colliding with one of its wingmen in a spectacular explosion.

In a matter of seconds, half the enemy squadron had been decimated. The survivors, realizing they were outmatched, turned tail and fled, only to be picked off by other Hooligan flights as they retreated.

Soren allowed himself a small smile. The unorthodox tactics they had developed during their training sessions were paying off. The enemy, used to fighting against more predictable opponents, was struggling to adapt to the Hooligans' fluid, unpredictable style of combat.

But even as he took pride in the performance of his fighters, Soren knew the real battle was being fought between the capital ships. He turned his attention to the larger conflict, where Strike Forces Seven and Eight were engaged in a brutal slugging match with the enemy fleet.

The space between the opposing forces was a storm of

destruction. Railgun rounds crisscrossed the void, their paths marked by brief flashes as they passed through pockets of ionized gas. Missiles streaked back and forth, leaving trails of exhaust in their wake. Shields flared constantly as they struggled to repel the relentless barrage.

Soren's eyes were drawn to a pair of Valkyries from Strike Force Eight, their hulls scarred and blackened from previous impacts. They were pushing hard, driving straight for the heart of the enemy formation. It was a bold move, perhaps even reckless, but Soren understood the strategy. They were trying to disrupt the enemy's cohesion, to create an opening that the rest of the fleet could exploit.

The enemy responded with a withering hail of fire. Railgun rounds slammed into the lead Valkyrie's shields, each impact sending ripples of energy cascading across the protective barrier. For a moment, it seemed as though the ship would weather the storm.

But then a missile slipped through an area where the shields had failed. It detonated against the Valkyrie's port side, the explosion briefly outshining the nearby stars. The ship's shields collapsed under the strain, leaving it vulnerable to the follow-up barrage.

Railgun rounds tore into the exposed hull, puncturing armor plating and wreaking havoc on internal systems. Secondary explosions blossomed along the Valkyrie's flank as power conduits overloaded and fuel lines ruptured. The ship began to list, trailing debris and venting atmosphere.

Its companion, seeing the fate of its partner, tried to break off. But the enemy, sensing blood in the water, pounced. A concentrated volley of fire overwhelmed its shields, and a pair of missiles struck home in quick succession. The Valkyrie's reactor containment failed, and the ship simply ceased to exist, consumed by a miniature sun of its own making.

Soren felt each loss keenly, knowing that hundreds of

brave men and women had just perished. But there was no time for mourning, not in the heat of battle. He forced himself to focus on the tactical display, searching for a way to turn the tide or better direct his forces. Commodore Clarey directed her ships with efficiency, her strategy sound. Captain Ling, following her lead, held his own better than Soren might have expected.

A pair of enemy Valkyries suddenly found themselves in trouble. They had pushed too far forward, breaking formation in an attempt to press their advantage. It was a mistake that would cost them dearly.

Strike Force Seven's two destroyers, including Clarey on the flagship, pounced on the isolated ships, their weapons blazing in perfect synchronization. The first enemy Valkyrie's shields held for a few precious seconds before collapsing under the onslaught. Railgun rounds punched through its hull, wreaking havoc on its internal structures. A lucky hit must have struck something vital because the ship suddenly went dark, all its systems shutting down at once. It drifted lifelessly, no longer a threat.

The second Valkyrie fared little better. It managed to get off a few shots, scoring glancing blows against one of the FUP destroyers. But it was too little, too late. A spread of missiles found their mark, detonating in a series of brilliant flashes. When the light faded, all that remained of the proud warship was an expanding cloud of superheated gas and debris.

"Captain," Ethan's voice crackled over the comm, tinged with excitement. "The vortex cannon is back online!"

Soren felt a surge of anticipation. This was the moment they had been waiting for, the chance to turn the tide decisively in their favor. "Excellent work, Ethan," he replied. "Keira, prepare to fire. Let's make this shot count."

"Aye, Captain," Keira responded.

"Sang, bring us sixteen degrees to port, cut mains, reverse

thrust ten percent. Fire starboard vectoring thrusters at twenty. Pitch down nine degrees and yaw left thirty-three."

Soren called out the angles with the smoothness of years of experience, his eyes on the sensor grid, lining up the shot. He could see the battle in his head, looking a few seconds into the future with almost preternatural skill. His lips parted, ready to give the word at the precise moment.

"Fire!"

Once again, the modified vortex cannon roared to life. But this time, the enemy was prepared. As soon as the Wraith de-cloaked to fire, every nearby hostile ship began redirecting to fire back with everything they had.

The space around the Wraith erupted in a storm of weapons fire. Railgun rounds and missiles streaked towards them from multiple vectors. Impacts rocked the ship as some of the incoming fire found its mark. Soren gripped his chair tightly, fighting to maintain his composure as alarms blared across the bridge.

"Shields at thirty percent but holding!" Keira shouted over the din.

But even as the Wraith absorbed punishment, its own attack struck home. The cone of swirling, destructive energy swept across the enemy formation, engulfing multiple ships in its fury.

The effect was devastating. Two enemy destroyers crumbled immediately, their structures unable to withstand the awesome power of the vortex cannon. A Valkyrie-class cruiser fared little better, its hull splitting open like an egg.

But it was the fourth ship, a Komodo-class battlecruiser, that suffered the most spectacular demise. The vortex energy tore through its shields as if they weren't there, ripping great chunks out of its armored hide. For a moment, it seemed as though the massive vessel might survive the onslaught. Then, its reactor containment failed.

The resulting explosion was blinding, momentarily overwhelming the viewscreen's filters. When the light faded, nothing remained of the once proud warship.

"Four enemy ships destroyed!" Mark called out, his voice tight with a mixture of excitement and disbelief. "Sir, I think we've done it. The enemy fleet is in disarray!"

Soren leaned forward, studying the tactical display intently. Mark was right. The devastating strike had broken the back of the enemy's resistance. Their formation had collapsed, individual ships now fighting for survival rather than victory.

"All ships, press the attack!" Soren ordered, his voice carrying across the comm channels to the entire FUP fleet. "Don't let up! Take them down!"

The response was immediate and overwhelming. FUP ships surged forward, weapons blazing as they fell upon the disorganized enemy. Fighters and drones swarmed around the larger vessels, picking off stragglers and harrying those that tried to flee.

Soren watched with grim satisfaction as the battle turned into a rout. A Valkyrie-class cruiser, its engines crippled by a lucky shot, found itself surrounded by three FUP destroyers. It fought valiantly, its weapons lashing out in defiance. But it was a hopeless fight. Within minutes, the proud vessel was reduced to a drifting hulk, venting atmosphere and trailing debris.

Nearby, a wing of Pilums caught an enemy destroyer trying to disengage. They swarmed around it like angry hornets, their railguns and missiles slowly but surely wearing down its defenses. They ruthlessly pressed their advantage, pouring fire into the wounded leviathan until its hull finally gave way.

All across the battlefield, similar scenes played out. The once-mighty enemy fleet was being systematically disman-

tled, unable to mount an effective defense against the coordinated FUP assault.

"We've done it," Jack breathed beside him, his voice
filled with a mixture of relief and disbelief. "We've actually
done it."

Soren nodded, allowing himself to relax slightly for the
first time since the battle began. "It's not over yet," he
cautioned. "But yes, I think we've won the day."

As if in response to his words, the last enemy Komodo-
class battlecruiser suddenly went dark, its systems overloaded by a concentrated barrage from three FUP ships. It
drifted lifelessly, joining the growing field of debris that
marked the site of their victory.

A cheer went up across the bridge, the crew's jubilation
impossible to contain. Soren felt it too, a sense of triumph
and relief washing over him. They had faced difficult odds
and emerged victorious. The rift, and the threat it represented, was now within their grasp.

But even as he prepared to give the order to secure the
area, a flicker of movement on the tactical display caught
his eye. He leaned forward, squinting at the readout.
"Mark," he called out, a note of urgency in his voice. "What
am I looking at here?"

Mark enhanced the sensor feed. His face paled as he
interpreted the data. "Sir," he said, his voice barely above a
whisper. "We've got multiple new contacts emerging from
the rift."

Soren felt his blood run cold. He turned to the main
viewscreen, where the distortion that marked the rift's location was now clearly visible. And through that shimmering
curtain of warped spacetime, dark shapes were beginning
to emerge.

"How many?" Soren asked, dreading the answer.

Mark swallowed hard. "At least thirty capital ships, sir.
Maybe more. They're still coming through."

The jubilant atmosphere on the bridge evaporated in an instant, replaced by a palpable sense of dread. They had won the battle, but it seemed the war was far from over.

Soren stared at the repopulating grid, weighing options and discarding them just as quickly. Their forces were depleted, their ships damaged. The vortex cannon was drained and would need two more minutes at least to recharge. They were in no condition to face a fresh enemy fleet, especially one of this size.

There was only one thing they could do.

CHAPTER 24

"Keira," Soren barked, his voice cutting through the stunned silence that had fallen over the bridge. "Activate the cloak. Now!"

"Cloak active, Captain," she reported.

Soren felt a small measure of relief. At least now they had a slim chance of escaping detection.

"Samira," Soren continued, his eyes never leaving the tactical display where the enemy fleet continued to pour through the rift. "Open a channel to Clarey and Ling."

"Channel open, sir," Samira replied a moment later.

Soren took a deep breath, steeling himself for what he had to say. "Commodore, you and Captain Ling have done your part. We're heading for the rift. You need to get out of here before it's too late and report back to Admiral Montoya."

There was a moment of stunned silence before Clarey's voice came back, tight with barely contained emotion. "Understood, Captain. We'll warn the Admiral. But how will you get through that blockade?"

Soren's jaw clenched. He knew what Clarey was really asking. Could the Wraith make it to the rift without support? He wasn't sure. The enemy ships were spreading out, creating a net that would be difficult to slip through undetected. But they had to try.

"We'll make it through, Commodore," Soren said, injecting more confidence into his voice than he felt. "We have to."

"Captain," Ling's voice cut in, his tone urgent. "With all due respect, we can't take any chances. After what happened on Proxima and Tau Ceti, how can we run away and risk failure? The enemy is too powerful, too prepared. You came here to go through the rift and find a way to stop the Convergence. I think this proves it's our only chance."

Before he could respond, Clarey spoke again, her voice filled with grim determination. "We'll create a diversion, Captain. Give you a clear shot at the rift."

"Commodore, no," Soren protested, even as he recognized the strategic logic of her plan. He couldn't ask her to make that sacrifice. "Your ships are damaged, your crews exhausted. You can't hope to stand against a force of that size."

"We don't have to stand against them, Captain," Clarey replied, a hint of fire creeping into her voice. "We just have to keep them busy long enough for you to slip through. It's the only way."

Soren closed his eyes, the weight of command pressing down on him like a physical force. He knew Clarey was right. He knew that sacrificing Strike Forces Seven and Eight might be the only way to ensure the success of their mission. But knowing that didn't make it any easier to accept.

"Understood, Commodore," he said at last, his voice heavy with the burden of the decision. "Whatever happens, I'll always remember you as a hero. May the stars watch over you all."

"And you, Captain," Clarey replied softly. "Good hunting."

As the channel closed, Soren turned to his crew, seeing the determination, fear and even grief on their faces. They all understood the gravity of what was about to happen, the sacrifice being made on their behalf.

"Sang," Soren said, his voice steady despite the turmoil in his heart, "get us to the rift. Stick to the edges of the battlefield, and watch out for wayward debris. Too much damage to the hull will compromise the cloak."

"Aye, Captain," Sang replied.

"Mark, keep a close eye on those enemy ships. I want to know the second they so much as twitch in our direction."

"Yes, sir," Mark nodded, his eyes glued to his sensor readouts.

"Minh, follow us through if you can. We'll pick you up on the other side."

"Aye, Captain. We'll be right behind you."

With a final glance at the tactical display, where the icons representing Strike Forces Seven and Eight were now moving to engage the emerging enemy fleet, Soren gave the order. "Take us in, Sang."

The Wraith began to move, accelerating slowly to avoid creating a detectable wake in the sea of debris now surrounding them. On the main viewscreen, Soren watched as the battered but unbroken ships of Strike Forces Seven and Eight formed up for their final, desperate attack.

Clarey's flagship, the Die Hard, took point. Even from this distance, Soren could see the scars of battle etched into her hull, the flickering of her shields as they struggled to maintain integrity. But she moved with purpose, her weapons blazing defiantly as she led the charge against the overwhelming enemy force.

The space between the fleets erupted in a furious exchange of fire. Railgun rounds and missiles crossed the void, creating a deadly lattice of destruction. Shields flared and failed, hulls buckled and broke. It was a slaughter, but one that bought precious time.

As the Wraith crept closer to the rift, using the chaos of battle as cover, Soren found his eyes drawn again and again to the Die Hard. Clarey was fighting with everything she had, her tactics brilliant even in the face of certain defeat. She led her ships in intricate maneuvers, maximizing their firepower while minimizing their exposure.

For a moment, it seemed as though they might actually hold their own. A pair of enemy destroyers fell to a concentrated barrage from Clarey's group, their reactors going critical in twin flashes of artificial sunlight. But for every enemy ship they managed to damage or destroy, still more emerged from the rift to take its place.

"We're almost to the rift, Captain," Sang reported, her voice tight with concentration as she guided the Wraith through the debris field.

Soren nodded, unable to tear his eyes away from the unfolding tragedy on the viewscreen. He watched as a Valkyrie-class cruiser from Strike Force Eight succumbed to a withering hail of fire, its hull splitting open like overripe fruit. The ship's death throes sent it spinning into the path of a friendly destroyer, the resulting collision taking both vessels out of the fight.

The battle raged on, a symphony of destruction on a scale that made Soren's heart ache. Clarey's flagship, the Die Hard, continued to fight valiantly, its weapons never ceasing their relentless barrage against the overwhelming enemy force. But with each passing moment, the odds stacked higher against them.

Soren watched in growing horror as a coordinated attack from three enemy destroyers focused on Die Hard. Railgun rounds hammered at her shields, creating holes the enemy exploited mercilessly. Missiles slipped through these gaps, detonating against the flagship's hull in a series of devastating explosions.

Die Hard's return fire weakened, its weapons barely managing to return a fraction of the incoming barrage. Soren could almost feel Clarey's desperation as she fought to keep her ship together, to buy just a few more precious seconds for the Wraith.

"No," Soren whispered, his voice barely audible as he watched Die Hard's shields fail. The enemy redoubled their assault. Railgun rounds tore into the exposed hull, ripping through armor plating and vital systems alike.

Suddenly, secondary explosions began to blossom along Die Hard's length. Soren watched, his heart in his throat, as Clarey's flagship began to break apart, consumed by the unforgiving vacuum of space.

The loss of Die Hard broke the remaining FUP ships. Their formation began to falter, individual captains ordering desperate retreats. The enemy ruthlessly pressed their advantage, their weapons never ceasing their relentless barrage.

"Captain," Sang's voice cut through Soren's shock, reminding him of the grim reality of their situation. "We're approaching the rift."

Soren forced himself to focus, to push aside the grief and anger that threatened to overwhelm him. There would be time for mourning later. If they survived. They had a mission to complete, a universe to save.

"Understood," he replied, his voice steady despite the turmoil in his heart. "All hands, brace for rift transit. We have no idea what to expect in the midst of it or on the other side."

As the Wraith closed the final distance to the rift, Soren took one last look at the battlefield they were leaving behind. Strike Forces Seven and Eight were nearly destroyed, their sacrifice buying the precious seconds the Wraith needed to reach its goal.

The rift loomed before them now, a shimmering curtain of distorted spacetime that bent the fabric of reality around it. A momentary flash of fear washed over Soren. They had no idea what lay on the other side, and there was no way to predict what would happen when they crossed that threshold.

But they had no choice. The fate of their entire universe rested on what they would find beyond that gossamer veil.

The Wraith surged forward, crossing the invisible line that separated their reality from another. For a moment, nothing seemed to happen. Then, with a lurch Soren felt in his very bones, the universe seemed to twist around them.

The viewscreen exploded in a riot of color and impossible geometries. Soren felt a wave of vertigo wash over him, his mind struggling to process what his eyes were seeing. It was as if they were falling through the heart of a kaleidoscope, reality fragmenting and reforming with each passing second.

And then, as suddenly as it had begun, it was over. The viewscreen cleared, revealing a star field that was both familiar yet alien.

They had done it. They had crossed over into another universe.

But as Soren's eyes adjusted to the new vista before them. A handful of enemy ships had yet to complete the crossing. If not for their cloak, they would be in deep trouble.

"Captain!" Keira cried out in alarm. "The rift disrupted the cloak. I think they can see us!"

"Oh no," Jack breathed beside him, giving voice to the fear that gripped them all.

"Keira, drop the cloak and raise shields!" Soren barked, reacting instantly to the news, even as the enemy ships slowed their approach on the rift to engage them. "All weapons hot!"

The Wraith's cloaking field dissipated, replaced by the shimmering barrier of its shields.

"Targets acquired," Mark reported, his voice tense but steady. "Three Valkyrie-class cruisers and a Komodo-class destroyer."

Soren nodded, a grim smile tugging at his lips. This was their chance. "Keira, get us a firing solution on that Komodo. Sang, bring us about, get us a clear shot."

"Aye, Captain," they responded in unison.

The Wraith surged forward, its engines flaring as Sang expertly maneuvered the ship into position. The enemy vessels had finally slowed enough to avoid the rift and were turning to bring their weapons to bear.

Too late for their survival.

"Fire!" Soren commanded.

The Wraith shuddered as its missile tubes emptied, sending a deadly swarm towards the Komodo. At the same time, its railguns opened up, the hypervelocity rounds slamming into the destroyer's shields before the missiles even got there.

The space between the ships lit up with explosions as the missiles found their marks. The Komodo buckled under the sudden combined onslaught. Several missiles penetrated, detonating against its hull in a series of brilliant flashes.

"Vortex cannon charged and ready, Captain," Keira reported.

Soren's eyes narrowed as he assessed the battlefield. The Komodo was damaged but still fighting, its weapons starting to return fire. The Valkyrie they'd been focusing on was nearly crippled, but the other two were moving to flank them.

It didn't matter. They were all in range.

"Sang, come about forty degrees hard to starboard!" Soren snapped.

His restraints held him in place as the Wraith slipped along its trajectory as though it were on ice, the bow turning to line up the cannon shot. Railgun rounds flashed out toward them, digging into the already weakened shields. They could only withstand so much of it, and once the enemy had their missiles locked...

"Fire!"

The vortex cannon roared to life, the cone of destructive energy lancing across space. It struck all four ships, but hit one of the Valkyries the hardest. The cruiser seemed to crumple in on itself, its hull unable to withstand the awesome power of the weapon. In a matter of seconds, only debris remained.

The other ships fared better, but not well enough. The cannon defeated their shields, punching holes that left them damaged and venting atmosphere without completely removing them from the fight.

"Press the advantage!" Soren called out. "Sang, bring us around. Keira, finish them off."

The Wraith moved with deadly grace, its weapons never ceasing their relentless assault. A damaged Valkyrie, already on the brink of destruction, succumbed quickly to a final barrage of railgun fire.

The Komodo, despite its earlier damage, proved to be a tougher nut to crack. It fought back fiercely, its weapons scorching Wraith's shields. But it was faltering, and Soren could see fear in its erratic movements.

A spread of missiles streaked toward the Komodo, followed closely by a barrage of railgun fire. The destroyer's shields finally failed, and the missiles struck home, their explosions tearing into the ship's engine section.

Seeing the tide of battle turn decisively against them, the last Valkyrie began to retreat. "Don't let them get away," Soren commanded. He knew they couldn't allow any of these ships to escape and warn their command of the Wraith's presence. "Sang, pursuit course. Keira, finish off the Komodo, then focus everything on that retreating Valkyrie."

The Wraith surged forward, closing the distance to the fleeing cruiser. The Komodo, now little more than a floating hulk, was dispatched with a final volley of railgun fire.

As they closed on the last Valkyrie, Soren felt a moment of regret. Even if they came from a different universe, these were fellow humans they were killing. He pushed the thought aside. They had started this war and invaded his universe. He would do whatever it took to protect his people. His reality.

"We have a firing solution on the last Valkyrie," Keira announced.

Soren opened his mouth, ready to give the order to fire.

There was no need.

The Hooligans came streaking through the rift in formation, all twelve of the piloted craft intact, though they had lost most of their drones. Without invitation, they targeted the fleeing Valkyrie, unleashing hell on the stricken ship.

Strafing past, they left the vessel dark, its systems offline, as they circled back toward the Wraith.

"Scratch one tango, Wraith," Minh said over the comms. "Permission to come home to roost?"

"Granted," Soren replied. "Nice work out there, Hooligans."

He relaxed back into his seat and exhaled sharply. The fight was over. They had made it through the rift alive.

His thoughts returned to Commodore Clarey and Captain Ling and their crews. They hadn't made it through alive. They had made the ultimate sacrifice to ensure the Wraith's mission could continue.

He would do everything in his power to ensure that sacrifice wasn't made in vain.

CHAPTER 25

As the adrenaline of battle began to fade, Soren took a deep breath, centering himself before addressing his crew. The bridge hummed with subdued activity, each officer focused intently on their stations, assessing battle damage and what remained of their weapons stores.

"Ethan, restore all primary systems to full power and provide a status report," Soren said over the comms, his voice steady despite the lingering tension in the air.

"Primary systems restored," he replied from engineering. Immediately, artificial gravity pulled Soren more fully into his seat, and the bridge lighting regained its normal hue. "As for status, well, the shields took a severe beating. They're currently at thirty-eight percent capacity and fluctuating. We'll need to make some repairs to the generation and transfer equipment. Several power conduits are showing signs of stress, and two of the auxiliary emitters were knocked offline during the fight." He paused, a note of pride creeping into his voice. "Hull integrity is still at one hundred percent, Captain. I don't think any other ship in the fleet could run the gauntlet we just did and come out the other side in better shape."

"Thanks in large part to Sang's flying," Soren said, relief washing over him. The Wraith had proven her worth once again, standing strong where other ships might have faltered. "How long for repairs to the shields?"

Ethan hesitated, considering the damage and his available techs. "We should have them back up to full strength in about three days, but as you know we can't work on any of the external generator damage inside a fold."

"How much of the damage is external?" Soren asked.

Ethan paused again, no doubt consulting his readouts. "About a third. We'll need another solid day to get it all patched up right."

Soren absorbed the information, his mind racing through potential scenarios. They were vulnerable now, in a universe not their own, with unknown threats potentially lurking around every corner. But they couldn't afford to remain defenseless.

"Do what you can on the interior right away," he ordered. "We'll finish repairs as soon as possible, but we can't linger here. Bobby, plot us a course to their Wolf system."

The navigator's head snapped up, surprise evident in his expression. "The Wolf system, Captain?"

Soren nodded. "Lacking any other leads, we might as well go see what's going on there. Go back to the scene of the crime, so to speak. It's relatively close, and we might find some answers there. Or at least a clue as to where to go next."

"Aye, Captain." Bobby set to work calculating the jump coordinates.

"Harry," Soren said next, contacting his quartermaster. "What does our ordnance supply look like after that trip through hell?"

"Better than I might have hoped," Harry replied.

"Railgun ammunition is down fifteen percent, and our missile stocks have been reduced by only five percent."

Soren raised an eyebrow, pleasantly surprised by the relatively modest expenditure. "Not bad, considering the intensity of the engagement. Keep an eye on the spare parts we loaded, too. I want to know if we run low on anything. We might not have a chance to replace it, and it's good to know all of our potential weaknesses ahead of time."

"You know me, Captain. Nothing gets used without going in my ledger."

"Good man." Soren cut that connection and made another. "Phoebe, what's the ordnance status for the Pilums?"

"Captain, we're still reviewing the individual fighters, but most will need almost a full reload. They were running on empty. Fortunately, they all came back. Unfortunately, we lost over fifty percent of the wingman drones."

Soren grimaced. He had hoped the programming updates they had made to the semi-autonomous ships would have improved their performance. Then again, considering what they had just gone through, retaining half of them felt like a victory.

"Get those fighters restocked asap," Soren said. "And make sure you report all stock depletions to Harry."

"Aye, Captain."

Soren's gaze swept the bridge, taking in the faces of his crew. They were tired, yes, but there was fire in their eyes, a determination born from their hard-fought victory. He felt a surge of pride, tempered by the weight of responsibility that pressed down upon him.

"A word, Soren?" Jack asked quietly.

"What's on your mind, old friend?" Soren asked, though he had a pretty good idea of what was coming.

Jack sighed before speaking, his voice low and urgent. "Do you realize just how much trouble our universe is in,

Soren? They just sent nearly a hundred more ships through the rift in addition to the two fleets we've already seen. At this rate, they'll have our universe conquered within a month."

Soren's jaw tightened, the memory of the brutal battle still fresh in his mind. "I know, Jack. Believe me, I know. But we did make it. And we learned a lot in the process."

"We're lucky to be alive," Jack pressed on, his eyes boring into Soren's. "If it wasn't for those tactics we worked on, the modifications to the vortex cannon..." He trailed off, shaking his head.

"We passed those tactics on to Montoya. Some of them worked, and might help slow the tide."

"But no amount of tactics will stop them."

"No. That's why it's up to us. We need to know what's causing the Convergence, and we need to stop it." He paused, a thought striking him. "Speaking of the vortex cannon." He activated his comm patch. "Tashi, switch the vortex cannon from shotgun back to spear mode."

"Aye, Captain," Tashi replied. "Are you sure?"

"The shotgun configuration was effective, but it drained too much power. And we might need the focused beam for precision strikes in the future."

"Aye, Captain."

"And Tashi…"

"Aye, Captain?"

"See if you can come up with a means to speed up the switchover process, or even automate it. Bonus points if you can line it up with the time it takes for the cannon to recharge."

"Sure, Captain," Tashi said excitedly. "I'll get on that right away. I might be able to cook up something."

"Coordinates laid in, Captain," Bobby announced. "Ready to initiate jump on your command."

"Initiate jump," he ordered.

The familiar sensation of spacetime folding around them washed over the crew as the Wraith shifted into jump space. As the universe flared and then went dark, Soren allowed himself a moment of reflection. They had crossed an impossible threshold, venturing into a universe not their own. The enormity of their mission, the weight of an entire reality resting on their shoulders, threatened to overwhelm him.

But there was no time for doubt, no room for second-guessing. They had a job to do, a universe to save. And Soren was determined to see it through, no matter the cost.

"Jump initiated, Captain. Estimated time to arrival—five days, nine hours."

Soren nodded, activating his comms again. "Vic, I want you and your team to report to the bridge for an unscheduled rotation. Our current crew needs a break after the intensity of the fighting."

"Of course, Captain," Vic replied. "We're on our way."

Soren allowed himself a moment to relax while he waited, his body sinking into his seat, muscles finally fully releasing. They were safe for now, outside the boundaries of the visible universe.

"Lieutenant Commander Bashir reporting, sir," Vic said on entering the bridge with his crew, stopping near Soren and coming to attention.

"At ease," Soren said. "Sang, Keira, Samira, Bastian, Mark, Bobby, Jack, you're relieved of duty. Vic, you'll maintain our current status unless something changes. If anything out of the ordinary occurs, no matter how small, I want to be notified immediately."

"Understood, Captain," Vic replied, settling into the command chair as Soren relinquished it. "We'll keep a sharp eye out."

With a final nod to Vic and his team, Soren and the others left the bridge.

"Is it wrong for me to say that I never want to do that again?" Bobby asked once they were in the passageway.

"I think that makes seven of us," Samira replied.

"Unfortunately, that might be wishful thinking," Jack added. "Though you all handled yourselves beautifully in there."

"Agreed," Soren said. "And now I want you all rested and ready for whatever we might encounter in the Wolf system."

"Aye, Captain," Keira replied, the other nodding.

While they broke for the officer's quarters or toward the chow hall, Soren made his way down to the hangar bay. The rhythmic thud of his boots against the deck plating echoed in the relatively quiet passageways, a steady counterpoint to the roar of whirling thoughts in his head.

As the hangar bay doors slid open before him, Soren was greeted by a scene of controlled chaos. The maintenance and ordnance crews swarmed over the returned Pilums, beginning the process of repairing and rearming the fighters. The smell of scorched metal hung in the air, a reminder of the recent battle.

Minh stood off to the side with his pilots and two officers Soren couldn't recall seeing the last time he had come down. Commanders Gates and Puccini, no doubt. As Soren approached, he saw the squadron CO's face light up with pride, countering a bit of his obvious exhaustion.

"Captain," Minh called out, snapping to attention. "What brings you down to our humble bailiwick?"

Soren waved off the formality. "At ease, Minh. I wanted to come down and personally commend you and your pilots. The Hooligans performed exceptionally well out there."

A chorus of cheers and whoops erupted from the nearby pilots, who had paused in their postflight checks to listen in. Soren felt a surge of pride at their enthusiasm and their unbreakable spirit in the aftermath of the overwhelming odds they had faced and knew they would face again.

Minh's chest swelled with pride, a grin splitting his face. "Thank you, sir. But if I may say so, you haven't seen anything yet."

Soren raised an eyebrow, intrigued. "Is that so? Well, I look forward to seeing what else you have up your sleeves." He paused, his gaze sweeping over the assembled pilots and deck crew. "All of you should be proud. What you accomplished out there was nothing short of miraculous."

The gathered crew members straightened, their fatigue seeming to melt away under the weight of their captain's praise. Soren could see even more fire rekindling in their eyes. An uncurbed determination to face whatever challenges lay ahead.

"Get some rest," Soren continued. "We don't know what we'll be facing when we reach the Wolf system, but I need you all at your best when we get there." He turned to the space bosses. "Phoebe, Ettore, my apologies. I missed greeting you during our initial jump to Proxima."

"Thank you, Captain," Phoebe said. "We were last aboard, I think. Still stowing our gear in berthing when you arrived. But Captain Pham speaks highly of you, and of course, your reputation precedes you."

"Excellent work getting the Pilums and their drones prepped and launched so quickly," Soren said.

"Thank you, sir," Ettore said. "If you'll excuse us…" He motioned toward the starfighters. They obviously still had a lot to do.

"Of course," Soren replied. "Don't let me keep you from your duties."

Soren turned to leave, the hangar bay once again erupting into a flurry of activity. Stepping through the hatch into the passageway, he heard footsteps behind him and turned to find Minh coming to a stop, his expression serious.

"Captain," Minh said softly, "thank you. For coming down here and acknowledging our efforts. It means more than you know to all my pilots."

Soren nodded. "The greatest bonus I have the power to give is to offer my appreciation. And you and your squadron have earned it, Minh."

"Still, it's not something you had to do, but because you did, my pilots will fly to hell and back for you, sir. They're a good bunch."

"That they are."

With a final nod, Minh returned to the hangar bay, closing the air-tight hatch behind him, cutting off all the sounds of activity on the other side and leaving him alone in the quiet corridor.

As he walked, his feet carrying him towards his quarters almost of their own accord, the events of the past few hours played through his mind on an endless loop. The desperate battle at the rift, the heart-stopping journey into another universe, the frantic fight for survival against the enemy ships that had followed them through.

They had won, yes. But at what cost? The loss of all the brave men and women of Strike Forces Seven and Eight whose sacrifice had made this mission possible weighed him down. They had given the Wraith and its crew a fighting chance, but the huge cost threatened to crush him beneath its mass.

As the door to his quarters slid open and he stepped inside, the door closing with a soft hiss behind him, he felt the last of his energy drain away. For a long moment, his body protesting the hours of tension and combat, he simply stood there in the darkness, letting the quiet wash over him.

"Lights, low," he finally murmured, and the room illuminated with a soft, warm glow.

His eyebrows went up at the sight of a bottle and a single glass resting on his desk near the back of the main room. He walked over to it, picking up a small folded note resting just in front of it.

Thought you could use this.
Harry.

Soren smiled as he sank heavily into his chair and picked up the bottle, turning it so he could see the label. Hibiki Whiskey. Wondering where the hell Harry had gotten his hands on a bottle of such expensive hootch, he was tempted to contact him to ask him to come join him, but he knew the man had a lot on his plate right now. He would definitely thank him later.

Soren lifted the glass, studying the play of light through the amber colored liquid, "I'll find you, Dana," he whispered, his voice barely audible even in the quiet of his quarters. "I'll find you, and we'll stop the Convergence and end this senseless war. You, me, and Alex."

He took a sip, savoring the smooth burn as it slid down his throat. As the warmth spread through his chest, Soren leaned back in his chair, thoughts swirling.

The Wolf system. It was where this whole mess had started, where Dana and her team had first detected the anomalies that had led them down this rabbit hole. What would they find there? Answers? More questions? Or just another dead end in their quest to save their universe?

Soren knew he should rest, knew that his body and mind needed time to recover from the strain of the past few hours. But sleep felt like a distant impossibility, his thoughts too chaotic, too fraught with worry and speculation to allow for any real relaxation.

Instead, he activated his terminal, calling up the data the other Dana had provided. The calculations and conjecture that she claimed proved the Convergence had a source. If it had a source, then that meant it could be stopped.

He still wasn't so sure, but he had to believe it. What other choice was there?

The equations and algorithms didn't mean much to him, even after an hour of staring at them. He watched Dana's video, in part to see if he could glean anything else from what she had said, and in part just because he wanted to see his daughter's face again, even if the woman on the video wasn't exactly his daughter.

Finally, with the bottle of whiskey half-drained, he shut off the terminal, stripped out of his uniform, and fell— finally groggy enough to sleep—onto his bed. The future seemed bleak, but he refused to give up hope.

They would stop this madness.

They had to.

CHAPTER 26

Toweling his hair dry, Soren stepped out of his private head, a cloud of steam billowing out with him, into the cooler air of his quarters. Despite still having a faint headache after his early morning jog, he felt refreshed but far from rested. Even high-priced whiskey hadn't dispelled his monumental concerns over their mission and the fate of their universe long enough for him to remain asleep for long. His run through the corridors had at least gotten his blood pumping.

Quickly dressing in utilities, with an intention to grab some chow before heading to the bridge, he exited his quarters and made his way through the ship's corridors, nodding to crew members as he passed. The Wraith hummed around him, the subtle vibrations of her systems a comforting constant. As he approached the galley, the scent of coffee, eggs, and bacon wafted towards him, his stomach rumbling in response.

The galley was bustling with activity, preparing for the change in shifts. Soren's eyes swept the room, taking in the faces of his crew. Some looked more rested than others, but all of them sat with a determined posture that suggested their morale remained high, despite the losses the Navy had so far suffered. Noticing him, Sophie offered a respectful nod and smile, which he returned. Hiraku gave him a similar greeting when he walked past the yeoman's seat.

His gaze settled on a table near the back where Alex sat with the other Scorpions. Asha, Wilf, and Tashi were with them, engaged in what looked like an animated discussion. Soren felt a surge of pride at the sight of his son, followed by a pang of fatherly worry. He pushed it aside. He had a job to do, and so did Alex. That was all that mattered now.

He made his way to the chow line, grabbing a tray and nodding to the galley staff as he chose from the simple but hearty fare—reconstituted scrambled eggs, cultured bacon, and a slice of freshly baked toast. He filled a large mug full of coffee before turning to survey the room.

For a moment, he considered sitting alone, giving himself time to gather his thoughts and plan for the challenges ahead. But the laughter from Alex's table drew him in, a reminder that even in the face of unimaginable odds, life and camaraderie continued.

"You got room there for your old man?" Soren asked as he approached the table, making it clear he was sitting with them as Alex's father and an equal, not as their captain. Maybe unorthodox, but he preferred it that way, and it was, after all, his ship.

Alex looked up, a smile breaking across his face. "Always, Dad. Pull up a chair."

Soren set his tray down in the open spot between Alex and Asha, and then pulled a chair up to the table. "What's got everyone so animated this morning?"

Wilf's fingers twitched excitedly. "We were just discussing the Convergence, Captain. Trying to wrap our heads around what it might actually mean for two universes to... well, converge."

Soren took a sip of his coffee, savoring the bitter warmth. "And? Any breakthrough insights?"

Tashi shook his head, his expression a mix of frustration and fascination. "The more we think about it, the more complex and wild it all becomes. I mean, consider this—what happens if someone in our universe is married to one person, but their counterpart in the other universe is married to someone completely different?"

"I was under the impression that everyone in the two universes is married to the same person," Soren replied. "Alex and Dana still existed in this universe with me as their father, so I assume this universe's Jane is intact."

"But what if she isn't?" Malik asked. "What if you're married to Lucy, and she doesn't even look like Jane?"

"How would that work though?" Asha asked. "Alex, you saw your doppelgänger. You said he looked just like you. That means the same genetics. The same parents."

"She has a point," Alex agreed.

"Phew! And here I was worried maybe I was ugly in this universe," Jackson said.

"I'm sure you're ugly in every universe, J," Sarah shot, laughing. "But maybe only some people are married to the same person. I mean, not everyone can be doing exactly the same thing in both universes, so they wouldn't meet the same people, so they wouldn't marry the same people. Right?"

"But then how could their children have duplicates?" Wilf asked. "How would that work?"

"How does any of this work?" Malik asked. "It's all so freaking crazy."

"Even if the Captain is right and everyone has the same partner, what happens if they're not in the same location when the Convergence hits?" Zoe chimed in. "Like, one version is on Earth and the other is on Prox...?" She trailed off without naming the second planet. "Excuse me while I try to pull my foot out of my throat," she said, flushing.

"Bad example, but the point is the same," Alex said. "Which planet do they vanish from?"

"Or worse, are they half on one and half on the other?" Wilf asked. His fingers curled as if they were puking.

"Man, that is gross," Malik said, laughing. "Like, one planet has the skin and the other planet has the bones?"

"Or one planet has the head, heart, and lungs; and the other planet has their other organs and the legs," Jackson added. "Wouldn't they both die?"

"Okay, Scorpions," Alex said. "I'm sure my father doesn't want to listen to this bullshit."

"Your dad's career Navy," Zoe pointed out. "I'm sure he's heard worse, haven't you, Skipper?"

"Yes, indeed," Soren agreed. "Gallows conjecture notwithstanding, it's still an interesting question. Here's another. What if a pilot and his doppelgänger were to fly a Pilum through the rift from each side of it at the same time, what happens when they pass each other? Assuming they don't crash into each other, of course. ? Do they both survive? Does one die? Or do they merge into one person with one personality or two?"

"That's a good one, Captain," Tashi said. "And in the same line of thinking, what about us? My duplicate is here in this universe with me, somewhere."

"I'm willing to bet not everything and everyone has a duplicate," Soren said. "But it's close enough to be a problem. We didn't start this war because we didn't know about the Convergence. But if we had learned about it first, would we be the ones on the attacking side now? Nobody wants to lose who they are."

"The more we discuss it, the more I go back to the thought that if the Convergence is real, when there are two versions of a person, either one version will die or both versions will die. More likely both. It's hard to see how two distinct consciousnesses could just become one."

A somber silence fell over the table as they all contemplated the implications of Alex's words. The enormity of what they were facing, the potential loss of life on an unimaginable scale, weighed heavily on them all.

Asha was the first to break the silence, her voice soft but determined. "But that's why we're here, isn't it? To stop this from happening. To find a way to prevent the Convergence before it's too late."

Soren nodded, feeling a surge of gratitude for the young medical officer's optimism. "You're right, Asha. That's exactly why we're here. Speaking of which..." He turned to Tashi. "I've been looking over those algorithms Dana provided, the ones she claims prove the Convergence is happening. Most of it is beyond my comprehension. What do you make of it?"

Tashi ran a hand through his hair in a gesture of frustration. "To be honest, Captain, most of it is over my head, too. Whoever developed these algorithms is either insanely brilliant or... well, just insane. The math involved is all so advanced. I'm trying, but..." He shook his head.

"Let's hope it's crazy smart, and not just crazy," Soren said, a wry smile tugging at his lips. "We're betting a lot on Dana's information being accurate."

"If I may, Captain," Wilf interjected, his fingers fidgeting nervously, "even if we can't fully understand or verify the math, the fact that we've seen evidence of another universe, that we've actually crossed over into it...doesn't that lend credence to Dana's claims?"

Soren nodded slowly, considering Wilf's words. "It does, to an extent. But we still don't know for certain that these two universes are actually converging. We've seen evidence of invasion, yes, but that's not the same as convergence."

"But why would they invade if not in preparation for

the Convergence?" Alex asked, leaning forward intently. "Why go to all this trouble, mount such a massive offensive, if there wasn't something bigger at stake?"

"That's a good point," Soren conceded. "But it's also possible that they believe the Convergence is happening when it's not. Or that they're using the threat of convergence as an excuse for invasion and conquest."

The table fell silent again as they all pondered this possibility. The implications were staggering. Could they be fighting a war based on a misunderstanding or an intentional lie?

"So what do we do?" Asha asked, her voice barely above a whisper. "How do we know what's real and what isn't?"

Soren took another sip of his coffee, buying himself a moment to gather his thoughts. "We keep pushing forward," he said finally. "We gather more information, we seek out answers. And most importantly, we stay vigilant. Whether the Convergence is real or not, the threat to our universe is verifiably real."

The others nodded, determination replacing the uncertainty in their eyes.

As they finished their meals, the conversation drifted to lighter topics. Funny stories from training, playful debates about the best way to spend their limited downtime on the ship, and other simple banter.

Finally, as the galley began to empty out, Soren stood, gathering his tray. "Thank you all for the company and the conversation. It's good to be reminded that even in the face of adversity, we can still find moments of normalcy."

The others bid him farewell, and Soren made his way out of the galley. As he walked through the corridors towards the bridge, his mind churned with the paradoxes of convergence they had discussed.

What would it mean for two versions of a person to merge? Would one consciousness dominate, or would they somehow blend? And what of the physical implications? If one version was missing a leg or arm and the other wasn't, what would happen to the merged body? The thought reminded him how the attackers had taken such care to preserve the domes of Proxima. If one dome were cracked open and the other wasn't, the enemy at least believed the crack would carry over, or there would be no reason for the caution.

The questions seemed endless, each one leading to a dozen more. It was maddening, trying to comprehend something so far beyond their current understanding.

But as frustrating as it was, Soren knew they couldn't afford to ignore these questions. If the Convergence was indeed real, if it was truly happening, then understanding its mechanics might be key to stopping it.

Because no matter how the universes resolved all of their questions, if the Convergence was real, if the Convergence happened, it would be disastrous for everyone in both universes.

He didn't know much, but he knew that beyond a doubt.

CHAPTER 27

The four days of folded space travel passed with a semblance of normalcy aboard the Wraith, though an undercurrent of tension ran through the crew like an electric charge. Every officer and enlisted member threw themselves into their duties with renewed vigor, acutely aware of the stakes they faced in this alien universe.

As the days progressed, Soren spent less time trying to unravel the mysteries of the Convergence and more time focusing on the immediate challenges they faced. The paradoxes and unanswerable questions about merged consciousnesses and overlapping realities had begun to feel like a distraction from their primary mission.

Instead, he poured over status reports, checked and double-checked his crew's readiness, and waited eagerly to reach the Wolf System. He knew that their survival, and potentially their entire reality, depended on their ability to adapt and respond to whatever they encountered.

On the evening of the fourth day, Soren stood on the bridge, his hands clasped behind his back as he stared at the main viewscreen.

"Captain," Ethan's voice came over the comm. "I'm

pleased to report that all internal shield repairs are complete."

"Excellent work, Ethan. You and your team have outdone yourselves."

"Thank you, sir. We'll be ready to tackle the external repairs as soon as we complete the jump."

"Let's hope we have that luxury," Soren murmured, more to himself than to Ethan.

As the hours ticked down to their arrival in the Wolf System, the tension on the bridge ratcheted up noticeably. Crew members sat stiffer at their stations, and a heavy silence permeated the atmosphere.

"Two minutes to arrival," Bobby announced, his voice tight with anticipation.

Soren took a deep breath, centering himself. "Keira, be ready with the cloak the moment we complete the jump. Sang, I want evasive maneuvers plotted and ready to execute at a moment's notice."

"Aye, Captain," they responded in unison.

The final seconds ticked away, each one feeling like an eternity. Then, with a flash of light on the viewscreen, the Wraith dropped out of folded space.

"Initiating sensor sweep," Mark said, his eyes glued to his readouts.

Soren leaned forward, his gaze locked on the main viewscreen as it resolved to show the Wolf System. His first impression was one of eerie familiarity. The stars and planets were exactly where they should be.

And yet, as the seconds ticked by and Mark's sensor sweep continued, a growing sense of unease settled over the bridge.

"Captain," Mark said, his voice tinged with confusion. "I'm not picking up...anything."

"Clarify," Soren ordered, though he had a sinking feeling he knew what Mark meant.

"No ships, no debris, no unusual energy signatures. Nothing, sir. The System appears to be completely uninhabited."

"Are you sure?" Jack asked. "No signs of recent activity? No particle displacement that might indicate ships have been here recently?"

Mark shook his head. "Nothing, sir. If anyone was ever here, it was long enough ago for any traces to have dissipated completely."

A heavy silence fell over the bridge as the implications of this sank in. Soren felt a chill run down his spine. The coordinates were exactly the same as in their universe, but everything else...it was as if they had never been here at all.

"Well," Jack said quietly, "I think this proves almost beyond a doubt that we really are in another universe."

Soren nodded grimly. "So it would seem."

"Captain, the cloak is active," Keira reported.

"Not that it matters," Soren said. "It appears we're completely alone out here. Mark, if Galileo had been here two months ago, would there still be PD traces?"

"Possibly," Mark replied. "But we'd need enhanced sensors to pick them up. Wraith is advanced in some ways, average in others. Her sensor suite is standard fare."

"Understood."

"Captain, should we consider using the vortex cannon to search for hidden objects?" Ethan asked. "It worked for us before, in our universe."

Soren considered the suggestion for a moment before shaking his head. "Not yet, Ethan. It's too risky. We don't know who or what might be out there, and firing the cannon would give away our position instantly."

"Understood, sir."

Jack turned to Soren, his expression troubled. "Are we sure there's anything to find here at all?"

Soren's jaw tightened as he considered Jack's words.

"There has to be," he said finally. "Think about it. This universe's Dana was in the Wolf System when she put out the distress call. Why did she go to the Wolf System, when she could have jumped directly to Earth? That can't be a coincidence. She was leading us here, I'm sure of it."

He studied the sensor grid, his gaze drawn to nearby Wolf 1061 C. The planet the other Dana's Valkyrie had been found orbiting. Could it be?

"Sang, bring us into orbit around the planet."

"Aye, Captain," she replied.

"Bastian, when we reach orbit, launch a full complement of drones and scan the surface for anything out of the ordinary."

"Aye, Captain," Bastian replied.

Soren activated his comm. "Phoebe, Ettore, prepare the Pilums for launch."

"Aye, Captain," they replied.

"Minh, I need you and the Hooligans to join our drones in a reconnaissance mission over Wolf 1061C. Work in conjunction with them to search the planet's surface. If there's anything to find down there, I want it found."

"Copy that, Captain," Minh's voice returned, tight with anticipation.

The Pilums and drones were ready to launch when Sang guided Wraith into orbit, hanging over the large, dry, rocky planet. In the viewscreen, drones and starfighters launched from the hangar bay, immediately descending toward the planet below.

"Captain, given the size of the planet and our available resources, it'll take three full days to complete a full sweep of the surface," Bobby said.

"Six then," Soren replied. "I won't have Minh and his team flying twenty-four seven. Hopefully, we'll find something before then."

"If there's something to find," Jack said.

"There has to be," Soren answered, firm in his conviction despite the doubts he sensed not only Jack but the rest of the bridge crew.

The hours crawled by with agonizing slowness as the drones and fighters methodically swept the planet. Soren found himself pacing the bridge, unable to sit still as the search dragged on without results.

"Anything?" he asked for what felt like the hundredth time.

Mark shook his head, frustration evident in his voice. "Nothing yet, sir," he answered.

"Captain," Ethan said. "This might be a good time to begin those external repairs. If this area hasn't been visited for some time, the odds that the enemy will arrive here now aren't very high."

"Especially since they're all busy destroying our universe," Soren muttered. Then louder, "Good idea. Make it happen."

"Aye, Captain," Ethan replies, getting to his feet and leaving the bridge.

"Keira, keep our railguns ready, just in case."

"Aye, Captain."

The hours wore on. By the time eight hours had passed without success, Soren decided to call back the Hooligans. It wouldn't do to have a squadron of exhausted fighter pilots. At least they were making progress on the shield repairs.

And there was always tomorrow.

Just as he was about to ask Samira to open a comm to Minh, her voice cut through the tense silence. "Captain! Incoming comms from Captain Pham!"

"Put him through," Soren replied.

Minh's voice filled the bridge, excitement evident in his tone. "Captain Strickland, this is Hooligan One. We've found something, sir. You're going to want to see this."

"What is it, Minh?" Soren asked, leaning forward in his chair.

"It's...well, it's hard to describe, sir. Sensors have detected what appears to be a tunnel entrance on the surface of Wolf 1061 C. Only, it's definitely not natural. And there's more. We're picking up faint energy readings from inside."

Soren's heart rate kicked up. This was it. This had to be what Dana had led them here to find.

"Good work, Minh," he said. "Mark down the coordinates and come on home."

"Yes, sir."

"Bastian, send a drone into the tunnel and call the rest back to the ship. I want to know what's down there."

"Aye, Captain. I'm redirecting one of the drones."

"Put its feed on the secondary display."

The drone feed appeared on the secondary, descending toward a rocky outcropping as Minh's Pilum peeled away and ascended past. Bastion slowed the drone when it neared the surface, the tunnel coming into view up ahead.

Barely eight feet in diameter, it was too perfectly round to be naturally made, not much more than a dark spot against the low face of a ridge. It was so tucked away that Soren was amazed Minh had spotted it at all. The drone angled toward it, still slowing as it neared. A headlight activated on the drone's front, the light sinking a short distance into the tunnel. Carved rock, smoothly bored, the floor lined with a drab metal often used to provide footing to magboots.

"Definitely manmade," Jack commented. "Someone put this here for a reason."

The obvious question: what reason?

The drone advanced into the tunnel. It had only gone about ten meters when the image from the feed froze. A few seconds later, Bastian barked out a curse.

"Damn it!" He looked at Soren over his shoulder. "We lost the network link to interference."

"Whoever did this, they didn't want probes poking around," Jack said.

"Agreed," Soren replied. "We'll have to do this the hard way. Bastian, once the Pilums and all the other drones are back in the hangar bay, head down there yourself and warm up the Stinger."

"Aye, Captain," Bastian replied. "Calling the drones back."

"Liam, Alex," Soren said, contacting them over the comms. "I have a job for you."

CHAPTER 28

Alex stood in the hangar bay, the Scorpions gathered around him, their faces a mirror of his own emotions behind their faceplates as they ran through the final diagnostic checks of their Karuta powered armor. The air was thick with the kind of excited, nervous tension that always preceded a venture into the unknown.

"Scorpions, comms check," he ordered.

"Scorpion Two online," Sarah replied. The others all answered in order.

"Sounds like we're ready to go, Gunny," Jackson said. "What's the hold up?"

"Yeah, don't these other jarheads know which way the armor goes on?" Malik asked.

He's just finished the question when the hangar doors slid open and the rest of the Marine contingent filed into the hangar bay, moving with disciplined precision, their faces set in masks of professional detachment. It was a sharp contrast to the Scorpions, who carried themselves with a more casual, predatory grace.

Liam led the unit in, and he stopped a short distance back, waiting for both teams to line up beside one another.

"Sergeant Strickland," he said, nodding to Alex. "Your team ready?"

"Yes, sir," Alex replied. "We're good to go."

Liam's gaze lingered on the Scorpions for a moment longer before he turned to address the entire group. "Alright, Marines. We're heading into unknown territory here. Hopefully, you go for a little uneventful stroll and make it back home by chow time. Stay sharp and watch each other's backs. Any questions?"

A chorus of "No, sir!" echoed through the hangar.

"Good," Liam said. "I'll be observing and providing direction with Captain Strickland on the bridge. Move out."

As they filed onto the Stinger, Alex felt a familiar thrill run through him. This was what they were made for, what they had trained countless hours to do. Whatever lay at the end of that mysterious tunnel on Wolf 1061C, the Scorpions would be ready for it.

But what about the other Marines? Like his team before the invasion of Jungle, they'd only ever practiced in the simulators, and they didn't have the benefit of the more advanced programs he and his team had found too easy. Would they keep their wits about them if things went sideways? Before their more recent training, he might have worried more. But they'd all held up well under the intense training the Scorpions had put them through. He had little reason to doubt them, but there was still a tiny niggling qualm or two swirling around in his gut.

"Wow, this is so much nicer than the drop seats of an Armadillo," one of the regular Marines commented, settling into one of the Stinger's seats. "Don't you think so, Gunny?"

"I think I'd rather have a real dropship," Alex answered. "Safer for everyone that way. But I'll take what I can get."

Bastian's voice came over the intercom as they strapped

themselves in. "Next stop, creepy alien tunnel. Please keep your arms and legs inside the ride at all times."

A ripple of nervous laughter ran through the Marines. Alex couldn't help but smile.

Alex felt the familiar pull of acceleration as the Stinger's engines roared to life. Through the viewports, he watched as the Wraith's hangar bay fell away, replaced by the vast emptiness of space. Then, slowly at first but with increasing speed, the rusty red surface of Wolf 1061C filled their view.

"So," Jackson said, breaking the nervous silence, "anyone want to place bets on what we'll find down there? I'm hoping for an ancient alien super weapon."

"Nah," Malik countered, shaking his head. "It's totally going to be a portal to another dimension. You know, because this whole 'two universes' thing isn't confusing enough already."

"Oh, yeah," Jackson agreed. "What about a portal to a room and the only way out is another portal, which is in another room whose only way out is a portal which brings you back to where you started."

"Exactly!" Malik laughed.

Zoe rolled her eyes. "You're both idiots. It's probably just some old FUP outpost that got abandoned and forgotten."

"Really?" Jackson raised an eyebrow. "And they just happened to hide it in a tunnel that blocks all our sensors? Seems a bit excessive for an ordinary outpost, don't you think?"

As the Scorpions traded hypotheticals, Alex noticed some of the regular Marines listening in, their expressions a mix of amusement and bewilderment. One of them, a young corporal with a fresh-faced look that suggested this might be his first real mission, leaned over to Alex.

"Are they always like this?" he asked, nodding towards the other Scorpions.

Alex grinned. "Pretty much. It's their way of dealing with the stress. You'll get used to it after a while."

Once the argument about what was in the tunnel wore out, Malik leaned forward, a mischievous glint in his eye as he addressed the regular Marines. "Hey, you guys want to participate in an old Scorpion tradition?"

"What tradition?" a young corporal with a fresh-faced look asked.

"Yeah, Mal," Sarah said. "What tradition?"

Malik grinned. "We always trade mom jokes on the way down. Keeps things loose, you know? Anybody got a good one?"

The Marines exchanged glances, amusement and confusion on their faces. Finally, one of them, a barrel-chested sergeant, cleared his throat.

"Alright, I'll bite," he said. "Your momma's so fat, when she fell I didn't laugh, but the synthcrete cracked up."

There was a moment of silence, then Malik burst out laughing, the sound echoing through the Stinger's cabin. "Oh man, that's a good one! I'm definitely stealing that one."

Encouraged by Malik's reaction, another Marine chimed in. "How about this—your momma's so old, her birth certificate is stamped 'expired'."

This time, it was Jackson who snorted with laughter. "These guys are alright," he said, nodding approvingly.

Not to be outdone, a third Marine offered, "Your momma's so ugly, she made an onion cry."

The joking continued as they entered the planet's thin atmosphere.

"Two minutes to touchdown," Bastian's voice came over the intercom. "Hope you all enjoyed the trip. Please remember to tip your pilot on the way out."

As they neared the landing site, the atmosphere in the Stinger shifted. The jokes and banter died down, replaced by a focused silence. Alex felt the adrenaline beginning to pump through his veins, his senses sharpening as they prepared for deployment.

The Stinger touched down with a gentle bump, its landing struts absorbing most of the impact. "Ladies and gentlemen," Bastian announced, "welcome to Wolf 1061C. Local time is...well, who the hell knows? But it's probably time to get moving. Out you go, kiddies."

The Stinger's port side hatch hissed open, revealing the alien landscape beyond. Alex took a moment to survey their surroundings as they filed out onto the planet's surface. The landscape was stark and forbidding, all rust-colored rock and windswept plains. The sky above was a deep, dark red, giving everything an eerie, otherworldly cast.

"Charming place," Sarah muttered. "Remind me to book my next vacation here."

Alex grinned behind his helmet. "I hear the weather's lovely at Christmastime."

Liam's voice came in over the comms. "Alright, Marines. Let's move out. Strickland, you and your team have point. The rest of you, fan out and keep your eyes open."

"Copy that," Alex replied. He signaled to the Scorpions, and they moved forward as one. The planet's lower gravity allowed them to bound ahead, moving in graceful synchronization with one another. Behind them, the Marines managed the lower weight with less agility and more disorganization.

As they approached the entrance to the tunnel, Alex felt a prickle of unease run down his spine. All joking aside, there was something strange about the small, manmade hole on an uninhabited planet in an uninhabited star system. His father had been certain they would find a clue in the area. This had to be it.

Or it could be a trick. A trap planted by the Soren Strickland of this dimension. He couldn't rule it out. They couldn't afford to rule anything out.

"Entering the tunnel now," he reported, his voice calm and professional despite the tension coiling in his gut.

The tunnel mouth yawned before them, a perfect circle cut into the rocky cliff face. As they stepped inside, their suit lights automatically activated, illuminating the smooth, bored walls.

"Four-degree decline," Zoe reported, reading off the data scrolling across her HUD. "Slight curve to the left. Sensors are...huh, that's weird."

"What's weird?" Alex asked, immediately on alert.

"Sensors are getting weaker the further in we go," Zoe replied. "It's like the rock is absorbing the signals or something."

Alex frowned. "Lieutenant, are you getting this?"

There was a moment of silence, then Liam's voice came through, slightly distorted. "Copy that, Gunny. Captain says we lost a drone in there. Any sign of it?"

"Not yet," Alex replied.

They continued down the tunnel, the slight decline making it feel to Alex as though they were caught in a tractor beam, being dragged inward instead of advancing. Alex kept a close eye on his HUD, watching as the sensor readings grew weaker and weaker.

After about thirty meters, he spotted the drone up ahead, landed cleanly on the metal floor of the tunnel. "I have eyes on the drone, Lieutenant," Alex said. "Retrieving it now."

"Say again, Gunny," Liam replied. "You're breaking up."

"I have eyes on the drone," he repeated. Liam didn't answer this time, the communications completely failing.

The lower gravity allowed Alex to easily lift the drone. He picked it up and turned back, the other Marines ducking under its short wings as he brought it back within comms range.

"Lieutenant, do you copy?" Alex asked.

"Confirmed," Liam replied.

Alex placed the drone on the floor and turned back. "Continuing down the tunnel. Two, I need you to hang back here. Establish a relay point so we can maintain contact with the ship."

"Sure, Gunny," Sarah replied, taking up position just inside the range of their comms.

They pressed on, the tunnel seeming to stretch endlessly before them. Every fifty meters, they were forced to leave another Marine behind, creating a chain of communication relays back to the surface.

As their numbers dwindled, Alex could feel the tension ratcheting up. The silence in the tunnel was oppressive, broken only by the sound of their breathing and the muted clank of their armor echoing in the confined space and thin air. There had to be a reason the tunnel was so deep, and lined with something to scramble their comms.

Whatever that reason might be, he was pretty sure he didn't like it.

Soon enough, Alex and Zoe found themselves alone, the last of their team left to press forward. The tunnel had been curving more sharply now, and Alex's sense of unease had grown with every step.

"I've got a bad feeling about this," Zoe murmured, her voice tight with tension.

"You and me both," Alex replied. "But we're close. I can feel it."

As if in response to his words, their suit lights landed on the end of the tunnel. A door blocked their path, set flush with the wall, its surface smooth and featureless.

"We've got something," Alex reported back through the comms chain. "Looks like a door of some kind."

"Can you open it?" Liam's voice came back, distorted but audible.

As they approached the door, Alex studied it carefully. Unlike the smooth, featureless walls of the tunnel, the door had a distinct control panel set into its surface.

"Are you seeing this, Lieutenant?" Alex asked.

"We see it, Gunny," Liam replied. "Can you open it?"

Alex approached the door's control panel. "I'm going to try to crack it," he said, recovering his DA from a protected compartment in his armor.

Lines of code scrolled across the DA's screen as the software went to work. Minutes ticked by in silence that seemed to stretch for an eternity.

Finally, Alex had to admit defeat. "No good," he said. "This dimension's door controls are different enough that I can't crack them."

A longer pause followed. Alex pictured his father and Liam arguing over their next course of action. At last, Liam's voice came through again. "Force it open. We need to know what's in there."

Alex hesitated, glancing warily at Zoe. Something about this felt wrong, rushed. But orders were orders.

"Copy that," he replied. "Stand by."

He and Zoe took up positions on either side of the door. "On three," Alex said. "One... two... three!"

They slammed their armored fists into the edge of each door panel, creating indentations that gave them leverage to pull. With a screech of protesting metal, the door gave way, sliding aside to reveal a small, dark chamber beyond.

As their suit lights penetrated the darkness, Alex's eyes widened behind his visor. A simple metal table rested in the center of the room, a black disc the size of a dinner plate resting on top. A single red light in the disc's center flashed at equal intervals.

"What the hell is that?" Zoe breathed.

"I have no idea," Alex replied. "Lieutenant, we've found something. Some kind of device. I can't identify it."

Soren's voice came through. "We see it, Gunny. Stand-by." After a longer delay, his voice returned. "Ethan thinks it might be a transponder of some kind. The tunnel's signal-blocking properties would explain why it was hidden so deep. It's likely designed to activate and send out a signal as soon as it's removed from the tunnel."

Alex felt a chill run down his spine. "A signal to who?"

"That's the question, isn't it?" Soren replied, his voice tight. "Was this left here by the other Dana and her people? Or by this universe's version of the FUP?"

The implications hung heavy in the air. If they removed the device, they could be walking into a trap. But if they left it, they might be passing up their only lead.

"Wait a sec," Zoe said. "If we bring the transponder with us, won't that render our cloak useless to whoever it's sending its signal out to?"

"Yeah, I think so," Alex replied. "Captain?"

Alex could almost hear the gears turning in Soren's mind as he weighed their options. The silence stretched on, each second feeling like an eternity as they waited for a decision.

Finally, Soren's decision came. "Gunny, I need you to hold your position. Don't remove the transponder yet."

"Sir?" Alex questioned, surprised by the order.

"We can't risk being discovered too soon," Soren explained. "Ethan and his team need to complete the external repairs on the Wraith first. Once we're at full defensive capability, then we'll bring the transponder aboard."

Alex exchanged a glance with Zoe, both of them realizing what this meant. "Understood, Captain. How long should we expect to wait?"

There was a pause before Soren replied, "Estimated time to complete the repairs is six hours."

"Yes, sir," Alex responded, his voice firm despite the sinking feeling in his stomach. "We'll be here."

As Alex relayed the orders to the rest of the team, he could imagine their frustration and resignation. Six hours sitting on their butts in this claustrophobic tunnel wasn't anyone's idea of a good time.

The hours crawled by with excruciating slowness. Unable to move because it would break the comms chain, the Marines at first took to sharing more mom jokes to pass the time before moving on to limericks and other increasingly raunchy fare, doing their best to stay strong during the hardest type of mission.

A waiting game.

The Scorpions, used to long periods of inactivity during missions, fared better, but even they felt the strain.

As the sixth hour approached, the tension in the group was palpable. Everyone was on edge, tired and irritable from the long confinement.

Finally, Soren's voice came over the comms. "Gunny, shield repairs are complete. You're clear to move out. Bring the transponder and return to the Stinger immediately."

A collective cheer of relief swept through the team as they got to their feet. Alex stretched, his joints protesting after hours of inactivity. "Alright, people, you heard the Captain. Let's move."

As they carefully lifted the transponder, Alex couldn't shake the feeling that they were crossing a point of no return. Whatever happened next, there was no going back now.

With the device secured, they began their long trek back up the tunnel. The weight of their discovery, both literally and figuratively, seemed to make each step harder than the last. As they passed each Marine relay point, the Marine posted there fell in behind them.

The journey back to the surface felt interminable, the

tension ratcheting up with each meter they ascended. By the time they emerged into the harsh, reddish light of Wolf 1061C's sky, Alex's nerves were stretched to their breaking point.

And the transponder's red blinking light was now a solid green.

"Whoever it's trying to contact, it's got a signal," Alex said.

"Benevolent overlords, I hope," Zoe offered, the joke falling flat.

As the Stinger lifted off, carrying them and their mysterious cargo back to the Wraith, Alex wondered if they had just opened a new can of worms.

The answer, he feared, would come all too soon.

CHAPTER 29

Soren stood in the Wraith's hangar bay, his posture rigid with anticipation as he waited for the Stinger to return. Beside him, Ethan fidgeted nervously, his fingers tapping an erratic rhythm against his thigh. Lina and Tashi stood a short distance away, equally nervous by their expressions. Liam completed their small welcoming party, his eyes fixed on the hangar doors.

The low hum of the ship's systems seemed unnaturally loud in the tense silence. Soren found himself straining to hear the first signs of the Stinger's approach as it passed through the bay's outer force field, knowing that every second they waited was another second for potential enemies to close in on their position.

Finally, the faint whine of engines could be heard. The Stinger glided in smoothly, touching down as gently as a feather. As soon as the engines cut off, the side hatch opened and Marines began to file out.

Alex was the first to exit, the mysterious transponder clutched tightly in his arms. He approached Soren and the others, appearing uncomfortable with the device he held. "Captain. Lieutenant," he said. "Here it is."

Soren's gaze fixed on the innocuous looking black disc. Its steady green light seemed to mock him, a constant reminder of the unknown threat it might represent. "Ethan," he said, turning to the engineer. "I want you to take a look at this thing. See if you can figure out where and even better, who it's connected to."

Ethan stepped forward, taking the transponder from Alex with careful hands. He turned it over, his eyes narrowing as he examined every inch of its surface. After a few moments, he looked up, his expression a mixture of frustration and curiosity.

"Well, on the outside at least, it looks like a standard FUP transponder," Ethan said. "Serial number and all. Nothing obviously out of the ordinary. But without opening it up and getting a look at its internals and software, I can't really tell you who it might be communicating with or what kind of information it's sending."

Soren frowned, weighing their options. They needed answers, but every moment they spent with the active transponder was another moment they risked discovery. "How long will it take you to crack it open and analyze its contents?"

Ethan shrugged. "Hard to say. Could be a few hours, could be a day or more. Depends on how complex the internals are and how well it's encrypted."

Soren nodded, coming to a decision. "Alright. Ethan, I want you to take that thing to your workshop and start working on it immediately. Alex," he turned to his son, "I want you to go with Ethan and his team. If any hostiles show up while they're working, I want you to destroy that transponder immediately. Understood?"

Alex nodded, his hand instinctively moving to where his sidearm was stowed beneath a layer of armor. "Yes, sir."

As Ethan, Alex, and the tech team moved to leave the

hangar, Soren felt a presence at his elbow. Liam stood there, an unreadable expression on his face.

"Captain," Liam said, his voice low. "Do you have a moment?"

Soren nodded, curious. "Of course. What's on your mind?"

Liam seemed to hesitate for a moment before speaking. "I just wanted to say...I think we worked well together on this operation. I know we had our differences at first, but I'm glad we were able to find common ground."

A smile tugged at the corners of Soren's mouth. "In all honesty, I didn't initially think the two of us would get along." Liam had seemed too rigid, too by-the-book for his more unorthodox style of command. But over the course of their mission, they had found a way to complement each other's strengths. "I'm glad we were able to settle our differences. In times like these, we need all hands working together."

Liam nodded, a ghost of a smile crossing his face. "Absolutely, sir. I'll let you get back to it. I just wanted to clear the air."

With a final glance around the hangar, Soren exited, making his way back to the bridge. The ensuing hours crawled by with agonizing slowness, and he found himself constantly checking the long-range sensors, half-expecting to see a fleet of enemy ships appearing at any moment. But the system remained eerily quiet, the Wraith alone in its silent vigil.

As the tension began to wear on the crew, Soren forced himself to remain outwardly calm. He knew his people were looking to him for strength and guidance. If he showed any sign of doubt or fear, it would ripple through the entire ship.

"Captain," Vic said, nodding respectfully. "I'm here to relieve you for the next shift."

Soren looked over at the commander. He'd been staring at the projected sensor grid for so long, he'd lost track of the time. He hesitated, reluctant to leave his post. What if something happened while he was gone? But he knew he couldn't stay on the bridge indefinitely. He and his bridge crew needed rest.

Just as he was about to stand and relinquish command, Samira's voice cut through the quiet hum of the bridge. "Captain! We're receiving a tranSat communication!"

Soren's fatigue vanished in an instant. "Put it through," he ordered, leaning forward in his chair.

A voice warbled over the speakers, distorted and broken. "You've…traced... turn off... immediately..."

"Can you clean that up?" Soren asked.

"Working on it, sir," Samira answered, pausing briefly. "Here it is, Captain."

The voice came again, clearer this time. "You've been tracked. Turn off the transponder immediately."

Soren's blood ran cold. The message was cryptic, offering no clue as to whether the speaker was friendly. Once again, he found himself faced with a crucial decision. Should he trust this mysterious warning?

The speaker said they were tracked. Whether the tracker was good or bad didn't make a difference now. They could sort that out when they actually arrived. He activated his comm. "Alex, destroy the transponder. Now."

There was a moment of silence, then Alex's voice came back, tight with tension. "Are you sure, Captain? Ethan thinks he's close to—"

"Do it!" Soren barked, cutting him off.

In the background, he could hear Ethan's voice, pleading. "No, wait! We're so close to—"

The sound of a gunshot and shattering electronics cut him off. "It's done," Alex reported.

Soren allowed himself a moment of regret for the lost

opportunity, but he knew he had made the right call. Better to err on the side of caution than risk the safety of his entire crew.

"Sir!" Mark's voice interrupted Soren's thoughts. "New contacts just appeared on the grid. I'm counting twelve ships, sir."

"Already?" Soren replied. They'd just finished destroying the transponder. Had they done it in time, or had their cloaked position been compromised? His eyes locked onto the incoming ships on the sensor grid. "Configuration?"

"Four Komodos, eight Valkyries, sir," Mark said. "Consistent with alt-FUP designs."

"Captain, should I prepare the vortex cannon?" Keira asked.

"No," Soren replied. "We can't stand against that. Bobby, prepare to jump. Set a course for anywhere but here."

"Aye, Captain," Bobby replied.

The ships continued advancing toward the planet. Toward them. Neither their formation nor posture gave any indication whether they had or hadn't located Wraith before Alex shot the transponder to pieces.

"Course set," Bobby said. "Ready to jump on your command, Captain."

Soren stared at the ships as if he could divine their intentions by looking at them long and hard enough. If he jumped away from friendlies, they might never find a way to reconnect. But wouldn't friendlies have tried to hail them by now?

"Captain, we're being hailed," Samira said.

Soren almost laughed out loud at the timing.

"Captain!" Mark snapped. "More new contacts. Another twelve ships."

His gaze returned to the grid, where a second flotilla

had appeared. Static at first, they began moving toward the first group of incoming ships.

"Captain, we're being hailed by a second ship now," Samira said.

Soren's eyes narrowed. What the hell was going on here? The odds of two groups of ships arriving so close to one another were so slim. Then again, the last two months had shown him things he would have thought were much more improbable.

"Soren," Jack said. "Two hails wouldn't come from one side."

"No," Soren agreed. One flotilla had to be friend, the other foe. He still had to decide whether to keep Wraith static and jump away or put the ship in motion and commit to a fight.

He needed answers, and only one of those options might provide them.

They had no choice but to fight. But to fight whom?

CHAPTER 30

"Sang, full burn," Soren ordered, his voice cutting through the tense silence on the bridge. "Get us out of orbit, now."

"Aye, Captain," Sang replied.

The Wraith's thrusters flared within their protective covers, the ship surging forward with a burst of acceleration that pressed Soren back into his seat. On the viewscreen, the rusty surface of Wolf 1061C peeled away as they vectored for deeper space.

"Samira," Soren continued, his eyes fixed on the sensor display where the two fleets were rapidly closing on each other. "Answer those hails. In order."

"Aye, Captain," Samira replied, working her console. "First hail is coming through now."

A familiar voice filled the bridge, causing Soren's eyebrows to shoot up in surprise. "This is Commodore Clarey of the Federation of United Planets Navy. Captain Strickland, I know you're here, somewhere. My fight isn't with you. Stand down and clear the area. We can speak after we've handled the interlopers."

Before Soren could respond, the space between the two fleets erupted in a fury of weapons fire. Brilliant flashes of light lit up the viewscreen as missiles streaked between the opposing forces. Shields flared and buckled under the onslaught, the initial salvos pounding relentlessly against the ships' defenses.

"They're really going at it," Jack said, watching the battle unfold.

"One of them is sympathetic to Dana's cause," Soren replied. He knew they couldn't stay neutral for long. Sooner or later, they would have to choose who to side with. "But which one?"

"Clarey did say she was with the Navy."

"That's not a lot to go on, especially when the stakes are so high if we're wrong."

"Second hail coming through," Samira announced, her voice tense.

"Put it on," Soren ordered.

The voice that came through the speakers next sent a fresh jolt of shock through the bridge. "This is Admiral Jack Harper. Captain Strickland, Soren, we need your help. We don't have the resources to go toe-to-toe with these Navy forces. Please, I can give you the answers you're looking for, but not if I'm dead."

Jack's face drained of color as he heard his own voice coming through the speakers. "Now I know how you felt when the other Soren contacted you," he muttered, shaking his head in disbelief.

Soren stared at the sensor grid. Already, one of the Valkyries on one side had gone dark, and the other ships in that flotilla seemed to be struggling to keep up the pace of return fire. But if his interaction with his alternate self had taught him anything, it was that this dimension was more ruthless than theirs.

As if sensing Soren's hesitation, Admiral Harper's voice came through again, more urgent this time. "Soren, listen to me. Your Dana is safe. She's with us. Help us win this fight, and I swear I'll bring you to her."

Dana. The name hit Soren like a physical blow. His daughter, the reason for this entire mission, was alive and supposedly within reach. But could he trust this other Jack?

Time seemed to slow as Soren weighed his options. The battle raged on around them, ships trading fire in a deadly dance of destruction. He knew he had to make a choice, and quickly.

"Keira," he barked, his voice sharp with sudden resolve. "Target Clarey's ship with the vortex cannon. Sang, get us into position. Fire when ready."

"Aye, Captain," they both replied.

"You're going to trust me, Soren?" Jack asked. "I'm not sure that's a good idea."

Jack's tone of voice made Soren laugh despite himself. "It hasn't been so far," he replied. "But I figure we're due."

Sang guided the Wraith in a wide, dipping arc, seeking to approach Clarey's Komodo from below. Meanwhile, a second ship went offline in the flash of a failed reactor that broke the vessel apart from the center, sending each piece careening off in a different direction. The ships in the paths of the debris were forced to break off their attack to maneuver around them.

"We're in position, Captain," Sang announced.

"Drop the cloak and fire," Soren replied softly.

The vortex cannon released in a brilliant lance of destructive force. The beam cut through space, crossing the distance to Clarey's ship in the blink of an eye. The spear of swirling spacetime slammed into its shields, overwhelming them in an instant. The ship's hull buckled and twisted under the awesome power of the weapon, secondary explosions blossoming along its length as internal systems overloaded and failed.

In a matter of seconds, Clarey's flagship ceased to exist.

"Captain, we're target locked," Mark announced.

"Shields up," Soren replied. "Sang, get us a good angle. Keira, ready all weapons."

Missiles launched from the nearest Navy ships in accelerating flares of thrusters, streaking across the distance and digging into Wraith's freshly repaired shields. They shrugged off the hits with ease as Sang guided them into position to return fire.

"Keira, hit that Komodo with everything we've got," Soren ordered.

"Aye, Captain," Keira replied.

The battle around them intensified, both sides seeming to recognize the game changing presence of the Wraith. Additional Navy ships began to break off from their engagements, turning to face this new, more formidable threat.

"Missiles away!" Keira announced as the Wraith unleashed its first salvo.

A spread of high-yield warheads streaked towards the targeted Komodo. Within seconds, they detonated against the destroyer's shields in a series of brilliant flashes. The ship's defenses held, but they were visibly weakened, energy cascading across their surface in flickering waves.

Keira didn't relent. The Wraith's railgun batteries opened up, hypervelocity rounds streaking across space to slam into the Komodo's already strained shields. Under the relentless barrage, the enemy ship's defenses finally failed, leaving it vulnerable.

"Their shields are down!" Mark reported, excitement evident in his voice.

"Finish them," Soren ordered, his voice cold and determined.

Keira needed no further prompting. Another spread of missiles leaped from the Wraith's launch tubes, this time finding no barrier between them and their target. They struck home with devastating effect, tearing into the Komodo's unprotected hull.

Explosions rippled along the length of the enemy ship as internal systems overloaded and ruptured. Its engines flared one last time in a desperate attempt to stabilize, then went dark. The destroyer began to drift, venting atmosphere and debris into the void.

Already, the tide of battle had shifted dramatically. With the Wraith's unexpected support, Admiral Harper's forces pressed their advantage. The Navy ships suddenly found themselves caught between the hammer of Harper's fleet and the anvil of the Wraith's devastating firepower.

A Valkyrie-class cruiser, attempting to flank one of Harper's destroyers, found itself in the Wraith's sights. Soren didn't hesitate.

"Keira, target that Valkyrie. Full spread."

The Wraith's weapons spoke again, a combination of railgun fire and missiles streaking toward the enemy cruiser. The Valkyrie's shields held initially, but after taking damage from Harper's ships and under Wraith's sustained assault, they quickly flickered and failed.

Soren noticed movement on the grid as the cruiser's hull began to break apart under the Wraith's relentless fire. The remaining enemy ships were starting to pull back, desperately trying to disengage.

"They're retreating," Jack observed, a note of disbelief in his voice.

Soren nodded. "Let them go. We've done enough damage for one day."

As the Navy fleet limped away, moving far from the field before stopping to jump, Soren took stock of the battlefield. The space around them was littered with debris, the remnants of destroyed ships from both sides. But it was clear who had come out on top.

"Damage report," Soren called out.

"Shields at 72%," Keira reported. "Barely a scratch."

Soren allowed himself a small sigh of relief. They had come through the battle relatively unscathed, a testament to Sang's piloting skills and the Wraith's advanced technology.

"Captain," Samira interrupted. "We're being hailed by Admiral Harper."

Soren straightened in his chair. "Put him through," he ordered.

Admiral Harper's voice filled the bridge once more. "Thank you, Captain Strickland. Your intervention turned the tide. We owe you a debt of gratitude."

"Save your thanks," Soren replied, his voice tight. "You promised me answers. And Dana. Where is she?"

There was a pause before Harper responded, his tone cautious. "Not here, I'm afraid. We need to talk first, Soren. I suggest we jump to another region of space to avoid any Navy reinforcements. I'll transmit the coordinates."

Soren's eyes narrowed. "You promised you would take me to Dana."

"And I will," Harper replied quickly. "I assume you encountered this dimension's version of you, and if so, I understand why you might be hesitant. But there's more going on here than you realize. Please, trust me a little longer."

Soren exchanged a glance with his Jack, seeing his own frustration and suspicion mirrored in his old friend's eyes. But what choice did they have? They had already committed to this course of action.

"Agreed," Soren said at last. "Send us the coordinates."

"Thank you," Harper's relief was palpable. "As a show of good faith, I'll give you a head start so you can activate your cloak before we arrive. Transmitting coordinates now."

"Fine. We'll see you there, Admiral."

As the communication ended, Soren turned to his crew.

"Bobby, set a course for the coordinates Admiral Harper provided. Keira, be ready to activate the cloak as soon as we complete the jump."

"Aye, Captain," they responded in unison.

"Bobby, what's the ETA?"

"Seven minutes, Captain. We're not going too far."

"Just far enough that the Navy won't be able to find us," Jack said. "Unless we do something reckless like activate another transponder.

"Live and learn," Soren replied in defense. "It had to be done."

The familiar sensation of spacetime folding around them washed over the bridge as the Wraith initiated its jump. In a flash of light, they left behind the debris strewn battlefield, charging headlong towards an uncertain future and the promise of long awaited answers.

The few minutes passed quickly, the Wraith emerging back into the universe in a second burst of light. The viewscreen activated, revealing their new surroundings. They were still in the Wolf system, but had emerged near 1061 D, a massive gaseous planet.

"Sensors are clear, Captain," Mark announced right away.

"At least the other me kept his word on giving us a head start," Jack said. "That's a good sign."

"Cloak active, Captain," Keira reported soon after.

"Excellent," Soren replied.

The minutes ticked by in silence as they waited for Admiral Harper's flotilla to appear.

"Contact!" Mark's voice cut through the quiet. "Multiple ships. Configurations match Admiral Harper's fleet."

"We're being hailed, Captain," Samira reported.

Soren took a deep breath, steeling himself. This was it. The moment of truth. "Put it through," he ordered.

Admiral Harper's voice filled the bridge once more.

"Soren. I hope the head start we gave you was sufficient to make you feel...well, if not safe, at least a bit more secure."

Soren exchanged a glance with his Jack before responding. "We're here, Admiral. Now, I believe you owe us some answers."

"Indeed I do," Harper replied, his tone serious. "I'd rather we keep this between us, if you don't mind."

Soren glanced at Jack, who shrugged. It was a strange request, but Soren didn't see the harm in honoring it. "Give me two minutes," he said.

"Of course," Harper replied. "Take your time."

Soren nodded to Samira to pause the comms. "Vic," he said, turning to the commander, who had remained nearby.

"Aye, Captain?" he replied, approaching.

"You have the conn. If you get any hint that those ships can locate us, get us out of here."

"Aye, sir. I have the conn."

Soren slipped out of the command chair to let Vic take his place. "Jack, you're with me. I want you to listen in to whatever this dimension's version of you has to say."

"I was hoping you would let me tag along," Jack replied.

Soren exited the bridge, Jack walking beside him. "There's something off about all this, isn't there?" Jack asked.

"I'm glad I'm not the only one who feels it," Soren replied. "If this conversation doesn't lead to Dana, there's going to be hell to pay."

CHAPTER 31

Soren and Jack made their way to the ready room. As the door slid shut behind them, Soren moved to his desk while Jack took up a position near the display feeding in the view outside the ship, his eyes fixed on the distant stars.

"Samira," Soren said, activating his comm. "Put the other Jack through to my ready room."

"Aye, Captain," Samira replied, her voice crisp and professional.

A moment later, Admiral Harper's voice filled the room. "Soren, thank you for agreeing to speak privately. I know you have many questions, and I promise to answer them to the best of my ability, though I have to admit, it feels strange talking to you like this, knowing you're not...well, not the Soren I know."

"From what little I knew about your Soren, maybe that's not a bad thing," Soren replied.

Harper sighed. "He wasn't always like that. But the Convergence...it changed him. He was so desperate to protect our dimension, he elected to do anything to come out on top. And I take it he tried." It was more a sad deduction than a question.

"To kill me and my son, you mean? He did try. And they both paid for it with their lives. They could have come to us. We could have worked on this together."

"Maybe from your perspective. I'm sure you've learned that our universes aren't exactly identical. The differences can be...stark, at times."

"He killed his own daughter for trying to warn me about the Convergence," Soren pointed out. "That's not me by a country mile."

"I don't really know what to say to that," Harper replied.

Soren leaned back in his chair, his eyes meeting Jack's for a brief moment. "Let's just start at the beginning, Admiral. How did all of this come about? In our universe, no one ever heard of an inter-dimensional rift or the idea of convergence. We're still trying to wrap our heads around the whole concept while your dimension is sending an extermination force across the rift to wipe us out."

There was a pause, and Soren could almost picture the other Harper gathering his thoughts. When he spoke again, his voice was heavy with the weight of memories.

"It's a long story, Soren, but I'll try to give you the condensed version," Harper began, sounding weary. "It all started over six years ago. Dana was on an expedition aboard the Galileo when they first encountered the rift. As she relayed it to me, they nearly flew right into it before they even realized a shimmering curtain of disturbed spacetime was even there. She and her expeditionary crew, mostly scientists and analysts, spent the next week taking measurements and trying to figure out what it was. I've met your Dana. She's a lot like ours. So I'm sure you know what happened next."

"She grew impatient with the theories and questions, and went through the rift," Soren said.

Harper laughed. "Exactly. She was always more impulsive than cautious. But in this case, her recklessness paid off. At first she didn't know she had crossed into another universe. She thought she had just gone harmlessly through the other side. She realized something was off when she tried to reach out through tranSat over encrypted channels, and couldn't make a connection. Flew right up to a relay, made sure it was operational, and went through every channel to every receiver she knew. It was one of her scientists, I don't remember which one, that figured out the encryption was different."

"That doesn't cry out that you're in another dimension to me," Soren said.

Harper chuckled, the identical chuckle that his Jack used. "No, me neither. But you know how scientists are. They just think differently."

"They do, but how did they really figure out they had moved into another dimension? Why would they even consider the possibility?"

"The Internet."

"You lost me."

"Dana looked you up. In your universe, you're supposed to be retired. Our Soren loved the Navy too much to retire. Just like me. I'm sure it was a struggle for her and her crew to wrap their minds around, but it was the only thing that made sense. After she figured out what the rift was, she went back through and came to me."

"To you?" Soren asked. He glanced at Jack, who remained silent, his face a mask of concentration. "Why not go through official channels? Or to her father? That doesn't sound like the Dana I know."

"She trusted me," Harper explained, his voice softening. "And she knew her father would go right to Admiral Montoya. Plus, I had the resources and connections to help her set up a proper research operation without too many questions being asked. At least at first. You have to understand, Soren, the implications of what she'd discovered... well, they were earth-shattering. We couldn't risk the information getting into the wrong hands before we understood what we were dealing with."

Soren nodded slowly, processing this information. "So you oversaw the research? Kept it all under wraps?"

"That's right," Harper confirmed, a note of pride entering his voice. "For the next year, I handled all the research done on the rift. Discreetly. Dana was in charge of the teams we put together. Brilliant minds from all over the Federation, working in secret to understand what we were dealing with. It was...well, it was exciting and terrifying in equal measures."

"And what did you discover?" Soren asked, leaning forward, his curiosity piqued despite his lingering suspicions. "I'm assuming it was more than we've managed to figure out in the past couple of months."

"You could say that," Harper said with a humorless chuckle. "It was one of our scientists, a man named Lukas Mitchell, who made the breakthrough. Brilliant guy, but a bit...intense. He determined the true nature of the rift and hypothesized the Convergence. Lukas believed that if his calculations were correct, the rift would increase in size over time, and new rifts would begin to appear in other places. He even provided estimated locations for where these new rifts might appear."

"You're saying there's more than one rift?" Soren asked, surprised.

Harper chuckled again. "Soren, there are hundreds of them, at least. Maybe even thousands or millions. The universe is a big place, and we gave up looking for them after we ended up over a hundred light years out and counted our sixth anomaly. It was...well hell, it's still terrifying to be honest. The idea that our entire universe might be on a collision course with another. Can you imagine what that was like, Soren? Knowing what was going to happen in years to come but being powerless to stop it?"

Soren sat back, considering Harper's words. It all made a twisted kind of sense, explaining why this universe seemed so much more prepared for the conflict than his own. They'd had years to see it coming. To prepare. But something still didn't add up.

"You said you kept all this under wraps. So who spilled the beans?"

"Our brilliant scientist, Lukas Mitchell. He wanted his fifteen minutes of fame. Also, he felt slighted because he had a thing for Dana, and she wasn't interested."

Soren shook his head in disbelief. All of this because of a rejected love connection?

"And the Joint Chiefs decided war was the answer? To invade our universe and wipe us out before we could do the same to you? What kind of logic is that?"

Harper released another heavy sigh. "It wasn't that simple, Soren," he said, his voice tinged with regret. "And it wasn't actually the military brass who made that call. It was the politicians. The President, specifically. He saw it as necessary for survival. He put the gears of war in motion, diverting resources to building more ships, pushing conscription through the Senate. They've spent the last four years throwing everything they had, and I mean every-thing, into this conflict."

Soren's jaw clenched, anger rising in his chest. He glanced at Jack, seeing his own fury mirrored in his friend's eyes. "And you went along with this? You and Dana? I find that hard to believe."

"No," Harper said quickly, a note of desperation entering his voice. "Well, not entirely. I watched it happen, yes. And I'll admit, I saw the logic in it at first. And your counterpart in this universe—my Soren—didn't just accept the strategy, he favored it. But Dana...she was never comfortable with the idea. She and Lukas had a theory that the Convergence was no accident, that there might be a way to stop it without resorting to violence."

"Wait, I thought Lukas outed the whole thing. Why is he still in this story?"

"Did I mention that he's brilliant? He came up with all of these algorithms and computations that he said proved something physical was messing with spacetime and pulling our universes together. The equations don't mean anything to me, but he was adamant."

"And let me guess," Soren interjected, his voice dripping with sarcasm. "When you tried to convince the powers that be, they decided they couldn't take that chance. Too risky to bet the fate of your universe on a scientist's math equations, right?"

"Exactly," Harper confirmed. "They couldn't risk the fate of our entire universe on a theory. So they moved forward with their plans for war. You have to understand, Soren, the fear that was driving these decisions."

"I do understand the fear," Soren snapped. "I felt it when I arrived in orbit of Proxima, our Proxima, and saw that your military is using chemical warfare to kill civilians," Soren said, each word sharp as a knife. "Millions dead on that one planet alone. Millions more on Tau Ceti, and plans to kill every human being in our dimension so that you all stay unique. So our collective consciousness doesn't merge with yours. How can you justify that, Harper? How can you sleep at night, knowing you're part of this...this insane genocide?"

There was a long pause before Harper responded, his voice soft and somber. "I can't justify it, Soren. It's monstrous. I'm not happy about it. None of us who know the truth are. But now that you're here, maybe we can find a way to stop it. If we can find the source of the Convergence and reverse it, we can end this war before it's too late. Before more innocent lives are lost."

Soren stopped his pacing, turning to look at Jack. His old friend's face was a mask of conflicting emotions—anger, disbelief, and a glimmer of hope. Soren took a deep breath, trying to calm the storm of emotions raging inside him.

"And if we do manage to stop the Convergence," Soren said slowly, choosing his words carefully, "will that be enough to end the war? Or is it already too late? Has too much blood been spilled? I've seen the devastation, Harper. I've seen worlds burned and populations decimated. How do you come back from that?"

Harper's response was immediate and forceful. "It has to be enough, Soren. We have to make it enough. The alternative is the complete annihilation of one universe or the other. Or both, if the Convergence proceeds unchecked. I know it seems impossible now, but if we can stop this, if we can find a way to reverse the Convergence, at least we can set things right for everyone who's left. I know that's a lousy outcome, but it still beats the alternative."

Soren nodded, even though Harper couldn't see him. It was a compelling argument, but something still felt off. He couldn't shake the feeling that there was more to this story than Harper was telling them.

"You mentioned Dana earlier," Soren said, changing tack. "Where is she now? You promised to bring me to her, and I've got to say, Admiral, my patience is wearing thin. I want to see my daughter."

There was another pause, longer this time. When Harper spoke again, his voice was cautious. "She's not here, Soren. She's with the other rebels. She's working with Lukas to locate the source of the Convergence. I can give you the coordinates, but..."

Soren's eyes narrowed. Here it was, the catch he had

been waiting for. "But what, Harper? What aren't you telling me?"

Harper's next words sent a chill down Soren's spine. "I need you to do something for me first, Soren. Something you're not going to like."

"What's that?"

"I need you to kill your Jack Harper."

CHAPTER 32

The ready room fell into stunned silence. Soren's gaze snapped to Jack, who had gone pale, his eyes wide with shock and disbelief.

"What did you just say?" Soren asked, his voice dangerously low. "Because I could have sworn you just asked me to murder my best friend. Please, Harper, tell me I misheard you."

"You heard me correctly," Harper replied, his tone grim. "Your Jack Harper needs to die."

Soren's hand clenched into a fist, anger boiling up inside him. "Why do you think he needs to die?"

"I'm sorry, Soren," Harper said. "I didn't make this clear to you. The convergence…it's pretty far along. In fact, the whole thing can collapse at any moment."

"What?" Soren hissed, his blood immediately running cold.

"Exactly," Harper replied. "We weren't ready to launch the attack. The government wanted another year, a hundred more capital ships, more troop transports, the whole thing. But Lukas said we're out of time. We're balanced on the razor's edge here, Soren. And I know how this sounds, but number one, I don't want to share my existence with another version of me. And number two, that's still just a theory, anyway. According to Lukas, there's a fifty-fifty chance the Convergence will kill anyone who has a duplicate."

Soren exhaled sharply. Of course, they had considered the possibility. It chilled him further to know it could still happen.

And at any moment.

"How am I supposed to kill him?" Soren asked. "He's back on Earth."

Harper laughed. "We both know that isn't true."

Soren glanced at Jack, both wearing confused looks. "How do you know that isn't true?" he asked Harper.

"You can feel it when your duplicate is close. You probably did too, you just couldn't place the sense of wrongness, so you bundled it up with whatever situation you were in. Now, I can't pinpoint him and defeat your cloak that way, but I'm confident he's with you. Probably on the conn right now, if I had to guess." He sighed. "I don't want us to be enemies, Soren. We're on the same side. But I do need to hedge my bets."

"You've always been pragmatic," Soren said.

"That's the deal, Captain Strickland. You kill Jack, I lead you to Dana."

"And how do I know you won't add another condition once that's done?"

"Because you know I'm a man of my word. And you have my word. Those are the only terms. Take it or leave it."

"If I leave it, the Convergence will happen, and you won't get what you want."

"No, but neither will you. Jane's alive and well in this universe, Soren. What about yours?"

Soren stiffened, the fury almost more than he could bear. He looked to Jack, who shook his head sadly.

"I need time to think about this," Soren said.

"You have an hour. Just remember, every second counts, so the sooner you make up your mind, the better it is for all of us."

"I'll be in touch." Soren slammed the disconnect button on his terminal.

"The better it is for everyone except me," Jack said, meeting Soren's angry gaze. "Soren, there's only one—"

"No," Soren interrupted. "I'm not going to kill you so that asshole version of you can live."

"No, you'll do it so you can reunite with your daughter and stop all of this madness before every innocent person in two universes is either combined into one or dead."

Soren stared at Jack, shaking his head. "There has to be another way."

"He can sense me, Soren. And since he mentioned it, I can sense him too, now that I know what that feeling means. He'll know when I'm gone. And if you don't kill me, he'll know that I'm not dead."

He sighed heavily, reminding Soren of Harper's sigh. So many people were being pushed into decisions they didn't want to make. Into directions they didn't want to go.

"I'm an old man, Soren," Jack continued. "Older than you. I've lived a good life. Served my purpose. I don't fear dying the way this Jack seems to. I don't need to feel powerful the way he apparently does. This dimension isn't like ours. The other Dana was right. It's cold and ruthless and filled with fear." He shook his head. "I'm not afraid."

"I can't kill you, Jack," Soren said. "And I won't ask anyone else to do it, either."

"Then give me a pistol. I'll do it myself. It'll be worth it to get you and Dana back together. And hopefully, to save your Jane and my son."

A heavy silence fell over the ready room. Both Soren and Jack turned to the viewscreen, staring out at the stars together.

"No," Soren said after a few minutes. "I'm not letting it end like this."

"There's no other choice."

Soren put his hand on Jack's shoulder, turning him until their eyes met. "Yes, there is. I have an idea."

Jack's eyes narrowed. "What kind of idea?"

Soren tapped his comms. "Liam, Alex, Tashi, I need you in the conference room immediately."

"Aye, Captain," Tashi replied, followed by acknowledgements from the others.

"What are you up to, old friend?" Jack asked.

Soren smiled. "The game is afoot, my friend."

CHAPTER 33

Alex stepped into his Karuta power armor, pressing his right foot forcefully down into the sensor-laden gel padding of the armored boot. Balanced on one foot, he repeated the same procedure with his left foot and then leaned forward, pushing his hands into the similarly padded arms until the armored gloves fit tight over his fingers. His chest sank into padding of its own, and servos in the rear hinges whirred, automatically bringing the back of the suit up and closed with a soft thump. Sensing his weight, the suit's augmented musculature came online, allowing him to move as freely as if he were naked.

The rest of the Scorpions were already in various stages of donning their own armor, the familiar routine providing a sense of normalcy in the face of their extraordinary mission. Alex watched as Malik struggled to convince the open back to seal, cursing under his breath.

"Need a hand there, big guy?" Alex asked, a hint of amusement in his voice.

Malik grunted, finally managing to convince the sensors he was fully embedded. "Nah, I got it. Just this damn suit trying to remind me who's boss." He paused, his expression growing serious. "Hey, Gunny...you really think we can pull this off?"

Alex felt the weight of his team's expectations settle solidly on his shoulders. He took a moment to consider his response, knowing his confidence would set the tone for the entire operation.

"We've done these types of sims before," Alex replied, his voice steady and assured. "We've trained for scenarios just like this."

"Yeah, but not against a friendly," Malik countered, voicing the concern that had been nagging at all of them. "This isn't some computer generated enemy we're going up against. These are real people, with real skills and real stakes."

Sarah chimed in, her voice muffled as she dropped her helmet over her head, where it locked onto the body of the armor. Immediately, a HUD activated over her faceplate as electrodes in the padded cover began reading her brain waves, ready to pick out subconscious instructions passed to the bucket and through it to the suit. "If we can't do it, then no one can. That's why they picked us, remember?"

Alex nodded, grateful for Sarah's vote of confidence. "She's right. We're the best of the best, and we've got the element of surprise on our side. Plus, we're not looking to hurt anyone. We just need to get in, complete the objective, and get out." He grabbed his helmet and put it on as he spoke, twisting it slightly to lock it in place. "Comms check. Sound off."

The Scorpions reported in one by one, their voices clear in Alex's helmet.

Satisfied with the comms check, Alex opened a channel to the bridge. "Control, this is Scorpion One. We're suited up and ready to proceed."

Soren's voice came through, calm and focused. "Copy that, Scorpion One. Tashi has completed the calculations, and Sang is prepared to move us into position upon your signal."

"Understood," Alex replied. "We're headed to the hangar bay now." Reaching it within a few minutes, they continued past the racks of Pilums to the outer bay doors before reporting they'd reached them.

"Opening outer bay doors now," Soren replied.

The doors groaned lightly as they peeled back, the shimmering force field keeping the atmosphere in while allowing ships and personnel to pass through. Beyond it, Alex could only see the outer edge of the cover that kept the ship invisible even with the bay doors open.

"Alright, team," Alex said, his voice low and intense. "Out and up."

The Scorpions moved to the edge of the open bay doors. Alex pushed off first, triggering his suit's jump jets. The boost pushed him toward the cover, the others behind him. As he neared his objective, he activated the magnetic locks on his boots and somersaulted over the edge of the cover. The locks clamped on as he landed, his knees flexing slightly to absorb his weightless momentum. The others did the same on either side and behind him. From there, they walked along the cover, out to the far edge of the ship and down the other side. Star-spangled space loomed beyond, beautiful and deadly, their target in sight.

"Control, Scorpion One. We're in position," Alex reported, stopping and holding his fist up to halt his squad behind him.

Liam's voice came through this time, crisp and professional. "Copy that, Scorpion One. Stand by and be ready to move on my signal."

Alex acknowledged the order and then turned to his team. "This is it, Scorpions. Nice and easy. Just like we did it in the simulator."

Alex took a moment to survey Admiral Harper's flotilla

as his team ran through their final checks. The six ships hung there, a collection of sleek, deadly warships. The Admiral's Valkyrie-class cruiser was easily identifiable by its protected position in the group's center.

The Wraith began to move slowly, almost imperceptibly at first, gradually gaining velocity. Alex was immediately impressed with Sang's piloting skills. As she guided the massive ship closer to the cruiser, her almost imperceptible course corrections incredibly precise, the Valkyrie grew more prominent in their field of view, its hull details becoming clearer with each passing second.

"Scorpion One, this is Control," Liam's voice cut through the tense silence. "You are clear to proceed on my mark."

Alex's muscles tensed, ready to spring into action. He could feel the same coiled energy radiating from his team.

"Three... two... one... mark!"

The Scorpions deactivated their magboots and fired their jump jets in perfect synchronization. The sudden acceleration pressed Alex back into his armor as they streaked through the void, approaching the Valkyrie. Their HUDs displayed the telemetry and trajectory needed to hit their intended target, which Alex marked for the team with just a thought. Automated systems helped guide their inception, jump nozzles making thousands of minuscule adjustments to ensure they landed on target.

"Whoooo!" Malik cried out. "This is better than the sims!"

As the Valkyrie's hull rushed up to meet them, Alex maneuvered around so he dropped feet first toward it. The others did the same. Their jump jets that had sped them to the target slowed them now, firing full bore to reduce velocity and allow them to land with practiced ease. Their magboots engaged, automatically securing them to the

Valkyrie's surface within a few feet of one of the ship's airlocks.

"Scorpion One to Control," Alex reported. "We've successfully landed on target. Moving to breach point now."

"Copy that, Scorpion One," Liam replied. "Proceed with caution. We're withdrawing to a safe distance. Good hunting."

"Alright, team," Alex said, his voice low and focused. "Let's get to work. Zoe, you're on point. Get us inside."

Zoe nodded, moving towards the airlock with purposeful strides. "This might take a minute, Gunny," she reported, withdrawing a multitool from her armor. She began unscrewing the cover over the control panel for the outer hatch.

The rest of the team huddled around her as Alex kept a watchful eye on their surroundings. He couldn't shake the feeling of exposure. Every second they spent on the hull increased their chances of detection.

"Jackson, hold this," Zoe said, passing him the cover once it was removed. Exposed wiring sat underneath, and she confidently clipped one of them. "Okay, Gunny, I've bypassed the alert system. We can crack open this can now without setting off any alarms."

"Good work," Alex said. "Jackson, Malik, get that door open."

The two Marines moved into position. The enhanced strength in their suits allowed them to manually override the airlock's locking mechanism. They pulled the outer hatch open with a silent groan that Alex felt through vibrations in his boots.

"Inside, now," Alex ordered, ushering his team into the airlock. Once inside, the small space felt confined with five fully armored Marines packed shoulder-to-shoulder. A mix of exertion and nervous energy, Alex could hear his squad's rapid breathing over their comms.

"Zoe, get ready to work your magic on the inner door," he said as he and Sarah sealed the outer door behind them. "Everyone, be ready. We don't know what's waiting for us on the other side."

As Zoe set to work on the inner hatch controls, Alex ran through the mission parameters in his head. Their objective was clear, but the path to achieving it was fraught with potential complications. They needed to move fast, stay undetected, and complete their task before anyone realized they were aboard.

"Inner hatch is good to go, Gunny," Zoe reported. "Whenever you're ready."

Alex took a deep breath, centering himself. This was it. The point of no return. He stepped up behind Zoe. "Open it up," he ordered. "Let's do this."

The inner hatch opened inward with a soft hiss, revealing a dimly lit corridor.

Alex stepped through first, his senses on high alert for any sign of movement or detection. "Clear," he whispered, motioning for the others to follow.

The Scorpions filed into the corridor behind him, Alex couldn't help but marvel at the similarities between this ship and the vessels he was familiar with. The layout, the design aesthetics. It was all so familiar, yet subtly different in ways he couldn't quite put his finger on.

"Control, this is Scorpion One. We're in."

CHAPTER 34

"Copy that, Scorpion one," Liam replied through the comms. "Proceed."

"Roger." Alex's heart pounded as he turned back to his team. "Alright, this is it. Remember, our objective is to secure and not hurt anyone if we can avoid it. These spacers are supposedly on our side."

Each of his squadmates nodded before following Alex through the passageway and down the next one, careful to keep their armored steps as quiet as possible. Every inch forward felt like a potential misstep that could blow their cover.

They heard footsteps and then voices as they approached the second intersection. Alex held up a fist, signaling the team to halt.

"I'm telling you," they heard a crewman say, "something weird is going on. Did you see how tense the Admiral was after that last comm?"

"Keep your voice down," another guy more quietly replied as the two crew members rounded the corner just a few feet ahead. "You know we're not supposed to—"

The man froze as he saw the armored Marines standing

directly before them. Before he could act, Alex pulled his sidearm and fired a stun charge that knocked him to the deck, temporarily paralyzed. Jackson took care of the other one.

"Four, Five, get them out of the passageway," Alex ordered. Malik and Zoe sprang into action, lifting the stricken crew members easily and depositing them in an empty compartment further back the way they had come.

Alex led the Scorpions deeper into the ship's bowels, the familiar yet alien corridors seeming to exacerbate their palpable tension as they moved with practiced coordination toward their objective. Every step, every turn, brought them closer to the bridge.

And to a confrontation with Admiral Harper.

As they rounded the next corner, they nearly collided with another set of crew members. These two were heading in the same direction, their heads down as they studied data pads, oblivious to the armored intruders a few feet behind them. They never knew what hit them. With lightning speed, Alex and Malik grabbed them in choke holds, hanging on until the man and woman both sagged in their arms. They dropped them to the deck, out cold.

As before, the team worked quickly, stashing the unconscious spacers in a nearby maintenance closet. They continued their advance, Alex still unable to shake the nagging feeling that their luck couldn't hold out forever. They had managed to avoid major detection so far, but all it would take was one wrong move, one stroke of bad timing, and their entire operation could unravel.

His fears were realized as they approached the last junction leading to the main corridor that would take them to the bridge. Multiple footsteps echoed towards them—a larger group this time, moving with purpose.

"Incoming," Alex hissed, readying his stunner. "Prepare to engage."

The Scorpions spread out, taking up defensive positions as a squad of six Marines rounded the corner. For a split second, they froze, startled by the unexpected encounter.

Then all hell broke loose.

The Marines reacted with trained efficiency, reaching for their weapons. The Scorpions were already bringing their stunners to bear. Alex fired his, dropping the Marine who made a desperate lunge for a nearby comms panel. Beside him, Sarah and Zoe unleashed a barrage of stun blasts, their precision aim felling two more.

The remaining Marines surged forward, closing the distance to engage in hand-to-hand combat. Malik met the charge head-on, his armored fist connecting with a Marine's jaw in a sickening crunch. The man crumpled, unconscious before he hit the deck.

Jackson grappled with another, using his enhanced strength to slam the Marine against the bulkhead. A quick strike to a pressure point, and another opponent slumped to the deck.

The last Marine, realizing the tide had turned, backpedaled and then turned, breaking into a dead run. Alex's heart leapt into his throat. The kid was little but fast as greased lightning, his mouth opening to sound the alarm.

With a burst from her jump jets, Sarah closed the distance in a heartbeat. Her armored hand wrapped around his head, clamping down on his mouth and dragging him to a stop. A swift, calculated blow to the temple, and the final opponent collapsed.

The entire encounter had lasted less than ten seconds.

"No time to hide these guys," he ordered. "We need to reach the bridge before one of them wakes up and sounds the alarm or someone else finds us."

The team surged forward, their enhanced speed carrying them swiftly down the remaining corridor. They encountered one more crew member right before the corner nearest the bridge, leaving him paralyzed in the passageway. Alex signaled for the team to hold position as he peeked around that final corner.

"Scorpion One to Control," he said over his comms. "We've reached the corridor outside the bridge."

There was a moment of tense silence before Liam's voice came through. "Stand by, Scorpion One. Captain Strickland will make contact with Harper. Hold your position and be ready to move on my command."

Alex acknowledged, then turned to his team. "The corridor's clear," he said, his voice low but intense. "Now, we wait for go ahead." Alex didn't need them to respond to know they would follow his order. He could feel the nervous energy radiating from them as they remained piled up at the corner, ready to make their move. This was what they had trained for, but the stakes had never been higher.

Nearly a minute ticked by while Alex remained ready to spring into action at a moment's notice. The plan was for his father to ask Harper to speak to him in private so he could relay his decision about kiling Jack. He would need to move to his ready room for privacy, and when he did, the Scorpions would grab him. Simple. So why the hell was it taking so long?

Finally, Liam's voice crackled in his ear. "Scorpion One, prepare to move. Harper is on his way."

Alex's heart rate spiked. This was it. He signaled to his team, and they shifted into position, ready to strike.

The bridge doors hissed open. Alex tensed, ready to spring—but before Harper could fully emerge, a shout rang out from inside the bridge.

"Admiral! Security breach!"

"Go!" Alex roared, his enhanced muscles propelling him forward around the corner with explosive force.

Harper's eyes widened in shock as the armored figures

rushed around the corner, headed straight for him. He spun on his heel, diving back towards the bridge. At the same moment, alarms began blaring throughout the ship, the sudden cacophony shattering the tense silence.

Alex activated his jump jets. The sudden burst of acceleration sent him hurtling towards the closing bridge doors. Time seemed to slow as he twisted in midair, angling his body to slip through the narrowing gap. For a heart-stopping moment, he thought he had miscalculated. The edges of the doors scraped against his armor, threatening to pin him there. But then he was through, tumbling onto the bridge in a controlled roll.

He came up in a crouch, his sidearm already drawn and leveled at the stunned bridge crew. Behind him, he heard the rest of his team slamming against the closed doors, working to force them open.

"Nobody moves!" Alex barked, his voice amplified by his armor's external speakers. His gaze locked onto Harper, who stood frozen near the command chair, his face frozen in shock and anger. With lightning speed, Alex closed the distance to Harper, his armored hand clamping down on the admiral's shoulder with enough force to make him wince. "Don't try anything stupid," Alex growled. "A lot of lives are at stake, including yours."

The bridge doors groaned and then slid open with a hydraulic hiss. The rest of the Scorpions poured in, their weapons trained on the bridge crew.

"Secure the room," Alex ordered. "Two, Three, watch the doors. Four, Five, get helm and tactical away from their stations." His squad moved efficiently, removing weapons from anyone who had them and making them retake their seats. Within moments, the bridge was fully theirs.

Alex tapped his comm. "Scorpion One to Control. We have Harper and control of the bridge."

"Well done, Scorpion One," Liam's voice came back,

tight with barely contained excitement. "Stand by for Captain Strickland."

As if on cue, the screen at the comms station changed to indicate an incoming hail. Alex turned to Harper, his grip on the man's shoulder tightening slightly. "I suggest you answer that, Admiral," he said, his voice cold.

Harper's jaw clenched, a flicker of something... Resignation? Fear? ...passed across his face. "Put it through," he ordered his comms officer.

Soren's voice, calm but laced with steel, filled the bridge. "Admiral Harper. I trust my team has made themselves comfortable on your bridge?"

Harper's eyes narrowed. "Strickland," he spat. "I should have known you'd try something like this. You're more like our Soren than I expected."

"I have new terms for you. Simple ones. Give me the coordinates to Dana's position, or there will only be one Jack Harper in this dimension." Alex was surprised by his father's dark tone when he finished his statement. "And it won't be you."

The color drained from Harper's face as the implications of Soren's words sank in. His gaze darted around the bridge as if searching for some way out of his predicament. Finding none, his shoulders slumped in defeat.

"All right, Strickland," he muttered. "You win. Well played." He paused, taking a deep breath. "You don't need me to send you coordinates, you already have them. The skunkworks space station where you picked up your ride." Harper smirked smugly when Soren didn't respond right away.

"Your Soren destroyed our version of the station," Soren replied.

"He wanted to scuttle the Wraith before it fell into the wrong hands."

"He nearly succeeded. So you have a Wraith in this universe?"

"Ours never made it into service. It suffered from power fluctuations during testing, and when they live-fired the main gun the reactor overloaded and the ship exploded."

"How did you know our version wouldn't explode, too?"

"We didn't. But you know Soren."

"He wasn't taking any chances."

"No."

"Does that mean the cloaking tech is in heavy usage across your Navy?"

"Only the Basilisk had it. The paint job cost too much."

Soren laughed. "Whatever the dimensions, it's always the bean counters. In any case, thank you for your cooperation. Alex, make sure the good Admiral sets a course for the station as well. I want his ships leaving right alongside us."

"Understood, Captain," Alex replied. He turned to Harper. "You heard the man, Admiral."

Harper hesitated, his face a storm of conflicting emotions. For a moment, Alex thought he might refuse. But then, with a resigned sigh, he called out to his navigator. "Set a course for the R&D Skunkworks."

"Aye, Captain," the officer replied. Then, soon after, "Course set, Admiral."

"Comm, advise our ships to follow." Harper raised an eyebrow, waiting.

"Scorpion One to Control," he said into his comm. "We're ready to initiate jump on your mark."

"Understood, Scorpion One," Liam's voice came back. "Stand by."

The next few moments passed in tense silence. Alex could feel the eyes of the bridge crew on him. He ignored their disdain. By breaching the Valkyrie and taking the bridge, he had saved his Jack Harper's life.

It was more than worth it.

"Admiral," Soren said over the comms. "Initiate jump."

"Fine, Strickland," he replied. "Initiate jump."

"Jump initiated," the officer said.

Alex felt the familiar lurch as the ship's jump drive engaged. The viewscreen flared with a brilliant light, then settled into the darkness of folded space. They were on their way.

As the jump sequence stabilized, Alex allowed himself a moment to breathe. They had pulled it off—infiltrated the ship, captured its commander, and set course for what he hoped would be a reunion with Dana. But he knew better than to celebrate too soon. Would this Harper be so cold as to send them all headlong into a trap? "How long until we reach the coordinates?" he asked.

"Approximately six days, fourteen hours," the navigation officer replied.

"There's no need to continue holding us hostage," Harper said. "You and your father won, Alex. We're on our way home. I would have brought you to the same place if you'd agreed to my terms."

"Your terms were monstrous," Alex replied.

"What measures would you take to survive? To ensure the people you loved survived? The only reason you're not in my shoes is because you didn't know any better, at least until now, and your duplicate is already dead."

"But theirs..." Alex paused, looking at his team scattered across the bridge. Had they killed their counterparts back on Jungle, or was the rest of this dimension's Scorpion Squad still out there? They'd left the planet before they had a chance to ID the enemy dead.

"Theirs are gone, too," Harper confirmed. "Odds are, you're the ones who killed them.

"It wouldn't have changed me if I hadn't killed your Alex," Alex insisted. "I'd still be here looking for a solution, not trying to ensure my survival when the Convergence comes."

"But what if you had a chance to do both?"

Alex stared at Harper without answering. After giving the question real consideration...he just didn't know.

"Now I think you're beginning to understand," Harper said. "Again, you don't need to hold us prisoner, and we don't need to be enemies. You won this round, and we have a much bigger fish to fry, as it were. What do you say?" He put out his hand, if not in friendship, then at least as an ally.

Alex's gaze bored into Harper's, searching for signs of deceit. He didn't see any, but he wasn't taking any chances.

"One of us stays with you at all times," he said. "You go to the head, one of us goes with you. Agree to that, and we can put this ship back to normal operations."

"Of course," Harper said. "Deal."

CHAPTER 35

Soren sat at the command station on the bridge of the Wraith, his eyes fixed on the dark viewscreen. Three days had passed since their confrontation with Harper's fleet. Three days of tense anticipation as they hurtled towards their destination. The prospect of seeing Dana again after so long filled him with a mixture of excitement and apprehension that made it hard for him to sit still.

So close, after all this time.

"Exit from hyperspace in two minutes, Captain," Bobby announced from the nav station.

Soren nodded, his fingers drumming an unconscious rhythm on the arm of his command chair. "Thank you, Bobby."

"Should I prepare to cloak?" Keira asked when Soren didn't immediately give the order.

"No, not this time," he replied. "I don't want whoever is in charge of station defenses to get the wrong idea about us. Although, I do wonder about Harper's intentions."

"You're overthinking it," Jack said quietly from beside him. "Harper knows when he's beaten. He's a pragmatist, just like... well, just like me."

Soren turned to his old friend. "Maybe," he conceded.

"Thirty seconds to exit," Bobby called out.

The final seconds ticked away. Then, with a lurch Soren felt in his bones, the Wraith dropped out of hyperspace. The stark white on the viewscreen resolved into a field of stars, and the skunkworks station was looming large before them.

Soren momentarily stared at the station, having forgotten how large it was. Like its copy before its destruction, it dwarfed the Wraith, its angular form bristling with sensor arrays and docking arms.

But it was the ships already docked at the station that truly captured his attention.

"There she is," he said, heart suddenly pounding, voice barely above a whisper as he pointed to a familiar silhouette. "The Galileo."

Jack leaned forward, squinting at the viewscreen. "By the stars, you're right. She's here."

A wave of emotion washed over Soren—relief, joy, and a renewed hope. If the Galileo was here, then Dana...

His thoughts were interrupted by Mark's urgent voice. "Captain, multiple contacts emerging from hyperspace. It's Harper's flotilla."

Sure enough, space behind them flickered as Harper's ships exited their folds, the sleek forms quickly settling into a defensive formation.

"Incoming transmission from Admiral Harper's flagship," Samira reported.

Soren nodded. "Put it through."

"Captain Strickland," Harper said by way of greeting. "I trust your journey was uneventful?"

"As uneventful as one might expect," Soren replied. "I see you've kept your word about bringing us here."

"I'm a man of my word, Captain. Even when that word is given under... less than ideal circumstances." He paused.

"We're being hailed by the station. Shall we proceed with docking?"

Soren hesitated for a moment, weighing his options. Every instinct screamed at him to be cautious, to demand more assurances. But Jack's advice and the sight of the Galileo, so tantalizingly close, made the decision for him.

"Agreed," he said at last. "We'll follow your lead, Admiral."

Harper nodded, and the transmission cut out. Moments later, the admiral's flagship began its approach to one of the station's massive docking arms.

"We're being hailed, Captain," Samira said.

"Open the channel," Soren replied.

"Wraith, this is Omega Station Control," a husky female voice said. "You're cleared to dock at arm sixteen. Follow the marker."

"Copy that, Control," Soren replied. "We're vectoring for landing." He nodded to Sang to bring them in.

"Confirmed, Wraith. Welcome to Omega."

The docking procedure went smoothly, the ship shuddering slightly as the magnetic clamps engaged. Soren rose from his chair, turning to address the bridge crew.

"Maintain ready stations," he ordered. "I want us prepared to disengage at a moment's notice if things go sideways." He nodded to Jack, then tapped his comm. "Liam, assemble a security detail and meet us at the airlock. We're going aboard."

Minutes later, Soren stood before the airlock, Jack at his side and Liam's Marines arrayed behind them. The airlock cycled open with a hiss of equalizing pressure, revealing a stark, utilitarian corridor beyond.

"Here we go," Soren said, exhaling sharply as they stepped onto the station. His heart continued to race, every fiber of his being eager to lay eyes on Dana, to take her in his arms and hold her tight. To tell her he loved her and was proud of her because he never said it enough and didn't want to waste a second chance.

They had barely cleared the docking arm when they encountered Harper and his entourage, including Alex and the Scorpions in their powered armor. The two groups came to an abrupt halt, eyeing each other warily. For a long moment, no one spoke.

It was Jack who finally broke the silence. "Well," he said, a note of dark humor in his voice, "this is certainly awkward."

Harper raised an eyebrow. "Indeed," he replied. "I must say, it's... disconcerting to see oneself from outside the body, as it were."

Soren watched the exchange with a mixture of fascination and unease. The two Jacks were mirror images of each other, down to the way they carried themselves. It was, as Jack had said, profoundly awkward.

Harper turned to Soren, his expression softening slightly. "Captain Strickland, I...I owe you an apology. You too, Jack. Asking you to kill my double was unconscionable. I can only hope you understand the desperation that drove me to make such a request. I'm sorry, to both of you."

Soren's jaw tightened, the memory of Harper's "deal" still raw. But before he could respond, Jack stepped forward.

"Water under the bridge," he said, his voice firm. "We've got bigger fish to fry. Stopping the Convergence is more important than grudges or personal vendettas."

Harper blinked, clearly taken aback by Jack's magnanimity. "I...thank you," he said at last. "You're right, of course. We need to focus on the task at hand."

Soren turned his attention to his son. "Alex. Are you alright? How was the trip?"

Alex shrugged. "Uneventful," he reported. "Admiral

Harper was a pretty gracious host, all things considered. We had some... interesting conversations."

Soren raised an eyebrow, glancing at Harper. "Is that so?"

Harper shrugged. "Your son is...dare I say it, a better Alexander Strickland than the one I knew. Insightful, principled. He helped me see some things from a different perspective."

"He's a natural leader," Soren agreed, unable to keep the pride from his voice."We've all made mistakes, driven by fear and desperation. But if we have any hope of stopping this convergence, we need to put aside our differences and work together."

"Agreed," Harper replied, extending his hand. "Partners?"

Soren stared at the offered hand for a long moment before clasping it firmly. "Partners," he repeated. "Now, where's Dana?"

"I'm sure both you and Alex are eager to see her," Harper said. "Follow me."

With the tension between the two groups somewhat defused, they began moving deeper into the station. As they walked, Harper filled them in on the station's purpose.

"We've been working to figure out the nature of the Convergence from this station for over three years," he explained. "We've enlisted some of the brightest minds from across the Federation to find a solution."

"But the FUP doesn't know you're here?" Soren asked.

Harper smirked. "As far as the FUP knows, Omega Station was scuttled three years ago. They've never stopped by to check that the station does in fact still exist."

"How do you bring in supplies without anyone becoming the wiser?" Jack asked. "And how did you manage to snag a whole fleet worth of warships, while we're at it? And then account for your whereabouts?"

"You know me, Jack," Harper replied. "I've always been resourceful. I pulled some of the ships from scheduled breaking, and negotiated the rest from the Outworlds. But I'm sure you noticed during our rescue, if you could call it that…we don't have the best supply of ordnance. We can't match up against the FUP, and we don't really want to. What you saw back in the Wolf System was our first tussle against our own people. We've done everything we could to stay out of their way. They think I'm on TAD, temporarily assigned to the Basilisk."

Soren smirked. "You should be glad you're not. That ship doesn't exist anymore."

"I guessed as much."

"So why did you decide to help us out back there against your FUP?" Soren asked. "I'm sure you know we could have cloaked and escaped."

"An error in judgment," Harper replied. "We knew once you activated the transponder, the FUP would pick up the signal, too. We didn't expect them to be so close to Wolf. As we planned it, our little party would have been over before the Navy ever arrived."

"Bad luck," Jack said.

"Extremely," Harper agreed, leading them to an elevator. They descended several decks before stepping out into a corridor that looked just like the last.

"Is Rashad here?" Soren asked as they continued walking.

"Sadly, our Rashad was killed when our Wraith exploded," Harper replied. "He was a great man. A real genius."

"He was."

"You'd probably like to know. Since she got here, your daughter and her crew have been leading one of our most promising research teams." He paused as they reached a set of heavy doors. "Are you ready to see her?"

Soren's heart thundered in his chest. After all this time,

all the hardship and loss, all the worries, he was moments away from reuniting with his daughter. He took a deep breath, steadying himself.

"I'm ready," he said.

CHAPTER 36

Harper pressed his palm against the scanner beside the doors, and they slid open with a soft hiss, revealing a large, circular chamber. Banks of computer terminals lined the compartment walls, their screens alive with scrolling data and complex simulations. In the center of the room stood a holographic projection of what Soren assumed to be the rift, its swirling energies casting an ethereal glow over the assembled scientists.

And there, bent over one of the terminals, her face a mask of intense concentration, was Dana.

Soren felt his breath catch in his throat. "Dana," he called out, his voice barely above a whisper.

She looked up, her mouth falling open slightly as her eyes widened in shock. For a moment, neither of them moved, the rest of the world fading away as father and daughter regarded each other across the gulf of time and space.

Then, with a cry that was a half sob, half laugh, Dana launched herself across the room. Soren caught her in his arms, holding her tight as months of pent-up emotion came pouring out.

"Dad," Dana choked out, her voice muffled against his chest. "You're here. You're really here?"

"I'm here, sweetheart," Soren murmured, stroking her hair. "I'm here. I was so worried about you. I love you. Your mom sends her love, too."

"I love you both, too," she answered.

As they embraced, a weight lifted from Soren's shoulders. Whatever challenges lay ahead, whatever dangers they might face, in this moment, everything felt right with the world.

But even as he reveled in the joy of reunion, a small part of Soren's mind remained vigilant. They had come so far, overcome so much. But the true test, he knew, was yet to come.

The convergence loomed on the horizon, a threat unlike any they had faced before. And as Soren held his daughter close, he silently vowed to do whatever it took to stop it. To save not just Dana, not just his family, but both universes from the catastrophe that threatened to engulf them all.

The moment stretched on, neither Soren nor Dana willing to be the first to break their embrace. It was only when Jack cleared his throat softly that they finally pulled apart, though Soren kept one arm wrapped protectively around his daughter's shoulders.

"Jack," Dana said, her voice thick with emotion as she reached out to hug him as well. "I can't believe you're both here."

"We couldn't very well let you have all the fun, now could we?" Jack replied, his attempt at levity barely masking his own relief at seeing her safe.

As Dana stepped back, her gaze fell on Alex. Her eyes widened in surprise. "Alex? But how...?"

Alex grinned, stepping forward to carefully embrace his sister. "It's a long story, sis. Let's just say I wasn't about to let Dad have all the glory rescuing you."

Dana laughed, the sound brightening the room. "Of course you wouldn't. I should have known."

Soren watched the exchange with a heart full to bursting. His family, all except for Jane, reunited against all odds. But as wonderful as the moment was, he knew they couldn't afford to lose focus on the larger issues at hand.

"Dana," he said gently, drawing her attention back to him. "I hate to cut this short, but we need to talk. About the Convergence, about everything that's happened in our universe."

Dana's expression sobered immediately, the joy of reunion giving way to the gravity of their situation. "Of course," she said, nodding. "You're right. There's so much to catch you up on, too."

She led them to a large conference table at the far end of the room, motioning for them to take seats. The other scientists in the room, seeming to sense the importance of the moment, quietly excused themselves.

As they settled around the table, Harper took up a position at the head, his posture straight and professional. He turned to Dana. "Why don't you start by bringing your father up to speed on our current situation?"

Dana nodded, her expression growing serious as she activated a holographic display in the center of the table. A complex web of energy patterns sprang to life, swirling and pulsing in a hypnotic dance.

"This," she began, "is our best model of the Convergence process. As you can see, it's far more complex than we initially believed. The rifts we've detected aren't just passive gateways between our universes. They're more like...wounds in the fabric of reality itself."

She manipulated the display, zooming in on one particular section. "These energy patterns here? They're not random. They're structured, almost like they're being guided by some sort of intelligence."

Soren leaned forward to study the display. "And this is why this dimension's version of me believed that someone or something is deliberately causing this."

Dana nodded, a grim smile playing at the corners of her mouth. "I don't know that we can claim this is being done on purpose but otherwise, that's exactly what we're saying. We don't know who or what is behind it, but we're certain this isn't a natural phenomenon."

The implications of her words hit Soren like a physical blow. He exchanged a glance with Jack, seeing his own shock mirrored in his old friend's eyes.

"If it's artificial," Jack said slowly, "then that means it can be stopped."

"Theoretically, yes," Dana agreed. "But it's not that simple. The process has already progressed much further than we initially realized. The boundaries between our universes are becoming increasingly unstable. If we don't find a way to reverse the Convergence soon..."

She trailed off, but Soren could fill in the rest. Total annihilation of both universes. The thought sent a chill down his spine.

"How long do we have?" he asked, dreading the answer.

Dana's expression tightened. "Based on our current models? It should have happened already."

The room fell silent as the weight of her words settled over them. Soren felt a knot of fear forming in his gut, but he pushed it aside. Fear wouldn't help them now. They needed solutions.

"So why hasn't it?" Alex asked, raising the question on most of their minds.

Dana shook her head. "We don't know. It's almost as if it's...waiting for something."

"That's not ominous," Malik quipped.

"Alright," Soren said, his voice steady despite the

turmoil in his mind. "What's our plan? How do we stop this?"

Harper leaned forward, his eyes intense. "We've identified what we believe to be the epicenter of the Convergence. A point in space where the energy patterns are most concentrated. We think if we can reach that point, we might be able to disrupt the process."

"Might?" Alex interjected, his tone skeptical. "That doesn't sound very promising."

"It's the best lead we have," Dana said. "And time is running out. We need to act, and soon."

Soren nodded, his mind already racing through potential strategies. "Where is this epicenter?"

Harper tapped a command into the table's interface, and the holographic display shifted to a star map. A red dot appeared near the center of the map, pulsing ominously.

"There," Harper said, pointing to the dot. "It's in a region of space we've come to call the Eye. No stars, no planets. And at the heart of it is the epicenter of the Convergence."

"How far?"

"About four weeks," Dana replied.

"Four weeks?" Jack said. "When the Convergence should have already happened?"

"That's not even the biggest problem we face."

"Of course it isn't," Jack muttered. "When is it ever that simple?"

Dana managed a small smile before continuing. "The Eye isn't just empty space. It's...well, we're not entirely sure what it is. Our probes have detected massive gravitational distortions, unpredictable energy surges, and temporal anomalies that defy explanation."

"In other words," Harper added, "it's a navigational nightmare."

"A deadly navigational nightmare," Dana agreed.

Soren leaned back in his chair. "So we need a ship that

can withstand these conditions. Something tough enough to punch through whatever the Eye throws at us, but agile enough to navigate the distortions." He paused, a realization dawning. "You need the Wraith."

Harper nodded, a glimmer of respect in his eyes. "Exactly. Your ship's advanced shielding and maneuverability make it our best hope of reaching the epicenter. But Dana, my Dana, believed we needed more than the Wraith. She believed we needed Soren Strickland, but ours was too dead set on war to be of any help to us. When she looked you up and saw that you were retired, she knew you were different. That you would put saving as many people as you could first. Which is also why I should have never asked you to do what I asked you to do, and why I wasn't all that surprised when you sent your Marines over to shed light on the errors of my ways."

"That sounds like an interesting story for another time," Dana said. "Even with the Wraith, even with you, Dad, it won't be easy."

"When is it ever?" Soren replied dryly. "What happens when we reach this epicenter? How do we actually stop the Convergence?"

Dana's expression grew uncertain. "That's...where things get a bit theoretical. Based on our models, we believe that the epicenter is some kind of focal point for the energy driving the Convergence. If we can disrupt that energy, introduce a counter frequency or possibly even deliver a massive nuclear blast, we might be able to unravel the whole process."

"Might," Alex repeated, his tone skeptical. "There's an awful lot of 'might' and 'maybe' in this plan."

"It's the best we've got," Dana shot back, a hint of frustration creeping into her voice. "We're dealing with forces and phenomena that push the boundaries of our understanding. Every theory, every potential solution, is a shot in the dark."

Soren held up a hand, forestalling any further argument. "It doesn't matter. We have to try. The alternative is to sit back and watch both universes be destroyed." He turned to Harper. "What resources can you provide for this mission?"

Harper straightened, his demeanor shifting from collaborative scientist to military commander in an instant. "Whatever you need, Captain. My entire fleet is at your disposal, as is everything and anything we have on this station."

"We'll need to coordinate closely. If we're going to pull this off, we'll need every advantage we can get."

"Agreed," Harper said. "I suggest we begin preparations immediately. Every moment we delay brings us closer to the point of no return."

"We're already past the point of no return. Every single second counts."

CHAPTER 37

As the others struck up side conversations related to Dana's presentation, Soren found his gaze drawn back to the holographic display of the Convergence. The swirling energies seemed to mock him, a visual representation of the chaos threatening to engulf everything he held dear.

He felt a hand on his shoulder and looked up to see Dana watching him, concern etched on her face. "Are you okay, Dad?"

Soren managed a small smile. "I'm fine, sweetheart. Just...processing everything. It's a lot to take in."

Dana nodded, understanding in her eyes. "I know. When I first realized the full scope of what we were dealing with, I...well, I didn't handle it well. But we can't afford to be overwhelmed. Not now."

"You're right," Soren agreed, straightening in his chair. "We need to focus on the task at hand. One step at a time." He turned to face her. "What happened out there? In the Wolf System. Our Wolf System."

Dana's expression hardened. "I met a version of you that I'm very glad you aren't."

"I met him, too. He tried to kill me."

"I want to hear all about how you ended up here, but I think I can guess most of it. I can just imagine you glaring stoically at a viewscreen, mentally promising that whoever hurt me would pay dearly."

Soren smiled. "It's amusing now that I found you."

"Maybe we can talk history later," Dana said. "We should talk shop right now."

"Agreed. I'm proud of you, Dana. For coming here. For all of this." He waved his hand at the hologram.

"Most of this is the other Dana's work. And Lukas'. You need to meet him, Dad. He's...incredibly bright. The most brilliant man I've ever met."

Soren immediately noticed there was something in the way she spoke about the scientist. In the way her eyes lit up. Maybe this dimension's Dana hadn't found him that alluring, but it appeared perhaps his Dana did. "Where is he?"

"We split up the teams. He's trying to figure out how to stabilize the Convergence, while my group is trying to stop it."

"Can it be stabilized?"

"Something is preventing it from happening right now. If we can figure out what that is, then maybe we can ensure it stays that way. There's still so much we don't know. But I'll definitely make sure you meet him soon. He's... amazing."

Soren wasn't quite as willing to agree to the claim, after Harper had told him Lukas was the reason the FUP found out about the Convergence. Without his hubris, their two universes wouldn't be fighting each other for their lives. "The FUP of this dimension went through the rift, Dana. They're attacking our dimension. They already took Jungle, Proxima and Tau Ceti within a month's time. Lukas may be great, and this may all seem exciting, but people are fighting and a lot of them are dying because of his ego trip. I just want to be sure you understand that."

Dana nodded somberly, her eyes glistening. "I didn't know it had started. We were hoping to figure all of this out before this dimension's FUP attacked. I know Lukas is the reason the government learned about all of this. That a lot of what's happening on our side is his fault. He knows it, too. He's doing everything he can to minimize his mistake."

"I hope it will be enough."

"Me, too."

"Alright," Soren said, his voice cutting through the ongoing conversation as he rose to his feet. "Let's lay out a concrete plan of action. Dana, I need you and your team to give us as detailed a report on these anomalies inside the Eye as possible. Once that's done, we can bring it to Ethan and Tashi to get their opinions on what we need to improve Wraith's capabilities. Admiral Harper, if we're going into the unknown, we'll need as many probes as you have to confirm whatever theories we leave here with. Alex, I want you to act as a liaison between our two groups, make sure nothing gets lost in the translation. I know that's not the same as Force Recon, but it's an important job. One I think you're well equipped to handle. Jack, head back to Wraith with the security detail and the Scorpions. I could be wrong, but I don't think they want to spend the rest of their lives in that armor. I'll be along shortly."

"We'll get right on it," Dana said, smiling proudly as she turned away to consult with her team.

"I'll speak to my techs," Harper said.

"Whatever I, and the rest of my team, can do to help, Captain," Alex said. "But yeah, it would be nice to get out of these tin cans for a while."

"It would be nice for me to be able to hug my brother properly," Dana added, smiling at Alex.

Soren felt a familiar sense of purpose settle over him.

The odds were stacked against them, the dangers ahead almost unimaginable. But they had faced impossible odds before and had come out on top.

They would do so again. They had to. The very fabric of reality depended on it.

As the others left to handle their assigned tasks, Harper approached, his expression serious. "Captain Strickland, a word before you go?"

"You can call me Soren if you'd like. I'll call you Harper, if you don't mind, just to keep me from becoming confused. What's on your mind?"

"Soren," Harper said, "I know you don't completely trust me. I don't blame you for that. But I need you to understand something. What we're about to attempt isn't just dangerous. It's probably suicidal. And the odds of success are…" He trailed off.

Soren's eyes narrowed. "Are you having second thoughts, Admiral?"

Harper shook his head vehemently. "No. This is our only shot, and we have to take it. But I need to know that you're prepared for what might happen. If we fail, if the Convergence can't be stopped…"

"Then both our universes will be doomed," Soren finished for him. "I'm well aware of the stakes, Harper."

"Are you?" Harper pressed. "Because it's more than just the fate of our universes at stake here. If we fail, if the Convergence happens, we have no idea what it will do to us as individuals. Will we merge with our counterparts? Will one version cease to exist? Or will we all simply be obliterated in the cosmic collision?"

Soren felt a chill run down his spine at Harper's words. He had considered these possibilities, of course, but hearing them laid out so starkly brought the true horror of their situation into even sharper focus.

"What are you getting at, Harper?" he asked, his voice low and intense.

The Admiral met his gaze unflinchingly. "I'm saying that we need to be prepared for every eventuality. Including the possibility that we might have to make some very difficult decisions in the heat of the moment."

Soren's jaw clenched as he understood Harper's implication. "You're talking about sacrificing one universe to save the other."

Harper nodded. "It may come to that. And if it does, we need to be ready to make that call. No hesitation, no second-guessing. The fate of billions, maybe trillions, could hang in the balance."

For a long moment, Soren said nothing, wrestling with the moral implications of what Harper suggested. Could he make that kind of choice? Sacrifice an entire universe, potentially including alternate versions of everyone he loved, to save his own? Or, on the flip side, could he sacrifice his universe, including Jane, for this one?

Finally, he spoke, his voice tight with emotion. "I hear what you're saying, Admiral. And I understand the reasoning behind it. If we have to make a decision like that, then let's agree to put our personal motives and desires aside. We pivot in whatever direction saves the most lives. Agreed?"

Harper studied him for a moment, then nodded. "Agreed. I just needed to know where you stood on this. For what it's worth, I hope it doesn't come to that."

"So do I," Soren replied. He turned to leave, then paused at the door. "And Harper? If it does come down to making that kind of choice...it won't be your call to make. It'll be mine."

With that, he strode out of the room, leaving a stunned Harper in his wake. The weight of command had never felt heavier, the stakes never higher.

CHAPTER 38

Soren stood at the head of the conference table aboard the Wraith, his gaze sweeping over the assembled bridge and engineering crew. A palpable sense of anticipation hung over the room as they waited for him to speak. He took a deep breath, centering himself before beginning.

"I know you're all wondering what we've learned," he began, his voice steady and measured. "The situation is...complex, to say the least. But I'll do my best to bring you up to speed."

Over the next hour, Soren laid out everything they had discovered about the Convergence, the nature of the rifts, and the desperate race against time they now found themselves in. He watched as expressions of shock, disbelief, and determination played across the faces of his crew.

"The Eye," he concluded, "is our destination. It's where we believe we can stop this madness once and for all. But it won't be easy. We're facing dangers we can barely comprehend, let alone prepare for."

A heavy silence fell over the room as the crew absorbed the enormity of what they were facing. Ethan finally broke it, leaning forward with a determined glint in his eye.

"So, what's our next move, Captain?"

Soren allowed himself a small smile. This was why he had chosen this crew and trusted them with his life. No matter the odds, they were always ready to face the challenge head-on.

"Dana and her team are working on a detailed report of the anomalies we can expect to encounter in the Eye," he explained. "Ethan, I want you, Tashi, and Wilf to come with me back to the station. Once we have that report, I need you three to start working on ways to improve Wraith's capabilities. We need every edge we can get."

Ethan nodded. "We'll make it happen, Captain. Whatever it takes."

"Good," Soren replied. "I'll make sure to keep the rest of you apprised of the situation as it develops further. In the meantime, do what you can to hone your skills. Even the smallest improvement could be the difference between success and death."

As the crew dispersed to their tasks, Soren motioned for Ethan, Tashi, and Wilf to follow him. They made their way back to the station, the corridors seeming more ominous now that they understood the true scope of the threat they faced.

They found Dana and her team hard at work in the main research lab, holographic displays flickering with complex equations and swirling energy patterns. She looked up as they entered, a tired smile spreading across her face.

"Dad," she said, stepping away from her workstation. "I was hoping you'd be back soon."

Soren nodded, then gestured to his companions. "Dana, I'd like you to meet Tashi and Wilf. They're two of the brightest minds we have aboard Wraith. And of course, you remember Ethan."

Dana's eyes widened in recognition. "Ethan? It's been years! The last time I saw you, I was just a little girl."

Ethan chuckled, a warm smile crinkling the corners of his eyes. "I remember bouncing you on my knee. You've grown up quite a bit since then. Though I have to say, you're still causing just as much trouble."

Dana laughed, the sound brightening the somber atmosphere of the lab. "Some things never change, I guess." She turned to Tashi and Wilf, extending her hand. "It's great to meet you both."

Tashi shook her hand enthusiastically, his eyes wide with excitement. "It's an honor to meet you. The Captain went through so much to find you. It's obvious how much he loves you."

Wilf nodded in agreement, his fingers twitching with nervous excitement. "I wish I had somebody who cared about me that much. Thanks to your father, I kind of feel like I do, now. He's a great man, so I'm sure you're a great woman. And of course, your work on the Convergence is… just…wow." He trailed off awkwardly.

Dana blushed slightly at the praise. "Thank you, both of you. But I can't take the credit. A lot of this work builds on what the other Dana started. And of course, Lukas has been instrumental in pushing our understanding forward."

At the mention of Lukas, Soren felt a flicker of unease. He pushed it aside, focusing on the task at hand. "Speaking of your work, how's that report coming along? Ethan and his team will need it to start working on upgrades for the Wraith."

Dana nodded, her expression growing serious. "We're close to finishing. The anomalies in the Eye are difficult to model. But I think we've managed to categorize the main types of phenomena we're likely to face."

She led them to the large holographic display, manipulating the controls to bring up a swirling vortex of energy. "This is our best model of the Eye's interior, based on the algorithms we've produced. Of course, we have yet to visit in person to confirm our math is right, but all indications are that it is. As you can see, we're dealing with extreme gravitational distortions, unpredictable energy surges, and temporal anomalies that defy our current understanding of physics."

Wilf leaned in, closely following the movements of energy within the eye. "Those patterns don't look random."

Dana shook her head. "You have a good eye, Wilf. They're not random. There's a structure to them, almost like they're being guided by some kind of intelligence. It's part of why we believe the Convergence isn't a natural phenomenon."

"Do you have preliminary estimations on the force of the energy surges within the Eye?" Ethan asked. "That'll give us an immediate idea of what kind of power requirements we might need for shielding."

"Of course," Dana said. She tapped on the terminal connected to the display. The movement came to a stop, and a list of properties appeared beside each of the events inside the Eye. "You can review this before the report is finished, if you'd like."

"Thank you," Ethan said. "We'll get to work on this right away."

The three engineers quickly fell into a deep discussion on the various measurements and speculating on potential countermeasures. Soren watched them for a moment, a spark of hope kindling in his chest. If anyone could find a way to navigate the impossible, it was this team, with the help of the researchers and scientists on the station.

He turned to Dana. "You look like you could use a break. How about we take a walk? Get a little one-on-one time."

Dana hesitated for a moment, glancing back at her

work. Then she nodded, a look of relief crossing her face. "You're right. I could use some fresh air...well, as fresh as it gets on a space station."

They excused themselves, leaving Ethan, Tashi, and Wilf engrossed in a discussion with Dana's team. As they walked through the station's corridors, Soren exhaled some of his residual tension. Despite the monumental challenges they faced, he had his daughter back. It was more than he had dared to hope for when Montoya interrupted his morning at the lake.

"So," he said softly as they walked, "is now a good time for me to ask you what happened to you in our Wolf System?"

"It's as good a time as any," she replied. She took a deep breath, her eyes distant as she recalled the events. "We were within a few days of the Wolf System when we picked up a distress signal over common frequencies. An unencrypted transponder signal that suggested a private vessel had gone somewhere it shouldn't have and ran into trouble. Being the closest available ship, we altered course to investigate. That's when we found a prior generation Valkyrie-class cruiser dead in space. Well, worse than dead. It had been torn apart, like a fish that wound up at the wrong end of a shark."

She paused, her expression growing somber. "We sent over a probe to investigate. That's when I saw her. The other Dana. She was in the command chair, but her face...it had been ruined by shrapnel. I didn't recognize her at first."

Soren felt a chill run down his spine at the thought of seeing his daughter like that, even if it wasn't really his Dana. "What happened then?"

"We were so focused on the Valkyrie that we didn't notice the other ship until it was too late. The Basilisk. It must have been cloaked, though we didn't know about that technology at the time. One moment, we were alone. The next, there it was, right on top of us."

Dana's voice grew tight as she continued. "They demanded our surrender. We didn't have much choice. They docked with us, and then...he came aboard."

"The other me," Soren said softly.

Dana nodded. "At first, he was angry. Furious, even. But then he saw me, and it was like something broke inside him. All the anger vanished. The commanding attitude crumbled. His eyes filled with tears."

They reached the elevators at the center of the station. Dana called one, indicating she had a clear destination in mind for their journey.

"That's when I learned who the commander of the Valkyrie was. He told me everything. About the Convergence, about the coming war. About what he had done to his own daughter and why. He said after seeing me, he regretted the decision. That he should have spared her and killed me instead. But...but he didn't want to leave both universes without a Dana." She shook her head. "The whole conversation was strange. He told me about his plans to kill you, Dad. And then he told me where to find the rift."

Soren's jaw clenched at the mention of his alternate self's plans. "Why didn't you send back a warning? To let us know what was coming?"

Dana turned to face him, her eyes glistening with unshed tears. "Don't you think I wanted to? He disabled Galileo's comms. We couldn't send any messages. He gave us one choice and one choice only. Go through the rift to the other Wolf System."

She took a shuddering breath. "He said he didn't want to have to kill Dana twice, but he would if I tried to warn anyone. There were too many lives at stake for him to put mine first. I didn't know what else to do, so I agreed. He set the course in Galileo's nav computer himself to ensure we went in the right direction. I...I was terrified, Dad. This dimension's Soren was...broken, in some way. It was awful."

Soren pulled her into a tight embrace, his heart aching for what she had been through. "You did the right thing, sweetheart. You survived. You found a way to keep fighting."

Dana nodded against his chest. "Admiral Harper found me not long after I arrived in this dimension's Wolf System. He brought me here, to the station. We've been working ever since to find a way to stop the Convergence." She pulled back, wiping her eyes. "What about you, Dad? How did you end up here?"

They exited the elevator, continuing through the station. Soren started at the beginning, telling Dana about the desperate search for her, the discovery of the Wraith, their encounter with the other Soren, and Alex's ordeal on Jungle. Everything, all the way up to the moment they docked at Omega Station.

It took nearly an hour, and Dana listened with rapt attention. By the time he finished with what happened on Proxima, they had settled near a viewport, standing together on either side of it and looking out at the ships docked to the station and beyond.

Now, they stood in silence, each lost in their own thoughts, both thankful to be together. The enormity of what they faced seemed to press in around them, the weight of two universes resting on their shoulders.

The sound of a door sliding open broke the quiet. They turned to see an average-height, slightly-built man with a mop of curly brown hair emerge from one of the nearby labs, his head bent over a data pad. As he looked up, his eyes widened in shock.

"Dana!" he exclaimed, a bright smile spreading across

his face. But as his gaze shifted to Soren, that smile faltered, replaced by a look of terror. "Cap...Captain Strick...Strickland, sir. I...uh...I..."

Dana quickly stepped forward. "Lukas, it's okay! This is my father, Soren. From my dimension."

The man immediately relaxed, though a wary expression remained on his face. He approached cautiously, extending a hand.

"Captain Strickland," he said, his voice tight with barely contained emotion. "I...I can't begin to tell you how sorry I am. For everything. If I hadn't been so foolish, so desperate for recognition..."

Soren studied the man before him. This was the brilliant mind behind their understanding of the Convergence. The man whose actions had inadvertently set in motion the events that now threatened both their universes.

For a moment, Soren felt a surge of anger. It would be easy to blame this man, to make him a scapegoat for all their suffering and loss. But as he looked into Lukas' eyes, he saw genuine remorse, and a desperate desire to make things right.

Soren took Lukas' offered hand, shaking it firmly. "What's done is done," he said, his voice level. "We can't change the past. What matters now is what we do going forward. Can you help us stop this?"

Lukas nodded vigorously. "Yes. Yes, absolutely. I've been working non-stop, trying to find a way to reverse the process. With Dana's help, I think we might be close to a breakthrough."

"Good," Soren replied. "Because time is running out. We need solutions, and we need them fast."

"Yes, sir. We're all giving two hundred percent. I haven't slept more than four hours a day in months. Sometimes I think Dana is the only thing that's kept me sane."

Soren's eyes narrowed. "What are your intentions toward my daughter, Lukas?"

Lukas swallowed hard, frightened once more. "What? Oh…well. I mean…I…"

"Now doesn't seem like the best time for romance," Soren pressed.

"Dad!" Dana complained. "I'm an adult. You don't need to—"

"Dana, you have more important things to devote your time to," Soren said directly to her. "That goes for both of you and anyone else on this station."

"I won't lie, I think your daughter is amazing," Lukas said. "But you're right, romance can wait until we stop the Convergence."

"We've already arrived at that conclusion," Dana added. "So you can spare us any lectures."

Soren took a deep breath, embarrassed by his outburst. "Of course. My apologies to both of you. I shouldn't have presumed."

"The Soren Strickland I knew would never have apologized to anyone for any reason," Lukas said. "I respect your humility, sir. Dana's told me so many wonderful things about you, it isn't unexpected."

"It's okay, Dad," Dana added. "We're all under a lot of pressure here. And I know you mean well. Let's just all stay focused on the Convergence, and save any personal drama for later."

Soren nodded. "Agreed."

She turned to Lukas. "Any progress on the stabilization theories?"

"Unfortunately, no," he replied. "That's why I have my pad in hand. Going to the chow hall for a working lunch. Would you two care to join me?"

"We should get back to my lab to check on things," Dana said. "But I'm sure I'll catch up with you later."

"Of course. It was an honor to meet you, Captain Strickland."

"You as well, Lukas. Enjoy your chow."

Lukas smiled sheepishly. "Probably not, but at least it'll keep me alive." He nodded to Dana, touching her arm before he hurried off.

She immediately turned to him. "Really, Dad? Did you have to do that?"

"I can't just turn off being an overprotective father," Soren replied.

She laughed. "Embarrassing in the moment, but I wouldn't have it any other way. Let's go see if your team has come up with anything."

CHAPTER 39

"Captain!" Ethan's voice came through Soren's comm, tinged with excitement. "Could you come down to the research lab? We've got something you need to see."

"On my way," Soren replied, his curiosity piqued. He lowered his data pad to his desk aboard the Wraith and got to his feet. After three days of waiting for news from the combined engineering and research teams, it appeared they had finally had a breakthrough.

He made his way through the Wraith's corridors, through the airlock and across to Omega Station in short order. Nodding to everyone he passed—crew and technicians alike—his presence on the station was no longer a strange sight for the researchers who had either known or heard about the Captain Strickland of the other dimension.

As the doors to the research lab slid open, Soren was greeted by an unexpected sight. Gathered around a large holographic display were not just Ethan and his team and Dana and hers, but also Lina, Sophie, Lukas, Harper, and Alex. They all looked up as he entered, their serious expressions suggesting they had been deep in weighty discussion only minutes before.

Soren approached the table, his eyes immediately drawn to the detailed schematic floating above the surface. A cross-section of the Wraith, it showed every system and component of the ship laid bare in intricate three-dimensional detail.

"Captain Strickland," Harper said. "Thank you for joining us on such short notice."

"I've been waiting for this meeting for days," Soren replied, circling the table to the last remaining empty seat. He turned to Ethan as he sat, noting the barely contained look of excitement in his chief engineer's eyes. "Alright, Ethan. I know that look. You have a solution."

Ethan's face lit up as he leaned forward to use the terminal attached to the table. "Captain, we've been crunching the numbers based on the algorithmic estimates of the Eye's energy patterns and running them up against Rashad's tables for shield power transfer rates and electricity availability, plus maximum generator absorption data and other vital calculations."

"And?" Soren asked.

He zoomed in on the Wraith's shield generators, the hologram flickering and reforming to show the intricate network of power conduits and emitters. "Well, what we discovered is that, assuming the estimates Dana's team have made are close to correct, the only way we have even a snowball's chance in hell of surviving those energy surges in the Eye would be to double our shield resistance."

"Even though Wraith has some of the most powerful shields ever installed on a starship?" Soren asked.

"Scary, right?" Tashi said. "Well…I mean, not scary. That's probably a bad word. But—"

"Yes, Captain," Ethan interrupted. "Her shields are powerful, but we're pretty sure they won't be enough. Our best estimate is that the Wraith can survive inside the Eye for three minutes, at most."

"But that should be enough time to get in and set off whatever device or weapon we want to fire on the Eye, shouldn't it?" Soren asked.

"Possibly," Lukas said. "It depends on how large the Eye really is. We've estimated the volume, but if the numbers are off…"

"Meaning it's risky to go in without the added shielding," Dana said. "And less risky with it."

"Doubling the shields won't double our time," Ethan said. "It'll quadruple it. We'll have twelve minutes instead of three."

"Estimated," Soren said.

"For now," Harper answered. "Once we reach the Eye, we can use the probes we're bringing to try to verify the numbers and get a more precise survival time, but there's no way to account for all of the variables."

"Bottom line, Captain," Wilf said. "More shields can't hurt." His fingers nodded in agreement.

"Understood, Wilf," Soren answered. "Correct me if I'm wrong, but won't doubling the shield strength put more of a strain on our reactors?"

"Absolutely," Ethan replied. "Too much strain, in fact. But we've put together a plan. It's crazy, it's ambitious, and it just might work." He used the controls to highlight sections of the schematic. "We want to install a third reactor, Captain. Right here…" He pointed to the location of choice. "…in this cargo bay near the core."

He shifted the hologram, showing an animation of a massive reactor. Tashi spoke up before Ethan could continue, his voice rising with excitement. "We can't put it directly in the core without a major overhaul, but we can route the power effectively from that cargo bay. It'll be tight, but we can bring it in through the hangar bay doors without compromising the outer hull and risking our cloaking ability."

Lina picked up the thread, her normally calm voice tinged with a hint of nervousness. "Once the reactor's in place, we'll need to beef up the shield generators. We're looking at installing either significantly heavier wiring or a second, parallel circuit to handle the increased load."

Soren absorbed the information, considering the implications. "If this is possible, why hasn't the Navy implemented something like this in their ships?"

Harper let out a dry chuckle. "In a word? Money. The resources required, the man-hours, the equipment...it's a logistical nightmare that the beancounters have deemed too costly versus the chance of survivability."

"Because every spacer has a price tag on them," Soren agreed.

"Even you," Alex added.

Ethan nodded in agreement, his expression growing serious. "It's not just a matter of doubling our output, Captain. To achieve double the shield strength, we're looking at seriously upgrading our power generation and distribution systems. The material requirements scale logarithmically. We're talking about three times the resources for twice the effectiveness."

Soren's jaw tightened as he considered the enormity of what they were proposing. "And how long would all of this take to implement?" he asked, his voice low and intense. "Remember, we're already out of time."

The room fell silent for a moment, the weight of the question hanging in the air. It was Harper who finally answered, his voice gruff. "With everyone working around the clock, pushing themselves to the limit? We're looking at about six weeks."

Soren's hope faded as quickly as it had risen. Six weeks. In the face of a convergence that could happen at any moment, it felt like an eternity.

"We might be able to cut that down to four weeks," Ethan said. "If we put the Scorpions to work, we can speed up some of the heavy lifting."

"How can we help?" Alex asked.

"We need a lot of heavy materials moved and bulkheads torn down, and while standard equipment can do the job, I think your team in your power armor can do it faster."

Alex considered the idea. "Yeah, I think we can make it work. The Scorpions are definitely up for the challenge."

Soren turned back to the group, his gaze intense. "Assuming we can pull this off in four weeks, will it be enough? Will it give us a fighting chance inside the Eye?"

"Captain, I wish I could say yes with absolute certainty," Lukas said. "The truth is, there's nothing we can do to fully protect against everything we think you'll encounter inside the eye. The temporal distortions and shifting magnetic and gravitational fields don't care about physical shields and are beyond our current technological capabilities to directly counteract. Fortunately, that doesn't mean we can't at least give ourselves more of a fighting chance. What we can do is update and upgrade Wraith's sensors to better identify these anomalies. With improved detection, you should be able to steer around the worst of the distortions. It's not perfect, but it's the best we can do with the time and resources we have."

Harper placed his hands on the table. "Bottom line, Soren, it's still going to be risky as hell. We're talking about flying into the heart of a cosmic storm with nothing but theories and hope to guide us. But with these upgrades, we're looking at a fighting chance instead of certain failure. It's a long shot, but it's the only shot we've got."

Soren looked around the room, taking in the determined faces of his crew and their allies. They had come so far, overcome so much. Now, they stood on the precipice of their greatest challenge yet. The weight of two universes rested on their shoulders, the fate of countless lives hanging in the balance.

He straightened, his voice filled with resolve as he spoke. "So," he said, a hint of a smile tugging at the corners of his mouth, "what are we waiting for?"

CHAPTER 40

Alex wiped the sweat from his brow, the faceplate of his Karuta power armor retracting momentarily to allow him the simple pleasure. The air inside the Wraith's corridor was thick with the smell of plasma and melted metal, a reminder of the grueling work they had been engaged in for the past two weeks.

"How much further, Gunny?" Malik asked over the comm, his voice tinged with fatigue but still carrying that undercurrent of enthusiasm that seemed inexhaustible with him.

Alex closed his faceplate again to consult the schematic projected on his HUD. "We're almost there," he replied, his eyes tracing the intricate network of power conduits and structural supports. "This should be the last bulkhead before we reach the entry to the core."

The corridor behind them was a mess of exposed wiring and pulled-up deck plating. The Scorpions had been working tirelessly, using their armor's enhanced strength and plasma torches to carve a path through the Wraith's innards. It was challenging work, requiring a delicate balance between brute force and surgical precision.

"I never thought I'd say this," Sarah chimed in, her plasma cutter sputtering as she expertly sliced through part of the bulkhead, "but I'm starting to miss dodging enemy fire."

Jackson laughed, the sound echoing strangely through their helmet comms. "Careful what you wish for, Two."

"Alright, Scorpions," Alex said. "Let's make this final push count. Sarah, Malik, you're on point with torches. Jackson, Zoe, be ready with the support struts. The last thing we need is to botch this and compromise structural integrity this close to the core."

The hiss and smell of ozone from Sarah and Malik's torches filled the air. The concentrated plasma easily dug into the bulkhead, leaving glowing red lines of slagged metal behind. Once they cut out part of the bulkhead, they carefully pushed the bottom inward with their feet and caught the top in their hands, easily lifting the cut pieces' substantial weights and moving them aside. The current supports blocked their path, so Jackson and Zoe moved in with custom-made replacements, positioning them further out and using the strength of their armor to shift them into place.

"Ready," Zoe said, backing away. Sarah and Malik replaced them, slicing through the supports first. Alex helped remove the thick beams and move them aside before Sarah and Malik replaced him again.

"Breakthrough in ten seconds," Malik called out, his voice steady despite the strain evident in his posture.

Alex tensed, ready to react if anything went wrong.

"Five... four... three... two... one... Breakthrough!"

With a resounding crack, the bulkhead gave way. A rush of cooler air swept over them as the pressures equalized.

"Good work, Four," Alex said, clapping Malik on the shoulder. "Alright, team. Let's secure this opening and—"

"Nice work, Scorpions," a familiar voice interrupted. "Right on schedule."

Alex turned to see Ethan and Tashi approaching from the newly opened corridor.

"Chief," Alex greeted, his faceplate retracting to reveal a tired smile. "Tashi. Come to check up on us?"

Ethan nodded, his eyes roving over the exposed circuitry and structural supports. "More like we're here to finish the connection in your wake."

Tashi, meanwhile, had pulled out a data pad and was furiously comparing the real-life results to the schematics they had been working from.

"How's it looking?" Alex asked, a hint of nervousness creeping into his voice. They had been working non-stop for days, pushing themselves to the limit to finish the work as quickly as possible. He could only hope they hadn't made a mistake.

Tashi looked up, a grin spreading across his face. "It's all right on target. I'm impressed, Gunny."

Ethan nodded approvingly. "You've done good work here, Alex. All of you have."

"I noticed we bypassed some of the emergency bulk-heads to create this opening," Alex said. "If any of those sections suffer a breach, we won't be able to seal them off from the core."

"I know," Ethan replied. "A necessary evil, I'm afraid. We couldn't find a way to make the connections work otherwise."

"Beats the hell out of being torn apart in the Eye," Malik said.

"Besides, with your father at the conn, we won't have any hull breaches," Tashi said confidently.

"So, what's next?" Alex asked.

Tashi consulted his data pad again. "Well, now that you've broken through to this corridor, we can start running the heavy wiring from the engine room. It's going to be a tight fit, but with the pathway you've created, we should be able to make it work."

Ethan nodded in agreement. "We'll take it from here, Alex. You and your team have done the heavy lifting, quite literally. Now it's time for some delicate work." He paused, a thoughtful expression crossing his face. "Actually, why don't you check in with Lina? Last I heard, she was working on some upgrades to the shield generators on Deck Four. I'm sure she could use some muscle there as well. Unless you need a break?"

"No, we're good," Alex replied. "The sooner we get this work done the better. Just say the word if you need us back here."

As Ethan and Tashi moved past them to inspect the newly opened pathway, Alex turned to his team. "Let's head to Deck Four and see what Lina might have for us."

They made their way through the ship's corridors, their armored forms drawing glances from the crew members they passed. The Wraith was a hive of activity, everyone working tirelessly towards their common goal. The sense of urgency was palpable, hanging in the air like an invisible fog.

As they approached a junction, Alex caught sight of a familiar group coming from the opposite direction. His father was deep in conversation with Lukas and Dana, their expressions intense as they pored over a data pad.

"Dad," Alex called out, causing the trio to look up.

Soren's face softened slightly as he saw his son. "Alex," he greeted, his voice warm despite the evident strain in his features. "How's the work progressing?"

"We just finished creating the pathway for the new reactor's power conduits," Alex reported. "Ethan and Tashi are taking over from here. We're on our way to help Lina with the shield generators."

Dana's eyes lit up at the mention of the shields. "You finished already? That's perfect. We were just discussing some adjustments we need to make to the probes. The latest data from the probes outside the Eye...well, it's not great."

Alex felt a chill run down his spine at his sister's words. "Not great...how?"

Lukas stepped forward, his face a mask of barely contained worry. "We've noticed a subtle shift in the energy patterns. It's concerning, to say the least."

"Concerning how?" Alex pressed, dreading the answer but knowing he needed to hear it.

Lukas exchanged a glance with Soren before continuing. "The patterns we've been observing, they're becoming more erratic. More unstable. If our calculations are correct, it could mean that the Eye is starting to collapse."

The implications hit Alex like a physical blow. "And if the Eye collapses...?"

"The convergence begins," Soren finished.

Alex looked at his father, seeing the lines of worry etched deep in his face. For a moment, he was struck by how much older Soren looked, the strain of command and the burden of their mission aging him almost overnight.

"How long?" he asked, dreading the answer but knowing they needed to face the reality of their situation.

Dana shook her head, frustration evident in her voice. "It's hard to say for certain. The data is changing rapidly. We're extrapolating based on speculative models that were never truly meant to handle this kind of phenomenon."

"Our best estimate," Lukas added, his voice tight, "is that we have maybe twelve weeks before the Eye reaches a critical point of instability. After that..." He trailed off, the unspoken consequences hanging heavy in the air.

Alex felt his heart sink. Twelve weeks. They had barely started the upgrades to the Wraith, and already their timeline was shrinking. "That's cutting it close," he said, struggling to keep his voice steady. "Too close."

Soren nodded, his jaw set in a determined line. "Which is why we're on our way to speak with Ethan. We need to see if there's any way to speed up the upgrades. Every hour, every minute counts now."

"What can we do to help?" Alex asked, gesturing to his team. "Just say the word, and we're there."

A ghost of a smile flickered across Soren's face, pride shining in his eyes despite the gravity of the situation. "Keep doing what you're doing. Your work with Lina on the shield generators is crucial. We'll need every ounce of protection we can get when we enter the Eye."

Alex nodded, straightening his posture. "Understood. We won't let you down."

"I know you won't," Soren replied softly. He placed a hand on Alex's armored shoulder. "Be careful, son. All of you. We can't afford any accidents, not now."

"You got it, Dad," Alex said, his voice thick with emotion. "You be careful, too."

With a final nod, Soren, Dana, and Lukas continued on their way, their hushed voices fading as they rounded the corner. Alex stood there for a moment, watching them go, a maelstrom of emotions churning inside him.

"You okay, Gunny?" Zoe's voice broke through his reverie, concern evident in her tone.

Alex took a deep breath, centering himself. "Yeah, I'm good. Just... processing."

"It's a lot to take in," Sarah added, her usual bravado subdued. "We were already out of time, but now we seem to have a hard deadline."

"Yeah, too soon," Alex agreed. He turned to face his team, taking in their worried expressions. Even through the armored faceplates, he could see the uncertainty in their eyes. It was a look he had seen too often lately, one that he felt mirrored in his own chest.

"Listen up, Scorpions," he said, his voice taking on the firm, confident tone he used when rallying his team. "I know the odds are stacked against us. But we've faced impossible situations before, and we've come out on top. This is no different."

"But Gunny," Malik interjected, "this isn't just another mission. We're talking about the end of everything. Both our universes. How do we even begin to face something like that?"

Alex nodded, acknowledging the weight of Malik's words. "One step at a time. That's how. We focus on what's in front of us. Right now, that means helping Lina with those shield generators. We do that job, and we do it well. Then we move on to the next task, and the next. We keep pushing, keep fighting, until we succeed." He looked at each of his team members in turn, willing them to feel the conviction in his words. "We're Scorpions. We don't quit. We don't give up. No matter the odds, no matter the enemy. We stand together, we fight together, and we win together. Is that clear?"

"Oorah!" The response came in unison, a chorus of resolve that echoed through the corridor.

Alex felt a surge of pride and affection for his team. They had been through so much together, and now here they were, ready to stare down the end of the universe itself.

"Alright then," he said, a hint of a smile in his voice. "Let's not keep Lina waiting. We've got a ship to upgrade and two universes to save."

As they resumed their journey to Deck Four, Alex couldn't shake the nagging worry in the back of his mind. Would they make it in time? Would all their efforts, all their sacrifices be enough?

He pushed the doubts aside, focusing on the task at hand. They had a job to do, and he would see it through. No matter what.

The Scorpions moved through the ship with purpose, their armored forms a reflection of the strength and resilience they would need in the days to come.

They would make it. They had to. The alternative was unthinkable.

As they approached Deck Four, the familiar hum of the Wraith's systems took on a different quality. There was an underlying tension, a sense of urgency that permeated every corner of the ship. Everyone knew what was at stake, and everyone was pushing themselves to the limit.

"There's Lina," Sarah called out, pointing towards a cluster of activity near one of the main shield generator access points.

Alex nodded, leading his team towards the chief of maintenance. Lina was bent over a complex array of circuitry, her fingers moving with practiced precision as she made adjustments to the delicate components. She looked up as they approached, a tired smile crossing her face.

"Scorpions," she greeted, straightening up with a wince. "Ethan told me you were headed my way. We've got our work cut out for us here."

"What do you need from us?" Alex asked, his team forming a semicircle around her.

Lina gestured to the exposed innards of the shield generator. "We're upgrading the power transfer modules to handle the increased load from the new reactor. It's delicate work, but we also need to move some of the heavier components. That's where you come in."

She pointed to a nearby stack of large, cylinder-shaped objects. "Those are the new superconducting coils. We need to install them in place of the old ones, but they're too heavy for standard equipment to maneuver in these tight spaces. With your armor, you should be able to place them precisely where we need them."

Alex nodded, already assessing the best approach. "Understood."

As his team moved to their assigned tasks, he couldn't help but marvel at the complexity of the work before them. The shield generators were a marvel of engineering, a delicate balance of raw power and precise control. And now they were pushing that technology to its absolute limits, all in a desperate bid to survive the unimaginable forces they would face inside the Eye.

"Overall, how's it looking, Lina?" he asked, watching as Malik and Zoe carefully maneuvered the first of the superconducting coils into position. "Are we going to make it in time?"

Lina's expression tightened, a flicker of worry crossing her face before she schooled it back into professional calm. "It's going to be close, Alex. We're making good progress, but these upgrades are pushing the boundaries of what's theoretically possible. Every system we touch, we're finding new challenges, new problems to solve."

She paused, watching as Sarah and Jackson delicately reconnected a series of power couplings. "But we're not giving up. Not by a long shot. Your father's got the entire crew working in shifts around the clock. If anyone can pull this off, it's us."

Alex nodded. The Wraith's crew had always been exceptional, but in the face of this crisis, they were proving themselves to be truly extraordinary. He attributed at least some of that to his father's calm demeanor and steady hand. He knew how to push the right buttons with people to get the most out of them.

"Careful with that coil, Malik," he called out, noticing a slight wobble in the massive component as his teammate maneuvered it into place. "We can't afford any mistakes, not with these tolerances."

"Got it, Gunny," Malik replied, his voice strained with effort even through the armor's systems. "This thing's heavier than it looks."

For the next few hours, Alex and his team worked tirelessly alongside Lina and her engineers. The work was grueling, a constant dance of brute force and microscopic precision. Every component they replaced, every system they upgraded, brought them one step closer to their goal. But with each passing minute, Alex couldn't shake the growing sense of urgency that gnawed at the back of his mind.

As they were finishing up the installation of the final superconducting coil, a loud, repeating gong came from the ship's speakers, immediately joined by flashing red lights along the entire corridor.

"Is that a red alert?" Jackson asked, looking away from the coil.

"All hands to battle stations. Captain to the bridge," Vic said, his voice quivering slightly over the loudspeakers. "I repeat, all hands to battle stations. This is not a drill."

"Sounds like a red alert to me," Zoe said.

"Alex, we're good here," Lina said. "Whatever's happening, go do what you can to help."

CHAPTER 41

Soren stood in Wraith's hangar bay, his eyes scanning the bustling activity around him. The space echoed with the sounds of machinery and urgent voices as crew members rushed to complete final preparations. Beside him, Dana and Lukas huddled over a data pad, their faces illuminated by its soft glow as they pored over the latest sensor readings from the Eye.

"These energy fluctuations are intensifying faster than we anticipated," Dana murmured, her brow furrowed in concentration. "We might need to recalibrate the drone sensors again to account for the increased instability."

Lukas nodded as he made rapid calculations on his pad. "Agreed. If we adjust the filters, we should be able to compensate."

"Captain," Phoebe said. He turned to see the aerospace boss approaching, a determined set to her shoulders. "We've finished loading the last of the modified drones. They're primed and ready for deployment on your order."

"Excellent work, Commander," Soren replied, nodding his approval. "How many do we have now?"

Phoebe's expression tightened slightly. "Twenty-seven, Captain."

"There are more on the support ships," Dana said, looking up from the data pad. "We have nearly a hundred drones altogether, with updated sensors and software packages."

"We'll need them," Lukas said. "Once we launch a drone, we'll be lucky if it lasts thirty seconds out there."

Soren opened his mouth to respond, but before he could, a loud, repeating gong came from the ship's speakers, immediately joined by flashing red lights throughout the hangar bay.

"All hands to battle stations. Captain to the bridge," Vic said, his voice quivering slightly over the loudspeakers. "I repeat, all hands to battle stations. This is not a drill."

Soren's blood ran cold, but he was on his way before he could take his next breath. He hit the bulkhead vertically adjacent to the hatch, pushed off it and leaped through it into a mass of crew members rushing to their duty stations. He pushed past them, slid sideways, and darted around others. Red lights flashed down the corridor, and the alarm was still blaring.

"Captain!" Mark's urgent voice erupted in his ear. "Sensors just picked up multiple contacts entering the system."

"Hostiles?"

"It looks that way, sir," Vic replied. "Their configurations match other FUPN ships we've encountered from this galaxy."

"Understood. I'm on my way."

"Aye, Captain," Vic's voice came back, steady despite the gravity of the situation.

"Dad!" Dana shouted from right behind him, her voice raised over the din from the loudspeakers. "Lukas and I need to get back to the station!"

"No," Soren shot back over his shoulder without

breaking his stride. "We don't know the intentions of the incoming fleet, and you're safer on board Wraith than anywhere else."

"My crew is on the station!" Dana argued, keeping up with him.

"So is my team!" Lukas added.

"I'm not having this argument with you right now! There's no time!"

"You're right. We need to go!"

Dana surged past Soren, Lukas right behind her. Soren watched her go for a moment, torn between his desire to protect her and allowing her to return to the station. He'd always tried to do the right thing. The professional thing. But as she approached the exit to the hangar, he knew he couldn't do both.

And he would be damned if he'd lose her again.

"Corporal!" he snapped, drawing the attention of the Marine standing guard at the exit. "Stop them!"

The Marine turned toward them, spread his legs, and rotated his rifle, bringing it up across his chest to completely block the exit before Dana and Lukas arrived. Soren stopped as she spun around to move around Lukas and confront him. "You have no right!"

"I have every right, not only as your father, but as your superior officer. You're both too valuable to this mission for me to allow you to leave. You can either accept that peacefully, or I can confine you to quarters."

"We don't have quarters here," Dana argued, her lips clamped tightly together.

"I'm sure we can accommodate you. Now, I don't have any more time for this." He bit down, his back teeth opening his comm. "Liam, send a pair of Marines to the exit to the station to collect Commander Strickland and Doctor Mitchell. They're to locate quarters for them and confine them there until I say otherwise."

"Aye, Captain," Liam replied. "They're on their way."

With a final glance at Dana, doing his best to absorb her furious glare, he hurried to the exit and sprinted towards the bridge. His heart pounded, a mixture of adrenaline and dread coursing through his veins.

He burst onto the bridge less than a minute later, immediately taking in the tense atmosphere. Jack stood near Vic, who occupied the command chair. Their face's were pale as they listened intently to a conversation playing over the main speakers. Soren recognized the voices immediately. Admiral Lane and Admiral Harper.

"...harboring the enemy, Harper," Lane's voice crackled with barely contained fury. "It's treason, plain and simple."

"Damn it Lane, listen to reason!" Harper pleaded, his usual composure cracking under the strain. "Don't you understand? We're trying to stop the Convergence. To save our galaxy. And we're running out of time."

Soren moved to stand beside Jack, his eyes fixed on the sensor display. The Fourth Fleet's ships loomed ominously, their weapons undoubtedly primed and ready. He felt a chill run down his spine as he realized just how precarious their position had become.

Lane's voice cut through the air again, sharp with skepticism. "Oh? And how much time do we have left, then?"

"Twelve weeks, at best," Harper shot back, his voice tight with desperation. "But it could be any minute now."

There was a pause, heavy with tension. When Lane spoke again, his voice was cold, calculating. "Twelve weeks, you say? Well, Admiral Harper, I have news for you. In twelve weeks, the other dimension will be ours. We're having great success against our counterparts. Their defenses are crumbling, their worlds falling one by one."

Soren's fists clenched at his sides, anger and disgust roiling in his gut. How many innocent lives had been lost already? How many more planets would fall before it was over?

Harper's voice came again, a note of pleading entering his tone. "We have a plan to stop the Convergence, Lane. A real chance to end this madness without more bloodshed. There's no need to keep killing innocent people!"

"We can't take that risk," Lane replied, his voice hard as steel. "It's the only way to ensure our survival. I won't jeopardize everything we've accomplished on the slim chance that your theories are correct, and you know the President won't, either."

"The President is wrong!" Harper snapped.

Soren exchanged a glance with Jack, seeing his frustration and fear mirrored in his old friend's eyes. They knew where this was heading, and the options were rapidly dwindling.

Lane's voice came again, filled with cold finality. "No, you're the one who's wrong. This is your last chance, Harper. Surrender the station and turn over the enemy, or you will be fired upon. The choice is yours."

"Just give me a minute, damn you," Harper growled, pausing the connection before Lane could answer.

Immediately, Samira's voice rose past the tension on the bridge. "Captain, we're being hailed. It's Admiral Harper."

Soren nodded sharply. "Put him through."

"Captain Strickland, I'm afraid we've run out of time and options. You need to make a run for it. Head for the Eye. You have the equipment. It won't be as easy, but you can finish the upgrades en route."

Soren's jaw clenched, the implications of Harper's words sinking in. "If we run, Lane will attack the station. You'll be killed."

A dark smile tugged at the corners of Harper's mouth. "Then you'd better stop that convergence, Captain. Make sure I don't die for nothing."

He thought of Dana, and then of the Galileo and its crew. "What about the Galileo? I can't just leave them to die with you."

Harper's expression softened slightly, a flicker of understanding passing between them. "We'll cover their escape as best we can. It's not much, but it's the best we can do under the circumstances."

Soren nodded, his mind already racing through potential strategies. "Understood, Admiral. And...thank you. For everything."

"Good luck, Captain," Harper replied. "We're all counting on you. Jack, it was nice knowing me."

As the transmission cut out, Soren turned to Vic. "I have the conn."

"Aye, Captain," Vic replied, moving out of the command seat. "You have the conn."

Soren replaced him at the station before tapping on his comms. "Ethan, do we have power?"

"Aye, Captain," he replied. "But the third reactor isn't connected yet."

"What about shields?"

"Starboard side is still under repair. Cloaking system and vortex cannon are operational, but with the state of the re-wiring, I can't guarantee we won't have stability regressions."

Soren winced. It wasn't an ideal situation, but there was nothing to be done about it. "Bobby, plot a course for the Eye. Be ready to execute on my mark. Keira, prep the cloak and the cannon. Sang, prepare to get us out of here. Mark, get us detached from the station and buttoned up."

The bridge crew responded with a chorus of, "Aye, Captain."

As the Wraith hummed with building energy, Soren's gaze was drawn back to the sensor display. Harper's small fleet had taken up defensive positions around the station, their weapons charged and ready. On the other side, the Fourth Fleet loomed, a wall of steel and firepower poised to unleash destruction.

"Admiral Lane," Harper said, resuming his original contact, Wraith still synced in. "You're making a huge mistake. Please, we can stop the Convergence. And even if we can't, what harm is there in letting us try?"

"You attacked your own," Lane replied coldly. "You're working with the enemy. You should be thankful I even gave you the option to surrender. Stand down immediately or be destroyed."

"So be it," Harper replied.

For a moment, silence reigned on the bridge. Then, without warning, brilliant flashes of light erupted from Harper's ships as they opened fire on the Fourth Fleet.

"All ships, defensive formation Delta," Harper's voice crackled over the comms. "Protect the station at all costs. Wraith! Galileo! Get the hell out of here. Now!"

CHAPTER 42

Soren's voice cut through the chaos on the bridge, sharp with urgency. "Sang, get us out of here!"

"Aye, Captain," Sang replied.

The Wraith lurched as its main thrusters flared, while vectoring thrusters pushed them away from Omega Station. Clearing the docking arm, Sang sent the ship accelerating through the void.

"Sang," he ordered, "keep our starboard side away from the enemy fleet at all costs."

"Aye, Captain," Sang replied, rotating the ship to ensure the unshielded starboard side remained safe from the oncoming barrage. Soren felt the deck shudder beneath his feet as the first volley of railgun fire slammed into their shields. The energy barrier flared a brilliant blue, absorbing the hypervelocity rounds without complaint.

"Shields stable, Captain," Keira reported from her station.

Soren nodded, his attention drawn to the larger battle raging beyond their immediate vicinity. Harper's small fleet had engaged the Fourth Fleet with a ferocity born of desperation. The vastly outnumbered ships had closed the distance with the larger formation, using the close quarters to limit the firepower Lane's ships could bring to bear. Their weapons blazed in defiance of the overwhelming odds, burning through what little ordnance they had left.

Soren's jaw clenched as he watched the uneven battle unfold. It was clear from the outset that Harper's forces were outmatched. Despite their valiant efforts, the Fourth Fleet's superior numbers and firepower would slowly grind down the defenders.

Even as he watched, a Valkyrie-class cruiser from Harper's fleet unleashed a devastating barrage against one of Lane's, its railguns digging hard into the larger ship's shields and threatening to punch through. For a moment, it seemed the smaller vessel might score a lucky hit. But then, a pair of Fourth Fleet Komodos shifted their firepower in the Valkyrie's direction, tearing through the smaller vessel's shields and ripping it apart in a silent explosion of light and debris.

"Mark," Soren called out, his eyes never leaving the projected sensor grid, "give me a location on the Galileo."

"Aye, Captain," Mark replied. A moment later, the ship was highlighted on the grid. "There she is, sir. Still docked at the station."

Soren nodded. At least the ship was still intact, for now. But they needed to get moving, and soon.

"Bobby," he said, turning to the navigation officer, "do you have our course plotted?"

"Yes, sir," Bobby answered, his voice steady despite the tension evident in his posture. "Course for the Eye is locked in and ready."

Soren's lips thinned into a determined line. "Hold that course for now. We don't leave until the Galileo is safely away."

"Captain," Jack interjected, his voice low and urgent, "we can't afford to wait too long. The longer we stay here, the more damage we'll take. We need to be at full strength to enter the Eye."

"I know," Soren replied. "But I won't abandon them." He turned back to Keira. "Keep the vortex cannon charged and ready. If any ship so much as looks at Galileo the wrong way, I want it taken out. Understood?"

"Aye, Captain," Keira responded.

Harper's fleet was putting up a hell of a fight, but the outcome was becoming increasingly clear with each passing moment. A Fourth Fleet Valkyrie erupted in a brilliant fireball as one of Harper's ships broke through to its reactor core. But that ship went dark a moment later as a barrage of missiles pounded through the shields and breached the hull in multiple places, the holes venting atmosphere and crew. It was the same across the entire battlefield.

The space around Omega Station had quickly become a maelstrom of destruction. Debris from shattered ships tumbled through the black, punctuated by the staccato flashes of railgun fire and the brilliant flares of exploding missiles.

Amidst the chaos, Soren's attention was drawn to a flicker of movement on the grid. The Galileo was finally on the move, its engines flaring to life as it pulled away from the beleaguered station.

"Captain," Mark called out, his voice rising with urgency, "There's an enemy Komodo vectoring to target the Galileo!"

Soren found the ship on the grid. "Sang, bring us about but maintain heading and velocity. Keira, prepare to fire the vortex cannon."

The Wraith turned sharply, its maneuvering thrusters

firing in precise bursts as Sang guided the ship into an optimal firing position, leaving them flying backward, away from the scene. On the main viewscreen, Soren could see the massive form of the enemy Komodo, nearly in position to unleash its fury on the comparatively tiny Galileo.

"We have a solution, Captain," Keira reported, her voice tight.

Soren's eyes narrowed. "Fire."

The Wraith shuddered as the vortex cannon discharged, its spearlike beam of displaced spacetime and furious energy lancing out across the battlefield. It struck the Komodo dead center, the destructive vortex tearing through shields and hull plating. For a brief moment, the massive ship seemed to implode, its structure collapsing in on itself before erupting in a spectacular explosion that lit up the surrounding space.

"Direct hit," Keira reported, a note of satisfaction in her voice. "Enemy Komodo destroyed."

Soren allowed himself a grim smile. "Recharge the cannon."

"Aye, Captain."

With the immediate threat neutralized, the Galileo accelerated away from the station, pushing its thrusters to their limit as it sought to escape the battle zone. Soren watched its progress intently, acutely aware that the rest of the Fourth Fleet was regrouping, their attention now split between Harper's dwindling forces and the Wraith.

"They're backing off, Captain," Mark observed, gesturing to the grid where the enemy ships were indeed giving the Wraith a wide berth. "Looks like that little demonstration with the vortex cannon has them worried."

"Good," Soren replied. "But don't let your guard down. They'll be looking for any weakness they can exploit."

As if to underscore his words, a brilliant flash erupted

from the heart of the battlefield. Soren's eyes widened in horror as he realized its source.

"Omega Station," Jack breathed, his voice barely above a whisper. "It's gone."

The research station that had been their base of operations, their last hope for understanding and stopping the Convergence, was now nothing more than an expanding cloud of superheated gas and debris. And with it, Soren knew, had gone countless lives—brilliant minds dedicated to saving not just one universe but two.

Before the shock of the station's destruction could fully register, another explosion rocked the battlefield. This time, Soren recognized the ship instantly. Harper's flagship, a Komodo-class destroyer, erupted in a violent detonation as multiple missile hits overwhelmed its failing shields.

Soren felt a pang of grief for the other Harper. Despite their differences, despite the mistrust that had colored their initial interactions, the man had ultimately proven to be a staunch ally. And now he was gone, along with so many others, in a war that should never have been fought.

"Samira, hail the Galileo," Soren said.

"This is Lieutenant Commander Von," came the answer a few seconds later. "Captain Strickland, what are your orders, sir?"

"Von, I need you to take Galileo back through the rift. It's imperative that you tell Admiral Montoya everything that's happening here. Tell him what we're trying to accomplish. It will give them some hope they sorely need."

"Sir, what about Dana?" Von asked, obviously worried for her commanding officer.

"Dana is here on the Wraith. We need her here. We'll take care of her."

Relief washed over Von's face, quickly replaced by renewed resolve. "Understood, Captain. We'll make for the rift immediately."

"We'll cover your escape. Godspeed, Commander."

As the transmission ended, Soren turned to his crew. "Keira, I want a full spread of missiles ready to launch. Coordinate with the railgun batteries. We're going to give the Galileo every chance we can to get out of here in one piece."

"Aye, Captain," Keira replied as she prepared the Wraith's formidable arsenal.

"Sang," Soren continued, "keep us between the Galileo and Lane's fleet. Do whatever you can to stay out of their firing solutions."

"Aye, Captain," Sang acknowledged, already adjusting their course.

The next few minutes were a blur of frantic action. The Wraith danced through space, its engines straining as Sang pushed the ship to its limits. Missiles streaked from its launch tubes in coordinated salvos while the railguns spat hypervelocity rounds in a near-continuous stream of fire.

Lane's ships pressed their attack, seemingly enraged by the destruction of the Komodo and determined to prevent the Wraith and Galileo from escaping. But between the Wraith's covering fire and their newfound caution regarding the vortex cannon, the enemy fleet struggled to land any significant hits.

"Galileo's approaching jump coordinates," Bobby reported, his eyes fixed on his navigational displays.

Soren nodded, a mixture of relief and tension coursing through him. They were almost there. Almost safe. But the most dangerous moment was yet to come.

"Sang, bring us to a full stop once the Galileo reaches its jump point," he ordered.

"Aye, Captain," Sang replied.

The moments stretched as the Galileo closed the final distance to its jump coordinates. Lane's fleet, realizing their prey was about to escape, redoubled their efforts. A barrage of railgun fire and missiles streaked towards both ships, the space between them lighting up with deadly energy.

"Galileo's at jump coordinates," Bobby announced. "They're preparing to jump now."

"Match their position," Soren commanded. "Keira, status on the vortex cannon?"

"Fully charged and ready, Captain," Keira responded.

Soren's eyes narrowed as he studied the tactical display. Lane's ships were closing fast, their weapons blazing. But they were still out of optimal range for the vortex cannon. He needed to time this perfectly.

"Galileo's jumping," Mark reported, a note of excitement in his voice.

Soren watched as the science vessel seemed to elongate for a brief moment before vanishing in a flash of light. One problem solved. Now they just had to save themselves.

"Captain," Keira called out, urgency in her tone, "enemy ships are entering optimal firing range for the vortex cannon."

Soren's lips curled into a dark smile. "Then let's give them something to remember us by. Fire."

For the second time, the Wraith shuddered as the vortex cannon discharged its awesome power. The beam lanced out across space, not aimed at any particular ship but rather at the center of the enemy formation. While no ships were destroyed outright, the powerful attack forced them to spread their formation and ease off on their velocity for fear of being struck by the next attack. It wouldn't stop them for long, but it would buy the Wraith the precious seconds it needed.

"Captain, we're clear to jump," Sang announced.

"Bobby, execute!" Soren barked.

Soren felt the familiar lurch as the Wraith's jump drive engaged. The viewscreen flared white, and then they were gone, leaving behind the chaos and destruction of the battle at Omega Station.

And headed directly into the unknown.

———

Thank you for reading! I hope you enjoyed the book! For more information on the next installment in the series, please visit mrforbes.com/convergencewar3

OTHER BOOKS BY M.R FORBES

Want more M.R. Forbes? Of course you do!
View my complete catalog here
mrforbes.com/books
Or on Amazon:
mrforbes.com/amazon

Starship For Sale (Starship For Sale)
mrforbes.com/starshipforsale

When Ben Murdock receives a text message offering a fully operational starship for sale, he's certain it has to be a joke.

Already trapped in the worst day of his life and desperate for a way out, he decides to play along. Except there is no joke. The starship is real. And Ben's life is going to change in ways he never dreamed possible.

All he has to do is sign the contract.

Joined by his streetwise best friend and a bizarre tenant with an unseverable lease, he'll soon discover that the universe is more volatile, treacherous, and awesome than he ever imagined.

And the only thing harder than owning a starship is staying alive.

Forgotten (The Forgotten)
mrforbes.com/theforgotten
Complete series box set:
mrforbes.com/theforgottentrilogy

Some things are better off FORGOTTEN.

Sheriff Hayden Duke was born on the Pilgrim, and he expects to die on the Pilgrim, like his father, and his father before him.

That's the way things are on a generation starship centuries from home. He's never questioned it. Never thought about it. And why bother? Access points to the ship's controls are sealed, the systems that guide her automated and out of reach. It isn't perfect, but he has all he needs to be content.

Until a malfunction forces his wife to the edge of the habitable zone to inspect the damage.

Until she contacts him, breathless and terrified, to tell him she found a body, and it doesn't belong to anyone on board.

Until he arrives at the scene and discovers both his wife and the body are gone.

The only clue? A bloody handprint beneath a hatch that hasn't opened in hundreds of years.

Until now.

Deliverance (Forgotten Colony)
mrforbes.com/deliverance
Complete series box set:

The war is over. Earth is lost. Running is the only option.

It may already be too late.

Caleb is a former Marine Raider and commander of the Vultures, a search and rescue team that's spent the last two years pulling high-value targets out of alien-ravaged cities and shipping them off-world.

When his new orders call for him to join forty-thousand survivors aboard the last starship out, he thinks his days of fighting are over. The Deliverance represents a fresh start and a chance to leave the war behind for good.

Except the war won't be as easy to escape as he thought.

And the colony will need a man like Caleb more than he ever imagined...

Man of War (Rebellion)
mrforbes.com/manofwar
Complete series box set:
mrforbes.com/rebellion-web

In the year 2280, an alien fleet attacked the Earth.

Their weapons were unstoppable, their defenses unbreakable.

Our technology was inferior, our militaries overwhelmed.

Only one starship escaped before civilization fell.

Earth was lost.

It was never forgotten.

Fifty-two years have passed.

A message from home has been received.

The time to fight for what is ours has come.

Welcome to the rebellion.

Hell's Rejects (Chaos of the Covenant)
mrforbes.com/hellsrejects

The most powerful starships ever constructed are gone. Thousands are dead. A fleet is in ruins. The attackers are unknown. The orders are clear: *Recover the ships. Bury the bastards who stole them.*

Lieutenant Abigail Cage never expected to find herself in Hell. As a Highly Specialized Operational Combatant, she was one of the most respected Marines in the military. Now she's doing hard labor on the most miserable planet in the universe.

Not for long.

The Earth Republic is looking for the most dangerous individuals it can control. The best of the worst, and Abbey happens to be one of them. The deal is simple: *Bring back the starships, earn your freedom. Try to run, you die.* It's a suicide mission, but she has nothing to lose.

The only problem? There's a new threat in the galaxy. One with a power unlike anything anyone has ever seen. One that's been waiting for this moment for a very, very, long time. And they want Abbey, too.

Be careful what you wish for.

They say Hell hath no fury like a woman scorned. They have no idea.

ABOUT THE AUTHOR

M.R. Forbes is the mind behind a growing number of Amazon best-selling science fiction series. Having spent his childhood trying to read every sci-fi novel he could find (and write his own too), play every sci-fi video game he could get his hands on, and see every sci-fi movie that made it into the theater, he has a true love of the genre across every medium. He works hard to bring that same energy to his own stories, with a continuing goal to entertain, delight, fascinate, and surprise.

He maintains a true appreciation for his readers and is always happy to hear from them.

To learn more about me or just say hello:

Visit my website:
mrforbes.com

Send me an e-mail:
michael@mrforbes.com

Check out my Facebook page:
facebook.com/mrforbes.author

Join my Facebook fan group:
facebook.com/groups/mrforbes

Follow me on Instagram:

instagram.com/mrforbes_author

Find me on Goodreads:
goodreads.com/mrforbes

Follow me on Bookbub:
bookbub.com/authors/m-r-forbes

Made in United States
Orlando, FL
08 December 2024